Why Don't You Keep Me

Rae Knight

This book is a work of fiction. Similarities to any person, place, or theory are in no way intended or to be inferred as fact or reference. Any reference to actual events, locations, organizations or people are entirely coincidental.

All rights reserved. No portion of this book may be reproduced in any form without written permission from the publisher or author, except as permitted by U.S. copyright law.

Contains adult situations not suitable for those under the age of 18.

Cover by Juniper Hall

Edited by Michelle Hester at Enchanted Edits LLC

Copyright © 2025 by Rae Knight

Content Warning

Please thoroughly read this list of trigger/content warnings before you dive into this book. As much as I want you to read my work, I want you to enjoy it and if any of these things seem like they wouldn't be nice to read about, please stop here.

This is purely fictional, and should be read that way.

Attempted rape, drugging, physical violence, and torture. Group scenes, power dynamics, and anal sex. Attempted kidnapping, mentions of past kidnapping, and killing, as well as bullying. Psychological manipulation, and gaslighting. Lastly, gang/mob/mafia violence, guns, shipments, etc.

To all the guys and gals who love their females strong, and their guys at their side supporting them, I wrote this one for you.

Now spread those pages and take it all in like a good girl.

Or maybe like a good boy ;)

1: TORI

You're a badass bitch.
You're a badass bitch.
You're a badass bitch.
Saying things three times makes them true, right? Or is that just for memorizing things?

I'm doing my best to remind myself why I decided to do this—to take the criminal route, the risky life, but my heart is pounding and my nerves are shot as we pull into one of Diablo's estates. So instead, I've made a song, and it goes:

I'm a badass bitch.

That's all I got.

Diablo has estates. Plural. Because why have one gigantic, intimidating house when you can scatter a handful across the country like oversized Monopoly hotels? And this one is the one he's decided we'll be living in.

The car bumps along the cobblestone driveway, and I try to convince myself that the twisting in my stomach is excitement.

It's totally not.

"Do you think this one has a secret basement?" Ryder says, his grin tugging at the corner of his mouth.

"If it does, you'll be the first one in it," Blaze replies flatly, tucking his phone into his pocket. He's been in hyper-focused mode all morning, like he's bracing for whatever fresh hell Diablo has planned for us.

The car rolls to a stop in front of the main entrance. I take a breath, the song in my head looping back.

I'm a badass bitch.

I don't feel like one.

"Tori." Thorne's voice is low, grounding. He's watching me from across the car, his dark eyes quiet but knowing. He doesn't say anything else—doesn't have to.

He knows. Of course he knows. Fucking mind reader, this one.

"I'm fine," I lie, pushing the door open before I can second-guess myself.

The manor is sprawling, all sharp angles and towering windows. Ivy crawls up the stone like it's trying to escape, and the fountain out front burbles obnoxiously, as if to say, *'This is wealth. Suck it.'*

The doors swing open before we can knock, revealing one of Diablo's well-trained staff members. "Welcome, Señorita Victoria. Your father is waiting for you," he says, moving aside.

We step in, and the foyer is exactly what I expected—marble floors polished to a shine, walls lined with gold-framed mirrors, and a chandelier so massive it could probably take out a small car. My boots squeak against the floor as we walk in, and I fight the urge to cringe.

Ryder leans in, glancing around. "This place brings back memories of getting yelled at for leaving fingerprints on mirrors." He stands straight again, wiggling his eyebrows at me before he speaks from the side of his mouth. "Feels like home."

Blaze gives him a pointed look. "Do us all a favor and don't touch anything."

"Relax," Ryder says, his grin widening. "I know better now. No fingerprints. Just smudges."

I roll my eyes, but the corners of my mouth twitch. "Can we just focus? The last thing we need is to give my father a reason to change his mind about having you guys here."

Before anyone can respond, Diablo steps into view at the top of the staircase. He looks exactly the same as the last time I saw him—sharp suit, colder-than-ice expression, and a presence that makes my pulse jump even when he's not saying a word.

"You're late," he says, his tone clipped as he starts to descend the stairs.

"Nice to see you too," I reply, forcing a smile. My voice doesn't crack, so I'm calling that a win.

His eyes flick to the guys, lingering just a second longer than necessary on each of them. I don't miss the slight downturn of his mouth.

"Well," he says, his voice cutting through the tension like a blade, "let's address a few things immediately. First, this will be the last time you're late. I expect punctuality as a standard, not a courtesy." His words are directed at everyone, but his sharp eyes land on me last, like a hammer coming down. "Since my time is valuable, I won't be at your side every moment. I've assigned trusted workers to handle the smaller details. You'll meet with me once a day. Sundays excluded. That day is for rest."

"Trusted workers?" The words leave my mouth before I can stop them. Images of Juan flit through my mind. He wasn't terrible, but the vibe was...strained.

"They, unlike you, arrived on time," he replies coolly. "They're waiting in the den. Follow me."

He pivots and strides down the hall with the kind of confidence that makes the rest of us look like amateurs. We follow, the soft click of his shoes against the floor the only sound until he stops in front of a set of white French doors. With a motion so smooth it's almost theatrical, he pushes them open. Inside are four people.

Not one. Nope. Not two, but four. Four fucking people.

The room itself is a modern den that feels entirely out of place with the rest of the estate. Sleek furniture, clean lines, and soft neutral tones make it look like something ripped from a catalog. It's too perfect. No one actually lives in spaces like this.

The four standing near the far wall, however, look like they belong here—perfectly poised. My stomach tightens.

"These are the individuals I've assigned to assist you," Diablo announces, gesturing toward the group like he's presenting a prize-winning team. "Each has been chosen for their specific skill set and will be indispensable to your training."

"Indispensable," Ryder mutters under his breath. "Fancy word for 'babysitters.'"

I shoot him a warning look, but I know he's not wrong. I turn my attention back to the group as they step forward one by one, and it's immediately clear Diablo isn't playing around.

The first is a tall woman with sharp features and an even sharper suit. Her hair is pulled into a severe bun.

She's got to have a massive headache all the time with that thing.

It's practically giving her a face lift.

Her gaze lands squarely on Blaze, sizing him up like she's preparing a report. "Eve Harper," she says curtly. Her voice is smooth but clipped, no-nonsense.

Next is a petite brunette clutching a folder so tightly it looks like she's afraid to drop it. Her wide eyes dart nervously to Thorne, and I can practically see the damsel-in-distress act unfolding in real time. "Mia Delgado," she says softly, her voice barely above a whisper.

Then there's the blonde. She steps forward with a confident air about her that radiates mischief. Her gaze locks onto Ryder, and her smirk deepens. "Lila Carter. Looking forward to working with you." Her tone drips with easy charm, and I want to gag.

My gaze narrows on her. I recognize a Sadie type anywhere.

She's going to be a problem.

Finally, Diablo gestures to a man lingering slightly behind the others. His posture is relaxed, but there's a sharpness in his light blue eyes that makes my skin prickle. His dark hair is split down the middle, loosely hanging down either side of his head. "This is Gabriel Morales. He'll be working as your personal guard."

"Guard?" I say, unable to hide the skepticism in my voice.

"Yes, guard," Diablo replies, his tone curt, as though the question itself is an offense. "Clearly, these three can't be trusted with your safety, given what happened with Nico." His gaze sweeps over Blaze, Ryder, and Thorne, lingering long enough to make it clear he doesn't hold any of them in high regard.

Heat rises in my chest, but before I can shoot back, he continues.

"Gabriel is also to help teach you, but now I'll be able to rest easy knowing my only daughter is safe with him."

The statement lands like a hammer. *My only daughter.* There's something unsettling in how easily he says it, like he didn't just meet me last month.

I clench my fists, trying to keep my expression neutral, but I can see this for what it is...a way for him to try to tear us apart. I mean come on, how are these three girls supposed to teach the guys anything? I'm all for woman power, but Mia here looks as fierce as a kitten, Eve looks more like a business major than a gang affiliate, and Lila, well, she might fit the bill—conniving. "That's...thoughtful of you," I manage to grit out.

Gabriel steps forward, his movements fluid, almost predatory. "It's a pleasure to meet you, Señorita Victoria." His voice is smooth, polite, but there's a weight to it that makes me uneasy.

"Tori," I correct automatically, not missing the faint smile that tugs at his lips.

Diablo claps his hands once, the sound echoing off the high ceilings. "Now that introductions are done, you'll begin familiarizing yourselves with your roles. I've decided to use your natural talents to my benefit."

Natural talents, huh?

I'm not sure I have any of those. Unless getting yourself into life-or-death situations is one.

"Blaze," Diablo continues, his gaze cutting to him sharply, "you'll be working with Eve to audit one of my logistics operations. Ensure everything runs like clockwork."

Blaze gives a curt nod, his face unreadable.

"Thorne," Diablo says, shifting his focus. "You and Mia will investigate a warehouse where I suspect there's been some...pilfering. " His tone makes it clear what dealing with it entails.

Mia's eyes dart to Thorne, who doesn't react beyond a slight narrowing of his gaze.

Am I expected to believe that Mia's natural talent is fixing these kinds of problems? She's about as intimidating as a basset hound puppy.

"Ryder," Diablo continues, "you'll accompany Lila to a negotiation tomorrow with potential allies. Charm them, convince them to see things my way."

"Charm," Ryder echoes. "That, I can do."

Diablo's expression doesn't change. "Don't mistake this for a game."

Ryder's grin falters a bit, but he recovers quickly, nodding. "Got it. Serious charm."

"And you, Tori," Diablo says, turning his full attention to me. "You'll be with Gabriel. He'll take you through the finer points of managing operations from the top. Consider this a crash course in leadership—something you desperately need."

Ouch. I thought dads were supposed to be encouraging.

"Leadership," I repeat, my voice flat.

"Yes," he replies smoothly, as if my tone doesn't bother him in the slightest. "You'll be reviewing schedules, inspecting my businesses, and ensuring everything runs as it should. Gabriel will teach you what to look for—and what to eliminate."

"Eliminate?" The word slips out before I can stop it.

His gaze sharpens, and his lips curl into something resembling a smile. "I trust you'll understand the implications when the time comes."

Fantastic. Nothing vague and ominous about that.

I mean, come on, Tori. You've already killed someone. Maybe it gets easier?

Yeah, no. That's never going to be a thing.

Diablo steps back, clasping his hands behind his back. "These tasks begin tomorrow morning. You'll report to me with your progress each evening. And remember, failure is not an option."

Because nothing motivates like a thinly veiled threat.

Before any of us can respond, he turns on his heel and strides toward the door. Gabriel moves to follow, but Diablo pauses, glancing back over his shoulder.

"Oh, and Gabriel?"

"Yes, sir."

"Keep a close eye on her." His gaze flicks to me, cold and calculating. "I don't trust anyone else to ensure her safety."

Gabriel inclines his head. "Understood."

The door clicks shut behind Diablo, leaving an almost oppressive silence in his wake.

Gabriel clears his throat, stepping into the center of the room. "Well," he says, his tone calm but firm, "it seems we have our work cut out for us."

Ryder snorts. "Yeah, no pressure or anything."

Blaze glares at him, but Ryder doesn't seem fazed.

Eve speaks up next, her sharp gaze cutting to Blaze. "We'll start with a detailed review of the supply chain first thing tomorrow. I expect you to be ready by eight."

Blaze nods, his expression unreadable. "I'll be ready."

Mia hesitates, clutching her folder like it's a shield. "Thorne," she says softly, her voice barely above a whisper, "I'll prepare the documents we'll need for the warehouse investigation. I can meet you here at—"

"Seven," Thorne interrupts, his tone calm but final. "We'll go early."

Her cheeks flush, but she nods quickly. "O-okay."

Lila leans casually against the edge of the couch, her gaze fixed on Ryder. "I'll prep you tonight," she says, her voice laced with teasing. "Gotta make sure you're not totally hopeless at diplomacy."

Ryder smirks, the kind that screams trouble. "Hopeless? I wrote the book on charm." His gaze flicks my way, a glint of hunger sparking in his eyes. "Besides, I'll be a little busy tonight."

Heat shoots straight to my core, and I'm instantly regretting the fact that I didn't prepare myself for Ryder being...well, Ryder.

"So," he adds casually, still holding my gaze, "I'll see you in the morning. Nine sound good? I like my sleep."

Lila raises a brow, her lips tightening, but she shrugs. "Nine it is. Don't be late, Prince Charming."

Ryder chuckles, leaning back into the couch with a self-satisfied air that makes me want to smack him—and maybe kiss him, depending on the moment.

Blaze exhales through his nose, clearly unimpressed, but says nothing. Thorne, ever the watchful one, shifts his gaze between Ryder and me, the faintest crease in his brow giving away his thoughts.

The girls all exit the room then, heading for the door, but Gabriel lingers.

He steps forward, commanding attention without a word. His eyes meet mine, calm but unyielding. "Señorita Tori, we'll begin at six tomorrow morning. I'll be sure to wake you. There's much to cover."

"Wake me?" I arch a brow, leaning back a little. *The bodyguard does wake-up calls?*

"Yes, wake you," he says evenly, like it's the most natural thing in the world. "The girls won't be living here, but as your bodyguard, I will. I can't exactly leave your side if I'm meant to protect you."

The air shifts. Blaze's shoulders go rigid, Ryder's grin evaporates, and Thorne—oh, Thorne—takes on that too-calm demeanor that sets my nerves on edge.

"Living here?" Thorne's voice is quiet, measured, but there's no mistaking the sharp undertone. His dark eyes narrow a bit, his entire stance screaming danger.

"Yes," Gabriel says simply, unaffected. "It's necessary."

Blaze steps forward, his chest puffed as he fixes Gabriel with a hard stare. "Necessary? Or convenient?"

Gabriel turns his attention to Blaze, his posture steady. "Both. Your track record with Señorita Tori's safety isn't exactly flawless. Nico proved that."

The silence that follows is deafening. Ryder shifts, his fists clenching as he glances at me. Thorne's expression doesn't change, but the tension in the room feels like it's seconds away from snapping.

"That's enough," I cut in, holding up a hand before the storm brewing between them has a chance to break. "There's nothing we can do about it. Diablo put him here, and we're not going to let it change anything." I stare at each of them, meeting their eyes with an unflinching, reassuring glance.

Ryder is the first to break, his shoulders relaxing a bit as he lets out a breath. "Fine," he mutters, though his tone is anything but happy. "But I don't like it."

"Noted," I reply sharply, moving my gaze to Blaze. He doesn't speak, but the tightness in his jaw makes it clear he's holding back.

Comments like Gabe's affect him the most. No matter how many times I tell him it wasn't his fault Nico took me, he still blames himself. That guilt is eating him alive, carving into him piece by piece, and I don't know how to fix it.

I hold his gaze a moment longer, hoping he can see what I can't say right now—that I don't blame him, that I never have. His shoulders ease an inch, but the weight in his expression doesn't lift.

"Let's just deal with it for now."

Finally, I turn to Thorne, who's still standing there—too calm, too serious. His dark eyes meet mine, but there's a fury behind them that is unmistakable. After a long pause, he nods. "For now."

The words settle over the room, easing the edge of tension but not breaking it entirely.

Gabriel turns and leaves us, his voice carrying faintly from the hall, polite and conversational as he speaks to one of the staff. He might as well have shouted, 'I'm staying here, deal with it.'

We're all silent again until Ryder shifts his weight, and opens his mouth. "Well, this is shaping up to be a cozy little arrangement. Nothing like a live-in stranger to keep things interesting."

Blaze shoots him a glare, but Ryder's grin doesn't waver. If anything, it grows wider.

"Come on," Ryder says, throwing up his hands. "If we don't laugh, we'll spiral into a rage. And I'm not in the mood for group therapy."

Thorne's gaze flicks to me again, questioning. "You sure about this?"

I sigh, letting some of the frustration bleed into my tone. "We don't have much of a choice."

Ryder claps Blaze on the shoulder. "You heard the lady. We're shit out of luck. For now. So how about we go find some food before the bodyguard decides to assign us curfews."

Blaze shrugs off Ryder's hand, but he doesn't argue. He turns toward the hall with a sharp exhale, and Ryder follows, chuckling behind.

Thorne lingers, his eyes still on me.

"You sure you're okay?" His voice is gentler now, low enough that only I can hear.

"Not at all," I admit. "But I'll handle it. I always do."

His gaze softens, and he gives a short nod. "You're not alone in this. Remember that."

"I know," I say quietly. "Thanks."

He hesitates a moment longer before following the others.

You wanted this, Tori. You wanted to learn from your father. Well, here you go.

2: TORI

The kitchen smells too clean—lemony and metallic, like it's never seen a spill, a stain, or a splash of oil in its entire life. It's so pristine it practically begs to be ruined, which is exactly what's about to happen. The stovetop looks like it belongs in a sci-fi movie, more spaceship console than something a person would use to cook food. I've been glaring at it for the last five minutes, hoping it'll reveal its secrets to me if I stare hard enough.

"Who needs this many settings just to boil water?" I mutter, squinting at the controls.

"You do," Ryder says, perched at the island like he owns the place, spinning a knife lazily between his fingers like some delinquent circus performer. "I've seen you burn water before, Tori. This setup was probably designed with people like you in mind."

I whip around, glaring. "Excuse me?"

Blaze doesn't even look up from his phone. "To be fair, he's not wrong. You're better off letting someone else handle dinner before you burn this place down."

"Oh, gee. Thanks." I roll my eyes, planting my hands on my hips. "I'll have you know I've improved since the last time I cooked."

Thorne, leaning against the fridge with his arms crossed, raises one unimpressed brow. "Last time you cooked, Ryder was sick for two days."

You try to cook a man a nice meal for taking a bullet for you and you never live it down.

"That wasn't my fault," I shoot back, spinning toward the pantry to avoid their stares. "And for the record, I wasn't the one who told him to eat three servings."

"It wasn't three servings," Ryder says, beaming from ear to ear. "It was one—and it definitely felt like food poisoning."

"It wasn't food poisoning!" I yank the pantry doors open with more force than necessary, grabbing flour, sugar, and vanilla extract like they've personally offended me. "And maybe cooking isn't my thing, but baking? I could bake circles around all of you."

"Baking?" Blaze finally glances up, his tone full of skepticism. "As in...with measurements and precise timing?"

"Yes, baking," I reply, slamming a mixing bowl onto the counter for emphasis. "You think I was going to bake cookies for you guys while you were busy tormenting me back in high school? Please. And after Nico? Baking wasn't exactly at the top of my priorities."

That shuts them up. The air shifts slightly, the teasing replaced by an awkward silence. Blaze looks like he's about to say something, guilt flickering across his face, but Ryder beats him, jumping in, in typical Ryder fashion.

"Oh, this I've got to see," he says, leaning forward on his elbows, his grin back in full force. "You've got a lot to prove, Cupcake."

I grab a whisk and start cracking eggs into the bowl, ignoring the heat creeping up my neck. "You're all going to eat your words—and my cookies."

Blaze leans against the counter, arms crossed, full attention on me now, his guilt swallowed down. "This better not end in disaster."

Watch and learn, boys.

The teasing dies down as the scent of vanilla and sugar fills the kitchen. Slowly, the sharp edges of the moment soften. When I glance over my shoulder, I catch all three of them watching me. Ryder tilts his head like he's trying to figure out how I've been hiding this skill from them. Blaze looks almost... impressed.

Holy fuck.

Thorne, as usual, watches me with that quiet intensity that makes me feel like he sees more than I'd ever willingly share.

By the time the cookies come out of the oven, golden brown and perfect, Ryder grabs one immediately, ignoring the heat as he takes a bite.

"Holy shit," he says through a mouthful of cookie. "These are amazing."

Blaze takes one, inspecting it from all angles as if he's unsure how it could look so normal. He takes a very slow bite, chewing slowly before giving me a short nod. "Not bad."

"Not bad?" I cross my arms, glaring at him. "That's all I get?"

That's what he said about the fucking chicken wrap that I know was a lot worse than this.

Thorne picks up a cookie, his lips twitching into the faintest smile as he takes a bite. "Impressive."

I smirk, raising a brow at Blaze. "See? They appreciate me."

Ryder polishes off his first cookie and grabs another, speaking around the crumbs. "These are delicious. But this doesn't erase your cooking crimes."

I grab a dish towel and fling it at his head. He ducks with a laugh, and for the first time all day, the tension eases.

After we've thoroughly demolished the cookies—and the dinner Blaze insisted on making because "we can't live on sugar alone"—we migrate to the living room, the scent of vanilla and chocolate trailing after us like a cozy blanket.

The oversized sectional couch is impossibly comfortable, swallowing me whole the moment I flop down onto it. The cushions seem to mold around me, cocooning me in a way that feels far too luxurious.

I could fall asleep here.

Blaze takes the seat on my right, his arm brushing mine briefly as he leans back, as if he's still deciding how comfortable he's willing to let himself be. Thorne claims the spot to my left, his quiet presence grounding as always, his knee pressing lightly against mine.

Ryder, predictably, stops mid-stride, narrowing his eyes at the arrangement like he's just been told his favorite dessert is off-limits. "No fair," he mutters, his lips tugging into a pout that would be laughable if it wasn't so perfectly Ryder.

"Life's not fair," Blaze says without looking up, his tone as dry as the Sahara.

Ryder doesn't bother responding to Blaze. Instead, he drops down dramatically in front of me, grabbing my ankles and gently tugging my legs over his shoulders. "Fine. I'll take the floor. See? Problem solved."

I stare down at him, fighting a smile. "You're cute when you pout."

"Ridiculously adorable, you mean," he counters, leaning back and hugging my calves to his chest. "I now have the best seat in the house."

Blaze lets out a long-suffering sigh but doesn't comment, while Thorne just shakes his head faintly, his lips twitching as though he's trying not to smile.

From his spot by the doorway, Gabriel watches us silently. He's been hovering like a shadow since we moved into the living room, keeping just enough distance to make it clear he's not part of this scene but that he's still there. I can feel his presence like a prickle at the back of my neck—a constant reminder that, despite the comfort of this moment, our new reality isn't exactly normal.

I glance at the remote Blaze has picked up. "What are we watching?"

"Something tolerable," Blaze replies, scrolling through the options with practiced efficiency.

"No rom-coms," Thorne says, his tone as calm as ever but leaving no room for debate.

"What about *Mean Girls*?" Ryder asks, tilting his head back against my legs with a mischievous grin.

Blaze barely spares him a glance. "Absolutely not."

I roll my eyes, snatching the remote from Blaze before the argument can spiral. "If you can't agree, we're watching *Spirited Away*."

Thorne nods immediately, his expression unreadable. "That works."

I blink at him, surprised. "Seriously? You're okay with that?"

"It's a good movie," he says simply.

Ryder twists around to stare at him, his jaw dropping in playful astonishment. "Thorne's secretly an anime fan. I knew it."

Thorne doesn't respond, but the faint smirk tugging at his lips gives him away.

Ryder groans, resting against my legs again. "Fine. But next time, I'm picking."

The opening scenes of the movie fill the room with soft, whimsical music, and for a while, everything feels easy—normal, even. I forget about the supposed assistant my father brought in. I don't let my mind linger on the fact that I'll have another overprotective male lurking around. I even let myself forget, for just a moment, that I killed someone.

I tuck my legs a little more firmly onto Ryder's shoulders, leaning into Blaze's side as Thorne settles into me more comfortably, his hand resting on my thigh warmly. Gabriel remains by the doorway, silent and watchful, but again I don't let myself linger on him.

As the movie continues, my thoughts drift. This was supposed to be a new beginning, a fresh start. Instead, it feels like I'm walking a tightrope over an abyss.

Maybe I made the wrong choice?

Too bad, Tori. It's too late to change your mind.

I just need to remember why I chose this. How I felt when I accepted that dark part of myself. I need to lean into that feeling and embrace it fully. Maybe then this won't feel like a horrible choice.

"You're overthinking again," Thorne murmurs, his voice so low it feels like it's been plucked straight from my thoughts.

I glance at him, startled. His dark eyes meet mine, staring into my soul again. "How do you always know?" I whisper.

He doesn't answer, just tilts his head a bit, his lips curving just the slightest.

Ryder's commentary breaks the moment. "How is this frog guy the one in charge? He's got the leadership skills of a wet napkin."

I laugh softly, nudging his shoulder with my knee. "Shh. Just watch."

He falls silent, leaning forward as he gets caught up in the magic that is *Studio Ghibli*. When the credits roll, the room feels lighter, as though the tension of the day has been absorbed into the soft glow of the TV screen. Ryder stretches out dramatically, stretching and lifting my legs with a contented sigh.

Thorne stands first, reaching down to scoop me into his arms before I can protest. His grip is sure and steady, and I don't bother fighting it.

"You're tired," he says simply, cutting off my argument before it even starts.

Before we can leave the room, Gabriel steps forward, his gaze settling on Thorne. "Carrying her like that up the stairs might not be the safest option," he says, his tone calm but firm. "If you were to fall—"

Thorne stiffens, his dark eyes locking onto Gabriel's. The shift in his posture is subtle, but the weight of it is undeniable. "I'm not going to fall," he says, his voice low and threatening. "And if you think I'd ever let her get hurt, you don't know me."

The tension in the room crackles, sharp and electric, but Gabriel doesn't flinch. He holds Thorne's gaze for a moment longer before stepping back, his silence louder than any retort.

Thorne doesn't wait for another word. He adjusts his grip on me and carries me up the stairs, fighting back the stomping I'm sure he'd like to do.

He kicks the door shut with his foot once we're all inside my room, and then sets me down gently on the oversized bed. His hands linger at my waist for a moment before he steps back, his expression as unreadable as ever, but there's a tightness in his jaw that gives him away.

I've slowly learned how to read Thorne's all too serious face.

"I already don't like him," he mutters, his voice low.

"Who? Gabriel?" I ask, even though I already know the answer.

"Obviously Gabriel," Thorne replies, running a hand through his hair. "The way he looks at you like you're more than an assignment."

Ryder drops onto the bed beside me, stretching out like a cat claiming its territory. "Finally, something we can all agree on. The guy pisses me off, all arrogant and quiet. That's my act. Charming on the outside, devil on the inside."

Blaze leans against the door, quiet as ever, but when his gaze meets mine, the frustration in his eyes is clear.

"You don't like him either, do you?" I ask, tilting my head toward Blaze.

"No," he says after a pause. "I don't trust him. He's here for more than just to be your bodyguard. Diablo didn't send him to babysit; he sent him to watch." Blaze's gaze sharpens. "And report."

Great. Not only do I have a shadow, but my shadow is also wired for surveillance.

"I don't know," Ryder says, stretching out his arms like he's trying to take up even more space. "If I were Gabriel, I'd be suspicious of us too. Look at us—three ridiculously good-looking guys and one badass girl all wrapped up in this...whatever you call this." He gestures vaguely. "He's probably wondering how we haven't imploded yet."

I roll my eyes, nudging his leg with my foot. "This 'whatever you call this' is a relationship, Ryder. Keep up."

The lightness in Ryder's tone fades. "Still doesn't explain why Diablo thought we needed assistants. Or why they all look like they've been specifically tailored to us. I mean, did you see Eve? She's just Blaze with boobs and no penis."

Blaze snorts, crossing his arms. "She's not me."

Ryder raises an eyebrow. "Oh, come on, she's basically you in a business suit. You can tell she just loves planning. She's got silent, judgy vibes, the way she—"

"Don't," Blaze cuts him off, his tone clipped.

Ryder grins widely, clearly enjoying himself. "Fine, fine. But you can't deny the resemblance."

Blaze doesn't reply, but the tightness in his stance says enough. I glance between them, trying not to laugh. But Ryder isn't wrong. In fact, I'd say Lila is a lot like him, too. The only one who didn't have a female version of themselves would be Thorne, but he's a strange breed. *You can't duplicate Thorne.*

"And Mia?" Ryder continues, turning his attention to Thorne. "She practically screams 'save me, Thorne.' Don't tell me that doesn't push all your protective buttons."

Fuck, he's right. That's why she's with him. Thorne has a hero complex, always has. Well, except for those years he took part in my torment. Although he was the one doing the least of it.

Thorne's gaze darkens, his voice even but sharp. "Mia is not Tori. No one is Tori."

My stomach flips at his words, the sheer conviction in them making my chest ache. But Ryder doesn't miss a beat.

"Obviously," he says, shrugging. "But Diablo didn't just throw us random people. He knew exactly what he was doing. Tailor-made distractions. It's almost impressive."

"Almost?" Blaze arches a brow.

"Okay, fine. It's completely diabolical," Ryder admits, throwing his arms up. "No pun intended. But the point stands—none of them are Tori. He's testing us, and we're not about to fail."

"Testing us for what?" I ask, my voice quieter than I intended.

Blaze meets my gaze, his expression softening slightly. "To see if he can break us apart."

The weight of his words settles over the room, heavy and suffocating. I wrap my arms around my knees, suddenly feeling smaller than I'd like.

Don't be insecure, Tori. They're strangers. You've had years with these boys, even if the first few were hell.

Ryder shifts beside me, resting his elbows on his knees as he leans closer. "Tori, come on. You know we're not going anywhere, right? These assistants, Gabriel—they're just noise. Background extras in our movie."

I raise an eyebrow at him. "Pretty sure extras don't flirt with the leads."

Ryder's eyes flicker with mischief. "Flirting doesn't mean anything if the leads are unshakable." He gestures between us, then leans back smugly. "And babe, we're the freaking Titanic. Unsinkable."

"Terrible example," Blaze mutters, pinching the bridge of his nose.

Ryder falters for half a second. "Okay, bad metaphor. You know what I mean."

Blaze steps closer, his presence steady as always, his gaze sharp and focused. "He's right, though. Diablo can throw whatever he wants at us, but it's not going to work. We're solid, Tori. You know that."

"Do I?" The words slip out before I can stop them, and suddenly all their eyes are on me. My pulse spikes as I scramble to cover it up. "I mean, yeah, obviously I know that. I'm not questioning us or anything."

Good save, Tori. Real convincing.

Thorne's brows furrow, and his hand brushes mine where it rests on my knee. "You don't have to pretend with us."

"I'm not pretending," I lie, my voice sharper than I intended. *God, you're such a mess.*

Blaze sits beside me, his shoulder pressing into mine. "We haven't always treated you the way you deserve, Doll. But I promise you have nothing to worry about. We love you, and we'd burn this world down if you asked. You're the only thing we want."

I glance at him, surprised by the gentleness in his tone. For a guy who's all sharp edges and precision, moments like this always catch me off guard. "I know," I admit, my voice barely above a whisper. "It's just...hard. The thought of losing what we have because of someone else..."

"You're not going to lose us," Thorne says firmly, his dark eyes locking onto mine. "Not to them. Not to anyone. You're it for us, Tori."

Ryder leans in, playfully grinning again as he bumps my shoulder. "Yeah, they can try, but it's kind of hard to compete with perfection. And you, babe, are perfection."

The tension in the room eases, but the weight in my chest doesn't fully lift. I glance between them, my heart pounding as I try to find the words I need. "You're all so sure," I murmur. "But what if...what if I'm not enough?"

They didn't call me Icky for years for nothing. It's been months together, but it's not like we're on solid foundation here. We're still fucking building.

The silence that follows is deafening. My throat tightens, and I immediately regret saying anything. *Way to go, Tori. Just throw your insecurities out there like confetti.*

"You're more than enough," Blaze says quietly, his voice heavy with affection, cutting the tension instantly.

Ryder nods, his grin softer now. "He's right. You're everything, Tori. And nothing's going to change that."

Thorne doesn't say anything right away, but the way he looks at me—intense and unwavering—speaks volumes. "You're ours," he says simply, his tone leaving no room for argument. "And nothing is going to come between us. Not them. Not Diablo. No one."

The lump in my throat grows, and I bury my face in my hands, overwhelmed by the sheer certainty in their voices. "I hate you all," I mumble, my voice muffled.

"No, you don't," Ryder says, tugging my hands away from my face. "You love us. And you know we love you."

I shake my head, but the corners of my mouth twitch despite myself.

Blaze rests a hand on my shoulder, his touch grounding. "You don't have to doubt us, Tori. We're not going anywhere."

Thorne reaches over, brushing a stray strand of hair from my face. "You're stuck with us," he murmurs, the ghost of a smile tugging at his lips.

"Fine," I say, rolling my eyes. "But if you start getting distracted by the assistants, I reserve the right to stab you."

I might mean that.

Ryder throws an arm around my shoulders. "Noted. But picturing you with a knife is only turning me on."

I roll my eyes, shaking my head at his antics. "Sure it does."

"Let me show you."

Oh hell. It's going to be a long night.

3: BLAZE

Morning comes too fast. I wake up to the soft warmth of Tori's breath against my chest, her fingers curled lightly into my shirt as if she's clinging to me even in her sleep. Ryder's sprawled out on her other side, snoring softly, one arm draped over her waist. Thorne's at the edge of the bed, his arm over Ryder, and his hand resting protectively on Tori's hip like a sentinel on watch.

For a moment, I don't move. The house is still quiet, and this is the closest thing to peace I've felt since we got here. These fleeting moments of calm are rare, and I'm not in a hurry to lose this one. But reality waits for no one, and Diablo's orders are waiting.

I won't be the reason Tori worries about her decision to come here.

I carefully ease out of bed, making sure not to wake her. Ryder barely stirs, muttering something unintelligible, but he settles again, and I let out a quiet breath of relief. The floor is cold under my feet as I head to the bathroom, running through the day in my head.

It's going to suck. I already know it.

By the time I've showered and dressed, the others are starting to stir. Ryder is the first to sit up, rubbing the sleep from his eyes as he shoots me a wink. "Up early, as usual. I couldn't do it."

"It's called discipline," I reply, buttoning up my shirt.

"Sounds boring." Ryder swings his legs over the foot of the bed and stretches. "But I guess it's working for you."

Tori groans softly as she rolls onto her back, her eyes blinking open to find me. "You're already dressed? Give us normal people a chance to catch up, please."

I step closer to the bed, leaning down, brushing a kiss against her forehead. "Good morning, Doll."

She smiles sleepily, her fingers reaching out to brush against mine. "Morning."

Thorne stirs next, his dark eyes opening as he takes in the scene. He doesn't say much—he never does first thing in the morning—but the way his gaze lingers on Tori says enough. He moves to sit up as he adjusts to the waking world.

"We've got a long day ahead," I remind them. "Let's not waste it."

We've all got our own tasks, and Diablo made sure none of them would be together. *Already trying to tear us apart by keeping us separated.*

Ryder groans dramatically, flopping back onto the bed. "You sure know how to ruin a perfectly good morning."

"You're welcome," I reply dryly, earning a chuckle from Tori.

She sits up, stretching her arms over her head before swinging her legs over the side of the bed. "Fine. But if we're getting up, I'm at least getting a kiss first."

Ryder is the first to oblige, leaning in to press a kiss to her cheek. "There you go, KitKat. Now you're officially awake."

Thorne follows, his touch lingering as he presses a kiss to her temple. "Good morning," he murmurs softly, his voice low and warm.

I step closer, cupping her face in my hands as I kiss her properly, letting my lips linger against hers for just a moment longer than necessary. When I pull back, her cheeks are flushed, and there's a softness in her eyes that makes my chest tighten.

"Okay, enough of this lovey-doveyness," Ryder says, clapping his hands together. "Let's get moving before Blaze starts timing us."

I shake my head, but I can't help the small smile that tugs at my lips as they start to get ready. It's moments like this that remind me why we're here. Why we're doing all this. *For her.*

Once everyone is dressed and ready, we head downstairs for a quick breakfast. Gabriel is already there, standing off to the side like the world's most intimidating statue. He doesn't say anything as we pass, but his presence is impossible to ignore. It's like he's always watching, always assessing. It grates on my nerves more than I care to admit.

Tori glances at him briefly before focusing on me. "You okay?"

I nod. "Just ready to get to work."

She doesn't press further, but the concern in her eyes lingers. I press a quick kiss to her temple before heading out, leaving her with Ryder and Thorne. There's no time for distractions—not until I figure out exactly what Diablo has planned.

The office I was instructed to go to is exactly what I expected: pristine, orderly, and utterly lifeless. The desk is clear except for a stack of neatly arranged folders, the shelves are lined with books that look untouched, and the air smells faintly of polished wood. It's a space that screams clean, and while I should appreciate that, it only makes me feel more on edge.

Eve is already there, of course. She's seated at the desk, her tablet in hand as she reviews something with the kind of focus that feels almost robotic. Her hair is pulled back into a neat bun, not a strand out of place, and her tailored suit fits her perfectly. She looks like she belongs in a high-rise office, not here.

"Morning," she says without looking up.

"Morning," I reply, taking the seat across from her. "What do you have for me?"

She sets the tablet down and slides a folder across the desk. "I've been reviewing the logistics reports for the past quarter. There are some discrepancies in the shipping manifests—minor, but consistent."

I open the folder, scanning the data. The inconsistencies jump out immediately—adjustments in weight, missing items, small enough to avoid detection but frequent enough to be deliberate.

Why has this gone unchecked for so long?

Or maybe it hasn't and Diablo is just setting me up for failure?

"These shipments go through the north docks?" I ask.

"Yes," she replies. "Luis Ortega oversees the operation, but his team has seen some turnover recently. It's possible someone new is exploiting the gaps."

"Or Ortega's in on it," I mutter, closing the folder. "Have you flagged the shipments?"

"Of course," she says smoothly. "I've also arranged for us to inspect the docks later today. I assumed you'd want to see the operation firsthand."

I nod, but something about her tone sets me on edge. She's too prepared, too perfect. It's like she's been given a script for the day and she's doing her best not to deviate from it.

"You've been with Diablo's organization for a while, haven't you?" I ask casually, leaning back in my chair.

"Long enough to understand how things work," she replies, her expression neutral.

"And yet you're here now. With me." I tilt my head, watching her closely. "Why is that?"

She doesn't flinch, but I catch the briefest flicker of something in her eyes. "Because Diablo trusts me to help you succeed."

"Help me succeed, or report back on what I'm doing?" I press, my tone sharpening. "Let's skip the bullshit, Eve. Why are you really here?"

Her composure doesn't crack, but her voice is firmer now. "I'm here because I'm good at what I do. If you have an issue with that, you'll need to take it up with Diablo."

It's a deflection, and a clever one. She's not giving me anything to work with, and I hate how much that irritates me. I push back from the desk, standing as I gather the folder.

"We'll head to the docks in an hour," I say, my tone clipped. "Be ready."

She nods, gathering her things before leaving the room. The door clicks shut behind her, and I let out a breath of frustration, dragging my hand down my face.

She's good. Too good. And as much as I hate to admit it, I'm starting to see why Diablo picked her. But that doesn't mean I have to like it.

The hour between Eve leaving the office and our trip to the docks drags on like a bad lecture. I sift through the reports she left, checking and cross-checking the manifests, weights, and locations. Every number is just believable enough to pass, but the discrepancies are consistent—almost like whoever's responsible wanted them to be found by someone like me.

There's no way Diablo doesn't know about this already. He's testing me, seeing if I'll play his game or fail it. And Eve? She's part of the test. Whether she's here to help or sabotage, I haven't figured out yet.

By the time I make my way to the garage, she's already there, leaning against one of the black SUVs like she's posing for a corporate ad campaign. Her tablet is tucked under her arm, her expression as neutral as ever.

"Ready?" she asks, straightening as I approach.

"As I'll ever be," I reply, climbing into the driver's seat before she has the chance. If this is going to be a game of control, I'm not about to hand her the wheel—literally or figuratively.

Eve slides into the passenger seat without a word, her calm demeanor grating on me more than it should. I pull out of the driveway, the silence so uncomfortable I almost play music.

"You're quiet," she finally says, breaking the silence. "I assumed you'd have more questions."

"About what?" I ask, keeping my eyes on the road. "The discrepancies? Or you?"

"Both," she replies, her tone annoyingly even.

I glance at her, trying to gauge her expression, but she's as unreadable as ever. "You already know my thoughts on the discrepancies. Someone's skimming, and it's either Ortega or someone under him. What I'm interested in is why this hasn't been handled already. Diablo doesn't strike me as the kind of man who lets things like this slide."

Her lips curve into a faint smile, the kind that's more calculated than genuine. "Maybe he's waiting to see how you handle it."

"Great," I mutter under my breath. "Another test."

"If it is, you seem to be passing so far," she says lightly, her gaze shifting to the window.

I don't reply, instead focusing on the road ahead. The docks aren't far, but the weird atmosphere between us makes every mile feel longer.

"You didn't answer the second part of my question," I say after a moment. "Why are you here?"

She doesn't respond immediately, her gaze flicking back to me with the kind of patience that makes me want to slam the brakes just to rattle her composure. "I told you. I'm here to assist you."

"And you expect me to believe that?"

"I expect you to draw your own conclusions," she replies, her tone maddeningly calm. "I'm just here to do my job."

I grip the steering wheel tighter, biting back the retort that's on the tip of my tongue. She's playing this game too well, deflecting just enough to keep me guessing without giving me anything to work with.

We arrive at the docks a few minutes later, the sight of stacked shipping containers and the faint smell of saltwater hitting me like a familiar punch. Workers move between containers quickly, but by how high they keep their shoulders, I can tell they're all too tense to be natural.

Eve steps out of the SUV, her heels clicking against the pavement as she adjusts her blazer. I follow, scanning the area for anything that feels out of place.

"Where's Ortega?" I ask.

"Inside the main office," she replies, gesturing toward a squat building near the edge of the docks. "I've already informed him of our visit."

Of course she did.

We make our way to the office, the faint hum of machinery in the background. The man I assume is Ortega is waiting for us, his expression a mixture of weariness and irritation. He's an older man, his face lined with years of hard work and harder decisions.

"Señor Blaze," he says, extending a hand. "Señorita Eve mentioned you'd be coming."

"Ortega," I reply, shaking his hand. His grip is firm but not overcompensating. "I want to go over the manifests with you. There are some discrepancies I need you to explain."

I don't miss the way his eyes flick to Eve briefly before returning to me. "Of course. Let me show you to the records room."

The records room is a cramped, dimly lit space filled with filing cabinets and a single computer that looks like it hasn't been updated in a decade. Ortega pulls out a drawer, retrieving a stack of files that match the ones Eve provided earlier.

"These are the original manifests," he says, handing them to me. "Everything should be in order."

"Should be," I echo, flipping through the files. The discrepancies are there, just as Eve pointed out, but Ortega's calm demeanor doesn't shift. Either he's very good at playing dumb, or he genuinely doesn't know what's going on.

"You've had some turnover in your team recently," I say, keeping my tone casual. "Anything stand out? New hires causing problems? Suspicious behavior?"

Ortega shakes his head. "Nothing out of the ordinary. We vet all new hires thoroughly."

"That doesn't mean they're clean," I point out. "Sometimes the best way to exploit a system is from the inside."

Ortega's eyes flicker with unease, but he doesn't respond.

Eve steps forward, her voice smooth as she interjects. "If someone is skimming, they're doing it carefully. The discrepancies are small enough to avoid detection unless someone is specifically looking for them."

"And you just happened to notice," I say, glancing at her.

Her expression remains neutral. "It's my job to notice."

"Convenient," I mutter, returning my attention to the files.

Ortega clears his throat, his tone cautious. "If there's anything else you need, let me know. I'll cooperate fully."

"I'm sure you will," I reply, closing the folder. "We'll be conducting a thorough review of the operation. If there's anything you're not telling me, now's the time."

He doesn't flinch, his gaze confident. "You'll find everything in order."

I don't believe him, but I let it go for now. Eve leads the way back to the SUV, her expression blank as we climb inside.

"Well?" she asks once we're on the road again.

"Well, what?" I reply, keeping my eyes on the road.

"Your thoughts on Ortega."

"He's hiding something," I say bluntly. "Whether it's intentional or not, I'm not sure yet."

"And me?" she asks, her tone almost teasing.

I glance at her, my expression hardening. "You're hiding plenty."

She smiles faintly, the kind of smile that feels more like a challenge than an agreement. "Maybe. Or maybe you're just looking too hard."

I don't respond, focused on driving us back to the estate. The ride back is quiet again, the silence settling like a heavy fog. She's still as composed as ever, scrolling through her tablet without a care in the world. Whatever she's up to is hidden too well, frustrating the absolute hell out of me. The whole setup feels wrong, but without proof, I'm stuck playing Diablo's game.

As I pull into the estate, my mind drifts to the others. Ryder's probably charming his way through whatever task Diablo saddled him with, making it look easy even if it isn't. He's good at that—masking stress with humor pretending it doesn't even exist. Thorne, on the other hand, is likely overanalyzing every move, his permanently grumpy face hiding the fact that he cares about shit more than anyone realizes.

And Tori...I grip the steering wheel a little tighter at the thought of her. She was worried this morning, even if she didn't say it outright. I could see it in the way her eyes lingered on me when I kissed her, in the way her hand brushed against mine like she needed the reassurance.

I park the SUV and step out, barely acknowledging Eve as she heads to her car. I grab my phone from my pocket and lean against the hood of the car, scrolling through my messages until I find Tori's name.

> **Blaze**
> How's it going?

I hesitate for a moment before adding another line.

> **Blaze**
> I love you.

It's simple, but it's enough. I hit send and stare at the screen, half-expecting an immediate reply even though I know she's probably busy. The phone buzzes a minute later, and her response makes my chest ache in the best way.

> **Doll**
> I love you too. Everything okay?

> **Blaze**
> Yeah. Just wanted to hear from you.

Her reply is almost instant this time.

> **Doll**
> You're sweet when you're not bossing everyone around.

I can practically hear the teasing tone in her voice, and it's enough to make me chuckle.

> **Blaze**
> Someone has to keep Ryder in line.

> **Doll**
> Good luck with that.

She shoots back, followed by a winking emoji.

I tuck the phone back into my pocket, feeling a little lighter. Even with everything going on, she has a way of grounding me, making everything feel right again.

As I head inside, I catch a glimpse of Eve driving, offering a polite nod when she meets my gaze. She's a puzzle I'm not sure I want to solve, but I know I'll have to eventually.

For now, though, I need to focus. The discrepancies at the docks aren't going to explain themselves, and if Diablo is testing me, I intend to pass—with or without Eve's help.

4: THORNE

The smell hits me first. It's a mix of rust, saltwater, and something I can't quite place—something metallic and bitter, like old blood. The warehouse looms ahead, its rigid walls dented and streaked with grime, like the world gave up on it a long time ago. I can't say I blame it.

Mia stands beside me, clutching her bag for dear life, like she's scared of even being here. She's trying to look composed, but her grip is white-knuckled, and her eyes dart around like she's expecting the walls to collapse at any moment. The six-inch heels she's wearing does nothing to make her seem less out of place.

"You're quiet," I say, glancing at her as we approach the entrance.

"So are you," she counters, her voice softer than mine, but there's a thread of grit in it.

Fair enough.

I pull open the heavy steel door, the hinges groaning in protest. The air inside is worse than outside—damp and stagnant, thick enough to choke on. A cold dread creeps up my spine, putting me on high alert instantly.

"Stay close," I tell her as we step inside.

She nods, following a step behind me. For someone so fragile-looking, she's got more grit than I expected. Not that I'd admit it out loud. Diablo paired me with her for a reason, and whatever that reason is, I don't trust it. She's part of whatever test he's throwing at us.

The rows of crates stretch endlessly, stacked high enough to block out most of the overhead lights. I pick a random aisle and head down it, scanning the labels on the crates as we pass.

"This is where Diablo keeps his legitimate operations?" I ask, curious as to how much information she'll let slip.

She shakes her head, eyes wide, as if being afraid is her permanent state of living. "There's nothing legitimate about this place."

I frown, disappointed by the lack of useful details.

We stop at a stack of crates labeled with codes that mean nothing to me. Pulling a crowbar from a nearby rack, I pry the first one open. The lid comes off with a satisfying crack, revealing rows of neatly packed electronics—phones, tablets, and a few devices I can't immediately identify. At first glance, everything looks clean. But even knowing about the secret compartment beneath the fake merchandise, the numbers on the manifest still don't add up, and that's what we're here to investigate. The drugs and weapons in the crate should make it weigh more than it says. It's off—just enough to be noticeable to someone paying attention.

What exactly is inside the crates that don't match up?

"Find anything?" Mia asks, her voice closer now. I didn't even hear her move.

"Weights don't match the manifest. Either someone's skimming, or someone's screwing with me," I reply, finding nothing but stacks of hundreds in the hidden compartments.

"Or both," she says, and there's an edge to her tone that makes me glance at her.

She's standing a few feet away, her arms crossed tightly over her chest. Her gaze is on the crates, but there's something pensive in her expression that sets my teeth on edge. For someone who's supposed to be nervous and out of her depth, she's holding herself together a little too well.

"What about you?" I ask. "Notice anything?"

She hesitates for a second, then pulls out a small notebook from her bag. Flipping it open, she shows me a series of markings she's been writing down. "These crates have similar discrepancies. Not just weights, but also the codes. They're off by a single digit. It could be a mistake, but..."

"But Diablo doesn't make mistakes," I finish, my voice flat.

She nods, her lips pressing into a thin line. "Exactly."

I narrow my eyes at her, trying to figure out if she's good at her job or if there's something more to this. She's raising my suspicions further with every passing second.

"You're awfully observant," I say, letting my tone sharpen.

Mia looks up at me, her expression oddly neutral, considering she's looked completely terrified the entire time before this. "I take my job seriously."

"Right," I mutter, turning back to the crates.

The conversation dies there, but the tension lingers. I move to the next crate, prying it open to find more of the same—electronics, medical supplies, hidden money, sometimes hidden drugs. Mia stays close, scribbling in her notebook and muttering under her breath every now and then.

She's starting to creep me out.

When I find a crate with a completely different code—one that doesn't match anything on the manifest—I pause. It's marked with a simple red X, nothing else. Mia notices immediately, her gaze flicking to the crate and then to me.

"What is it?" she asks.

"Don't know yet." I pry it open, the crowbar digging into the wood. The lid pops off, revealing rows of unmarked black cases.

I pick one up, snapping it open to find stacks of cash, neatly bundled and organized.

"Well, that's not suspicious at all," I say dryly.

She ignores me as I open another case to find more cash. The crates were supposed to be filled with medical supplies only, not be entirely full of cash. Something is definitely off.

"We need to report this," Mia says, her tone urgent.

"To who? Diablo?" I close the case, my mind racing. "He already knows. This is his setup."

"Then why have you look into it?" she asks, her voice softer now.

"Because he can."

Her silence tells me she doesn't like that answer, but it's the truth. Diablo doesn't need a reason to test us. He does it because he enjoys watching us squirm, because it gives him power.

Because he doesn't want us with his daughter.

Maybe he thinks we'll quit and leave.

Clearly, he doesn't know anything about us if he thinks we'd ever leave Tori's side.

We move deeper into the warehouse, the air growing colder as the natural light from outside fades. The dim overhead bulbs do little to cut through the shadows, casting long, jagged lines along the floor and walls. Mia follows a step behind me, her earlier confidence slipping the farther we go. She stops suddenly, her hand clutching the strap of her bag tightly.

"What's wrong?" I ask, my voice low, keeping the edge out of it. I don't need to startle her more than she already is.

Mia hesitates, her eyes flitting to mine before she looks away. "Nothing. It's just...this place. It's suffocating." Her voice wavers, the veneer of composure cracking just enough for me to see through it.

I glance around the warehouse. It's nothing special—just rows of crates and the occasional piece of forgotten machinery.

"You want to wait outside?" I ask, softening my tone as much as I can manage. "I can handle the rest."

"No." She shakes her head quickly, her grip on her bag tightening. "I'm fine. Let's just finish this."

She's not fine. I've seen enough fear to recognize it, even when someone's doing their best to hide it. But I also know pushing her won't help. So I nod and keep moving, slowing my pace a bit so she doesn't have to rush to keep up.

Mia stays close, her steps quieter now, almost hesitant. The contrast from earlier is striking—yet again, she flips on me. *Maybe she has multiple personalities?*

For a brief moment, she reminds me of Vic, of how she used to be. Always breaking beneath the surface but never letting it show.

The thought hits me harder than it should, stopping me in my tracks. I glance back at Mia, her eyes scanning the area like she's bracing for something to jump out at her. It's not the same as Vic, not exactly, but it's close enough to twist something in my chest.

I remember the way Vic used to flinch when we got too close, how she'd fold in on herself to hide the cracks she didn't want anyone to see. I remember the nights she looked at me like I was the enemy, and I didn't know how to fix it. Seeing that same vulnerability now, in someone else, makes my stomach churn.

"Thorne?" Mia's voice pulls me out of my thoughts, her brows furrowing as she watches me.

"Sorry, it's nothing," I say quickly, shaking off the memory. "Let's keep going."

We reach another stack of crates, these marked with a different set of codes. I pry one open, letting the lid fall to the floor with a dull thud. Inside are rows of neatly packed medical supplies, just like the manifest said. No discrepancies here.

Mia steps closer, her eyes scanning the contents like she's trying to memorize every detail. Her hand brushes against the edge of the crate, and I notice the slight tremor in her fingers.

"You sure you're okay?" I ask, keeping my tone as neutral as possible.

She hesitates, her gaze lingering on the crate before she finally speaks. "It's not the warehouse," she says quietly. "It's...everything. This whole situation. I've never been in something like this before."

Her voice is steadier now, but there's a rawness to it that wasn't there earlier. She's not just talking about the task at hand—she's talking about all of it. Diablo, the assignments, the constant pressure to perform. It's a lot, especially for someone who looks like a simple breeze would blow her away.

"First time working in the big leagues?" I ask, taking a page out of Ryder's book and trying to lighten the mood without brushing her off completely.

She lets out a short, humorless laugh. "Something like that."

I lean against the crate, crossing my arms as I study her. "You'll get used to it."

She looks up at me, her expression hard to read. "Did you?"

It's a simple question, but it knocks the air out of me for a second. *Did I?* Vic floods my mind again, the way she's learned to carry the weight of everything we've put her through, and I wonder if it's the same for me.

"Eventually," I say, because it's the closest thing to the truth I can give her.

Mia nods, but I can tell she doesn't believe me. Not entirely. And honestly, I don't blame her.

We finish checking the crates in silence with my mind stuck in the past. By the time we're done, Mia's composure is fraying at the edges. But she's still standing, still trying, and I have to give her credit for that.

As we head back toward the entrance, I catch her glancing at me out of the corner of my eye. There's something in her expression I can't quite place—gratitude, maybe, or something close to it. I don't say anything, but I make a mental note to keep an eye on her. Liability or not, I can't ignore the fact that she's here, in this with me, whether I like it or not. For all I know, she's being forced to be here by Diablo.

The moment we step back out, Mia takes a deep breath, her shoulders relaxing somewhat as the fresh air hits her. I don't say anything as I watch her, but the image of Vic lingers in my mind, comparing the two of them when I know I shouldn't.

Whatever Diablo's game is, I'm starting to see the pieces fall into place. And I don't like it.

The ride back to the estate is quiet for the first few minutes. Mia sits stiffly in the passenger seat, clearly uncomfortable. I focus on the road until Mia suddenly sits up, pairs her phone to the vehicle and starts some music. My heart lurches as Deftones begins to play.

"I'm sorry. I really can't stand it when it's too quiet," she admits shyly, sitting back as she starts to uncoil. All I can do is nod my head, hating how Mia reminds me of a deep-in-trauma Vic.

The ride is rather calm until we hit a stoplight, and I notice her glancing at me out of the corner of her eye like she's debating whether or not to say something.

"If you've got something to say, spit it out," I command, keeping my tone light.

Mia startles, her grip tightening before she forces herself to relax. "I was just wondering...how long have you been doing this?"

I glance at her, noting the faint hesitation in her voice. "Depends on what you mean by 'this.'"

"This," she says, gesturing vaguely. "The...dangerous, illegal side of things. The kind of life where warehouses full of cash and drugs are just another unremarkable day."

Her attempt at humor falls flat, but I can tell she's genuinely curious. I consider brushing her off, but something about the way she's watching me—like she's trying to piece me together—makes me answer.

"Long enough," I say.

"That's vague," she replies, her voice soft but not timid.

"On purpose," I counter, smiling ever so subtly.

She doesn't push, but the silence that follows feels heavier. I tap my fingers against the steering wheel, my thoughts drifting back to the warehouse, to the way she froze and then flipped back into composure, like a switch had been thrown.

"What about you?" I ask, glancing at her again. "How long have you been working for Diablo?"

Mia hesitates, her fingers tightening around her bag. "A few months," she says finally.

"And before that?"

"Different jobs," she says vaguely, her gaze fixed on the passing scenery. "Nothing like this, though."

I raise an eyebrow, my suspicion piqued. "So, why this? Why now?"

She doesn't answer right away, and when she does, her voice is quieter than before. "Because I didn't have a choice."

The words hang in the air between us, heavy with unspoken meaning. I don't press her, but my mind starts turning, trying to connect the dots. She's scared, that much is obvious, but there's something else—something she's not saying.

We hit another stoplight and I glance at her again, noting the way she's staring down at her hands, her expression tight.

"Diablo forcing you to be here?" I ask, my tone sharper than I intended.

Her head snaps up, her eyes wide. "No," she says quickly. "It's not like that."

"Then what is it like?"

She hesitates, her gaze dropping again. "It's...complicated."

"Complicated," I echo, my voice flat.

She nods, her grip on the bag loosening a touch. "Let's just say I owe someone a favor, and this is how I'm paying it off."

It's a half-truth at best, but I let it slide for now. Pushing her won't get me anywhere, and I've got enough on my plate without trying to unravel her secrets.

"Fair enough," I say, my tone neutral.

We fall into silence again, but this time it's less strained as we continue to listen to her music. Mia leans back in her seat, her fingers tapping lightly against the strap of her bag. I keep my eyes on the road, my thoughts drifting back to Vic and the others.

Ryder's probably running his mouth somewhere, charming his way out of trouble or into more of it. Blaze is likely neck-deep in logistics, his perfectionist streak keeping him too busy to notice the cracks forming in the foundation of this entire operation.

And Vic...

She's strong, stronger than any of us give her credit for, but this place isn't safe—not for her, not for any of us. Diablo's playing games, and we're all just pawns on his board.

Mia's voice pulls me from my thoughts.

"You care about her, don't you?"

The question catches me off guard, but I don't let it show. "Who?"

"Tori," she says, her tone careful but not hesitant. "I saw the way you looked at her yesterday."

I glance at her, my expression revealing nothing. "What about it?"

Mia shrugs, her gaze meeting mine briefly before returning to the window. "Just an observation."

I don't respond, but her words linger. Of course I care about Vic. *Fuck that. I love her.* She's the reason I'm here, the reason I'm putting up with Diablo's bullshit.

"You think Diablo's testing her, too?" Mia asks after a moment.

I nod, my grip on the steering wheel tightening. "She may be his daughter by blood, but blood doesn't always make a family. He's testing all of us."

"Why?"

"Because he can."

The words come out harsher than I intended, but they're the truth.

Mia doesn't say anything, but her expression shifts, a flicker of unease crossing her features. I wonder, briefly, what her connection to Diablo is.

"Do yourself a favor," I say, my voice quieter now. "Don't trust him."

Her gaze flicks to mine, her eyes narrowing just a tad. "And I should trust you instead?"

The corner of my mouth lifts. "That's up to you."

She doesn't respond, but the tension in the car eases just enough. It's a small victory, but I'll take it. Maybe if I get her comfortable enough with me, make her believe I'm her friend, she'll open up more.

By the time we pull into the estate, the sun is dipping below the horizon. I can see Blaze is already back and so is Tori, but no Ryder yet. I park the car and cut the engine, glancing at Mia as she gathers her things.

"Get some rest," I tell her. "Tomorrow's probably going to be worse."

She nods, her expression unreadable as she steps out of the car. I watch her walk toward her vehicle, her shoulders squared but her steps slightly hesitant.

As I head inside, I can't shake the feeling that whatever game Diablo's playing, it's only just begun, and we're not the only pieces on the board.

5: RYDER

I hate suits.

They're itchy and restricting, but mostly they make me think of the way my father used to make me dress to meet his campaign donors. Fake smiles, fake love, and the perfect image of a family that didn't actually exist.

Suits don't mean shit to me, but to everyone else, a man in a suit screams power, intelligence, and authority. So here I am, stuffed into one, doing Diablo's bidding for no other reason than he said so.

Well, except for my KitKat.

I'm doing this for her.

This is what she wanted, and I'm sure as hell not going to be the one to screw it up. But that doesn't mean I won't take advantage of the situation. If Diablo has a hidden agenda—and I know he does—I'm going to figure it out, and Lila is going to be the one to crack.

I'm not here to charm investors. I'm here to charm her.

She wants my attention; I can see it. Hell, I can feel it—the way she practically vibrates with the need for me to notice her. All I have to do is give her just enough to keep her wanting more, then watch her unravel. People like Lila always do. And once she's putty in my hands, she'll tell me exactly what Diablo is planning.

"You're awfully quiet for someone who sounded so confident yesterday," she says, her focused green eyes flicking my way as she raises a brow. Her blazer hugs her figure too well to be professional, and the lack of a shirt underneath makes it clear she's playing a game of her own.

"Don't worry, babe," I flash her my signature smirk, the one that says 'I've got this in the bag.' "I don't need much pre-game to finish what I start."

"I guess we'll see." She mirrors my expression, unfazed by my arrogance, like she's been expecting it. "How about a little wager?"

I shouldn't bite.

I know I shouldn't.

But...

"A wager?" I arch a brow, the bait already too tempting. Besides, I always win. And when I do, she'll have no choice but to spill her secrets. "Alright. Name your terms."

Her lips curl into a confident smile, the kind that says she thinks she's already won.

Cute, but I'm going to mop the floor with you.

"We see who closes the deal the fastest," she says, her tone light but her eyes sharp. "If I win, you have to make me dinner."

I blink, caught off guard for a split second before I laugh—an actual laugh. "Dinner? That's it? Hate to break it to you, but I'm not exactly *Chef Boyardee*."

She shrugs, still smiling. "I don't care if it's PB&J, Ryder. It's the principle of the thing."

"Alright, fine." I lean back against the elevator wall, feigning nonchalance. Internally, though, my mind is already spinning. She thinks she's clever, and maybe she is, but she's underestimating me. "And when I win?"

Her confidence falters, just for a second, but it's enough to tell me she's not as certain as she pretends to be. "What do you want?"

I lean in, closing the space between us just enough to make her feel it. "When I win, you tell me what Diablo's planning. All of it."

Her eyes narrow, and for a moment, I think she's going to refuse. But then her expression smooths out, and she tilts her head, her arrogant grin back in place. "That's a steep price."

"Don't make wagers you can't afford to lose," I reply, my voice low and unwavering.

The elevator hums softly around us, the silence stretching between us for a moment. Finally, she steps back, straightening her blazer and lifting her chin. "Fine. But you'd better bring your A-game, Ryder. I don't lose."

I let her have this moment. "Neither do Ikm."

The elevator dings and the doors slide open, revealing a room filled with rich, law-breaking investors who think they're untouchable. But for once, I was a good little boy and studied them all.

Untouchable my ass.

They'll be eating out of my hand in seconds.

They're laughing, sipping expensive liquor, and trading stories about the millions they've made through their "ventures." The kind of people who have just enough power to think they're above consequence.

This is going to be fun.

Lila steps out first, her heels clacking against the marble floor like she owns the place. Her confidence is impressive, I'll give her that. But I don't follow immediately. Instead, I hang back just enough to watch her, to see how she interacts with the room.

She dives in smoothly, shaking hands like she's been doing this her whole life. It's an act, of course—one that Diablo no doubt trained her for. But I can see the cracks in her performance, the slight stiffness in her posture, the way her eyes dart around the room, cataloging every face. She's not as relaxed as she wants everyone to believe.

I step out of the elevator and into the crowd, plastering on my most charming smile.

Time to get to work.

I don't rush, don't make a direct line for anyone. Instead, I let my presence speak for itself. Heads turn, eyes flicker my way, and I catch a few curious glances as I take my time surveying the room.

I hate to admit it, but it's a trick I learned from watching my father in his senator days. They can't think I'm desperate. I have to wait for one of them to show interest, curiosity—something I can work with.

Before I get too comfortable, I search the room for Lila, finding she's still trying to find her target. I'm not exactly sure how she works her charm, but I'm sure the way she's dressed has something to do with it.

I stop near a group of investors standing in a loose circle, their conversation a muddled mix of buzzwords. One of them, a man with slicked-back hair and a watch that probably costs more than my bike, glances at me, his expression polite but guarded.

"Evening," I say smoothly, my voice just loud enough to catch the attention of the others without interrupting. "Hope I'm not late to the party."

Slicked-back raises an eyebrow. "And you are?"

"Ryder Hayes, and you?" The question catches him off-guard, as if I should know who he is, or at the very least know not to bother him.

You're my big tuna.

Target acquired.

The man straightens his posture, his ego inflating with the smallest puff of my attention. "Anthony Marston," he says, offering a hand. His grip is firm, practiced—the kind of handshake meant to dominate a room. I let my lips tilt into something faintly amused as I shake his hand, holding his gaze just long enough to flip the balance back in my favor.

"Pleasure, Marston," I say, letting his name roll off my tongue like I've heard it a hundred times before. "I've been hearing about you for years. It's good to finally put a face to the reputation."

Total lie.

Marston's chest swells, the corners of his mouth twitching upward. "And what reputation is that?"

"That you know how to make the best kind of deals," I reply, my tone easy, almost conversational. "Always in your favor. That's rare these days."

Gotta make you think you're in charge, but really I'll be feeding you the terms of the deal you don't even know we're about to make.

I catch a glimpse of Lila across the room, her lips curving into a faint smile as she schmoozes with some small-time in the corner.

Game on.

"Well, I do aim to be efficient," Marston says, his voice dripping with satisfaction.

"That's great, because cutting a deal with Diablo seems a daunting task, but at 5% revenue of his weapons dealings," I shrug, letting them mull over my words, filling in the blanks with what they want.

The others in the circle lean in subtly, curiosity lighting up their expressions. Marston preens under the attention, his ego inflating even more with every passing second. I keep my posture relaxed, as though I couldn't care less if they sign or not—*because that's how you reel them in.*

"Five percent may seem small," I say casually, "but when you consider Diablo's operations are expanding, it's less a percentage and more a golden ticket. Of course, it's not for everyone. Some people just don't have the stomach for this kind of business."

Marston's eyes narrow a bit, and I see the flicker of a challenge in them.

Just take the bait, man. You know you want to.

Marston glances around the circle, gauging the reactions of the others. Their silence is all the confirmation he needs. "Fine," he says, extending his hand. "Let's see what Diablo has to offer."

Gotcha.

It doesn't take long to move through the room after that. My eyes drift to Lila every time I do, seeing her speaking with the same man.

I've got this bitch in the bag.

The others in the room fall like dominoes, each conversation easier than the last as they sense the momentum building. By the time I'm done, nearly every investor Diablo sent me to charm is locked in. Nearly.

Because the only one missing is the old geezer Lila had been with the entire time.

Lila is tucked into a corner—alone—looking...bored? Her gaze meets mine, and she lifts a signed contract just enough for me to see it, a triumphant look on her face.

Fuck.

When?

I stroll over, keeping my expression neutral, but by her smug look I know she got a contract signed before me. She's all confidence as I approach, her posture relaxed and her smile sharp.

"Well, that was fast," I say, my tone light but laced with meaning.

"I'm not in the business of losing my bets," she replies, her voice smooth. She crosses her arms, tucking them beneath her breasts in a way that lifts them, then flexes her muscles so that she's squeezing them together, showing more through the blazer.

This is how she closed the deal so fast. She distracted that man so much with her body, she had him the moment he looked her way.

I glance at the paper in her hand, doing my best to school my features. "I see you, Lila."

She leans in just a fraction, her green eyes sparkling. "And here I thought you'd be happy for me."

I chuckle, though it's more for show. "Happy isn't the word I'd use."

She grins, lording around the fact I lost. "I guess that means I win our wager."

"Looks like it," I admit, keeping my tone steady. "Too bad it wasn't about anything worthwhile, like quality or quantity."

She tilts her head, her gaze flirtatious. "Don't worry, Ryder. There's always next time."

She smiles, leaving me with the bitter taste of defeat.

She played me, no question about it.

I'm so getting the shit beat out of me by Thorne and Blaze for this.

My mind flashes to Tori, picturing the hurt in her eyes when I tell her about my shenanigans. I wonder how upset she'll be, exactly.

Dammit! I shouldn't have taken the bait.

I should have known.

I let the guilt weigh heavy on me for a moment, but I don't show it. I don't want Lila to see how much this will actually affect me. But maybe that was the point, wasn't it? For her, I mean. She wants to see me rattled, or maybe she wants to see Tori hurt?

I'll kill her.

Lila steps closer, placing her hand on my chest with a tap of each finger. Her eyes flick up to mine with a confidence I don't need her to have. "Can't wait for dinner." She laughs as she walks off, leading the way to the elevator. We're done here, after all. And even though I passed Diablo's test with his business, I failed the test with his daughter.

Wait! Loophole.

Lila said I had to make her dinner. She didn't say we had to be alone, or that I had to stay and eat it with her. I'll have Tori by my side the entire time I make a poorly constructed sandwich. Then I'll throw said sandwich at Lila, tell her bon appétit and carry my dinner—a KitKat—to my room.

Sounds delicious.

The confidence is back in my stride as I head for the SUV Diablo is having us all drive. Blaze lost his sports car, Thorne his truck, and I my bike. But when business isn't involved, you can bet your ass Tori will be riding on the back of my bike soon.

"For someone who just lost a bet, you seem a little too happy," Lila es, entirely misinterprets my good mood. "Are you just excited to cook me dinner?"

I chuckle, leaning back against the elevator wall as the doors close, crossing my arms and letting my inner demon peek through my eyes. "I'm excited for something, that's for sure. But cooking you dinner is definitely not it."

She's smug, her shoulders pushed back to press her breasts out further, her eyes dancing with lust as she watches me. I'm not bothered by it, keeping my gaze straight on the doors until they open again.

I take the lead this time, being the first to step out into the attached parking garage. We're almost to the SUV when I spot a silver Dodge Tomahawk.

It's illegal on the streets, so what are the chances they'll report it stolen?

My lips twitch, stretching into a wicked grin as I eye the bike. The suit feels more constrictive now, like staring at this beautiful metal has reminded me of how binding this fabric is. I take the blazer off and toss it at Lila's head.

"I'll meet you at the estate. The keys are in the right pocket." I point to what I just threw at her. Taking my tie off and shoving it in my pocket, I slowly roll my sleeves up and unbutton the top two buttons of my shirt before I straddle the bike.

"What?" Lila whisper shouts at me, finally snapping out of the shock. She marches toward me, her eyes wide like she's about to scold me, but my mind's focused on how to get this thing started.

Can you hot-wire a bike?

I'm searching around, sleek metal beneath my fingers as I feel around. My fingers snag on a small compartment, sliding it open to find the keys.

I don't know who owns this bike, but I both want to laugh in their face and stick my tongue down their throat.

If I wasn't already on edge, if I wasn't already feeling so wound up and ready to explode, I might think my actions through. But right now I just need out. I need away from Lila, away from the suits and ass-kissing.

Lila is still spouting something, but I've tuned her out so much I don't even notice her when I take off. The bike is a fucking dream, faster than anything I've ever ridden before. It's intimidating, which means I love it even more.

I'm racing through the streets, weaving through the traffic as I make my way to the estate. My mind is focused on my KitKat, ready to wrap her in my arms and make her mine. Ready to show her that she matters most to me.

She needs to know that even though I like to be in control in the bedroom, she's the one who owns me.

The estate looms ahead, not exactly homey, but as long as I have Tori and the guys, it's enough. I park in the front, kicking the stand out with more force than necessary.

I note there are two SUVs, so I begin to wonder who's missing. With a nagging worry, I trudge my way to the front door, knowing I'm about to get a lecture from whichever guy is home. But when I open the door, I'm greeted by two dogs—at least it feels that way. Thorne stands up so fast, if he had a tail it'd be going a mile a minute. Blaze, on the other hand, comes running out of the kitchen into the hall.

That answers the question of who's missing.

Almost at the same time, all of our faces fall. "Not that I'm not happy to see you guys, but where the fuck is our girl?" I ask, closing the door behind me and stepping in.

"I thought you were her," Blaze mutters through gritted teeth, turning back and making his way to the kitchen. It smells good, so he's gotta be cooking.

I nod at Thorne and we follow the grumpy Blaze. He immediately takes his spot at the stove, stirring whatever heavenly stir fry he's got going on in the pot. Thorne and I crowd the island, leaning over it in silence. It doesn't take a genius to figure out what we're all thinking.

Is Tori okay?

"Has anyone texted her?"

"I did earlier. Everything seemed fine then," Blaze responds, keeping his attention on the food.

"Let's try to call her." I pull my phone out, and dial her number but get nothing in response.

We're all starting to worry now.

Blaze slams the wooden spoon against the edge of the pot, his jaw clenched so tight I can practically hear his teeth grinding. "If Gabriel screwed up—"

"Relax," I interrupt, though my chest feels as tight as his tone. "Tori's smart. If there was trouble, she'd handle it—or let us know."

"That's not the point," Thorne snaps, his voice sharp. "She shouldn't be in this position. What the hell is taking so long?"

My fingers twitch against the counter as I set my phone down. No answer. My thumb hovers over her contact again, but I don't press it. Instead, I force myself to keep my voice even. "She's with Gabe. He's...capable."

I think.

Surely Diablo wouldn't have him as her bodyguard if was total shit at doing his job.

Blaze snorts, his head snapping toward me. "Capable? That's the bar we're setting now? Because capable doesn't cut it if she's not home in five minutes."

"She's not a kid, Blaze," I remind him, even though my stomach twists at my own words. "She's more than able to take care of herself." *Right?*

"Still not the point," Thorne mutters darkly, crossing his arms and leaning back against the counter, his expression hard. "If she's hurt—"

"She's not hurt," I cut in quickly, trying to defuse the growing storm. "And if she is, we'll deal with it. Starting with Gabriel."

Blaze huffs, turning back to the stove and stirring with more force than necessary. "I don't like this."

"None of us do," I admit, though the words feel sour in my mouth. I glance between them, their frustration mirrored in my own chest. "But blowing up before we know anything doesn't help."

Thorne narrows his eyes at me, like he wants to argue but can't find the words. So, I gesture to the stool next to me. "Sit down and talk."

"About?" he raises an eyebrow in suspicion.

Blaze glances over his shoulder, clearly interested despite his attention being on the food. I drag a hand through my hair, knowing I need to tell them the stupidity of me.

"I, uh...lost a bet," I admit, keeping my voice light.

Blaze pauses, his spoon hovering mid-air. "With Lila?"

"Yeah."

Thorne's eyebrows shoot up, and Blaze mutters something under his breath that sounds suspiciously like, "Idiot."

"Thanks for the vote of confidence," I say dryly, leaning against the counter. "It's not a big deal."

"*You* lost a bet? *You?*" Thorne's disbelief is almost comical, but I don't laugh.

"Technically, yeah. She closed a deal before I could. A sneaky one." I shrug, playing it off even as my muscles coil. "Now I have to make her dinner."

"Dinner," Blaze repeats, his voice flat. "You've got to be kidding me."

"Oh, but I'm not." I grin, though it doesn't reach my eyes. "But I've got a plan. She said I had to make her dinner, not that I had to eat it with her."

Thorne groans, pinching the bridge of his nose. "You've got to stop thinking with your ego."

"It's not ego," I counter, though I know it's a lie. "It's strategy. She wants to play games? Fine. I'll play. But I'm not losing twice."

Blaze shakes his head, returning his attention to the stove. "This is going to backfire."

"Maybe." I shrug, though the nagging worry about Tori undercuts the bravado. "But tell me you don't have plans of your own to get Eve to talk."

Before Blaze can respond, the sound of tires crunching on gravel drifts through the open window. Blaze's head snaps up and Thorne straightens, both of them moving toward the front door like bloodhounds on a scent. I trail behind, my pulse spiking.

The SUV rolls to a stop, but it's not Tori—it's stupid fucking Lila. She steps out, looking annoyingly composed. Her sharp eyes sweep the driveway, and when they land on us, she looks smug as fuck.

Great. Just what I needed.

KitKat, I need you to hurry home—but also not be pissed when you get here and see her. Please.

6: Tori

Earlier that day

The drive out of the estate felt longer today, probably because Gabe drives like we're in a retirement parade. I swear I counted the same pothole three times, and my left leg won't stop bouncing. Not that Gabe notices—he's too busy being the world's most stoic chauffeur. If he gets any quieter, I'll have to start narrating my own thoughts just to fill the silence.

Okay, Tori, focus. This is fine. Everything is fine.

Except it's not. Diablo's "grand tour" of his empire is feeling less like a chance to learn and more like an audition for a reality tv show. Every building we've visited today has been crawling with people who'd sell their own mothers for a favor from him. I've smiled, nodded, and pretended I wasn't itching to grab a fire extinguisher and start swinging. But hey, I'm learning, right?

Learning that my dad's a control freak who probably sleeps with one eye open.

Gabe clears his throat, snapping me out of my spiral. His blue eyes flick to me briefly before returning to the road. "You okay back there?"

"Oh, you know," I say, waving a hand. "Just contemplating the existential horror of inheriting a criminal empire. No big deal."

His lips twitch, but he stays stoic as ever. Gabe never seems to smile. I'm convinced his face would crack if he tried.

"You'll get used to it," he says, like that's supposed to be comforting.

"Yeah, sure. Just like you get used to paper cuts or stepping on Legos." I cross my arms, slouching deeper into the seat. "What's next on the 'Tori Learns the Family Business' tour? Organ harvesting? Or is that too hands-on?"

"Funny," Gabe says dryly. "But no. Just more stops to show you how things operate."

I glance out the window, catching sight of a scraggly patch of forest we're passing. "Fascinating. Can't wait for the highlight reel."

He doesn't respond, and the silence stretches long enough for me to feel the itch of my own curiosity. "So," I say, leaning forward in my seat, "how did you end up working for Diablo? Did you, like, lose a bet or something?"

Gabe glances at me, his expression unreadable. "I was recruited."

"Recruited," I echo. "That sounds ominous."

"It's not a story you'd find interesting," he replies, his tone dismissive.

"Oh, come on," I press, resting my chin on my hand. "You've got that whole 'mysterious bodyguard' vibe going on. At least give me something. Did you grow up in this world? Were you, like, groomed to be the perfect soldier?"

His grip on the steering wheel tightens ever so slightly. "Something like that."

"Wow," I say, dragging the word out. "That was so specific and detailed. I feel like I know your entire life story now."

"You're relentless, you know that?" he mutters, though there's a faint note of amusement in his voice.

"It's a gift," I say, taking a small bow. "So, what's the deal with you and Diablo? Are you just his favorite henchman, or is there more to it?"

"Why are you so curious?"

"Because you're going to be around all the time, and I have to figure out whether you're a terrifying enigma or just really good at your job."

He lets out a low chuckle, surprising me. "I'll let you decide."

Before I can push further, Gabe's eyes narrow and he adjusts the rearview mirror. "We're being followed."

"What?" I twist in my seat, craning my neck to look out the back window. Sure enough, a dark SUV is tailing us, keeping a fixed distance but matching our speed.

"Stay calm," Gabe says, his voice sharp and focused. "It could be nothing."

"Yeah, because random cars following us is super normal."

He ignores me, his hands steady on the wheel as he takes a sharp turn onto a dirt road. The tires kick up a cloud of dust, and the car behind us speeds up, closing the gap.

"Uh, Gabe?" I say, gripping the door handle as the car jostles over the uneven terrain. "What's the plan here?"

"Hold on," he says, his tone leaving no room for argument.

Before I can demand a better explanation, a second SUV accelerates and slams into us with too much force not to leave a mark. My head smacks against the window, and for a second, stars explode in my vision.

"Son of a—" I cut myself off, rubbing my temple as Gabe yanks the wheel, trying to control the car.

"Are you okay?" he asks, his voice tight with concern.

"Peachy," I mutter, wincing as another jolt rocks the car. "What the hell is their problem?"

"Probably not fans of my driving," he says dryly, his focus laser-sharp as he navigates the narrow road.

Did he just make a joke?

"Stay down," he commands, driving like he's raced in Nascar before.

"Stay down?" I echo, my voice rising. "Gabe, it's not like they're shooting at us."

Another ram sends the car skidding, and I nearly tumble out of my seat. Gabe mutters a curse under his breath, jerking the wheel again to keep us on the road.

"Just trust me," he says, his voice hard.

"Trust you? You're the one who got us into a demolition derby!"

The SUV behind us revs its engine, preparing for another hit. Gabe slams on the brakes suddenly, and the car jerks violently. The SUV shoots past us, skidding to a stop a few yards ahead.

"Stay here," Gabe orders, unbuckling his seatbelt and reaching for his gun.

"Like hell I'm staying here," I snap, fumbling with my seatbelt. My head still throbs, but adrenaline is surging now, drowning out everything else.

"Tori," he says sharply, his gaze locking with mine. "I need you to trust me."

I hesitate, my fingers hovering over the seatbelt clasp. There's something in his eyes—something unyielding—that makes me pause. Finally, I nod, sinking back into the seat.

"Fine," I mutter. "But if you get yourself killed, I'm stealing the car."

And running everyone over.

He doesn't respond, already stepping out of the vehicle. My heart pounds as I watch him approach the other SUV, his gun drawn and his posture radiating calm authority. The driver's door opens, and a man steps out—a broad-shouldered figure with a shaved head and a scar running down one side of his face.

To my surprise, they don't start shooting. Nope, they exchange words, but I can't hear what's being said over the roar of blood in my ears. My fingers tap against the armrest, a nervous rhythm I can't stop. The passenger door of the SUV opens, and another man steps out, his hand hovering near his waistband.

"Gabe!" I shout, leaning out of the window. "Watch—"

Before I can finish, the second man lunges, pulling a knife. Gabe moves like lightning, disarming him with a swift motion and sending him sprawling to the ground. The first man charges but Gabe's ready, delivering a sharp kick to his knee that drops him instantly.

It's over in seconds, but my heart feels like it's been running a marathon. Gabe stands over the two men, his expression cold and impassive. He glances back at me, and I can't help but notice the way his jaw tightens.

"You okay?" he asks as he returns to the car, sliding into the driver's seat.

"Define 'okay,'" I say, my voice shaking slightly. "Because if it means having a minor heart attack, then yeah, I'm great."

He exhales sharply, running a hand through his hair. "We'll talk about this later. Right now, we need to move."

"Move where?"

"Anywhere but here," he says, starting the engine. "Buckle up."

I do as he says, though my hands are still trembling. As the car pulls back onto the road, I glance at Gabe, my mind racing with questions I don't even know how to ask.

"Gabe?"

"Yeah?"

"What the hell just happened?"

He doesn't answer right away, his focus on the road ahead. Finally, he sighs, his shoulders relaxing a tad. "Welcome to the family business."

I groan, rubbing the side of my head where it smacked against the car window. "Next time, I'm driving."

He doesn't laugh. *Big shocker.* Instead, his eyes dart to the rearview mirror for the hundredth time, his hands gripping the wheel like it's the only thing keeping us alive. Which, judging by the way my ears are ringing, might not be far from the truth.

"Is your head okay?" he asks, finally sparing me a glance.

"Oh, yeah, just great," I reply, even though my head's pounding and I'm pretty sure I'll have a window-shaped bruise to show off later. "Just another day in the glamorous life of Tori Reyes. You?"

"Could be better." His voice is clipped, his focus back on the road—or what's left of it. The dirt path we're bouncing along is narrow and lined with trees that look like they're ready to snatch us off the road. "You hit your head pretty hard."

"Yeah, well, the window hit back," I mutter, touching the sore spot gingerly. "Wanna actually tell me what happened now?"

"Not exactly." He hesitates, and that hesitation tells me everything I need to know: whatever's going on, it's bad.

"Gabe," I drawl, giving him my best 'don't screw with me' look. "Spill. Now."

He sighs, his shoulders slumping just an inch. "They're part of a group that's been trying to edge in on Diablo's territory. Small-time, but persistent. They've been causing problems at a few of his operations."

"And by 'problems,' you mean..."

"Attacks. Threats. Attempts to take over." He clenches his teeth, and his knuckles whiten on the steering wheel. "This wasn't random. They know who you are."

I blink, processing that little nugget of information. "So, what? They were hoping to kidnap me and use me as leverage? Because I killed the last guy that tried."

And it still makes me sick.

"You're more than leverage," he says, his voice quiet but firm. "You're his daughter."

I roll my eyes, even though my stomach twists at the thought. "Yeah, well, someone should send out a memo. 'Tori Reyes: she kicks, bites, and kills.'"

Gabe doesn't respond. Instead, he slows the car as we approach a clearing. The dirt road widens, revealing a small, dilapidated building that looks like it's one strong gust away from collapsing.

Great. Another stellar destination.

"Where are we now?" I ask, squinting at the place. The sign above the door is faded, the letters barely legible.

"One of Diablo's fronts," Gabe says, parking the car and cutting the engine. "A bar. Or it was, until someone decided they wanted to set it on fire. Now it's a rundown place we stash things in."

"And we're here because...?"

"Because places like this need to be checked on from time to time, and today is that time, seeing as I'm going to need more ammo than I originally thought." He opens his door, glancing back at me. "Stay close. And keep your phone ready, just in case."

I pull my phone from my pocket, only to notice the screen is destroyed, cracked to hell. Not exactly sure how that happened. "Yeah, about that. My phone's not exactly in fighting shape right now."

I only got to text Blaze a couple of times this morning and now I won't be able to text Thorne or Ryder and check on them.

Fucking goons.

Gabe glances at the shattered screen and frowns. "Stay close anyway."

We step out of the car, the cool air biting at my skin. The place is eerily quiet, the kind of quiet that makes your instincts scream at you to turn around and run. But, because I apparently have a death wish, I follow Gabe toward the building.

Inside, the air is stale and heavy, carrying the faint scent of spilled beer and something sour. The place is a wreck. Tables overturned, chairs broken, glass littering the floor. It looks like a tornado decided to stop for a drink and didn't like the service.

"Nice place," I mutter, stepping over a broken bottle. "Definitely has that 'welcome home' vibe."

Gabe doesn't reply. He's scanning the room, his posture stiff. "Stay here."

"Yeah, sure. Because splitting up in a creepy, abandoned bar is always a good idea," I mutter under my breath. But I stay put, watching as he moves deeper into the building.

This is how people die in horror movies.

They split up.

He disappears around a corner, leaving me alone with the broken furniture and my own thoughts. I fidget with the belt loops of my jeans, my mind racing. If those guys from earlier were willing to ram us off the road, what's to say someone else won't try something here? And with my phone out of commission, I'm basically a damsel in distress.

I'm about to call out to Gabe when a loud crash echoes from the back of the bar. My heart leaps into my throat, and before I can think better of it, I'm moving toward the sound.

Curiosity killed the cat, Tori. Like, literally, you could die.

"Gabe?" I call softly, my voice barely above a whisper.

Another crash. Louder this time. My pulse pounds in my ears as I round the corner, my eyes scanning the dimly lit hallway. Gabe's voice rings out, sharp and commanding, followed by a string of curses that definitely don't sound like him.

I step closer, peeking into the room at the end of the hall. Gabe is there, facing off against two guys who look like they've been bench-pressing cars for fun. One of them lunges, and Gabe moves faster than I thought possible, dodging the attack and countering with a punch that sends the guy stumbling back.

The second guy notices me before Gabe does, his eyes narrowing as he takes a step in my direction. My stomach drops, and I instinctively reach for the nearest object—a broken chair leg—holding it like a makeshift weapon.

"Tori, get back!" Gabe's voice is sharp, cutting through the chaos. But the guy doesn't stop, his focus locked on me.

Gabe moves like a storm, slamming into the guy and knocking him off balance. The first thug is back on his feet, charging at Gabe like a bull. Gabe sidesteps him, delivering a brutal elbow to his ribs that makes me wince just watching. The guy wheezes, clutching his side, but Gabe doesn't let up. He grabs the thug by the collar, slamming him against the wall hard enough to rattle the shelves nearby.

The second guy tries to capitalize on the distraction, lunging at Gabe from behind. But Gabe spins, his movements fluid and precise, and lands a kick to the guy's knee that sends him crumpling to the floor with a scream.

Maybe Gabe is John Wick in real life.

I'm sure there's a pencil somewhere around here...

"You want to keep going?" Gabe growls, his voice low and dangerous. He steps toward the first thug, who's still pinned against the wall. "Because I've got all day."

The guy's eyes dart between Gabe and his friend on the ground, calculating his odds.

They're not good.

"Alright, man. We're done," he mutters, raising his hands in surrender. Gabe releases him with a shove, and he stumbles toward the door, dragging his injured friend with him.

"Next time," Gabe calls after them, his tone cold enough to freeze water, "you'll wish you stayed home."

The silence that follows hurts my ears. Gabe turns to me, his expression a mix of anger and concern. "What part of 'stay here' did you not understand?"

"The part where you thought I'd actually listen," I shoot back, my voice shaky despite my attempt at humor.

His jaw tightens but he doesn't argue. Instead, he lets out a heavy sigh, his hand gripping my arm. "Are you okay?"

I nod, even though my knees feel like they might give out at any second. "Yeah. Thanks to you."

He studies me for a moment longer before his grip softens. "Let's get out of here."

I don't argue, watching him grab the ammo he needs, and then following him back to the car. My head's still spinning, but one thing is clear: if Gabe keeps this up, I might actually start trusting him.

We drive with the setting sun as our scenery, the orange and pinks easing my troubles for a moment. Thankfully, we're heading home, where I can finally be surrounded by the people I want to be around.

I wonder if it would have been better to go to college?

The estate comes into view, and my heart races with excitement, ready to bury my face into their chests and feel their arms wrap around me. I've missed them, and being away from them with Gabe has been torture.

The bump from the earlier car 'adventure' with Gabe hasn't stopped throbbing, and my patience for today is officially dead. I glance at my bodyguard as he parks, his expression neutral as always, but his finger taps against the steering wheel—a subtle sign he's bracing for impact. He knows he's about to have to deal with Thorne, Ryder, and Blaze.

The second the SUV comes to a halt, the front door bursts open. Thorne and Blaze storm out, their faces like thunderclouds. Thorne reaches the back door first, yanking the door open before I can even unbuckle.

"You okay?" he asks, his dark eyes scanning me for injuries. His hand hovers near my head, his thumb grazing the bump gently.

"I'm fine," I say, though the wince I fail to suppress probably doesn't help my case.

"Fine?" Blaze's voice is sharp as he rounds the car, his gaze zeroing in on the swelling. "That doesn't look fine, Doll."

Before I can reply, Gabe steps out of the driver's seat, drawing their attention like moths to a flame.

"What the hell happened?" Blaze demands, his tone icy. "You're supposed to keep her safe, not let her get banged up."

"It was unavoidable," Gabe replies evenly, though his calm demeanor only seems to stoke their anger.

"Unavoidable?" Thorne's voice drops to a dangerous low, his hand curling into a fist at his side. "You mean to tell me you couldn't avoid letting her get hurt?"

"She's here, isn't she?" Gabe's gaze doesn't waver, his tone unflinching. "Sometimes keeping her safe means taking calculated risks."

Oh, great. That word—calculated. Thorne's least favorite when it comes to anything involving me.

"Calculated risks?" Blaze echoes, his voice rising. "She's hurt, Morales. What part of that screams safe to you?"

I sigh, slipping out of the SUV while they're busy verbally mauling each other. Normally I wouldn't mind watching this unfold. But, really, I am fine, and my stomach is growling too loudly to ignore, reminding me that I've had exactly zero food since this morning. The bump on my head is annoying, sure, but my hunger is downright murderous.

Leaving the three testosterone tornadoes behind, I head for the kitchen. The familiar scent of something delicious wafts through the air, but the sound of hushed laughter stops me in my tracks.

Rounding the corner, I find Ryder and Lila at the kitchen island. She's perched on a stool, leaning in closer to him than necessary, her hand brushing his arm as she laughs at something he said. My hands clench into fists as I take in the scene. Lila's wearing a too-tight blazer, with no shirt underneath, and I swear I can feel the fire burning behind my eyes.

Oh, you've got to be kidding me.

Bitch stole my move.

Ryder, for his part, looks as entertained as the wall. My stomach twists, a mix of irritation and something sharper cutting through me. She knows that he and I are together, yet she's sitting here in *our* house—flirting. Not only does she look fucking pathetic, she's disrespecting me!

I'm about two seconds away from letting her know exactly what I think when Ryder's gaze shifts. His eyes meet mine, and the grin that spreads across his face is nothing short of devilish.

"KitKat," he says, his voice warm and teasing. "Perfect timing."

Lila glances over her shoulder, her expression faltering when she sees me.

Good. You ***should*** *feel awkward.*

Before she can say anything, Ryder grabs the sandwich he was holding and tosses it at her. She catches it awkwardly, her mouth opening and closing like a fish out of water.

"You enjoy your dinner," Ryder says, his tone light but laced with finality. "I'm going to go enjoy mine."

Then, with zero warning, he strides toward me, scoops me up, and slings me over his shoulder like I weigh nothing.

"Ryder!" I yelp, my fists pounding weakly against his back. "Put me down!"

"Nope," he replies cheerfully, his hand resting on the back of my thigh to keep me steady. "You're exactly where I want you."

"Ryder, I swear—"

"Relax, KitKat," he interrupts, his voice dipping lower as he carries me up the stairs. "You're going to love what I've got planned."

My protests die in my throat as his words sink in, heat blooming across my cheeks. By the time we reach the bedroom, my irritation is a distant memory, replaced by anticipation that has my heart racing.

I'm still hungry, but that can wait now.

Ryder kicks the door shut behind us, his grin widening as he sets me down gently. The way he's looking at me sends a shiver down my spine—like I'm the only thing that matters in the world.

"Now," he murmurs, his hands trailing up my arms, "where were we?"

I don't bother answering. Words aren't necessary for this.

7: RYDER

Tori's laugh is soft, almost teasing, as she sits on the edge of the bed, leaning back on her hands. The way her hair spills over her shoulders and the mischievous glint in her eyes have me grinning like I've already won this game of life. Which, let's be honest, *I have*.

"I've been waiting for my dinner all day, KitKat. You can't keep a man starved like this," I say, my voice low as I kneel in front of her.

She rolls her eyes, but the blush creeping up her neck gives her away. "You already know I can't cook."

"I don't think you get it. You're the meal, Kit...Kat," I stretch her nickname out, savoring it the way I'll savor her. My hands slide up her thighs, and she shivers under my touch, her breath catching just enough to stroke my ego. "So do me a favor, unwrap yourself for me. I'm hungry."

Her response is a sharp inhale, and then my mouth is on her, my hand holding her jaw steady as I taste her. She's sweet and intoxicating, and if I could bottle her up, I'd keep her all to myself, and every once in a while I'd share with Blaze and Thorne.

My fingers hook on her pants, pulling them down with her help, our mouths never breaking apart. Her hands race to the hem of her shirt, but I'm not ready to let her lips go. I slide my knees beside her, bracing my weight on them as I lift up just enough to fist her shirt in my hands. With a fast, hard pull, I tear her shirt open, feeling her gasp against my lips.

My hands instantly unhook her bra, snapping it open from the front and finding her beautiful brown nipples. My fingers dance around them, lightly swirling the buds between them. She moans, muffled against my lips. I take the opportunity to slide my tongue past her lips and deep into her mouth.

Her head presses back against the mattress as her back arches, matching my need. Slowly, tauntingly, I let my fingers trail down her abdomen and between her thighs. Her warmth calls to me, inviting me in with a promise of sleek wet want.

I insert a single digit into her, her walls clenching around it as if it's not enough. For the first time since we started, I break the kiss, loving the sight of her bruised, puffed lips.

"Are you ready to feed me, KitKat?" I ask, but she doesn't need to answer, not when my finger has already discovered the truth. Standing now, I place my hands on her knees and part her legs as I hold her gaze. With a grin so wide my cheeks hurt, I kneel before her, seeing her glisten with pure need.

I dive right in like a man starved for years. My tongue slides across, tasting her sweet, tangy flavor. Her hands fly to her breasts, playing with them as I continue to lick. I love watching her like this, seeing her so lost in the moment that she forgets to even think.

My finger slides back in as I suck on her sensitive clit. She pinches those beautiful brown pebbles in response as she bucks her hips. Slowly I slide my finger in and out, stroking her walls, coaxing her to build.

She's practically trembling when the door swings open.

"Ryder, have you seen Tori yet? She needs to eat and...oh, for f—" Blaze's voice cuts off as he finally takes in the scene, his feet frozen mid-step. His eyes narrow, though his jaw ticks in a way that tells me he's more annoyed at himself for walking in than at us.

"Dinner's already served, Chef," I say, turning back to Tori and licking my KitKat, my voice muffled against Tori's skin. "You're late."

"Ryder," Blaze growls, his tone carrying that familiar mix of exasperation and command. He's holding a plate—of actual food, I assume—and sets it down with a thunk on the nearby dresser.

Tori's half-laughing, half-mortified, her hand covering her face as Blaze's gaze flicks between us. "You could've locked the door, you know."

"Where's the fun in that?" I quip, finally leaning back just enough to shoot him a cocky grin.

"She needs to eat, Ryder," Blaze says, his voice softening just enough to betray his concern. His eyes flick to Tori, who's flushed and breathless but beaming from ear to ear.

"She's just fine," I say, then turn to Tori, arching a brow. "Aren't you, KitKat?"

She groans, her face flush, but there's no way she wants to stop now. "You're impossible."

Blaze mutters something under his breath, pinching the bridge of his nose. "Do you want me to leave, or...?"

I glance at Tori, tilting my head toward Blaze. "Your call. Want Chef here to join the menu?"

Her eyes widen for a second, but then she nods, her voice soft but certain. "Yeah. I do."

Blaze's brows lift in surprise, and for a second, he looks like he's debating whether to scold me or thank her. Then his expression shifts, his usual control slipping just enough to show the heat beneath. He shrugs off his jacket, rolling his sleeves up to his elbows as he steps closer.

"You're lucky I'm in a good mood, Ryder," he says, his voice low and steady. "She really should have eaten before you brought her up here."

"Lucky? Nah, I'm just irresistible," I shoot back, but I get serious as Blaze lays on the bed beside her and takes Tori's face in his hands, his touch reverent in a way that makes my chest tighten. His lips claim hers, slow and deliberate, and for once, I'm content to let someone else take the lead.

I watch her lean into him, her hands moving to his shirt, her fingers tracing the outline of his pecs through the fabric. He breaks the kiss and turns to me, his eyes dark with desire.

"Are you going to keep pleasuring our girl, or do I need to take over?" he bites out at me, reminding me I need to get back to work.

My tongue delves back into her sweet pussy. She squirms, and it's hard not to smirk against her slick skin. A moment later, Blaze's hand finds its way into my hair, his fingers gripping and tugging it.

"Ryder, don't tease her," he whispers.

"Who's teasing?" I say, leaning back against his hand, and looking him dead in the eyes. "If you're hungry, help yourself."

I see the moment of hesitation, but only for a second. In a swift motion, he's off the bed and kneeling next to me. My tongue is replaced by his, his long licks giving her the pressure she craves. I watch him devour her, the same look of hunger that I saw a minute ago, and it makes my heart hammer and my cock stiffen.

I lean back, letting him have his time, enjoying the sounds Tori's making. I unzip my pants and pull out my cock, slowly stroking myself.

"Oh God," Tori gasps.

"No," Blaze groans, his voice muffled against her. "God is the one you pray to. I'm the one you need to yell for, Doll."

Her hands grip his head, pulling him tighter, and she moans his name as his tongue works its magic. I lean back, watching them both, stroking myself a little faster.

"Fuck," she cries out, her body trembling.

"I got you, Doll," Blaze says, standing. He strips out of his clothes, his hard length already bobbing from the confines.

I take my spot on the bed, laying her on her side and pulling her into another kiss. Blaze climbs onto the bed behind her, his hand reaching between her thighs, and her hips rock in response.

"Is this what you want, Doll?" he asks.

"Please," she begs, her voice cracking.

"Don't worry," I whisper against her lips, my voice raspy with need. "He's going to take good care of you."

His eyes meet mine, and he nods once, and then positions himself behind her. Blaze holds her in place as his cock slides inside, her legs keeping him in a tight grip. My hand slips between her legs and my fingers begin to stroke her clit.

Her eyes close, and her head tilts back against Blaze, her face a mix of pleasure and pain. He's holding her against his chest, his hand cupping her breast as his hips start to move. I play with the other, sucking on her nipple like it's the best lollipop in the world.

She moans so loud, I hope Lila can hear it from the kitchen. I need her to know that Tori is the only woman for me.

The only one.

"That's it, Doll. Tell us how much you like it," Blaze coos, spurred by Tori's moans.

"Please don't stop. I need—" she pleads, fingers digging into my arms.

"You need what?" he asks, his voice low, his pace quickening.

"I need you. Both of you. So close. Don't stop," she manages to say between her panting breaths.

"We've got you, KitKat. We won't stop," I whisper, leaning in and kissing her.

Her hand goes around the back of my neck, holding me close as she kisses me. Her body writhes in pleasure, and the sound of her moans muffled by our lips is music to my ears.

We're fully lost in the moment when the door bursts open again.

"What the hell is going..." Thorne's voice dies mid-sentence as he takes in the scene, his expression swinging from shock to anger in record time.

And then I see Gabe, trailing behind him.

The guy is frozen in the doorway, his eyes wide, his face rapidly turning red as he tries not to look but can't quite figure out where else to direct his gaze. Thorne shoves him hard, sending him stumbling back into the hallway before slamming the door shut.

"Are you kidding me?" Thorne snaps, his voice sharp enough to cut glass. "You're doing this with the door unlocked? With *him* in the house?"

Blaze lets out a heavy sigh and his hips slow, his chest heaving. He leans his head against the crook of Tori's neck and she shudders, her hand gripping his thigh.

"I'll deal with him," Blaze says, and even in the dim light, I can see the muscles tensing along his jaw.

Tori whimpers, and I stroke her cheek, my touch gentle. "We can deal with him later. You need us right now, don't you, KitKat?"

She nods, her nails digging into Blaze's skin now, as if she refuses to let him go.

"You heard the lady," I tell Thorne, arching a brow. "We're busy."

Thorne's nostrils flare, his eyes flashing, and for a second, I think he's going to storm over and put me in my place. Which would be a damn shame, because Tori's right on the edge, and we need to finish her.

"Fine," Thorne grits out, his fists clenching at his sides. "I'll just take care of it myself."

He's turning, ready to march off when Tori calls after him in a voice so dazed with pleasure it hardens my dick to the point it hurts.

"Thorne, wait. I need you here, too."

His whole body goes still, and for a second, no one speaks. No one moves. It's like we're all waiting for him to respond, to breathe.

"Please," she says again, her voice breaking.

I don't know what to say or do, because if he says no, she'll be crushed.

But if he says yes, we'll have to buy Plan B tomorrow, because we used up the last of the condoms our first night here.

He finally turns back, his expression torn between lust and fury. He walks back and stands there, not sure if he should join in, or leave, or...

I don't give him a choice. I grab his wrist and tug him down, my hand fisting in his hair and pulling him toward Tori's breast.

"She said she needs you. Don't be a dick."

Thorne doesn't respond, but his mouth is on her, and then her mouth is on mine. I can't see him, but I hear the zipper of his pants and feel his weight settle on the bed, his knee pressing into the mattress.

It's enough.

She's moaning into my mouth, and it's taking everything in me not to break the kiss and watch everyone. I never realized how much I liked watching until I caught Tori pleasuring herself before the warehouse meeting with Valen.

Blaze starts to move inside her again, his arms wrapping around her waist as his thrusts become more desperate. Tori's cries fill the air, and it's a symphony to my ears.

"I'm- I'm-" she stutters.

"I got you, KitKat. Come for us," I whisper, feeling her tremble.

She comes hard, and I catch her cry with my lips, holding her tight.

"Doll," Blaze groans, his own release not far behind.

He pulls out, shooting ropes of cum on her back. His hands gently caress her as wipes her clean with the shirt he took off. She looks absolutely fucked and perfect, and we're not even done.

"Are you ready, Doll?" Blaze whispers, his voice strained.

"We want more." I land my hands on her hips. "But if you don't want to, say the word and we will stop."

"Don't stop," she pleads, her head shaking. "I need you all."

"Fuck," I hear Thorne curse under his breath, and when I turn, his hand is on his cock, stroking it. "How do you want us, Vic?"

"I need more. Just give me more," she pleads, and the tone of her voice makes me want to do whatever she asks.

Blaze moves off the bed, his body still glistening with sweat, his cock hanging limp.

"I'll be right back," Blaze says, his voice soft but firm. "Take care of her while I'm gone."

My brows furrow, but then Tori's hands are on me, and the only thing I can focus on is the feel of her nails scraping down my back and the soft, sweet taste of her tongue.

When he comes back, Blaze's hands are slick with lube. He sits behind her, eyes glued on her.

"Are you sure you're ready, Doll?" he asks, and it's almost comical how his voice has changed. It's no longer that of the boss, or even a lover.

No, it's that of a caretaker who wants to make sure his girl is taken care of.

"Just do it," she says, and I swear my heart stops for a moment.

He slides a finger inside, and I can hear the slick, squishing sound as he opens her, getting her ready for one of us. The question is, which one of us gets the pleasure of that tight, puckered hole?

Tori moans, her eyes fluttering closed, her mouth forming a perfect O. Her nipples are hard, her cheeks flush, and her pussy is so wet I can see her dripping for us.

Blaze takes his time, moving his finger in and out of her slowly, his free hand gripping his cock and pumping. He's going to come again, and I have to admit, I'm jealous.

"More," she breathes, her hips grinding against his fingers, and I swear, he's got at least three inside her.

He removes his fingers, and she whines in protest.

"She's ready for you." Blaze locks eyes with Thorne and I groan.

It's the piercings. I know it is.

He's not wrong. It's probably not the best idea.

Still I can't help but be disappointed. Maybe I'll take them out for her. Then I'd get to be inside her wherever I want.

Thorne takes his time, slicking himself and Tori up really well before he lines his cock up and slowly pushes inside.

We're all silent, the only sounds in the room are those of heavy breathing and skin on skin. Tori's head is thrown back, her eyes closed. Her hands grip the sheets in front of her as she stays laying on her side, Thorne thrusting from behind as he holds her back close to his chest.

Thorne is gentle, his strokes are slow, and every inch of his face is full of concentration. He's trying not to hurt the only other person he loves on this planet.

"Harder," she cries, and we all stare, slack jawed.

Thorne hesitates, but when she begs him again, he picks up the pace.

His hand grips her hip, his fingers digging in as his hips snap back and forth. I can't look away, can't stop watching, can't stop my hand from sliding down to grip my own shaft, stroking myself as I watch the two of them together.

Her eyes meet mine, her teeth caging her lips as she reaches for me.

"I need you too," she whispers, and it's all the permission I need to slowly—teasingly—slide my bare dick inside her sweet pussy.

I hiss at the contact, her slick walls gripping me. She lets out a soft cry, and I don't know if it's pain or pleasure.

"You okay, Doll?" Blaze asks, his eyes locked on where we're joined.

She nods, so lost to pleasure she can't even talk. Blaze sits near our heads, leaning down to slide his hand between Tori and I, rolling her pebbled nipples in his fingers.

"More," she gasps, and I'm not sure if she's talking about her breasts, or if she wants us both moving inside her.

We start a rhythm, the three of us rocking her body between us. I lean over, capturing her mouth, my hand wrapping around the back of her neck.

She tastes like sweat, and her mouth is swollen from kissing, but it's exactly the way I like it.

When her orgasm hits, her whole body trembles and her muscles clench, milking us both. I pull out of her, my cock aching and ready. I grip my shaft, pumping myself once, twice, before I explode, my cum spurting onto her stomach, the last few drops landing on her tits.

Thorne isn't far behind, his movements more frantic, and when he comes, he lets out a grunt, his entire body shaking.

The two of us roll her onto her back, admiring the sight of her.

"We should get her cleaned up," Thorne suggests, and I nod.

Blaze leads the way as always, getting everything ready, and we pamper our girl. We shower off, washing her from head to toe. She doesn't even have to lift a finger.

Why would she?

She's our queen.

When we step out, Blaze runs her a bath, but doesn't get in with her like I assumed he would.

"Take care of her. Thorne and I need to talk to a little pesky mouse that thinks he's some kind of lion," he says, his eyes burning holes through the walls and straight to Gabe, who I bet isn't far from the bedroom door.

"Give him a good punch for me." I nod, slapping his shoulder as I walk by.

"No punching," Tori interrupts, eyes closed as she floats in the jet tub and head resting on the edge. "I may have hit my head, but he did save me from being kidnapped...*twice*. One of which was completely my fault because—surprise—I didn't listen when he had told me to stay back."

"Doll," Blaze starts, but Tori won't have it. She shakes her head, cracking her eyes to stare right at him.

"I mean it," she speaks, her tone firm and final. "No fighting with him. Besides, what happened with him seeing us was totally our fault for not locking the door."

"Vic, it's more than that," Thorne argues, his tone dark and held back as he tries not to lash out his frustrations.

"If you need to fuel your egos, you're welcome to threaten and torment like you do, but no punching. At least not today, okay? Again, he did save me." She closes her eyes again as if to say 'this conversation is over.'

They grunt, but it's clear they got the message by the way they march off. I know they'll listen, but Gabe should still be worried. We know how to torment, and he's in our crosshairs.

That's not a place anyone wants to be.

8: BLAZE

A night with Tori will always be a highlight of my life, but trying to sleep in a bed crammed with Ryder and Thorne doesn't exactly lend itself to restful sleep. As usual, I'm the first one up, sitting in the kitchen nursing a cup of coffee while Tori still sleeps, sprawled out in a position that defies physics.

If I could, I would watch her sleep every morning, peaceful and beautiful. Thoroughly fucked.

It took everything in me not to punch Gabe right in the face. But Tori was right...he did save her. Which is more than I can say.

I let her get taken by Nico right in front of me.

Maybe that's what pisses me off the most—that he did something I couldn't do.

Either way, I may not have punched him, but I definitely threatened him. If she so much as gets another scratch on her, he's dead. I added on the bonus of never speaking a word of what he saw to her. He doesn't need to bring it up.

I've barely gotten a moment to breathe when Diablo calls. It's more of the same—assignments laced with vague threats and veiled insults. I'm no stranger to pressure, but this feels different. It's obvious he's up to something, but I can't tell what. All I know for sure is that he's playing a game, and I'm tired of being a pawn in it.

I'm going to make myself a player, figure out what he's up to, and then beat him.

While I'd rather disappear back into bed with Tori in my arms, I've been ordered to get to the docks right away. I leave a note on the counter for her, not wanting to wake her and knowing her phone is broken now. She swore she would get a new one today and text me the moment she did.

I then send a text to Thorne and one to Ryder with their own assignments for the day.

To my annoyance, I'm paired with Eve again. She's already waiting by the dock, tablet in hand and hair tied back in a pristine ponytail, not a hair out of place. She's the picture of professionalism, like she's ready to conquer the world—or at least micromanage it.

"Blaze," she greets, her tone clipped, straight to business. "We're scheduled to review inventory discrepancies and confirm shipment timelines."

"Good morning to you too," I reply, drier than the desert sand. My tone earns me a sharp glance, but she doesn't comment. Instead, she strides ahead, leading the way to the warehouse.

The docks are alive with activity. Crates are being unloaded, forklifts hum as they weave through narrow aisles, and workers shout over the constant grind of heavy equipment. It's a well-oiled machine on the surface, but the cracks are there if you know where to look.

And I always know where to look.

"We need to follow up on the flagged shipments," Eve starts as we enter the main storage area. "The discrepancies obviously suggest someone is tampering with the cargo, and we need to follow the trail before it gets cold."

"Fantastic," I mutter, already scanning the rows of towering containers. The scent of saltwater and oil mixes heavily in the air, carrying a faint metallic tang of rust. "Let's get this over with."

Eve leads me to a section marked "Priority," where the flagged crates are stored. She's efficient, directing the workers to bring down specific containers and logging the details on her tablet. I grab a crowbar from a nearby rack, prying open the first crate with practiced ease. Inside, neatly packed electronics sit in rows, their labels flawless.

"Looks clean," I say, though experience tells me otherwise. I tap one of the devices, checking for signs of tampering or hidden compartments. "You see anything off?"

Eve steps closer, her sharp eyes scanning the contents. "The serial numbers match the manifest, but the weights don't. There's something underneath."

I nod, lifting the top layer of electronics to reveal...cash. Bundles of it, neatly stacked and bound. My stomach tightens as I glance back at Eve.

"This shipment wasn't supposed to include currency," she says, her voice carefully neutral. "Someone's using Diablo's operation to move their own product."

"Or Diablo knows and wants to see if we're paying attention," I counter, my tone low. "Either way, it's bad news."

Eve's brow furrows as she types furiously into her tablet. "We'll need to flag this for review. But first, let's finish inspecting the rest."

The next few crates tell the same story—electronics hiding stacks of cash. By the time we're done, it's clear someone's running a side hustle through Diablo's channels. The question is whether Diablo's testing us or if we've stumbled onto something bigger.

Eve's efficiency borders on unsettling. She barely pauses between tasks, her focus razor-sharp. But there's a tension in her movements, subtle but telling. Something's eating at her.

"You've done this before," I remark as we secure the last crate. "You're too good at it to be new."

She straightens, her expression guarded. "I'm thorough. It's what Diablo expects."

"That's not an answer," I point out, leaning against the edge of a crate. "You've got a lot of experience for someone who's supposed to be a new hire."

Eve hesitates, her grip on the tablet tightening. For a moment, it looks like she's going to brush me off, but then she sighs. "Diablo doesn't hire amateurs. Let's leave it at that."

I don't press further, though her response only raises more questions. Instead, I focus on the task at hand, my mind already spinning with possibilities. If Diablo's testing us, we've passed. But if this is something else...it's a complication we don't need.

By the time we finish logging the discrepancies, it's late afternoon. Eve's demeanor shifts a touch, giving way to something almost hesitant.

"Blaze," she starts as we walk back to the dock office. "Thank you for...not pushing."

I glance at her, surprised by the sincerity in her tone. "You're welcome. But don't think I'm letting it go. I'll get my answers eventually."

She smiles faintly, a rare crack in her professional armor. "We'll see."

We're quiet as we make our way to a nearby café for a late lunch. It's not much—just a small, nondescript place by the water—but it'll do. We order our food and sit at one of the outside tables to enjoy the oceanside view.

"Do you think Ortega's behind this?" Eve asks, sipping her coffee.

"He's definitely hiding something," I reply, biting into my sandwich. "But whether he's the mastermind or just another pawn, I don't know yet."

Eve nods thoughtfully, her gaze drifting out to the water. "It could be someone under him. A new hire exploiting the system, maybe."

"Or someone higher up," I counter. "Someone who knows how to cover their tracks. Someone who has enough power to threaten Ortega."

She doesn't respond immediately, her expression pensive. "If that's the case, it'll be harder to trace. People at that level don't leave trails."

"Everyone leaves a trail," I say, my tone firm. "You just have to know where to look."

The conversation shifts as we eat, the tension easing somewhat. It's the first time Eve seems more human, less like a perfectly programmed machine. She even laughs at one point, a soft, genuine sound that catches me off guard.

"What's your story, Eve?" I ask, leaning back in my chair. "You're not exactly an open book."

She hesitates, her fingers tracing the edge of her coffee cup. "There's not much to tell."

"Bullshit," I say with a smirk. "Come on, everyone's got a story."

She sighs, giving me a look that's equal parts exasperation and amusement. "Fine. I grew up in Chicago. My dad was a cop, my mom was a teacher. Normal enough until my dad got killed on duty. After that, things got...complicated."

"Complicated how?" I ask, my tone gentler now.

"My mom couldn't handle it," she admits, her voice quieter. "She spiraled, and I had to grow up fast. Got a job when I was sixteen, dropped out to support us. Eventually, I started working in logistics. That's how I ended up here."

There's a weight to her words, a vulnerability she's trying to mask. "That's a hell of a journey," I say, meaning it.

She shrugs, her gaze meeting mine. "You do what you have to do. No point dwelling on it."

For a moment, the silence between us feels comfortable, like we've reached some unspoken understanding. But it doesn't last long. Eve straightens, her professional mask slipping back into place. "We should get back. There's still work to do."

"Right," I say, draining the last of my coffee. As we head back to the SUV, I can't shake the feeling that I've only scratched the surface with Eve. There's more to her story, more to why she's here. And I'm going to find out what it is—one way or another.

The drive to the office is silent—giving me too much time to think. My mind reels with thoughts of the crates, of what Eve is up to at the behest of Diablo, and what intricate web he's weaving. If I spiral too much into it, I'll lose focus, so I push the thought aside, focusing on the road ahead.

We pull into the lot of the office Diablo assigned us. The building is as unremarkable as it gets—gray concrete walls, narrow windows, and a door that creaks when you open it, like the building itself is sighing. Eve steps out of the car, her heels clicking sharply against the pavement. The sound grates, like nails on a chalkboard. She's too put together for this place, her tailored suit and flawless hair looking out of place against the building's bland, utilitarian backdrop.

I grab the folders from the backseat and slam the door harder than necessary. My mood is already sour, and her presence isn't helping. She's quiet, as always, but there's something about the way she walks ahead of me that feels like she's trying to insinuate she's the one in control here.

I'll let her believe it. For now.

As we step inside the office, Eve bends to pick up a piece of paper that's fallen near the doorway. The motion is deliberate—it has to be—because when she leans forward, her skirt rides up just enough to reveal the edge of her thigh, her ass cheeks peeking just beneath the hem of her skirt. My jaw tightens, and I look away, forcing my gaze to the desk instead.

"Did you get what you needed?" I ask, my tone sharp.

She straightens, holding up the paper with a neutral expression. "I did."

Of course, she's going to pretend that wasn't intentional. I grit my teeth and push past her, dropping the folders onto the desk with a thud. "Alright," I say, pulling out a chair. "Let's figure this out."

Eve moves to her seat, pulling out her tablet and setting it on the glass with the precision of someone who's done this a million times before. She's methodical, detached, like she's running through a script.

"We've flagged three shipments so far," she begins, her tone clinical. "All through the north docks, all under Ortega's oversight."

"We already know that," I snap, flipping open one of the folders. "What we don't know is who's behind it. Ortega seems too obvious of a choice."

She raises an eyebrow, but her composure doesn't falter. "You really think it's someone higher up."

"I think it's someone smart enough to make Ortega look like the scapegoat," I say. "And I think they're counting on us wasting time chasing him down while they keep skimming off the top."

"Interesting theory," she murmurs, leaning forward. The movement pulls her shirt taut across her chest, and for a split second, I'm certain it's intentional. My grip on the folder tightens as I force my eyes back to the papers in front of me.

"Stop that," I mutter.

"Stop what?" Her voice is all innocence, but when I glance up, there's a glint in her eye that tells me she knows exactly what she's doing.

"You know what," I snap. "If you think I'm stupid enough to fall for whatever game you're playing, you're dead wrong."

"Game?" she echoes, tilting her head. "Blaze, I'm just doing my job. If you're distracted, that's on you."

I let out a sharp laugh, leaning back in my chair. "Distracted? Trust me, sweetheart, I've dealt with your type before. You're not as subtle as you think you are."

Her expression hardens, but she doesn't back down. Instead, she leans across the desk to grab a pen, the movement pressing her chest against my arm. "Maybe you should ask yourself why you're paying so much attention in the first place," she says, her voice low and cutting.

I shove my chair back, standing abruptly. "Are you kidding me right now? You've been flirting since the moment we walked in here, and now you're trying to gaslight me into thinking it's my fault?"

She stands as well, crossing her arms and meeting my glare head-on. "Flirting? Blaze, if that's what you think, then maybe you need to take a long, hard look in the mirror. I've been professional this entire time. You're the one making things weird."

"Professional?" I scoff, gesturing to the desk. "Yeah, because pressing up against me and bending over like that is so professional."

Her eyes narrow, but her tone remains icy. "I bent over to pick up a paper. If your mind went somewhere else, that's on you. Maybe you should focus on the current task instead of projecting your issues onto me."

My fists clench at my sides, the urge to throw something rising with every word out of her mouth. But I force myself to take a deep breath, stepping back and shaking my head. "You're unbelievable."

"And you're paranoid," she shoots back, her voice like steel. "If you can't handle working with me, maybe you should ask Diablo to assign someone else."

"Oh, trust me," I mutter, grabbing the folders off the desk. "If I had that option, you'd be out of here in a heartbeat."

She doesn't respond, but the tension between us is so thick, it's suffocating. I move to the other side of the room, flipping through the files with more force than necessary. The numbers blur together, my frustration making it impossible to focus.

"Blaze," she says after a moment, her voice softer. "I know we don't trust each other, but we're on the same side here. Let's figure this out before things get worse."

I glance at her, surprised by the sudden shift in tone. For a moment, she looks almost sincere. Almost. But I've learned better than to trust appearances.

"Fine," I say, my voice curt. "But if you pull another stunt like that, Diablo will be the least of your worries. Got it?"

She nods, her expression unreadable. "Got it."

Before I can say anything else, my phone buzzes on the desk. I grab it, glancing at the screen. It's a message from an unknown number.

> **Unknown**
> I got a phone again!

I smile for the first time today, knowing it's Tori. I save her new number and send her a quick reply.

> **Blaze**
> Thank you for texting me, Doll. I'll give you a reward when we get home.

> **Blaze**
> Count on it being delicious.

The tension in my muscles seems to disappear at the thought of being home with Tori. My eyes flick up to Eve, who's just watching me.

"Anything of use?" she asks, preening her neck as if to get a better look.

"Not to you," I respond, ready for my time with her to be over.

Just as I tuck my phone back into my pocket, another buzz follows.

WHY DON'T YOU KEEP ME

> **Ryder:** I don't like what's happening today. Is there anything weird with your "assistant"? Mine is being more crazy than usual.

I look up at Eve and start to wonder what part of her behavior is her and what part is Diablo. Ryder's text definitely proves something, though...these girls aren't here to 'assist.'

I stare at Ryder's text, the words pulling me out of my spiraling thoughts. My fingers hover over the screen for a second before I type back.

> **Ryder:** Flirting. Boldly. Like she thinks I'm some clueless idiot who doesn't notice. You?

I glance at Eve, who's now scrolling through her tablet with that same unnervingly calm expression she always wears. Her shoulders are relaxed, her posture perfect, but there's something about her that's just a little too pristine—like she's trying too hard.

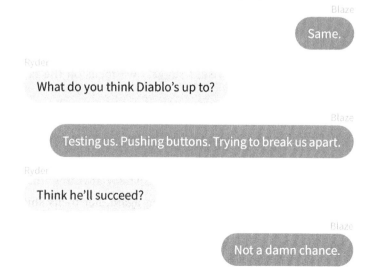

Ryder's reply is a thumbs-up emoji, but the tension in my chest doesn't ease. If anything, it tightens. I tuck my phone back into my pocket and fix my gaze on Eve, who's now typing something on her tablet.

"You're awfully quiet," I say, my tone casual but laced with meaning. "Not like you to pass up an opportunity to share your insights."

Eve glances up, her expression neutral. "I've found that silence can be more productive than chatter."

"Productive for who?" I take a seat again, leaning back in my chair, crossing my arms. "Because it seems to me like you've been working on more than just these shipments."

Her brow arches, but she doesn't falter. "And what exactly are you accusing me of, Blaze?"

"I'm not accusing you of anything," I reply smoothly. "I'm just curious about your...motivations. You've been awfully hands-on for someone who's supposed to be assisting. Makes me wonder what your endgame is."

Eve's lips twitch, but it's not quite a smile. "My endgame is the same as yours: getting to the bottom of these discrepancies."

"And if it isn't?" I press, my voice dropping a notch. "What happens if this all leads back to you?"

Her composure cracks just enough, a flicker of something unspoken passing through her eyes. "If you have evidence to back that up, feel free to share it. Otherwise, I suggest we focus on the task at hand."

I let out a low chuckle, shaking my head. "You're good, I'll give you that. But don't think for a second that I'm buying the act. Whatever game you're playing, it ends here," I say, my tone sharp.

Eve's expression hardens, but she doesn't say anything. Instead, she picks up her tablet and starts typing again, her focus shifting back to the files. I slip my phone back out of my pocket and send Ryder one last text.

> **Blaze:** Keep an eye on her. I'll do the same with mine.

> **Ryder:** Always.

I glance back at Eve, her profile illuminated by the harsh glow of the tablet. She's still as composed as ever, but there's a tension in her shoulders that wasn't there before. For the first time, I feel like I've managed to unsettle her, even if it's just a little.

Good. Let her squirm.

9: Tori

The care ride to Diablo's estate stretches longer than my patience, winding through perfectly trimmed hedges and fountains that probably cost more than my entire childhood. Gabe drives with both hands on the wheel, too tense for my liking, his sharp blue eyes scanning the grounds like he's expecting ninjas to jump out of the hedges and attack.

He hasn't met my eyes once today, and I'm fairly certain it's because of what he saw. The awkward tension in the air between us is thick, and I'm not exactly a fan of it.

So, what do I do? I poke the damn elephant in the room and just ask.

"Exactly how much did you see last night?" I question, stretching in my seat like I didn't just ask the most humiliating question ever.

"I don't know what you mean," he replies, his voice tight, his eyes avoiding me like they've just discovered the road has more answers to life than I do.

I roll my eyes, already knowing he's full of shit, but I push on anyway. "You know exactly what I mean. When you came into the room last night—how much did you see?"

"I didn't see anything. I was pushed out before I even stepped a foot inside." His voice is his gaze still glued to the road, pretending to scout the area.

"If that's the way you wanna play it, fine." I shrug, crossing my arms tightly, letting my gaze drift out the window, the cold air biting through the glass. "We can pretend it didn't happen."

He doesn't answer, which is fair. I'd ignore me, too. Instead, he pulls up to the estate entrance, where a pair of guards open the grand double doors before we even get out. Diablo doesn't do waiting, apparently.

Gabe is out first, rounding the car to open my door, a habit I pretend not to notice. "Try not to antagonize anyone important," he mutters as I step out.

"No promises."

As we step inside, a butler greets us and leads us through the halls toward the dining room, where Diablo's lieutenants are already gathered, eyes shifting my way.

Is it a hundred degrees in here?

No, just me?

Great.

Seated to Diablo's right is a woman who's watching me with casual interest, her elbow resting on the table, fingers lazily toying with the stem of her wine glass. She's stunning, auburn hair slicked back into a high ponytail, sharp green eyes scanning me like I'm a puzzle worth solving. Her suit is tailored within an inch of its life, the kind of precise, effortless look that makes it clear she didn't dress to impress—she just does.

"Tori," Diablo says smoothly. "Come, sit. We have much to discuss."

I slide into my seat, directly across from the woman who hasn't taken her eyes off me. I match her stare, not in a confrontational way, just a measured one.

If this is a game, I don't want to lose, even if I don't know the rules yet.

"You're the infamous Victoria Reyes," she finally says, voice smooth as silk. "I've heard a lot about you."

"Oh? And here I thought I was the family's best-kept secret," I say, reaching for my glass of water.

She grins, sharp but not unfriendly. "Not for long." She offers her hand. "Cassandra."

I shake it, her grip firm but not overcompensating. I appreciate that.

Lunch is a production, of course. The table is covered in dishes that belong in an art museum more than on a plate, and I spend half the meal trying to figure out if I'm supposed to eat the garnish or admire it. The conversation shifts between business updates and thinly veiled power moves, but my focus keeps drifting back to Cassandra.

She appears to be the kind of woman who can command a room without saying much at all. And unlike the others at this table, she doesn't seem interested in proving anything to me. If anything, she looks amused.

"So, how's the adjustment going?" she asks, cutting into something that looks too delicate to actually be food. "I imagine being thrown into this world isn't exactly seamless."

I huff a quiet laugh. "Oh yeah, real smooth. Kidnappings, death threats, moral dilemmas—just another Tuesday."

She nods like it's to be expected. "Sounds like you're catching on quick."

"Is that a compliment?"

"It's an observation," she says, sipping her wine. "Most people take years to learn how to navigate this world. You're doing it in weeks."

I shrug, glancing at Diablo, who seems busy with a side conversation. "Trial by fire. And pure stubbornness."

Cassandra tilts her head. "Good. You need both to survive."

She's easy to talk to, which surprises me. Most of Diablo's people treat me like an obligation or a liability. She treats me like...a person. Like I belong here. It's disarming, but not in a bad way.

As the meal goes on, our conversation drifts from business to something easier. We trade stories, and I find myself laughing more than I expected. She's quick-witted, with a dry sense of humor that makes me like her despite my usual reservations.

"So, what did you do before you were thrust into mob royalty?" she asks, her tone teasing.

I roll my eyes. "Oh, you know. Just your average barista. Taking orders and slinging coffees like a master."

Cassandra's hands fly to her mouth, trying to cover the laughter she's suppressing. "Definitely not what I was expecting you to say."

"What can I say? I was due for a career change. But what about you?" I ask. "Were you always a part of this life?"

She hums, considering. "Let's just say I didn't exactly have a traditional childhood."

There's something there, something unspoken, but I don't push. We all have things we don't talk about.

*Plus, I just met her. I have **some** boundaries.*

She shifts, leaning forward as she twirls the stem of her wine glass between her fingers. "You know, I think I like you."

I raise a brow. "Yeah? What was the deciding factor? My sparkling personality or my complete disregard for authority?"

She chuckles. "Both, actually."

It's that simple. That easy. Like we've known each other longer than just one conversation. And just like that, I realize something: I think I like her, too.

"Great. Because like I said earlier, I'm pretty stubborn, so those qualities aren't going anywhere." I take a drink of my wine—a swig, really, because I'm not classy.

Cassandra takes a slow sip of her wine, her eyes sharp with amusement. "You know, I have to admit, I didn't expect you to be so...easy to talk to."

I plaster on a smile, stabbing a piece of grilled chicken with my fork. "What did you expect, some scared little mouse, shaking in her seat?"

Cassandra laughs, the sound smooth and genuine. "Not quite, but I wasn't expecting someone I'd actually want to have a drink with either."

I clink my glass against hers. "Guess we're both full of surprises."

We eat in comfortable silence for a beat before she leans in slightly. "So, tell me, what's your angle in all this? You really planning to take over the empire, or is this more of a 'humor your dad' situation?"

I twirl my fork, considering my answer. "It started as something I was forced to accept. But I don't know...the more I thought about it, the more I didn't hate the idea of being in control for once."

Cassandra nods approvingly. "Good. This world isn't kind to women who hesitate. We have to be five steps ahead just to be considered competent. Ten steps if we actually want respect."

"Great. So just casual light work," I deadpan.

She laughs warmly, like she likes my sense of humor. "Exactly. But if you ever need an ally in all this, you know where to find me."

The sincerity in her tone catches me off guard. I expected politicking, maybe a few subtle power plays. But Cassandra? She seems like someone I could actually trust, which is rare in this world.

Before I can reply, Diablo clears his throat, drawing everyone's attention. "Tori, since you've met most of the table, I'd like you to make your rounds. Get familiar with the faces you'll be working with."

Translation: suffer through forced small talk with a bunch of older men who think I should be anywhere but here.

I paste on my best 'I'm totally engaged' expression and make my way around the room, shaking hands, exchanging pleasantries, and pretending to care about shipping routes and turf disputes.

Every conversation blends into the next—monotonous, self-important, and barely tolerable.

Through it all, Gabe remains my shadow, always within arm's reach, his gaze sweeping the room like a security camera. A few of the lieutenants give him curious glances, probably wondering why my bodyguard looks like he'd rather put a bullet in someone than be here.

Finally, after what feels like an eternity, Diablo seems satisfied. "That should be enough for now," he says, swirling the last of his whiskey. "Tomorrow, you'll accompany me to oversee a shipment. It's time you learn how these transactions are handled."

I nod, barely concealing my relief. Anything has to be better than sitting through more of these dull introductions. "Looking forward to it."

As we make our way toward the exit, Cassandra steps beside me. "Hey, Tori. Don't forget about my offer if you ever need help."

I nod, a real smile tugging at my lips. "I'll keep it in mind."

Gabe and I step outside and the fresh air feels like freedom. He opens the car door for me and I slide in, leaning back with a sigh. "Well, that was...exhausting."

Gabe shuts the door and rounds the car, sliding into the driver's seat. "You handled it well."

I watch him for a moment. The way his hands grip the wheel, his expression tight. Protective. Always watching. "You didn't look like you enjoyed yourself."

He scoffs, starting the engine. "I don't do small talk."

"Yeah, I got that."

As the car pulls away from the estate, I think about Cassandra's words. About allies. And for the first time in a long time, I wonder if maybe I've found one.

The road stretches ahead, bathed in the golden hues of late afternoon, and I roll my head against the seat, exhaling loudly. "God, that was painful. I think I lost brain cells listening to those guys talk about turf disputes."

Gabe hums in agreement, keeping his eyes on the road. "I was more concerned with making sure none of them tried anything stupid."

I snort. "Like what? Slipping something in my drink? Patting me on the head and telling me to run along? Please, I could handle them in my sleep."

A hint of a smirk tugs at the corner of his mouth, barely there, but I catch it. "No doubt. But that doesn't mean I would give them the opportunity."

I study him for a second, taking in the hard set of his jaw, the way his fingers flex against the wheel like he's still on high alert. "You always this intense, or is this a special performance just for me?"

He exhales sharply, but this time there's a ghost of amusement in it. "You're a unique case."

I press a hand to my chest in mock offense. "Wow. That almost sounded like a compliment."

He gives me a sidelong glance. "Don't let it go to your head."

Too late.

I prop my elbow on the center console. "You know, I think that was the first time I saw you smirk. Are we making progress? Do you, in fact, have a soul?"

His lips twitch again, like he's fighting it. "Debatable."

"Ah, so there is a real person under all that brooding." I stretch my legs, sighing dramatically. "I feel honored to witness this moment."

"I could still toss you out of the car," he replies, but there's warmth beneath the threat.

I tilt my head, eyeing him. "You wouldn't."

"No?"

"Nope. You're way too invested in keeping me safe. Pretty sure you'd dive after me before I even hit the ground."

His silence is telling. And then, to my absolute delight, he chuckles. It's low, rough, like he doesn't use it often, but damn if it doesn't do something to me.

"What?" he asks, catching my expression.

I shake my head, grinning. "I was right. You totally have a soul."

"Don't start getting ideas," he mutters, but there's no real bite to it.

I lean my head back against the seat, feeling lighter than I have all day. Maybe it's the relief of leaving that house behind, or maybe it's just Gabe finally dropping his walls enough for me to catch a glimpse of the man underneath all that steel.

Either way, I like it.

And I want more.

I glance at him again, watching the way his knuckles begin to relax against the wheel. "So, mystery man," I say, tilting my head. "If I'm such a unique case, does that mean you don't usually babysit 'mafia princesses?'"

His eyes flick to me, unimpressed. "You're not a princess."

"Oh, so you do pay attention," I tease, nudging his arm lightly. "Alright, then. If you're not a full-time glorified babysitter, what do you actually do for fun? Don't tell me you just sit in a dark room cleaning guns in your spare time."

His lips press together like he's considering playing dumb, but I see the way his brow twitches, like he's trying not to give in. "I read," he finally admits.

I blink. That wasn't the answer I was expecting. "Read? Like actual books? With words and pages and everything?"

"That is what reading generally entails, yes."

I narrow my eyes, suspicious. "What kind of books?"

He hesitates for a second, like maybe he regrets saying anything at all. "A little bit of everything."

"Uh-huh. That sounds fake. Come on, Gabe, what's your guilty pleasure book? Romance? Poetry? Maybe a little sci-fi?"

His silence stretches long enough that I'm about to give up when he sighs, shaking his head. "Greek mythology."

I stare at him, caught completely off guard. "Excuse me?"

"You heard me." He shifts in his seat, his grip on the wheel just a little tighter. "I like Greek mythology."

A slow grin spreads across my face. "You mean to tell me, all this time, I've had my very own brooding, modern-day Achilles as my bodyguard, and you're only just now sharing this?"

He exhales through his nose, fighting a smile. "You're impossible."

"Oh, this is fantastic," I say, grinning. "Alright, favorite story. Go."

He doesn't answer right away, but I can see the slight shift in his expression, the way his eyes darken in thought. "Orpheus and Eurydice."

My grin fades just slightly. "That's the one where he tries to save her from the underworld, right?"

Gabe nods. "But he looks back too soon. Loses her forever."

There's something heavy in his voice, something deeper than just a love of mythology. I study him, my stomach twisting with curiosity. "That's kind of a tragic choice, don't you think?"

He gives me a sideways look. "Not all stories have happy endings."

I watch him for a second longer, my heart kicking up for reasons I don't entirely understand. "Maybe not. But that doesn't mean they don't deserve one."

His grip on the wheel tightens again, and for the first time, I think maybe Gabe isn't just a bodyguard with a tragic backstory—he's someone who's still living it.

The silence that settles between us isn't uncomfortable. It's something else. Tense but not heavy, expectant but not urgent. Like we're both waiting to see who cracks first.

"So," I start, staring at him from my spot on the center console. "You gonna keep trying to dodge all my questions, or do I finally get to unravel the enigma that is Gabe Morales?"

His lips twitch. "That depends. You planning on giving up if I keep ignoring you?"

"Not a chance."

He exhales sharply, shaking his head as if he's somehow both amused and exasperated with me. "Fine. Ask your questions."

"Full name?"

"Gabriel Andres Morales."

I hum, rolling the name on my tongue. "Strong name. Sounds like you should be leading a rebellion or something."

"Not much of a rebel," he says dryly. "More of a survivalist."

That catches my attention. I straighten in my seat, interest piqued. "Survivalist, huh? What'd you have to survive?"

His grip on the wheel tightens, just for a fraction of a second, but I notice it. "Life."

"Wow, okay. Way to be dramatic."

He glances at me, one brow raising. "You're one to talk."

"Fair. But come on, throw me a bone. What was little Gabe like? Were you always this serious?"

His silence stretches long enough that I almost think he won't answer, but then, quietly, he says, "I didn't get to be little for long."

Something in my chest clenches. There's weight behind those words. A past I suddenly want to pry into, to pull apart until I understand every piece of what made him who he is.

Instead, I keep it light. "Alright, Batman. Then tell me about the present. What do you do for fun? Aside from reading."

He snorts. "Fun?"

"Yes, fun. You know, that thing normal people have?"

His hands flex on the wheel, and for the first time, I catch something that looks like hesitation on his face. "I don't have time for fun."

I scoff. "Bullshit. No one is that dedicated to their job."

He side-eyes me. "You are."

I open my mouth to argue, then promptly shut it. Dammit. *He has a point.*

"That's different," I argue anyway, because admitting defeat isn't in my nature. "I got thrown into this. You chose it."

"Did I?" The question is quiet, rhetorical, but it leaves something thick and unspoken between us.

I watch him for a long moment, studying the hard angles of his face, the sharp focus in his eyes, the way his body is always coiled, like he's never truly at rest. "So, if you could do anything else, what would it be?"

He doesn't answer right away. The road stretches before us, empty except for the occasional flicker of headlights in the distance. Finally, just when I think he won't say anything, he exhales and mutters, "Hiking."

I blink. "Hiking?"

Gabe shifts nervously, like he regrets answering. "Yeah. Being out in the open, no noise, no people. Just you and the land."

I never would've guessed that. "Wow. Didn't peg you for the nature type. Thought you'd be more of a 'brood in the corner of a dimly lit bar' guy."

His lips twitch again, and this time, the smirk does break through. "That too."

I shake my head, chuckling. "Alright, I'll bite. Where's your dream hiking spot?"

He hesitates, then says, "Torres del Paine."

I blink. "Where the hell is that?"

"Chile. Patagonia."

I gape at him. "Damn, alright, international man of mystery. Didn't expect you to have dream destinations."

"Everyone has dreams," he says simply. "Even if they don't talk about them."

That does something to me. I don't know what, but it makes my throat feel tight, makes my heart trip over itself in a way I don't like.

I swallow hard and look out the window, processing that. But before I can dwell too long, he speaks again.

"Your turn."

I glance back at him. "Huh?"

"You asked me mine. What's yours?"

I roll my eyes. "Gabe, I am not a nature person at all. I have never thought about hiking spots."

"That's not what I mean."

His voice is softer now, and something about it makes my stomach flip.

"What do you want, Tori?"

The only ones to ever ask me that have been Blaze, Ryder, and Thorne, and only just recently. To have Gabe ask me the same, well, it throws me off.

What the hell do I want? I thought I wanted this, but now I'm not so sure.

I wet my lips, suddenly uncomfortable. "I—"

The car jolts as Gabe suddenly swerves, his hand shooting out instinctively, landing firmly against my stomach to keep me steady.

The warmth of his palm, the way his fingers splay against my shirt, the way he doesn't immediately move away—it sends a jolt through me, sharp and unexpected.

"What the hell?" I snap, my voice higher than I'd like it to be.

His eyes flick to mine, something veiled in them before he finally removes his hand and grips the wheel again. "Pothole."

A goddamn pothole.

Except now my heart is racing for an entirely different reason, and suddenly the air in the car feels too thick.

He clears his throat. "You were saying?"

Right. What do I want?

I don't know. Not when I can still feel the ghost of his touch burning through my clothes.

10: Tori

My response to Gabe's question was a quick "I have what I want," because it's true. I have Blaze, Ryder, and Thorne. I have a family now, not with Diablo, but with them. And yeah, knowing who my dad is was something I always wanted, and I guess I have that too now. The rest of the ride is silent without my nagging questions, but my brain stays in overdrive.

The moment we pull up to the estate—I can't call it home yet—I jump out before the car is even fully parked. I don't bother looking back, my shoes marching against the gravel as I head straight for the door. I don't bother stopping even when Gabe shouts "Victoria!"

I step through the front door, barely taking two steps inside before Thorne is already there, his presence like a gravitational pull I can't resist. His hands find my waist as he presses a slow kiss to my temple.

"Missed you," he murmurs, voice low, his lips grazing my skin for an extra second.

Warmth spreads through me, making my shoulders relax for the first time all day. "Missed you too."

Before I can say anything else, Blaze appears behind Thorne, his dark eyes sweeping over me like he's memorizing every detail. "Took you long enough, Doll."

I roll my eyes, but the teasing lilt in his voice makes my chest feel lighter. "Trust me, if I could have left sooner, I would have."

Blaze huffs a quiet laugh before stepping forward, brushing his fingers through my hair like he's checking to make sure I'm still in one piece. Just as I'm about to lean into his touch, the door opens behind me.

Gabe.

He walks in carrying a couple of bags from the car, his jaw tight as he takes in the scene—Thorne close at my side, Blaze practically hovering. His gaze flicks to me, something guarded flaring behind his eyes before he schools his face into neutrality.

Blaze notices first. "We got it from here."

Gabe doesn't move right away, doesn't speak. Instead, his eyes linger on mine for a second too long, a quiet hesitation in the air. Like he wants to say something but knows better than to do it in front of them.

Ryder comes in next, clapping a hand against Gabe's shoulder in a way that's both casual and pointed. "Yeah, buddy. You're done for the day. Now scram."

Gabe clenches his teeth, but nods once. Without another word, he turns and heads down the hall toward his room. I exhale, flooded with relief.

Ryder drags my attention back. "That was fun."

I narrow my eyes. "You're an ass."

He slings an arm around my shoulders with that playful smirk of his. "Eh, only for you. C'mon, KitKat. We've got plans."

"Plans?" I arch a brow, letting him lead me further inside as Thorne and Blaze exchange some look I can't quite decode.

Thorne gives me a small yet comforting smile. "You've had a long day. We're running you a bath."

Blaze nods, his fingers brushing the inside of my wrist, like he's already thinking about stripping me down. "And we're helping you relax."

Oh.

Ryder's grip tightens playfully. "You up for it, KitKat?"

I swallow, pulse kicking up as I glance between the three of them, heat curling low in my stomach. "Do I even have a choice?"

Thorne leans in, lips ghosting over my ear. "Not really."

My breath catches, and just like that, my exhaustion is a thing of the past.

I lean against the bathroom counter, watching as the steam curls from the oversized tub, the scent of lavender and vanilla filling the air. Thorne rolls up his sleeves, testing the water with his fingers, while Blaze adjusts the towel on the rack like it's a puzzle only he can solve. Ryder lounges against the doorframe, arms crossed, eyes on me.

They're all fussing over this bath like it's a sacred ritual, and honestly, it's kind of cute.

"So," I start, tilting my head, "how was your day?"

Thorne's eyes flick to mine, too fast, too guilty. Blaze tenses. Ryder, however, snickers under his breath, looking downright irritated.

"Oh, you know," he drawls, rolling his eyes. "Just business stuff. Very professional. No distractions whatsoever."

Blaze shoots him a glare. "Shut up, Ryder."

I narrow my eyes, crossing my arms. "Oh? No distractions at all? That's funny, because you all look suspiciously like men who've been dodging something all day."

Thorne clears his throat, reaching for the bath salts like they're a lifeline. "It was fine."

Ryder lets out a dramatic sigh. "'Fine,' he says. Like we weren't being hunted down by Diablo's handpicked temptresses." He presses a hand to his heart. "Tori, it was brutal. I barely made it out alive."

Blaze pinches the bridge of his nose. "It wasn't that bad."

"Really?" I arch a brow. "Because Ryder's making it sound like you were thrown into a pit of seductresses."

"Oh, you mean like the pit we keep you in?" Ryder winks.

I roll my eyes, but I can't help the happiness that tugs at my lips. "Well, if it was so traumatizing, maybe I should've been there to protect you."

Thorne scoffs. "Trust me, they would've run the second you walked in."

I hum in agreement, stepping forward and running my fingers up his arm. "Good to know. But now I feel like I should be extra nice to you all after such a harrowing ordeal."

Ryder tries not to laugh as he speaks. "Oh, I like where this is going."

Blaze catches my wrist before I can get too close, his eyes darkening a bit. "Get in the bath first."

I pout. "Bossy."

"And yet, you love it."

I don't argue. *Mostly because he's right.*

With a slow stretch, I peel off my clothes, letting them drop to the tiled floor. The guys don't move, don't even breathe as I step into the bath, the hot water enveloping me in warmth. I sink in, sighing, stretching my legs along the porcelain.

The moment I'm settled, Thorne kneels beside me, rolling up his sleeves further, and scoops up a handful of warm water, letting it cascade down my shoulders. Blaze follows, grabbing a loofah and lathering it with soap. Ryder, on the other hand, just props his chin on his hand, watching with open appreciation.

"So, how exactly are you planning to 'be extra nice' to us, KitKat?" he muses.

I grin a little too wickedly, running a damp hand up Thorne's arm, feeling the muscles tense beneath my touch. "Well, I suppose that depends on how good you all are at taking care of me."

Thorne's gaze flickers with something molten. Blaze's lips twitch like he's trying not to get too excited. And Ryder leans in, voice low and teasing.

"Oh, we plan on taking very, very good care of you."

"I guess we'll see about that," I retort with a wink of my own.

Ryder only laughs, accepting the challenge as he shifts positions, rolling the legs of his pants up. He lays himself back on the thick edge of the tub, dipping one foot in the water while his fingers skim along my arm in lazy patterns.

I lean back, sinking deeper into the warm water as Blaze moves to kneel beside Thorne, hands tracing circles on my thigh beneath the water. I should be relaxed, floating in this little sanctuary they built for me, but my mind keeps drifting.

They notice. Of course they notice.

"You're thinking too much," Thorne murmurs, his voice that perfect low rasp that always has my stomach tightening.

"Yeah, KitKat," Ryder chimes in, his hand dipping lower, fingers pressing into my hip. "Kind of a mood killer when we're trying to spoil you and you're over there looking like you're trying to solve calculus."

I huff a laugh, shaking my head. "I don't think you understand how much I appreciate this."

"We do," Blaze says, lifting my hand out of the water to press his lips against my knuckles. "But you're still in your head."

I bite my lip, staring down at the rippling water. "Just...a lot happened today."

Blaze's fingers tighten faintly. "Anything we need to deal with?"

I shake my head. *Not yet, anyway.* "No. It's fine. I can deal with my own problems."

Ryder stops tracing for a moment, squeezing my arm in concern. "So you have them, then. Problems?"

Thorne's arms tense for a moment, like he's restraining himself from demanding every detail right now. "Did anyone give you a hard time?"

"No," I admit, tracing a droplet of water on Blaze's forearm, distracting myself. "I actually...met someone I liked."

Blaze's head tilts, his dark eyes narrowing. "Liked?"

I sigh, sensing the possessive waves rolling off of them already. "Not like that. Relax, cavemen."

Ryder smirks. "I don't know, Tori. You do have a habit of collecting people."

"Yeah?" I shoot back. "Want me to add another?"

Blaze makes a low noise in his throat, something between a warning and amusement. Thorne just sighs, pressing a kiss to my shoulder, his lips lingering there. "Tell us about them."

I hesitate for half a second before shrugging. "Cassandra. She's one of the lieutenants. She seems...different from the others. Smart, funny. Doesn't treat me like I'm some fragile thing."

Blaze hums, noncommittal. Ryder leans closer, nudging my cheek with his nose. "So you have a girl crush now?"

"Shut up," I mutter, shoving at him. He catches my wrist, bringing it to his lips and pressing a kiss to the back of my hand.

"You know you can tell us if you're feeling...off about all of this, right?" Ryder inclines, his blue eyes piercing me with his gaze.

I exhale slowly, letting my eyelids close for a second. "I know. And I'm fine, really."

Except maybe not. I don't know.

I do know that I don't like these girls around them, or Gabe at my side 24/7.

Blaze's grip on my thigh tightens slightly, a grounding touch. "You know we're here if you need anything."

The sincerity in his voice tugs something deep in my chest. I turn my head, catching his gaze. "Yeah?"

"Yeah," he confirms. "Now, can we stop talking about people who aren't in this bath and focus on the fact that we're currently worshiping the hell out of you?"

I laugh, rolling my eyes. "I had a different kind of worship in mind."

"Oh, yeah? Don't worry, KitKat, we're getting to that," Ryder teases, pressing another kiss to my hand.

Thorne reaches across, gripping my waist tightly as he shifts closer, his breath warm against my ear. "You trust us, don't you?"

My heart skips a beat at the question. "Of course I do."

Ryder hums, his fingers trailing down my arm in featherlight strokes. "Then trust us to take care of you the way you deserve."

Blaze's hands grip my thighs beneath the water, his thumbs brushing soft, teasing circles against my skin. "Starting now."

I barely get a breath in before Thorne tilts my head back, his lips capturing mine in a slow, possessive kiss, and just like that—I'm gone.

The world outside this bathroom ceases to exist. The only thing that matters is the heat of their touches, the way their hands anchor me, the way they strip away every lingering thought until I am entirely theirs. And fuck, do I love it.

After all, what's the point of having three men if you can't have all of them at once?

It starts slow, their touches lingering, fingers teasing, their mouths tracing lazy patterns on my skin. But then the water grows cold, and Blaze is pulling me out of the tub, soaked and without a care, his mouth devouring mine like a starving man.

He gently lays me on the bed, the mattress shifting around me as they each take their places. My heart's pounding, my core heating like molten lava, needing to be cooled before it consumes me whole.

Ryder's lips ghost across my shoulder, his hand sliding up my leg. "Fuck, KitKat. You're so goddamn perfect."

"The only woman who could ever handle us," Blaze mutters, his hands skimming up my sides as his mouth trails down my neck.

I lean into his touch, my breath hitching when Thorne's lips follow his path. "The only woman we'll ever need."

"Mine," I mutter, and their lips pause for a moment.

"Always," Thorne promises, and the heat inside me burns brighter.

It's too much.

Their hands, their lips, their bodies pressed against me, it's all so much, but it's still not enough. I need more. I want more.

My fingers reach for Ryder, gripping the fabric of his shirt and pulling him up to my lips. I can feel him smirk against me, and then he's kissing me like the world is burning and I'm the only one who can stop the flames.

His fingers dip down, circling my nipple and making me moan into his mouth. "What do you want, KitKat?"

I can't even think right now, let alone speak. Instead, I push his hand lower, and he chuckles against my lips.

"Use your words."

I groan, turning to glare at him, but I can't muster up any real irritation when I catch sight of his hooded eyes and swollen lips.

Too fucking sexy.

"Please," I gasp.

Thorne leans forward, his teeth nipping at my ear. "Please, what, Vic?"

"Make me come," I demand, my fingers curling around Ryder's wrist and shoving his hand down.

"You sure you want it that bad, Doll?" Blaze growls, and I feel the heat of his gaze on me.

"Yes," I hiss.

"You'll take whatever we give you," Thorne whispers, and I nod without a second thought.

Give it all to me.

I can't find the words, not when I'm so fucking turned on and they're not touching me where I want it most.

"Ryder," I moan, and the bastard fucking laughs.

"Ask nicely."

"Please," I whimper.

He grins. "Mmm. I love it when you say please."

Then his fingers finally brush against my clit, and I release a loud, guttural moan, my hips arching off the bed. Blaze's lips find mine, his tongue pushing into my mouth, muffling the sounds escaping me.

"Fuck, Tori," Ryder groans, his fingers working in quick, tight circles against my clit, sending me reeling.

My hips rock against his hand, desperate for release. He presses deeper, sweeping against that tender spot inside me just right. The pressure coils tight, and I'm so close already.

This might be a fucking record.

I try to hold out, but then Blaze's lips move down, and the second his tongue swipes at my nipple, the pleasure bursts through me, making me cry out.

"That's it," Thorne rasps, his fingers twisting in my hair. "Come for us."

My eyes squeeze shut, and I ride the waves of pleasure, body arching into their touch, needing more. Needing them.

When I finally come down, the air is hot, my lungs heaving for breath, and they're all watching me with hunger in their eyes.

None of us are done. Fingers just aren't enough anymore. They leave me hungrier, needing it all.

Needing them.

"I need..."

"What, KitKat?" Ryder coos, his fingers tracing patterns along my inner thigh.

"More."

"Oh, KitKat. We're going to give you everything."

"And we're going to make you scream our names," Blaze says, his eyes flashing.

"You want that, Vic?" Thorne asks, his hand skimming over my breast, squeezing lightly. "You want us to make you feel good?"

I nod, the words stuck in my throat, too busy panting to respond.

"We can't hear you," Ryder taunts.

I lick my lips, forcing out the words. "Yes. Please. I want it. I need it."

Ryder groans, leaning down to press a kiss to my lips, and then he's reaching for the bedside drawer, pulling out condoms and passing them out like we're at a frat party.

I reach for Blaze, and the moment our lips connect, he's tugging me up, shifting positions. Then his hands are on my hips, guiding me down his covered cock, stretching me wide.

I let out a moan, rocking my hips slowly as I adjust.

"Fuck, Blaze," I whisper, leaning forward to rest my head on his shoulder.

He hums, his fingers digging into my hips, keeping me still. "So fucking good."

"You take us so well, Victoria," Thorne mutters from behind me, his hand slipping down between Blaze and I to rub my clit, drawing a groan from me.

Don't think I didn't notice you using my full name there, Thorne.

I heard it. I feel the way it ran down my body and held tight, coiled in my center and melting me to my core.

"So damn responsive," Ryder mutters, his hands tracing patterns over my right breast.

I start rocking against Blaze, chasing the high. He's holding back, not letting me take control, and I can feel his restraint in the way his muscles tighten beneath me. The way he thrusts his dick so deep inside me, I almost cry out.

I'm so fucking sensitive, it feels like the smallest thing could push me over the edge again, and that's exactly what they're doing.

They're building me up, making me chase the pleasure.

I lean into Blaze, moaning against his skin, and the others move. Ryder's hand slides down my spine, Thorne's fingers slip from between us, to my back side.

His finger traces a path down my ass, and my breath catches, realizing where he's going. Ryder does too, reaching for oil they're apparently keeping in the drawer as well.

Do we have a sex drawer that I wasn't aware of?

I should be surprised, but I'm not.

"You want it, KitKat?" Ryder asks, and I can hear the smug confidence in his voice.

I nod against Blaze, and then Thorne's lips are at my ear.

"Use your words," he reminds me, his voice low, and a shudder runs through me.

"Yes," I moan.

I feel the pressure as Thorne inserts a single finger. The stretch is a lot, and the guys can tell. They take their time, letting me adjust before adding another finger, preparing me for what's to come.

It's uncomfortable, but the pain is quickly drowned by the pleasure building in my core. Thorne's not even inside me yet and I already feel like I'm going to burst.

Then, finally, Thorne withdraws his fingers, and the three of them adjust themselves. Blaze stands, still buried deep inside me as Thorne lays flat on his back. With ease, Blaze sits over his lap, adjusting me so that my ass is pressed against the tip of Thorne's dick. Blaze keeps his pace slow, grinding his hips, his grip on my hips almost bruising.

"You ready?" Thorne asks, and I nod.

"Please," I whisper, and Thorne's lips quirk up.

"Good girl."

Then he's sliding inside me, stretching me impossibly wide, and my body shudders at the overwhelming sensation.

"Fuck," I gasp, fingers digging into Blaze's arms, holding myself upright.

Thorne pauses, letting me adjust. It takes a second, but eventually, the pain subsides, and I start rocking against Blaze, feeling Thorne inside me, and a wave of pleasure washes over me.

"I'm feeling left out here, guys," Ryder complains.

"You hear that, Doll?" Blaze asks, sliding in and out of me with each word. "He's pouting."

"Maybe you should ask nicely?" I tease, using his words against him.

He growls, his fingers fisting in my hair and pulling back, forcing me to look up at him as he kneels beside me. "You wanna play, KitKat?"

Before I can answer, he's leaning down, his lips capturing mine in a bruising kiss. His hand grips my chin, holding me still.

I whimper, melting into the kiss. When he finally pulls away, we're both panting, our breaths mingling.

"You're lucky I love you," he says, and the words hit me like a freight train.

My chest swells, the warmth spreading through me. Before I can say anything, Ryder is standing on the mattress, his piercings staring me right in the face. Every beautiful rung sparkling under the light.

A bedazzled dick, just for me.

I almost laugh at my thought, but it's quickly pushed aside when Blaze and Thorne match strides. Instead I moan, too close to ecstasy to form any more coherent thoughts.

"Open wide, KitKat. I'm going to fuck that dirty little mouth of yours," he orders, stroking his bare dick in my face.

"You're such a fucking dick," I pant.

"Only because you want it so badly," he retorts.

I can't help it, I laugh, but it's short lived as Blaze thrusts his dick deeper.

"Fuck," I hiss.

Ryder's hand reaches down, his fingers curling around my chin. He forces me to look up at him as he grinds into me. "Tap my thigh if it gets to be too much, okay? Can't have you suffocating on my cock."

I nod, and he smirks, the same one I've grown so fond of. "Good. Now be a good girl and suck. And don't you dare come until we're done with you," he says, his fingers tangling in my hair and tilting my head back, sliding his cock past my lips.

His hips rock forward, his piercings dragging against my tongue, metallic and cold. I moan, and he curses under his breath, his fingers tightening in my hair.

Blaze's hips snap against mine, driving me forward and deeper onto Ryder's dick. All three of them set a brutal pace, fucking me from both sides, in all holes, and my mind goes blank. There's nothing except them. Nothing except the way they fill me completely, the way their hands hold me down, the way they fuck me like I'm the only thing they've ever wanted.

It's too much, and not enough. My muscles tense, my body shaking as the pleasure builds.

"Fuck," Ryder hisses, his hips stuttering as he fucks my mouth.

"God, Vic, you look so beautiful taking us," Thorne rasps.

I whimper, the sound muffled by Ryder's dick in my mouth. They keep pounding into me, their rhythm faltering as they all get closer.

"You're going to come for us, Doll," Blaze growls. "You're going to fucking scream our names when you do."

My thighs shake, and the heat coils inside me, tighter and tighter until finally—it snaps. I cry out, the sound smothered by Ryder's dick, and they curse, fucking me through my release.

"Vic," Thorne moans.

"Doll," Blaze growls.

"KitKat," Ryder hisses.

And then they're all coming, their bodies tense and shuddering as they find their own releases.

Look who's screaming whose name now, boys.

We all collapse, a tangle of limbs, our hearts pounding and bodies covered in sweat.

Ryder is the first to pull out, a long string of spit and cum stretching from his tip and connecting to my lips. Blaze follows, and I groan at the loss of contact.

Thorne is last, slowly pulling out, and I hiss, the pain returning.

"You okay?" he asks, cupping my cheek and brushing his thumb along the corner of my lips.

"Yeah," I murmur.

I'm more than okay.

He smiles, the kind that makes my heart ache, and leans down, pressing a soft kiss to my lips. When he pulls away, his dark eyes are swirling with emotions, and he swallows.

"I love you," he whispers, and a lump forms in my throat.

"I love you too," I whisper back.

11: THORNE

It's been two weeks of menial tasks and balancing acts. Doing things for Diablo alongside Mia while trying to make time for Vic every evening with the guys. She said she wanted us all to share, and that's what we've been doing. But I'd be lying if I said I didn't miss just having her to myself sometimes.

Now my balancing act is tilting, and not in the direction I want it.

A middle of the night call and here I sit, away from the person I want to be with most. Mia may not be the worst person to be around, and I definitely didn't plan on being stuck in a car with her for the rest of the night, but when Diablo called and said to stake out the warehouse where all these suspicious crates were coming from, I couldn't exactly say 'fuck off,' no matter how much I wanted to.

Vic, although annoyed, told me to go, and it's not like Blaze or Ryder were sad to see me go. Hell, they're probably happy sharing with one less person for a moment.

There's no getting enough of Vic...ever.

"This is pointless. He's already had this warehouse surveilled, so why have us do it too?" I complain, gripping my pants over my knees and digging my fingers in frustration. "Nothing turned up last week. What's different about today?"

Mia shrugs, her eyes fixed on the night sky, like she's wishing on a star. No clue what for, and that makes me more wary of her. "Orders are orders, so here we are."

"Yeah, well, these orders are bullshit."

"Are you always this impatient?" she questions, turning her gaze towards me.

I take a handful of M&Ms a little too aggressively and mutter "When there's better shit I could be doing? Yeah," before shoving them all in my mouth.

She smiles, almost as if she finds my answer amusing. "Like what? Holding Tori hostage in your bed?"

My eyes snap on her, but there's no malice in her tone, just wonder in her eyes. It's almost as if she's curious about what I do to her in the privacy of our room. "She's not a hostage," I respond, my tone clipped and cold. "She's the only thing worth my time."

"Must be nice to have that," she whispers, propping her chin on her palm as she rests her elbow on the door, and stares out the window.

We grow silent, watching the way the wind blows against the trees that beat on the warehouse bricks. The silence lingers until she breaks it, turning her attention to me again.

"You ever think about what you'd be doing if you weren't in this life?"

I huff a quiet laugh. "No point in thinking about shit that won't ever happen."

She nods like she understands, but there's something wistful in the way she stares out the windshield. "I used to dream about being a teacher," she says suddenly. "Back when I was a kid."

I don't know what to say to that. It's too normal. Too far removed from this world.

"You would've been a terrible teacher," I tell her, allowing the smallest twist of my lips to show.

She's too meek. Kids would eat her alive. They're more vicious than the kind of people we deal with in this career line.

She laughs softly, shaking her head. "Yeah, probably."

Another lull of silence. The wind picks up, rustling the trash littering the alleyway. A cat darts past the dumpster, but nothing human moves.

I want to go home.

I check my watch, sighing. "Another hour. If nothing happens, we call it."

Mia doesn't argue. Just leans her head back against the seat and closes her eyes. I keep my gaze on the darkness outside, waiting for something—anything—to give me a reason to be here.

But the warehouse remains unbothered.

"I know we're supposed to be stealthy and all that," Mia starts, but her attention is on her phone. "But I think I'll lose my mind if it stays this quiet. And you're not much of a talker."

She pairs her phone with the car's bluetooth and starts playing her music, which oddly sounds like Vic's playlist. The first thing on is *Paint the Town Blue* by Ashnikko, which Vic has been playing a lot as of late. Something to do with a tv show she really enjoyed watching.

Mia's boots tap against the floorboard as she tries to restrain herself from dancing, but in no time flat, her hands start beating against her lap and then she's humming along.

"I sometimes wish I was that bold. You know?" she randomly starts again, her eyes on the lot but her mind somewhere else completely. "Leave my mark everywhere."

"You know how superheroes have secret identities?"

She turns her head to look at me like I'm some weirdo for asking, even though she's the one who keeps saying random things. "Yeah," she responds almost wearily.

"Well, we have to be the same way. You don't want people knowing you unless you're ready to risk the people you love. So maybe leaving your mark isn't exactly what you want to do."

"Yeah, maybe not."

We grow silent again, and the very faint music keeps switching, a mixture of Ashnikko, Le Tigre, and Billie Eilish invading my ears for the next twenty minutes. I'm half tempted to tell her that we're going to stake the place out by walking around the warehouse's perimeter instead, but she cuts in again.

Her lips press together, something flickering in her eyes—frustration, maybe. Or something else entirely. "Do you ever question him?"

I scoff. "Every damn day since coming here. But questioning and disobeying are two different things."

Even Vic has learned that.

"Why did you come here?"

"It's simple." I grab another fistful of chocolate, but this time I pop it into my mouth one at a time. "Vic wanted to come."

"So just like that, you packed up and came here to work for *him?*" She's almost too shocked, like the thought of someone dropping everything for the person they love is too much to believe.

"Just like that." I nod, popping a blue M&M into my mouth.

Everyone says the colors don't have flavors.

But then why does blue taste the best?

"You must really love her," she whispers, sounding almost wishful, like she wants the same kind of care.

"More than she comprehends."

Mia hums softly, nodding like she understands that better than she should. I don't press. If she wants to talk, she will. If not, I'm not about to waste energy dragging it out of her.

Minutes pass, long and slow. The only sound is the low hum of Mia's music and faint creak of metal in the distance as the wind rattles the warehouse's siding. I glance at my phone, checking the time.

Such a waste of my fucking time.

I lean back, rolling my shoulders, but Mia's still tapping away beside me. Her gaze flickers across the lot like she's expecting something to jump out at any second and she's keeping her mind busy with music.

I'm ready to call it but before I can say anything, a sharp crack splits the silence—a gunshot, distant but clear. Mia jerks, sucking in a sharp breath, and for a second, she looks like she's somewhere else entirely, her hands trembling before she clenches them into fists.

*I know I said this was pointless, but that didn't mean I **wanted** it to have one.*

You're always against me, universe, aren't you?

"Mia," I say firmly, my hand already reaching for the door handle. "Stay in the car."

She shakes her head quickly. "What if—"

"Stay. In. The. Car." I cut her off, my voice edged with authority. "That's not a request."

Her breathing is fast, her hands white-knuckled against her lap, but she nods. Barely.

I don't waste another second. Pushing the door open, I step out, adjusting my grip on my gun as I scan the lot. The night just got a hell of a lot more tense.

With my gun held high, I creep my way through the lot, sticking to the shadows. It's stupid to go toward the sound of a gunshot, but here I am, doing just that. Because that's what belonging to a gang is like, running toward bullets to fireback.

I turn the corner ready to shoot, but there's nothing. In fact, it was never anything. What I thought was a gunshot turns out to be a pipe hitting against the siding.

My shoulders relax and I release the tension in my finger. I holster my gun, cursing myself for jumping the gun, quite literally.

I head back to the car, only a few feet away.

I'm almost there, the handle in reach, when I realize Mia is missing.

Was the pipe a distraction? Did someone want to take Mia? And if so, why?

I don't know enough about her to tell why she would be a target.

Fuck, fuck, fuck.

Where the fuck did she go?

I'm turning on my heel, spinning in circles and making myself dizzy. *What direction would they have taken her?* My ears strain, listening for sounds of an engine or tires screeching against the asphalt, but there's nothing. After another second, I make a decision, running down the road away from the warehouse.

A scuffle to my left catches my attention as a piece of tarp flaps in the wind, and there, hidden beside a large blue barrel tucked away by the tarp, is Mia. She's curled into a ball, shaking all over, but seemingly unhurt.

My feet pound against the earth as I race to her side, picking her up and taking her to the car. I quickly shove her into the passenger side, race around the hood, and take my seat, tires peeling away as I head for the estate.

I'm watching the rearview mirror the entire time, waiting for a car to start giving chase, but nothing happens. My body is tense, on edge and ready to pounce. I'm jumpier than ever as I turn down strange streets to try and lose the invisible car chasing after us.

"What did you see?" Mia suddenly asks, pushing against the door so she doesn't slide into it as I turn the corner.

"What do you mean?" My focus is torn between her, the road, and the people I'm sure will appear any second now.

"Why are you driving so crazy? What did you see back there?"

My foot hits the brake so fast and so hard, Mia almost hits her head on the dashboard from the sudden jolt. The tires screech, burning against the road, echoing through the night. "No one took you? You didn't almost get kidnapped?"

Suddenly, nothing makes sense. Then again, nothing seems to make sense anymore.

"What? No!" She shakes her head, brows furrowed, unable to comprehend how I ever got to that conclusion.

"Then why the fuck were you hiding?" I snap, because at this point, my frustration is overriding my tolerance of this entire thing.

"I..." she pauses, eyes swimming with uncertainty, searching me for something, some kind of symbol that will tell her she can trust me. "It was the sound," she admits in a whisper of shame.

"The sound of what?" My fingers pinch at the bridge of my nose, a headache brewing with this conversation—with this whole damn night, really.

"The gunshot."

I stare at her, waiting for more. When nothing comes, I exhale sharply, pressing a hand against the steering wheel to keep my grip from tightening into a fist.

"You're telling me," I say slowly, "that you hid like that because of a gunshot that wasn't even a gunshot?"

Mia swallows, turning her face toward the window. Her fingers dig into her sleeves, clutching the fabric like it's the only thing keeping her centered. "Yeah."

I wait, but she doesn't offer anything else. The silence between us stretches, thick and unbearable. My pulse is still hammering from the unnecessary panic, my adrenaline still dumping into my veins like I'm gearing up for a fight that isn't coming.

I drag a hand down my face. "You wanna tell me why? Because this line of work has gunshots ringing from all sides, so I'm guessing this isn't just a general fear of loud noises."

Mia flinches, like I hit too close to something raw. Her nails press harder into her sleeves.

"I was twelve," she says after a moment, her voice barely audible over the hum of the engine. "My dad was drunk. He was always drunk, but that night was worse. He was screaming at my mom, accusing her of things she never did. She tried to talk him down, like she always tried to do, but he wasn't listening."

Her breath shudders, and she shifts in her seat like she's trying to curl into herself. "He pulled out his gun. Waved it at her, at me, at my siblings. Said if she wanted to leave so bad, he'd make sure she never walked out the door alive."

My grip on the wheel tightens. I don't say anything. Don't interrupt. I just let her talk. All the while, the image of my drunk father invades my mind.

"My mom fought with him, and the gun fell. I don't know what happened after that. Something inside me just—snapped. I remember grabbing the gun. I remember the way it felt in my hands, too big, too heavy, but somehow I held it steady. And then—"

She stops, sucking in a breath like she's trying to force herself to keep going.

"I shot him. I just wanted him to stop. I wanted him to leave my mom alone, to leave *me* alone."

The words drop between us, stark and cold.

"I didn't even think. One second he was screaming, and the next, he was on the ground, bleeding. My mom was crying, shaking me, but I couldn't move. I just stood there, staring at the gun in my hands."

I don't look at her, but I can feel the weight of everything she's saying, seeing how close my story could have been to hers had my dad owned a gun. The quiet thickens long enough that I almost think she won't say anything else, but then she takes another breath, shaky and uneven.

"I was arrested. They called it self-defense, but I was still a kid with a record. Juvenile detention wasn't any better. It was just a different kind of hell. You learn quickly that no one cares why you did something—just that you did it. I spent six years in that place, trying to stay invisible, trying to survive. And when I finally got out, I had nothing. My mom didn't want to have anything to do with me, suddenly too afraid of me to let me stay with her. I had no home, no job, no money. Just a reputation that followed me everywhere."

I glance at her now, and she looks so much smaller than she usually does. Like the weight of that night still clings to her, wrapping around her like an old, tattered coat she can't take off, no matter how hard she tries.

"Cassandra found me," she continues, voice thick. *Tori's Cassandra?* "Took me in when no one else would. She said people like us don't get second chances—we have to take them for ourselves. So I did. I learned how to survive in this world because I didn't have another choice. Because being helpless once was enough."

Her hands are trembling. She shoves them between her knees like that'll stop it, but I still see it.

I exhale through my nose, staring straight ahead. "So that's why you were hiding."

She nods, barely moving. "Every time I hear it...it's like I'm back there. Like I'm twelve again, standing in that kitchen with the gun in my hands. I can't—I don't know how to stop it."

I don't know what to say to that. I've seen a lot of shit, lived through worse. I know what it's like to have a past that never really leaves you. But I don't know how to fix it. I don't even know if it can be fixed.

"You tell anyone else about this?" I ask, my voice quieter than before.

She shakes her head. "Cassandra knows. Diablo knows. But you're the first person I've actually told."

I glance at her again, surprised. But she isn't looking at me. Just staring out the windshield like she's afraid to see whatever's on my face.

I let out a slow breath, my grip loosening on the wheel. "I'm sorry you went through that. No one should have to."

Mia scoffs, but it's weak. "Yeah, no kidding."

The tension in the car shifts, not quite comfortable but not as suffocating as before. I reach for the center console, flipping it open, and pull out a pack of Skittles. I shake a handful into my palm and hold them out to her.

She blinks at me, confused. "What—"

"Just take it."

She hesitates before reaching out, plucking a few from my hand. I toss the rest into my mouth, crunching down, the sugar helping to cut through the leftover frustration knotting in my chest.

Mia stares at the candy in her hand before sighing and popping them into her mouth. "Thanks."

"Don't mention it."

She nods, and I start driving again, heading back home to Tori, to hold her close and pretend that what Mia told me didn't just drag up some trauma of my own.

I check the time. "We're leaving. If Diablo wants us to sit around and wait for nothing, he can come do it himself."

Mia doesn't argue, just leans her head back against the seat and closes her eyes.

I drive, my mind still turning over everything she just told me. And for the first time, I see Mia not just as Diablo's pawn, or some girl I was forced to deal with—but as someone who survived hell and still kept going.

Doesn't mean I trust her. But I understand her more now, and that's got to get me somewhere. Maybe soon she'll tell me the real reason she's always assigned to me.

12: TORI

It's been two long and gruesome weeks of training with Gabe in the mornings, afternoon lessons on how things run with Juan or Cass, and lunches with my dad on the daily. My evenings are spent trying to keep Blaze, Ryder, Thorne, and I all together, snuggled tight or fucking hard.

Either way, as long as they're with me, I'm happy.

"I think you get off on seeing me struggle to breathe," I complain as I stretch on the cold, blue mat beneath me, dying from my screaming muscles.

Gabe has been sparring with me to continue my self-defense lessons for a good hour now. My body aches, but the sting of my lungs with each breath I take is what's really doing me in.

Please, shoot me now.

"I don't *get off*," he air quotes with a shake of his head. "I am, however, happy to see you learn how to protect yourself."

I watch as he bends down, reaching for a bottle of water, hardly out of breath, and it makes me want to kick him. His Adam's apple bobs as he takes a few drinks before eyeing me with an arched brow.

"You forgot your water again, didn't you?" He sighs as he passes his bottle to me, and I give him a sheepish grin.

"About three weeks in and you already know me so well." I take the bottle and waterfall the precious liquid with reverence. "Tell me I'm at least improving? Star pupil material?" I quip as I hand him his bottle back.

He takes it, capping it before he lets a very small smile slip.

He's harder to crack than Fort Knox.

"You're my only student, Reyes," he says, extending his hand for me to take.

"All I'm hearing from that is that I'm your best student. Good to know." I grin playfully as I accept his help up, knowing my legs are weak little suckers that couldn't lift a feather at the moment.

"Come on. You need to shower before your lunch with your dad." He doesn't bother arguing with me, knowing it's pointless anyway. He just shoos me out of the at-home gym and cleans up as I head upstairs.

Sadly, Blaze, Ryder, and Thorne are all out of the house with stupid tasks. It doesn't matter that Thorne had to leave in the middle of the night and didn't return till almost dawn. Come nine o'clock, he had to go again.

The longer we're here, the busier everyone seems to be. I don't like how little time we have with one another. At first, we had the entire evening together, but as of late, we hardly get two hours.

Thankfully we're all night owls and stay up later than we should, talking, touching...fucking.

God, I love fucking.

When I reach my room, I throw open the closet doors and grab a black shirt and dark skinny jeans with purposeful holes. I'm not a sundress kind of girl, despite how desperately my father would like me to be.

Steam fills the bathroom as I shower until every surface has a nice sheen of humidity. I feel more like myself when I finally emerge, dressed and ready. My hair is plopped in a wet bun on top of my head, not having bothered to even try to style it right.

I came here to get to know my father better, and what I'm learning is that I might not like him at all. When we're together, I can clearly imagine what life with him would have been like growing up. There's this other version of myself, the one that grew up in his world, that acts snobby and arrogant, who just does what she's told.

That's never going to be me.

I know Diablo would love it if I would just listen and do as he says without question. But, you know, I have a brain of my own, and it works more than fine when I'm not getting myself into trouble. Which actually hasn't been as often here lately, because you know what? I'm growing, dammit.

And anyone who says otherwise can suck my left tit.

I huff at my own thoughts as I descend the stairs, seeing Gabe already there, waiting on me. He looks up, assessing my outfit choices and lets out the longest sigh.

He knows what I'm doing.

"You're really trying to make everyone's life hell, aren't you?" He exhales heavily as he shakes his head but knows telling me to change will only waste his breath.

"Why, whatever do you mean?" I feign innocence, batting my lashes and clutching my figurative pearls.

He doesn't respond, just leads the way to the car as usual, opening my door for me and gesturing for me to get in. I climb up, buckling up as he rounds the hood of the car and takes his place behind the wheel.

No other words are exchanged between us as he drives us to Diablo's estate. Only the hum of Sleep Token's *Caramel* keeps the ride from complete silence. The estate is still as intimidating as it was the first time, and no easier to navigate since I'm only ever in three areas—the garden, the dining room, and Diablo's office.

I'm not allowed to *explore* the rest of the place, and Diablo makes sure of that. Suffice it to say it's oddly suspicious and definitely not my favorite part of being here. But I know that after this lunch, I get to see Cass. She's got Tori duty this afternoon, and she's honestly the only person I vibe with in this dreary place.

Maybe because she's the only other woman here—like literally. We're the only estrogen in this bitch.

There's so much testosterone here I could drown in it.

Gabe leads the way, knowing I hate being the first one to enter this place. Everyone's eyes immediately fall on me every time, but when Gabe enters first, I get to hide behind him for a second longer. A second in which people lose interest and look away. It lowers the number of stares I get by a decent amount.

Look at me, being clever.

The estate seems emptier than usual as we head to the dining room. It's obvious something is going on, but of course, I'm clueless about it.

"Oh? Is there a company retreat? Some team building exercises going on?" I ask Gabe, as if he'd actually tell me something useful.

To my surprise, he does.

"Not exactly. We're making a show of force, so almost everyone is running around today."

I keep that information stowed away because it seems important. Something is going on, otherwise, why the big show?

Gabe opens the door for me again, gesturing for me to enter without him as I normally do. These lunches are just dear ol' dad and I, bodyguards unwanted. I know that Gabe won't venture far, though. He always just waits by the door for me like a good little doggy.

"Mija, I see you didn't get the dress I sent over," he remarks, his eyes twitching for a moment, like they want to narrow but he's fighting the instinct.

"Oh no, I got it." I take my seat before him, making sure it drags against the tile as I scoot it in.

He doesn't hesitate as he takes his place across from me, his frown firmly in place. "I see."

"Yeah. As I've said before, sundresses just aren't my thing." I pick my fork up, toying with the salad already set out for me. Meanwhile, his plate is stacked with a nice ribeye and some asparagus.

Um, excuse me, but I'd love a fucking steak.

Part of me just wants to reach across and switch our plates, but I've learned where the line is, and although I push at it at times, I know not to cross it. Grabbing his plate definitely crosses it.

With a forkful of spinach, I start our dull conversations. "So, what's new?"

"I sincerely hope that isn't how you plan on speaking to the other jefes if you're ever to take over." He quirks his brow, cutting into his steak more aggressively than he should, scraping the plate with his knife. The sound makes my skin crawl, raising the hairs on my arms.

"Terribly sorry. I thought I was talking to my father and not a *jefe*." I roll my eyes, already over this lunch and we're less than two minutes in.

Where are my guys to save me when I need them?

Surprisingly enough, Diablo indulges me and answers my earlier question. "There's another gang trying to move into our territory. I'm making sure they realize what a terrible idea it is." He takes a bite, chews, and swallows before he continues. All the while, I'm silent as a mouse, worried I'll spook him from speaking again. "It's easier to stomp out an ember than it is to stop a flame."

"I'll keep that in mind." I nod, realizing he's not going to say anything else on the matter, but it's more than I've gotten out of him before. "I have another question for you."

You're really testing your luck today.

"Go on." He waits on me, eyes fully locked with my own.

"What made you want to be in this kind of life? It honestly just seems really stressful all the time. Like *all* the time."

Watching him, and all of this, the past few weeks has made me realize just how untrusting of everyone he is. Even the people he claims to be his closest allies. I see the way he eyes Gabe or even Juan, how he's just waiting for them to turn on him.

I'm not sure I could live like that—unable to trust anyone around me.

I think my asshole would be so permanently puckered, I'd die from not being able to shit.

"It wasn't exactly my first choice, but when I was growing up, my options were slim. It was either work the fields and make an honest living that I would hardly be able to survive off of, or join a gang." He shrugs, like that isn't stating some very bleak and still too real of a scenario. "The risk is high, granted, but I knew if I could work my way up, it would pay off. And it did."

I chew on that for a moment.

Literally...since I'm still eating my salad.

"And if those weren't your only options?" He arches his brow at me like he doesn't understand what I'm asking, so I try again. "Like, if you could have chosen something else, what would you have wanted to be?"

He stays silent for a while—so long, in fact, I finish eating. I'm pushing my chair in, ready to leave, when he very quietly answers me.

"I would have liked to be an engineer."

His words linger as I head out, weighing on me for some unknown reason. I shouldn't care as much as I do—not after he's been such a controlling ass—but a big part of me feels sort of sorry for him.

Gabe is waiting for me as I expected, pushing off the wall and pocketing his phone.

"Ready?" he asks, a light in his eyes like he'd been so bored while I was gone.

I nod, my voice trapped in my throat at the weight of my sudden caring. My mind can't help but imagine what Diablo would be like had he had the chance to become an engineer. How life would have been for us both.

A nice, suburban home with white walls and a large yard. We'd have nosy neighbors who we would be polite to out of necessity, just to keep the peace. I would have gone to school and gotten straight A's, applied to colleges and gotten scholarships, because I would have never gone to that private school, would have never gotten bullied. I would be graduating as a doctor this year, smiling as my mom and dad yelled from the stands, so full of pride.

But then, I wouldn't have spent that year with Thorne in the group home. I would have never met Blaze or Ryder, never gotten to know this side of them. They may have fucked up my life, but they're also the only ones who would burn the world for me without question. Who can say that they have three people willing to maim, torture, or kill someone for them?

Me, that's who.

So, no. I didn't get to have the normal life that could have been. I didn't get to have the mafia princess life. I had the foster-home, never-loved, always-bullied life, and it made me stronger, made me capable.

I lift my head, feeling a surge of pride rush through my body as we round the corner, heading for the side doors that lead to the garden. I guess that's where Cass is today.

"Cass told me to bring you to the garden because she has something she wanted you to see," Gabe explains as he leads me outside into the bright sun. "Honestly, I think she just wants to talk to you where others can't hear."

I can tell that Gabe doesn't fully trust Cass, and I'm not sure why, but it kind of offends me. She's worked hard to get where she is, being the only female lieutenant in this joint. I can't imagine her breaking that trust after all that hard work.

"I don't mind spilling some tea in the garden," I laugh at my joke, seeing Gabe just roll his eyes at my antics.

I know you secretly love it, Gabe.

Life is dull without me, huh?

"Tori!" Cass greets me enthusiastically, stretching her arms out for a hug.

She's really affectionate, this one, but she tells me that's just how she grew up. Hugs. Kisses. Rubs.

Cass pulls me into a bear hug, and I can't help but smile. She smells like jasmine and something a little spicier, like cinnamon. It's a comforting mix that immediately makes me feel at home, or at least as close as I can get to home here.

She steps back, giving me a quick once-over before a soft grin creeps across her face. "How was lunch with the big guy?" She tilts her head, the question teasing but laced with genuine curiosity.

I roll my eyes, already over the entire ordeal. "We had the most riveting conversation. Mostly about what a disappointment I am because I refuse to wear the sundresses he keeps sending me." I cross my arms, shrugging it off like it's nothing, but I know Cass can see right through the casual exterior.

She laughs, but there's a knowing edge to it. "Yeah, Diablo's pretty set in his ways. But you can't blame him for wanting you to fit the picture he's got in his head. He's got expectations of you, Tori. And that's the real challenge: deciding whether you'll meet them on your own terms or his."

I let out a frustrated sigh. "I get it, but I don't need his approval. Hell, I've been doing fine without it. But I'm sick of playing by his rules. His rules don't feel right to me. I'm not some…princess he can dress up and show off."

Cass's smile shifts, a little more serious now. "You don't have to be a princess to get shit done, Tori. But you can't just rebel for the sake of it. You've got power in this world, but you have to know how to wield it, not just throw it around like a tantrum. Trust me, there's more than one way to make your mark here, but you've got to play the game a little bit before you can break the rules."

I huff, crossing my arms tighter. "That's the thing, though. I'm sick of playing games. I'm not even sure I'm learning what I'm supposed to. I don't want to be a puppet on anyone's strings. Least of all Diablo's."

Cass steps forward, her hands resting on her hips as she studies me. "You're not a puppet, but you sure as hell need to learn how to make the strings work for you. You're tougher than you think, but you need to stop letting your emotions decide everything for you. If you want to play in this world, you need to stop letting it control you. Take a breath. Take control."

I exhale sharply, staring down at my shoes for a second before I look back up at her. "And what about the rest of it? The whole...gang thing. What do I do there? How do I make a whole group of men listen to me when my own father won't?"

Cass softens a little more, crossing the short distance between us and resting her hand on my shoulder. "You've got to prove that you're more than just Diablo's daughter. You've got to show them you're capable of running things, of making moves on your own, not just in his shadow. You don't need anyone's approval, Tori. Just trust yourself."

I shake my head, feeling the weight of the pressure she's laid on me. "It's a lot, Cass. More than I thought I'd have to deal with."

"Yeah, it is," she agrees with a serious nod. "But you can do it. You've got this fire inside you. Just...don't let it burn you out before you've had the chance to use it."

I stare at her for a moment, the words sinking in. Cass has a way of cutting through all the bullshit and hitting me with the truth. I'm starting to get it. I've been so focused on the noise around me that

I haven't stopped to think about what I need to do to make sure I'm the one calling the shots.

"Thanks, Cass," I say quietly. "I think I needed to hear that."

"Anytime," she replies, then gestures toward the garden gates. "Now, how about we step away from all that heavy stuff for a minute? I've got a few tricks to teach you, and I promise, no sundresses involved."

I laugh, the tension easing out of my shoulders as I follow her. Maybe she's right. Maybe I just needed to stop fighting so hard against everything and start using what I've got to carve my own path. This place doesn't have to define me. I'm gonna make sure I do that on my own terms.

13: RYDER

"I'm sorry, you have to do what now?" Tori snaps, her brow arched and her hand placed firmly on her hip. I feel like I'm being scolded by my mother, and it's not something I like.

"KitKat, are you jealous?" I tease her, brushing her hair behind her ear as I lean closer to her face, a breath away.

"Of you having to pretend you're dating that Bratz doll who likes to throw herself at you?" *There's that witty humor of hers I love so much.* "I'm not jealous. I'm pissed."

"Ooo, talk dirty to me, baby." I laugh, faintly grazing my mouth against her neck. I can feel her pulse beneath my lips, calling on me to suck and leave a mark.

"Ryder, I'm serious!" She pushes at my shoulders, and I oblige, backing away with a groan of annoyance.

"It wasn't my idea, and I'm just as thrilled about it as you are," I admit, staring right into her fiery eyes. *She's so fucking hot when she's mad.* "I promise, you have nothing to worry about. Lila can't hold a candle next to you. You're a whole damn bonfire. You'd eat her alive."

"She better fucking know it. You better warn her to watch herself, Ryder, or I swear..." she doesn't finish. She doesn't need to finish; it's obvious by the way her body is shaking. Given the chance, she'd kill Lila if she tried anything.

"I'll make sure to mention how ferocious my kitty cat is."

"It's bad enough you call me KitKat, don't start calling me kitty cat." Her finger points at me, her eyes so serious I can't help the smirk that crosses my lips.

"Yes, ma'am!" I salute her, noting the way her shoulders drop a fraction of an inch. "It's just for one quick meeting. I won't let her lay it on too thick."

"You better not." She sighs, leaning against the counter as she sips the coffee she made us all this morning.

Her coffee is always the best.

"You really should talk to your dad about these girls. Then again, he probably wouldn't get rid of them." I shrug, reaching out toward her, resting my hands on her hips and pulling her toward me—coffee cup and all. "He's up to something. And I don't like it."

"Neither do I." Her brows pinch in such a way, it's clear she's stressed. "I'll be at his estate today before he sends me to some random place, I'll see what I can find out."

"Be careful," I warn, gripping her hips tight, like she could fade from existence before the day even begins. "He may be your father, but he's still a man we need to be wary of. A man who won't take kindly to you snooping."

Her eyes meet mine, a small smile tugging at the corner of her lips. "I love how you worry about me. But really, I got this."

"I know you do, Kitkitty."

She slaps my arm, half playful, half serious. "No. Bad boy," she scolds me, like a dog, so I pretend to whimper. "I swear. You're too much sometimes."

I know she's kidding. I can see it in her eyes, in the way her mouth tries not to curve. She loves the stupid shit I do or say.

I live to see her smile, to hear her laugh.

I live to annoy her, frustrate her, and then cool her off.

I live to be the fuel that ignites the fire inside her, to show her how she can bend but never break.

"You love me all the same," I say, before laying a kiss on the top of her head.

"Yeah. I do."

"Thought so." I pull back, memorizing her face this morning. *No makeup, messy bun, pj's, and still so fucking beautiful.* "Ugh. I better go. Go cuddle next to Thorne and go back to sleep like I know you want to."

Blaze was the first out this morning, leaving just as Thorne came in. Tori was up, wanting to show Blaze her love by making him coffee the way he likes. She stayed awake for my sake, but I know she's tired.

"I do love sleep." She nods, placing her cup on the counter. "But first..."

She grabs me by the back of the neck and pulls me toward her so fast and so hard we almost collide. Her lips land on mine, hungry, needy, passionate. She's kissing me with absolutely everything she's got, and it's so damn much.

My fingers dig into her skin through her pants, holding her hips so firm they may bruise. She doesn't break away, doesn't pull back, snaking her fingers in my hair and pulling lightly. My teeth graze against her lip, nibbling it the way I love, sliding my hands to her ass and squeezing tight.

She moans and I about lose my shit. But then she pulls back, sucking my very soul right out of my body. Her lips look more fuckable than before, puffy and red. Those sweet brown eyes of hers are hungry, and my little Stanley is ready to burst from my pants like a magnet pulled toward her.

"Remember this moment any time Lila gets too close, and if you're good, I'll let you tie me up today."

Oh shit. Oh fuck. My imaginary tail is wagging a mile a minute right now.

"Are you sure?" I ask, because I know she's still working through what Nico did to her. I need to make sure she's really ready—even though I would love nothing more than to tie her up and fuck her hard.

She nods, her eyes locked on me, wide and full of love, trust.

Yes! Motherfucking yes!

"You know just how to keep me in line, don't you KitKat?" I graze my knuckles against her cheek, leaning down and kissing her tenderly for a moment. "I promise I'll be a good boy. And when I get home, I'll be claiming my prize."

"I'll be waiting. Now go. I'm going to bed for another hour before Gabe forces me up." She rolls her eyes, but I catch the way she doesn't actually mind. It's obvious she's getting closer to Gabe, and it's freaking us all out.

I told her I wouldn't share outside of Thorne and Blaze, and I meant those words. Gabe would be a very dead man.

"Sleep good."

I race out, taking my bike for once, because this time Lila didn't come to collect me. We're meeting at Juan's place, and I can't wait to see that broody motherfucker.

It's been too long since I've been on my bike, and it's a long enough drive that I actually get to enjoy it. Between this, Tori's kiss, and her promise, my morning is the best one yet. If anyone brings me down from this high, well, I might just kill them.

Too soon, I'm pulling into a long winding driveway, finding a theme with all these estates—they like to see who's coming. When I pull up to the front of the pastel yellow house—*can I call it a house?*—Lila is waiting by the door for me. She's wearing a small, white sundress with thin straps and a sweetheart neckline. Her blonde hair is curled around her shoulders, and the way she's smiling at me is giving me the creeps.

She's going to push against my boundaries again today.

Someone save me.

I want my reward, dammit!

I sigh, kicking my stand out and slipping my helmet off. She's skipping toward me as I dismount my bike. My eyes roll at the show and I don't exactly hide it.

"Your acting skills still need improving, I see." She tries to tease as she plays innocent, holding her hands behind her back as she sways on the balls of her feet.

"I can act just fine, but there's no one to act for out here, Lila," I retort, heading inside before her.

She pouts, like dramatically pouts, lower lip out and all before she turns on her heel and follows close behind. As I enter, I catch sight of the big guy waiting on us, and Lila suddenly gets serious.

"I see you got to keep your leg," I start, feeling too comfortable given I helped save his ass. "That's probably for the best. A peg leg would make you even less approachable."

Juan's face is all serious, not even a little tug of a smile. "I see you haven't changed." He crosses his arms, like he's disappointed about this.

Way to bring the mood down, Juan.

"Why fix what isn't broken?" I shrug, ignoring Lila completely as she steps closer. Juan notices, his eyes suddenly fixed on her before returning to mine.

"Follow me and I'll give you the details of today's assignment and all the things you'll need," he orders, leading the way before he's even finished his sentence. "You'll be assuming fake identities for this. We figured having you act as a couple would make you less conspicuous. Diablo felt this assignment would be best for the two of you, given how well you did at sealing deals with our investors."

"Oh that?" I wave it off, "Light work."

He nods, but it's clear he doesn't believe it, or at least doesn't want to admit I am competent enough to have done it. "You'll be heading to a high-end club to try and find a supplier we think may be involved with our crate discrepancies. Your job is to snuff him out, corner him, get him to talk, and not get caught."

"Okay. What's the dress code? How much do I need to be rolling in with? And how do I spot the supplier? Got a picture?" I ask, finally matching my stride with his as we make it to what I'm assuming is his office.

"I have all that right here." He steps inside and throws a file down on the table, sliding it toward me.

I flip it open and am surprised at what I find.

Seriously?

"Wrong file, man," I point out as I close it and slide it back.

It seems Juan is on our side.

The file he first handed me was meant as a warning. I know it, seeing as the first pictures I saw were of Thorne, Blaze, or me. There's more in there, but I can't fan through it with Lila over my shoulder. A quick glance is all I could get without alerting her.

Warning served.

Thank you, Juan.

It looks like Diablo has been collecting information on us for a little while now.

"My mistake." He takes the file back, fishing through his drawer until he pulls out the real one. "This one should be it. I'm not much of a file guy. I guess I better start labeling them."

"Organization definitely helps make things run smoother," Lila chimes in, thinking she's being helpful, but all she is is annoying.

"I'll keep that in mind." Juan tries for a polite tone but it falls flat, annoyance so thick I could choke on it.

I have to hold back my laughter as he opens the folder to show pictures of our intended target. He's average on all accounts. Average height, brown hair cut in the latest style. The guy wears jeans and simple shirts. There is nothing remarkable about him, just another man in the background, and that's what makes him so good.

Being invisible in plain sight is a gift I was not given. Not with these baby blues, handsome-as-fuck face, and golden strands girls love to run their fingers through. I've learned how to make it work for me, how to turn it into an advantage in this world, but sometimes I wonder how much easier things would be if I could slip in and out of places unseen.

"And you're sure he'll be at this club?" I question, working through all the information as I hand Lila a picture of the guy.

This file contains not only pictures of the guy, but information on his usual spots and time of day. It would appear our supplier likes to have routines. Coffee at a local shop, a scone and an americano for breakfast. A walk through the park after, a couple of meetings, some work, lunch at the plaza where he adds spontaneity to his day by choosing a different food truck each day.

There's so much here, I'm surprised they need us for anything. But I guess the important stuff is missing. Who is he meeting with? Who's paying him to smuggle their things in with Diablo?

As I continue to dig through the file, I find the blueprint for the club. There's a list of workers alongside pictures and schedules, not to mention their daily tasks so you can know where all workers are meant to be and when.

If this were a test, this file is an easy cheat sheet, and I don't plan on letting it go to waste.

"How much time do we have before we need to be there?" I ask, needing to know exactly how long I have to memorize this golden nugget.

"You have until five this evening. He'll be there for dinner. Don't let the chance go to waste," Juan answers casually, but I can hear the caution in his tone.

Diablo wants you to fail, watch yourself.

"No problem." I nod, grabbing everything and moving to the couch in his office. "I'm making myself at home, Juanie, hope you don't mind."

Juan grumbles something incomprehensible under his breath as he rolls his eyes, but he doesn't tell me to fuck off, so I take it as a good sign. The next few hours are spent memorizing everything here, reading up on our fake identities for the night, and deciding on our relationship story. Don't want to fumble if some old coon decides to call us a cute couple and ask personal questions.

I've learned they really like to do that. Maybe because they're so bored with life at that point.

By three, Lila leaves, claiming she needs well over an hour to get ready. I let her go, not wanting her near me anyway.

You won't get a fight out of me.

At about four-twenty, I decide I should get ready. I find the white tux, black shirt, and red tie waiting for me in a room. It fits like a damn glove, hugging my muscles just right. Not too obvious, but enough to intimidate if I flex. The shoes are a glossy, polished black that only the most expensive of dress shoes can achieve.

I find the hair wax I like to use, rubbing it in my hands before I slick my hair back. Never flat against my head, my hair is too thick for that shit anyway. It's up and out of my face, with the longer pieces falling over the back of my head.

Good enough.

I slide my phone into my blazer pocket, switching out my ID and placing the fake one in my wallet. My real one's going in my bike on the way out. No way I'm getting caught with that.

I step out to find Lila in a similar color scheme to mine. Her dress is black, long with a mid-thigh slit on each side. Her bust is barely contained in the sleeveless, heart-shaped neckline. The heels they decided to torture her with are six inches tall, bringing her to just an inch below my height. They are a juicy red, matching the color of my tie.

She wastes no time, wrapping herself around my arm in a purposeful way as she presses her breasts against my bicep. I pull my arm out of her grip and eye her cautiously.

"Listen, we're pretending that we're dating for this assignment, but that doesn't mean you get to take advantage." I hold her gaze as I speak, needing her to know I'm putting down a line she shouldn't cross. "Don't be affectionate until we get there. Once we're there, you can hold my hand or my arm. Hell, you can even run your fingers through my hair. *But* there will be absolutely *no* kissing. You can't grab my ass or my dick, and you certainly can't make me grab your ass or tits. Don't press them up against me like you just did, either. Think of this as courting, okay?"

She pinches her brow, pressing her lips thin for a moment. "Sure, Ryder. We're really going to be selling the whole dating thing acting like that," she says with deep sarcasm as she rolls her eyes.

"We sure are." I plaster a smile so fake I feel like a Ken doll. "Now let's get this show on the road."

We take the white Lamborghini Diablo had sent to Juan's house for us and head for the club. Everything I memorized the last few hours floods my brain—planning, calculating.

I feel like Blaze.

Ew.

When we get there, we use the valet, because what self-respecting rich man parks his own car? Lila immediately latches herself to my arm, doing exactly what I told her not to and holding it across her chest so her breasts are essentially hugging my forearm.

I roll my eyes, but shoving her off now would raise more suspicions than I need.

Please give me my reward, KitKat. I promise I'm not enjoying this.

We enter the building and I slip the hostess a bill to sit us in the corner where we can see all the exits and entrances. She obliges, taking the money discreetly, and leads the way to our table.

My eyes are peeled as we head for our table, searching for our guy, but he's nowhere to be found. At least not yet. I hold Lila's seat out for her and push it, because it's a great way to show we're in a relationship without me being physical.

A point for Ryder, please.

Our waitress takes our drink order, a glass of wine for her and an old fashioned for me. I hate the drink, honestly, so I get it, knowing I'll nurse the hell out of it and not get drunk on the job, trying to keep pretenses up.

"So, you want to tell me why you're so adamant about keeping your distance? I've already told you, what happens on these tasks between us stays with us," Lila starts back up again, and I swear everyone can hear the sigh that slips out of my mouth.

"And I've told you, I'm not interested."

"That would be a first," she remarks, her confidence at an all-time high.

"It wouldn't be the first time I'm a girl's first." I wink at her, knowing no one can hear what we're saying but can see how we're saying it.

Act like you like her with your expression.

Talk about sending mixed signals.

She opens her mouth to speak, but she doesn't get the chance as our guy walks in. He's alone, no bodyguard, no entourage, and no girl. He's easy pickings if we can get him alone and cornered.

I'm so focused on the guy, I don't realize Lila has moved so close. Somehow she silently moved her chair beside mine, her arm pressed against mine with what little room she left. I try to keep my focus on our supplier while simultaneously and silently trying to scoot my chair away from her.

No luck.

Her hands cup my face, turning me to face her in such a way that my lips are immediately assaulted by her own. I've never wanted to hit a woman in my life, but Lila has just proven that the gene exists inside me. I want to push her away, to storm out, but with our guy three tables down. I can't do shit.

I go stiff, knowing no one can see my lips. I don't kiss her back, letting her practically eat my lips as I keep them glued together. By the way she digs her fingers in my cheeks, I can tell she's annoyed by my lack of response. After a few more torturous seconds she pulls away, doing her best to school her expression, frustration dancing in her eyes.

"You crossed a line, Lila, and you're going to learn what that means when we're done here."

She freezes as if it's just now dawned on her that there might be consequences for her actions. I'm pissed the hell off, and all I can imagine is running her over with the Lamborghini outside. Instead, I take a deep breath and turn my attention back to average Joe.

He's excusing himself, so I do the same, following him to the bathroom. He doesn't notice me, doesn't even look back once. Part of me worries there's more to this guy than I'm aware of. My danger radar is spiking and I'm not sure why, which is only freaking me out more.

Inside the bathroom, I take my spot two urinals down from his, trying not to look his way. There's really no telling how he'd react. He'd either think I was some creep, or he'd grow suspicious of me. I shake it, flush, and make my way to the sink just a few seconds before him. I'm thoroughly washing my hands when he passes me by.

Bro, are you really not going to wash?

His hand is on the handle, my chance to corner him slipping through my fingers. When the door swings open, Lila's there, pushing him back inside. In the mirror, over her shoulder, I can see a hulking figure make its way across the dining area toward the bathroom.

He does have a guard.

Immediately, I hop into action, pulling Lila all the way in and locking the bathroom door, the click resounding in the otherwise empty restroom.

"Dammit, Lila. There's a reason I didn't do it here." There's banging at the door within seconds and I know I need to make a decision soon.

Average Joe is trying to be invisible, but he's literally the target. *So, that's not going to happen, buddy.*

"So what? There's a window there. We get what we need and we're out." She shrugs like she did nothing wrong.

Ugh. Why was I stuck with you?

Am I this annoying?

"Fuck it. We don't have another choice now." My attention turns to the supplier and he blanches, so pale he could blend in with the walls. There must be something in my expression, because he's squirming way before I even reach for my gun.

"Start talking and I won't shoot." He's scared, but he's not stupid. "Talk fast enough and you can slip out of here without suspicion. She and I were having sex in here and blocking the door."

On cue, Lila starts banging back against the door and moaning. Her acting is spot the fuck on, but I shouldn't be surprised by that. *She's a psycho.*

"Tick Tock," I wave my gun side to side. "Who's paying you to slip their merch into Diablo's crates?"

He's shaking all over. "I—I can't."

"You're running out of time. She's getting close," I warn, pointing toward Lila, and she understands exactly what I need her to do.

"Oh. Fuck!" she yells. "Harder, harder."

Okay, Lila. Chill, we're not trying to get more attention.

"Give me a name."

"I—I don't know. She never told me. She used a code name."

*Of course they did. Or rather **she** did.*

"Keep talking."

"Uh—she's tall. She has, sh-sh-she has long hair."

I step closer, raising my gun to his forehead. "Come on, man. You're describing so many women right now. Give me something."

"She's high up in Diablo's line. She told me—she knows when the shipments come and which ones to switch." He steps back but meets the wall, my gun an inch away from his forehead now.

"There's gotta be more."

I'm getting a vague idea of who, but I need to make sure.

"I don't—I don't know!"

"Yes you do!" I press the gun beneath his chin, lightly squeezing the trigger. "Keep talking."

He's racking his brain, I can see it in the way his eyes flicker in panic. "One of her guys," he randomly spouts as if some revelation just hit him. "He called her Cas."

Fuck.

Dammit, KitKat. You got bad taste in friends.

14: TORI

Today's been a bust. All the snooping I've done at my dad's estate has revealed that Diablo is a paranoid man who must have the memory of a fucking elephant. The man doesn't have a single file, computer with hidden files, or books with coded messages.

Nada.

Zilch.

I don't know how he keeps track of things, but I know he's got it under lock and key. He's well guarded, not just physically but metaphorically as well. I may be his daughter by blood, but we're strangers nonetheless. He won't trust me just because we're related.

The afternoon sun is hanging low, giving way to the evening sky as Gabe drives me to the warehouse in question. Everyone knows about it at this point, so why shouldn't I get a look at it, too?

Because you're not as physically capable of defending yourself as others, Tori.

Because what the heck are you going to do?

I sigh, knowing inner me is my worst fucking critic but also right. With everything that's happened, I know I can rely on Gabe, but I shouldn't have to. I need to learn even more self-defense, learn how to fight and take care of myself out here.

I can't be weak in any sense of the word.

"You've been avoiding me," Gabe suddenly breaks the silence in the car, eyeing me from the rearview mirror.

That's right. I sat in the back, Gabe.

No touchy.

"That's literally impossible. You're my shadow," I say, rolling my eyes like he's an idiot for thinking that. But he's totally right.

I'm avoiding the shit out of you.

I don't like how easy I'm finding it to trust you.

I need distance.

"For about an hour or two, you were shadow free in your father's office," he points out, his gaze focused on the road again.

I scoff, leaning my head against the cool window, watching the scenery blur past. "And you think that was me avoiding you?"

"I know it was." His tone is so damn certain it grates on me. I don't answer, which is basically just proving his point, but I don't care. *Let him think whatever he wants.*

He sighs but doesn't push further, and I'm grateful for the silence. The drive is longer than I expected, the sun bleeding out behind the skyline, setting everything in a hazy gold glow. My stomach twists, nerves creeping in. I don't know why I suddenly feel antsy, but my gut is tight with unease, maybe because what I'm doing is dangerous.

We pull up to the warehouse, and the sight of it sends a ripple of excitement through me. This is where everything is happening, where all the answers are waiting. Diablo may keep his secrets locked away in his head, but this place? It might give me something to work with.

Gabe puts the car in park but doesn't turn off the engine, tapping his fingers against the steering wheel. "You stay close to me. Got it?"

I roll my eyes. "Yes, Dad."

His lips twitch, like he wants to smile but refuses to let himself. "Tori."

"Fine, fine," I grumble, already unbuckling. "I'll stay close."

The warehouse is buzzing with low murmurs as we step inside, workers moving around, crates being shuffled. It's dimly lit, shadows stretching across the floor like they're waiting to grab at my ankles.

"Stay behind me," Gabe mutters, his hand brushing my lower back as he moves ahead.

I nod absently, my eyes scanning the space, searching for something but not really sure what. In the distance, I overhear something that just makes my fucking day.

"Yeah, Harrow's been in and out all day, checking the inventory."

My breath catches. *Thorne. He's here.*

I don't wait for Gabe. The impulse is instant, pure instinct. I weave through the maze of crates, my pulse kicking up as I move deeper into the warehouse, my heart hammering at the idea of surprising him.

It's stupid, probably reckless, but excitement outweighs logic.

Then I see him.

My breath whooshes out in relief, in something warm and familiar. He's standing near a stack of crates, a hand stretched out like he's reaching for something I can't quite see. He looks good—*because he always does*—and the sight of him makes my chest feel lighter.

You're just so yummy, Thorne.

My steps quicken, eager to close the distance, to throw out some teasing remark, maybe even pull him aside for a stolen moment alone.

But then Mia steps forward.

And *kisses* him.

My feet stop so fast, it feels like I hit some invisible wall so hard it shattered everything inside of me. My brain short-circuits, like it can't process what I'm seeing. My heart clenches so hard it physically hurts.

What the actual fuck?!

It's a mistake. A misunderstanding. Thorne wouldn't—he *wouldn't*.

But my eyes don't lie. Mia's lips are on his, her hands resting lightly against his chest, her posture intimate in a way that makes my stomach turn. And worse? He hasn't pushed her away yet. He hasn't moved, hasn't *done* anything.

It's like my lungs forget how to work. My heart, my body, everything just—locks. A hollow ache spreads through my ribs, a slow, twisting knife that I *never* thought I'd feel again with him. Or maybe I did, and I fooled myself into thinking it wouldn't happen when I should have kept my guard up. But after everything we've been through, after the promises we've all made, I let myself believe.

Boy was I stupid, but what's new?

My fingers curl into fists at my sides, nails biting into my palms just to keep myself from unraveling right here. The pain is immediate, hot and blinding. It's a rush of emotions that hit like a punch to the gut—anger, hurt, disbelief. It claws up my throat, choking me, making my stomach churn. I feel like a fool. A fucking idiot for thinking that maybe this time, *this time*, things were safe. That I wouldn't get hurt.

I don't stay long enough to see his reaction. I don't care. I can't. My body moves on its own, spinning on my heel so fast I don't register my surroundings. My breath is coming too fast, my throat closing up, the pressure in my chest unbearable. I need out. I need air. I need—

I collide into something solid. No, not something. *Someone.*

My dear shadow—Gabe.

He steadies me immediately, hands gripping my arms, his warmth seeping into me, grounding me. "Tori?" His voice is soft but alert, sharp enough to cut through my spiraling thoughts.

I tilt my head up, and I know he sees it. The sheen in my eyes, the way my chest is rising too fast, the way my fingers are trembling at my sides. His face hardens, jaw tightening like he already knows something is wrong, like he already wants to fix it.

"Take me home," I whisper, my voice barely holding together. "Please, Gabe. Just...take me home."

He doesn't ask. He doesn't need to.

His nostrils flare, his grip on me tightening for just a second, like he wants to demand answers, to storm in there and take apart whatever just hurt me. But he doesn't. He just gives me a single nod, silent and sure, and then wraps an arm around me, guiding me back the way we came. I don't look back.

Each step away from that warehouse feels like a new weight pressing into my chest, but Gabe's arm is steady, anchoring me, shielding me from whatever storm is brewing inside of me. I don't say anything as we reach the car. It's impossible for me to form a coherent sentence without breaking down, and I can't do that. Not here.

He opens the door for me, and I sink into the seat, staring blankly ahead. The drive back is quiet, the hum of the engine the only sound between us. My fingers press against my temples, as if trying to erase what I just saw. *As if that will help.* My stomach twists, bile rising in my throat, but I swallow it down.

I won't cry. Not yet.

Gabe's grip on the wheel tightens. He doesn't look at me, but I can feel his tension, the way he's holding back words, questions. Maybe even anger. But he lets me have my silence. And for that, I'm grateful.

The ride back to the estate is suffocating.

I'm curled up in the backseat, my forehead pressed against the cool window, watching the city blur past, but I don't really see it. My vision is too hazy, my eyes burning too much from the tears that won't stop coming. Every time I blink, I see it again—Mia's lips on Thorne's, her hands on his chest. It's like a flash permanently burned into my retinas.

I can't breathe.

I suck in a sharp breath, then another, but it doesn't help. The pain sits heavy in my chest, an anchor dragging me deeper and deeper. I bite the inside of my cheek, trying to swallow it all down, trying to hold on to something solid before I completely spiral.

WHY DON'T YOU KEEP ME

From the front seat, Gabe is silent. His grip on the steering wheel is tight, his knuckles white even in the golden glow of the setting sun. He doesn't ask what happened. He doesn't push. But I can feel it—the storm raging inside him, the protective fire that's barely restrained.

It's almost as if he doesn't want to just protect me physically; he wants to protect me emotionally, too.

After a long moment, his voice cuts through the suffocating quiet. "Do you want to talk about it?"

I shake my head, barely managing to get the words out. "No."

His hands flex against the wheel, but he doesn't push. Just nods once, like he understands. Like he knows me well enough to recognize that anything he says right now won't fix the gaping wound in my chest.

The rest of the drive is silent, except for the occasional sniffle I can't stop. My fingers twist together in my lap, my nails digging into my palms to keep myself grounded. When we finally pull up to the estate, Gabe slows to a stop but doesn't move to get out.

I reach for the door handle, hesitating for just a second. "Wait here a minute," I whisper, my voice barely audible. I don't want him to hear what happened when I tell Blaze or Ryder. One of them is home, I can tell by the SUV, but I'm not sure who.

Gabe doesn't like that I asked him to wait—I can tell by the way his shoulders tense, his grip tightening on the wheel—but he nods. "I'll be here."

I step out before I can change my mind, the evening air cool against my tear-streaked face. Home. My safe place with them. The place where the people I love are. The people who love me.

Or at least I thought they all loved me.

Do any of them actually mean those words?

I shake off the thought and force myself forward, my shoes clicking softly against the pavement as I reach the front door. The second

I step inside, warmth surrounds me, the scent of something familiar—something safe—curling in the air. I exhale slowly, letting the comfort of the house settle around me like a shield.

The sound of a woman's laugh suddenly rings in my ears, and my body goes rigid.

No. Fuck, no! I refuse to believe I could be broken twice in one day.

The sound comes from upstairs, soft but distinct, followed by the low murmur of a voice I know too well. Ryder. My chest squeezes. It has to be nothing. It *has* to be nothing. I move on autopilot, my feet carrying me up the stairs even as my body begs me to stop.

But I don't stop. *I can't.*

I round the corner, my breath lodged in my throat—and then I see them.

Lila is pressed against Ryder, her hands sliding up his chest, her body molding against his. His head is tipped back against the wall, his posture lazy, his expression hazy. His arms hang at his sides, not wrapped around her, *not pushing her away.*

It's like all the air is sucked out of the room. My stomach twists, bile rising in my throat. My heart, already cracked from Thorne, shatters completely.

Not Ryder too.

My body moves before my brain catches up. I spin around, my vision blurring as I flee. I don't think, I don't stop—I just run. I need to get out, I need air. I need Gabe to take me away.

The second I step outside, twilight encompasses the sky, darkening by the second, just like my heart. My breath hitches, and then I collide straight into Gabe's solid chest. Warm arms wrap around me instantly, anchoring me, holding me up when my knees threaten to buckle.

I bury my face in his chest, my fingers curling into his jacket, a sob ripping out of me before I can stop it. He doesn't say anything—doesn't ask, doesn't push. He just *holds* me, one arm tight around my waist, the other cradling the back of my head like he's trying to shield me from the world.

"Take me away," I whisper against his chest, my voice breaking. "Please, Gabe. Just...take me away from here."

He doesn't hesitate. He scoops me up effortlessly, carrying me toward the car like I weigh nothing. His grip is firm, his body radiating warmth, safety. He sets me down in the passenger seat, buckling me in before rounding the car.

The second he slides into the driver's seat, he peels out of the driveway, his hands gripping the wheel so tightly I think he might break it. His whole body is taut, vibrating with restrained rage.

I stare out the window, tears slipping down my cheeks. My heart is in pieces, my world turned completely upside down. I don't know where we're going, and I don't care.

I just know I can't stay here.

Minutes stretch into miles, the city lights fading behind us as Gabe drives us somewhere unknown. The silence is thick, heavy, as my mind continues to torture me with images of Thorne and Mia, Ryder and Lila.

How could they?

We pull up to a quiet street, the houses dark except for the occasional porch light. Gabe cuts the engine, staring straight ahead, his fists tight on the wheel.

"This is a safe house we keep," he says quietly. "Come inside."

I follow him without question, stepping into some strange home, feeling more out of place than ever. It's small but neat, void of much life. I scan the room, my gaze catching on small details—books stacked neatly on a shelf, mugs hanging on hooks over a coffee pot, an empty coat rack in the corner.

Gabe watches me, his expression stoic. Then, finally, he sighs. "You want something to drink?"

I shake my head. I just want...I don't know what I want.

A time machine?

A new heart?

A new life?

He hesitates, then crosses the room, grabbing a folded blanket off the couch and draping it over my shoulders. The gesture is so gentle, so thoughtful, that my chest aches all over again.

"You want to talk about it?" he asks, his voice softer now, careful.

I let out a broken laugh. "What's there to say? I'm a fucking idiot."

His eyes darken. "You're not an idiot, Tori."

I let out a breath, shaking my head. "Then why does it feel like I am?"

He doesn't answer immediately. Instead, he sits beside me, his presence solid, unwavering. "Because people you love let you down," he finally says. "And that fucking sucks."

I swallow hard, looking up at him. "Has it happened to you?"

His jaw tightens, his gaze flicking away for just a second. "Yeah."

I hesitate, studying him. "What happened?"

His throat bobs, something unreadable flickering in his eyes. "Not tonight, Tori."

"I'll tell you what happened, if you tell me your story."

I don't look at him right away, just stare at the floor, fingers toying with the frayed hem of my sleeve. My voice is quieter than usual, but the edge is still there.

Gabe exhales, slow and measured. He doesn't answer immediately, and I start to think he won't at all. Then, finally, he shifts his stance, letting his shoulders fall, and motions for me to sit in the chair. I do so, and he follows by sitting on the couch opposite me.

"Alright," he mutters, the word barely above a sigh. "But you first."

Of course. Always making me do the hard part first.

I suck in a breath, my throat still raw from the betrayal I just ran from. "While we were at the warehouse," I start, my fingers gripping my sleeve tighter. "I heard one of the workers say Thorne was there.

I wanted to see what he was up to, which is when I ran ahead from you."

Gabe makes a noise—not quite a grunt, but something close. Like he already knows where this is going.

"I saw him," I continue, voice hollow. "And I saw Mia. And I saw..." My throat clenches around the next words, but I force them out. "Her kissing him."

Gabe doesn't say anything, but I can feel the air shift. He goes rigid again, muscles all taut, but not how he was before. No, it feels different, almost like...guilt? Like maybe he knew it would happen and he wishes he could have protected me from it.

"So, I left," I finish, my laugh bitter and sharp. "Ran into you. Asked you to take me home. And when I got there? Well, I ran upstairs and saw Lila was all over Ryder."

Gabe curses under his breath. "Dios."

"Yeah. Double homicide might be in my near future," I mumble. "But I ran instead. Came straight to you like some pathetic, heart-broken schoolgirl."

Gabe finally turns to look at me, blue eyes burning. "You're not pathetic."

I snort. "No? Because I sure as hell feel like it."

He holds my gaze, his voice steadier now. "You ran to the one person who could help. That's not pathetic."

Something tightens in my chest. I drop my gaze first, looking at my hands like they have all the answers. "Your turn," I say, needing to shift the attention. "Tell me why you're here. Why you're working for my father. Why you do what you do."

Gabe leans back, exhaling slowly through his nose. "I grew up in a shitty neighborhood. No father. My mother did the best she could, but she got sick when I was a teenager. Cancer. Didn't have the money for treatment, so I did what I had to do to take care of my little brothers and sister."

I stay quiet, letting him talk, processing everything he's telling me.

"I joined the military at eighteen," he continues, staring at the blinds covering the small window ahead of him, though his focus is somewhere else entirely. "Thought it'd give me a way out. A future. A chance to take care of them properly, even though it meant leaving them in the care of someone else. And for a while, it worked. Sent money home. Made sure they were okay. But when I got out, I had nothing. No skills that translated to a normal job, no options except the kind that came with blood money."

His fingers drum against the arm of the couch, a small, restless motion. "Diablo made me an offer. Work for him, and he'd make sure my family never had to struggle. That they'd have everything they needed. So, I took it."

I chew on my bottom lip. "Do they know?"

He shakes his head. "They think I work in private security. I keep my distance. Make sure they're comfortable, safe. That's all that matters."

A beat of silence stretches between us. Then, because I can't help myself, I whisper, "Do you ever regret it?"

Gabe doesn't answer right away. Instead, he tilts his head slightly, considering the question like it's one he's asked himself a hundred times before.

"No," he finally says. "Because they're alive. Because they have futures. And if that means I have to live in the dark so they don't have to, so be it."

Something about his words lodges themselves deep in my chest, settling right next to my own guilt. I stare at him, this man who was placed by my side since the moment I stepped into this world, and for the first time, I see him. Not just as my bodyguard. Not just as the one person who hasn't let me down yet.

But as a man who has sacrificed everything for the people he loves.

Before I can say anything else, headlights flash through the window, cutting across the dim room. Gabe tenses instantly, rising to his feet as the car outside screeches to a stop.

The front door swings open, and time stops and fast forwards all at once.

15: Tori

The moment the front door flies open, time snaps into hyper-focus.

My breath stills in my throat as men in dark clothing rush in, armed and raging like the Hulk. My body reacts before my brain catches up—I lurch to my feet, heart pounding like a war drum.

Gabe is already moving, placing himself between me and the intruders. His hand flies to his waistband, drawing his gun with a sharp, fluid motion. His voice is a snarl of command, deep, gravel.

Okay, dragonborn. Geez.

"Touch her, and you're dead."

The lead guy—big, bald, looks like he scares small children for fun—raises his hands like he's dealing with some scared civilians instead of a trained soldier and a not-in-the-mood-for-this-kind-of-shit mafia daughter. "No need for threats," he says smoothly, though the smirk curling his lips says he enjoys the game. "We just came for the girl."

Of course.

This day is such shit.

"I'm flattered," I deadpan, shifting a little behind Gabe, preparing myself. "But I'm really not in the mood for terrible company."

"You don't have a choice," the man states, taking a step forward.

Gabe doesn't wait for him to take another. The gunshot shatters the air, so loud in the confined space that my ears ring. The guy barely ducks in time, the bullet slicing past his shoulder and embedding into the wall behind him. The smirk vanishes from his face. And then the fight really starts.

The first guy lunges but Gabe sidesteps, grabbing him by the wrist and twisting so hard there's an audible snap. The man's scream is cut short when Gabe shoves him backwards into his own men, sending them toppling like dominoes.

A hand grabs my arm, and I react immediately. I twist, just like the guys taught me, driving my elbow into the guy's gut. He grunts, stumbling back, but he's fast. His grip tightens, yanking me toward him. My pulse spikes, adrenaline surging through my veins. I don't freeze this time.

I bring my knee up—hard, right to his precious jewels.

Don't pretend, Buddy. I know that hurt.

He chokes out a curse, releasing me as he doubles over. Without missing a beat, I grab the closest thing—a lamp—and swing it into the side of his head. The glass shatters, and he crumples to the floor, dazed but not out.

Gabe sees it. Sees me.

His eyes flash with something dark and veiled before he turns his fury back to the others. He moves like a predator, fast and unrelenting. Another man charges, but Gabe catches him mid-swing, deflecting the punch before landing one of his own—straight to the guy's jaw. A sickening crack echoes, and the man drops.

I barely dodge a second attacker. He swings a knife, the blade slicing through the air, inches from my face. My stomach clenches, but I force myself to move.

It seems between what Gabe and the guys have taught me, I'm really learning how to take care of myself in these fights.

That's right. 007 in training over here.

I duck under his arm, grab his wrist, and drive my fist into his ribs. He grunts, but his grip is strong. Too strong.

Gabe wrenches the guy back, slamming him into the nearest wall so hard the drywall cracks. "You even breathe in her direction again, I'll make sure you never take another breath," he growls, voice low and lethal.

The guy slumps, barely conscious, and Gabe turns to me, scanning me quickly for injuries. "You okay?"

My chest heaves, my hands shaking just a bit, but I nod. "Yeah."

The last remaining intruder is already scrambling for the door, not nearly as eager to take us on now that the rest of his team is either unconscious or groaning on the floor. Gabe lifts his gun and fires a shot just above the guy's head, making him freeze.

"Who sent you?" Gabe demands, stepping forward, towering over him like death itself.

The man swallows hard. "We—we were just following orders."

"Whose orders?"

A beat of hesitation. Then, "I don't know. Just a contract."

Gabe's fingers twitch on the trigger, but before he can decide whether to pull it, I step forward, wiping my bloody palm on my jeans. "Tell whoever hired you that I'm not easy to fucking steal," I say, voice flat, cold.

Not anymore, anyway.

I'll never allow myself to be taken again.

Gabe glances at me, something like pride flickering across his face. Then, with one last sneer, he lowers his gun and lets the guy bolt.

The room is wrecked. Furniture overturned, shards of the broken lamp littering the floor, blood smeared across the wood. I exhale sharply, rubbing my sore wrist, the reality of what just happened settling over me like a heavy fog.

"We need to go," Gabe says, his voice still edged with adrenaline. He's already moving, grabbing the keys and a duffel bag from behind the couch. "Now."

I don't argue. I follow him out the door, stepping over the unconscious bodies like they're just minor inconveniences. The second we're in the car, he peels out of the driveway, tires screeching against the pavement.

I let my head fall back against the seat, closing my eyes for a brief second. My pulse is still racing, my body still wired. I fought. I actually fought, and I won...mostly.

Blaze would be so fucking proud.

Blaze.

I need to call him. But...what if he betrayed me too?

I can't handle that right now.

Gabe's grip on the wheel is tight, his jaw clenched as he speeds through the empty streets. The tension rolling off him is thick, suffocating, but he doesn't speak. Doesn't even look at me.

After a few minutes, I crack an eye open, glancing at him. "You okay over there? Your brooding is on a new level."

His eyes narrow. "I should be asking you that."

"I'm fine." And weirdly, I think I mean it.

At least this is distracting me from the pain in my chest.

Gabe exhales through his nose, fingers tightening before he finally forces them to relax. "You fought well."

I blink. That...was not what I expected. "Did you just compliment me?"

A muscle ticks in his jaw. "Don't let it go to your head."

I smile, but it fades as I glance out the window. We're in a different part of town now, away from the city's chaos. The streets are quieter, lined with suburban houses, each one looking eerily similar.

I frown. "Where are we?"

Gabe pulls into a driveway, kills the engine, and finally looks at me. "My house."

He gets down as I process what he's said and where he's taken me, rounding the hood and opening my door before I blink back to life.

He leads the way to the door, pushing it open, and I follow, hesitating on the threshold before stepping into his world.

What kind of person are you really, Gabe? Am I going to find clothes everywhere? Or are you a neat freak like Blaze?

It's...not what I expected. I don't know what I expected, but a homey little place with a lived-in couch and the faint scent of coffee isn't it. It's weirdly normal.

He may be your bodyguard, Tori, but he's still a human. He can have a normal home.

"You gonna stand there all night?" he asks, raising a brow as he locks the door behind me.

"Just taking it all in," I mutter, shrugging off my jacket. "Didn't peg you for the cozy type."

He snorts. "Didn't peg you for the table-lamp-wielding type, but here we are."

I scowl, tossing my jacket onto a chair. "Hey, it worked, didn't it?"

He shakes his head, amusement flickering in his eyes before they darken, scanning me. "Sit down. Let me check you over."

I plop onto the couch, letting him crouch in front of me. His hands are careful, precise, as he takes my wrist, fingers skimming over the forming bruises. He doesn't say anything, but he has the same look the guys get when they see me hurt.

Protective. Pissed. Dangerous.

"I'm fine," I say, but my voice is softer this time, almost reassuring.

His eyes flick up to mine. "You shouldn't have had to fight like that."

I swallow, something thick lodging in my throat. "I wasn't gonna just let them take me."

His grip tightens, just for a second. "I can tell."

The air shifts, something heavier settling between us. He's still holding my wrist, thumb brushing over my skin in a way that's too careful. My pulse betrays me, kicking up, and I know he notices because his lips press together, his own breathing going a little uneven.

I clear my throat, desperate for something—anything—to break whatever the hell this is. "So, what now? You gonna tell me why you brought me here instead of another safe house?"

Gabe exhales through his nose, still watching me too closely. Then, finally, he leans back, running a hand through his hair. "Because there's something you need to know. And you're not gonna like it."

My stomach knots. "Great. Love that for me."

He doesn't smile. Doesn't joke. Just levels me with a look so serious it sends a chill down my spine.

"This isn't just about you, Tori," he says, voice low, measured. "This is about them—Lila, Mia, and Eve. About why they're here. About what your father is really planning."

And just like that, the air turns ice cold.

Everything goes quiet, even the world outside these four walls seems to grow silent as I wait for whatever shitstorm Gabe is about to let me in on. It's obvious my father has been up to something with my guys and these supposed assistants, but I'm not exactly sure what he hopes to accomplish, or why.

Gabe's fingers drum against his knees as he thinks, almost as if he's questioning whether or not he should really do this.

It's too late to change your mind now, Gabe. I won't let you.

"Well? Are you going to tell me? Or are you just stringing me along here?" My impatience shows as I arch a brow at him, waiting for him to start.

Today has been such utter shit. I can't take much more.

"I wouldn't string you along, Tori. I'm just worried about what you'll think of me by the end of it," he admits, his blue eyes meeting mine in a way-too-tender expression. It's almost as if he's pleading with me not to hate him with his eyes alone.

"You won't know until you tell me."

My stomach twists, tightening the knot that feels like it will never unravel. I can hardly breathe as is, and currently, Gabe is like my oxygen tank, only something tells me my supply is about to be cut off.

"From the moment you called to tell him you and your three boyfriends were coming, your father has been planning," he starts, resting his elbows on his knees as he leans forward.

I swallow hard, my mouth suddenly dry. "Planning what, exactly?"

Gabe exhales through his nose, shaking his head like he wishes he could tell me anything but this. "He doesn't see them as viable long-term partners for you, Tori. He never did. In his eyes, love makes people weak, and the fact that you're splitting yourself between three men? He thinks that's a disaster waiting to happen. He doesn't want you to just inherit his empire—he wants you to *own* it. Alone."

I scoff, crossing my arms. "Yeah, well, he can take that plan and shove it."

Gabe gives me a look that tells me my father is not someone who takes no for an answer. "You don't get it, Tori. He didn't just want to break you up. He wanted *you* to walk away, believing it was your choice."

Something cold slithers down my spine.

What kind of man gaslights his daughter like that?

That's an easy answer, Tori.

Clearly.

"How?"

"By making sure you saw them fail you, over and over again," Gabe answers, voice even, but there's anger simmering beneath it. "Those assistants weren't just random hires. They were chosen specifically to test your men in ways Diablo knew would hurt you the most."

My stomach clenches. "What does that mean?"

WHY DON'T YOU KEEP ME

Gabe's expression shifts, a mixture of frustration and guilt, as if he hates everything he knows. "Lila was meant to tempt Ryder with easy affection, someone who could match his energy without the weight of your shared past. She was instructed to be pushy, to make you doubt him, to get close enough that if he so much as hesitated, it would look bad."

I think of Ryder in that hallway, Lila pressed against him, his posture too loose, too relaxed. My fists clench in my lap.

"And Eve?" I force out.

"She was meant to appeal to Blaze's perfectionism, his need for control. She's calculated, intelligent, a master manipulator. She wasn't trying to seduce him, not in the way Lila was with Ryder. She was trying to *integrate* herself, to become indispensable to him. Someone he relied on, maybe even trusted more than you."

I swallow against the lump forming in my throat. "And Mia?"

Gabe hesitates. "Mia was a wild card. Your father knew Thorne wouldn't fall for seduction easily. So he gave him something else. A broken girl who needed saving."

I flinch like I've been slapped. Because *fuck*. I know exactly how that would work on Thorne.

"When your father realized the guys weren't falling for his traps, he probably ordered the girls all to help. To be more aggressive. That's probably what you saw today."

I want to believe what he's saying. That what I saw is nothing more than my father's manipulation, but Ryder and Thorne had to have played into it for it to work. I don't dwell on it, asking my next question instead.

"And you?" My voice is raw now, trembling. "What were you supposed to be?"

Gabe meets my gaze, his expression masked. "I was meant to be the things they weren't."

A cold laugh bubbles out of me, humorless. "And what's that?"

"Steady. Uncomplicated. Safe." His voice is quiet, but the words hit like a hammer. "He wanted me to be the constant while they fell apart. If they lost you, if they broke your trust, he wanted *me* to be standing there, the only one who never let you down."

I can't breathe.

Was every interaction with Gabe planned? Are we even really close?

Fuck me, Gabriel. I might not hate you, but I definitely don't trust you anymore.

My whole world tilts, my lungs shrinking inside my chest. My father didn't just want to split me up from the guys—he wanted me to be the one to leave them willingly. And worse? I played right into it.

I ran to Gabe. I let him be the one to comfort me. I *felt* something for him.

I'm realizing now it was never romantic. Maybe it was all just hero worship. Someone to lean on when I needed it.

"I know what you must be thinking, and it wasn't all a lie, Tori," Gabe says quietly, reading me like an open book. "I had orders, but at some point, I stopped following them."

I let out a hollow breath, my body vibrating with something too tangled to name. "Why?"

His lips press together, like he's deciding whether or not to say it. When he does, it's low, quiet. "Because I started to *care*."

I scoff, "Care? If you cared, you would have told me sooner. If you cared, you would have stopped Mia and Lila and Eve. You wouldn't have watched me turn into this self-doubting shell."

Gabe doesn't say anything at first, allowing me to vent, to get it all out. When he realizes I'm done, he leans forward, invading my space. His eyes are piercing mine with such intensity, it's like he's trying to drill a message into my head with his eyes.

"I care about you, Victoria Reyes. I may not have come out and said it, but I do care about you." When he feels I've understood that part, he leans back just a little, giving me room to breathe for a moment...even though my lungs are only half working right now.

"You have to understand, my siblings have always come first for me. They're the reason I live, and before I could tell you anything, I had to make sure to get them somewhere safe, with someone Diablo couldn't influence."

I guess I can understand it.

But can I trust it?

"And are they safe now?"

"Yes. They're with an old army buddy of mine who swore he'd watch out for them." Gabe takes my hand in his, his calloused fingers rubbing over my own. "I swear, Tori, you're important to me, too. I haven't just been guarding you. I've been watching you, seeing what kind of person you really are. You're nothing like your father, and that's a good thing."

Yeah, no shit.

"Good. I don't want to be anything like him. But how am I supposed to trust you now, Gabe? How can I even tell what was really you and what was just another order from my father?"

"I know I can't make you believe me, but I can show you how serious I am. I am on your side, Tori, and I'll help you get back at your father, if that's what you want to do." He leans in again, his breath fanning across my face as he crosses my personal space. His eyes never waver from my own. "You can trust this feeling. Trust that I will never let anything or anyone hurt you—physically or emotionally."

Silence stretches between us, thick and suffocating. My pulse thrums in my ears, my heart hammering against my ribs. I don't know how to respond, don't know what to do with any of this.

And then, headlights flash through the window.

Gabe stiffens instantly, rising from his seat, gun already in hand as he steps in front of me.

A car screeches to a halt outside. The front door swings open, and time stops.

Blaze.

His dark eyes lock onto me instantly, chest heaving, rage burning so hot off of him I feel it in my bones.

"Get away from her!" he growls, his voice raw, filled with something that sends a shiver down my spine.

I barely have time to process before he storms inside, and just like that, everything crashes down around me.

16: BLAZE

I storm through the door, fists clenched, heart hammering like a fucking war drum. My vision tunnels straight to Gabe, standing way too fucking close to Tori, and my rage boils over.

I don't think. I just move.

My fist is halfway to his face when Tori throws herself between us, hands splayed against my chest. "Stop!" she yells, her voice sharp, panicked.

My breathing is ragged, my muscles coiled tight. My gaze burns into Gabe over her shoulder. He's too calm. Too fucking steady. Like he knew I would try to hit him but couldn't give two fucks about it.

"What the hell did you do to her?" My voice is a growl, low and lethal.

When it was well past time for her to be home, I decided to track her phone. Thinking the worst, I came straight here without any backup, because Ryder was too fucking wasted to wake up, his pants halfway down like he tried to slip into bed but passed out before he could get down to his boxers.

Gabe doesn't flinch. He just stands there, completely unfazed. "Nothing," he says evenly. "She saw something she shouldn't have and needed space. So I made sure she had it."

Space. That word grates against my skull like nails on glass. "Space from what? Because the only person she needs space from is you! Always lingering behind her, trying to stay close even when we're home." My hands shake as I fight every instinct screaming at me to grab Tori and get her the hell away from him.

"He didn't do anything wrong," Tori snaps, shoving at my chest. "I *asked* him to bring me here."

I freeze.

The anger doesn't leave, but it shifts. My jaw clenches, my stomach tightens, and suddenly, I really *look* at her.

Her eyes are red-rimmed. Her hands shake but just barely. She's standing strong, but there's a fragility to her, like she's one wrong breath away from falling apart.

My chest tightens. "Tori," I say, softer now. "What happened?"

She looks away, her throat bobbing. That hesitation, that sliver of doubt flickering across her face—it guts me. She doesn't want to tell me, and that hurts more than anything.

Fuck.

I drag a hand down my face, exhaling hard. "You know you can tell me anything, Tori. Basement rules."

Her lips part, something in her expression *cracking* at the words, but I don't push. I just wait. And finally, she tells me.

"I saw Thorne," she whispers, her voice trembling. "And Mia. She kissed him."

It's like something inside me snaps.

I go completely still. The rage is instant—hot, searing, *fucking consuming.*

"What?" My voice is dangerously quiet.

Tori swallows hard. "I saw her. She kissed him. And he—he didn't pull away. And then..." she hesitates, her voice cracking. "And then I found Ryder. With Lila."

My blood goes ice cold.

Lila? She wasn't around when I got home, so was it before that?

I don't need to hear more. My body moves on its own, every nerve locked onto a single objective: get to Ryder and beat him within an inch of his life. Then do the same to Thorne when he shows up.

I turn toward the door, but Tori grabs me.

"Blaze, *no*."

Her grip is tight on my arm, her nails digging into my skin. My heart slams against my ribs. She looks up at me, wide-eyed, desperate.

"I can't—I can't do this right now," she whispers, voice raw. "I can't go back there and deal with this. I just—I don't have it in me."

I stare at her, my own fury pressing against my ribs like a knife. I want to wreck them. Make them bleed. But she's shaking. And she never shakes.

She comes first.

Always.

My teeth clench, but I breathe through it. Force myself to listen.

"You don't have to face them alone," I tell her, voice low. "You might not feel like you have the strength right now, but I know you do."

She blinks up at me, something unreadable in her expression. She nods once, almost imperceptibly, but then—

"I need Gabe to come, too."

My stomach drops.

I jerk back, recoiling like she just fucking slapped me. "You want *him* to come?" My voice is sharp, incredulous.

Tori nods, eyes pleading. "I need someone to be able to take me away, if it turns out I'm not as strong as you give me credit for."

I feel like I've been punched in the gut.

I *hate* this. I hate every fucking part of this.

But I *look* at her. At the way she's barely holding herself together. At the cracks she's trying to hide, and I fucking *hate* that this is what it's come to.

I force myself to breathe. To swallow my goddamn pride.

"Fine," I grit out. "But he stays at least six feet away from you."

Gabe doesn't react, just gives a silent nod.

I shoot him a look that makes it clear—one wrong move and I will end him.

Tori exhales, like she's finally releasing some of the pressure crushing her chest. And *fuck*, I want to reach for her. I want to hold her, fix this, erase whatever the hell they just did to her. But I can't. Not yet. Not until she knows—really knows—how much I really love her. How I would pick her over anyone. *Anyone.*

"Let's go," I mutter, turning toward the door.

Because I *will* get her through this.

And Ryder and Thorne are about to fucking pay for hurting our girl.

The drive back is too quiet. Tori sits in the passenger seat, her arms crossed, her nails digging into her sleeves. Her eyes are locked on the road ahead, but I can tell she's not really seeing it. Her mind is somewhere else. Somewhere that's tearing her apart.

I grip the wheel tighter, knuckles going white. I don't know how to fix this. I don't even know where to start. All I know is that every breath she takes like she's forcing herself to stay upright is another reason for me to punch my supposed best friends.

Thorne. Ryder. Those two are dead men walking.

I glance at her again, at the way the dim glow of the streetlights flickers across her face, casting shadows under her eyes. She looks exhausted. Hollowed out in a way I don't think I've ever seen before.

I can't take it.

"What's going on in that head of yours, Doll?" My voice is softer than I expect, but I don't correct it. I just need her to say something. Anything.

She exhales slowly, like she's debating whether or not to tell me. Her fingers twitch, curling into a fist before relaxing again. "I don't know," she finally mutters. "Everything. Nothing. I keep thinking about what happens when we get home."

I nod, keeping my eyes on the road. "And?"

She lets out a bitter laugh, shaking her head. "And what if this changes everything."

The words hit me like a goddamn wrecking ball.

I inhale sharply, gripping the wheel harder, willing myself to stay calm when all I want to do is pull over and make her look at me.

Instead, I keep my tone even. "It won't."

She lets out a shaky breath. "You don't know that."

"The hell I don't." My voice is firm now, no room for argument. I glance at her again, my chest tightening at the way she's biting her lip, holding back a breakdown. "Listen to me, Victoria. Nothing changes. Not for me. Not for you. Not for us."

She's quiet for a long time, but her breathing evens out, like she's trying to believe me. Trying to hold onto something real.

I'll be that something for her.

Always.

She shakes her head, like she's thought about it and she can't see how nothing changes after this. She's ready to argue. "I—"

I cut in before she can even start, my grip on the wheel finally relaxing. "I swear to you, no matter what happens, we're going to be okay."

She swallows hard, nodding once, but I don't miss the way her hand twitches like she wants to reach for mine.

I let out a slow breath. "Come here."

She hesitates, then finally shifts, leaning toward me just enough that I can grab her hand. My fingers wrap around hers and I squeeze gently, reassuringly. She squeezes back.

I keep my grip on her hand as we drive, the silence stretching between us. The weight of everything that's happened sits in my chest like a goddamn stone, pressing down hard. I hate knowing that the people who should have been her safe place are the ones who just broke her.

Her fingers twitch against mine, like she's still not sure if she should be holding on or letting go. I don't let her make the choice. I hold on tighter.

"Blaze..." she starts, then hesitates, licking her lips. "What if I can't look at them the same way? What if I can't forgive them?"

I shake my head. "That's not going to happen."

A small, breathy laugh escapes her, but it's humorless, like she doesn't quite believe me. "It's not that simple."

"It is," I insist, my grip tightening for just a second before I force myself to ease up. "Tori, you could set fire to the entire goddamn world, and I'd still be standing beside you. Thorne and Ryder? If they know what's good for them, they'll be doing the same, whether you forgive them or not. They'll grovel until you do, or until they die. Whichever comes first."

She exhales, leaning back in her seat. "I just...I need to be sure."

I shoot Gabe a look in the mirror. "Which is why we're going back. To make sure."

Gabe holds my stare for a beat before nodding. "Exactly."

But then, instead of letting it drop, he leans forward, eyes directed at me in the rearview mirror. "But maybe she shouldn't have to do this *right* now."

I blink. "What?"

Gabe's jaw tightens. "I'm saying maybe she doesn't need to face them tonight. Maybe she needs time. To think. To feel. Instead of diving headfirst into something she's not ready for."

My grip on the wheel tightens. "You don't know her like I do. That's not how she works. Tori doesn't hide from shit."

"Maybe she should," Gabe shoots back. "Maybe for once, she should get to take a breath instead of forcing herself to be strong for everyone else."

Tori lets out a quiet, "Guys—"

I don't hear her. My focus is on Gabe. "No. That's not what she needs. She needs to confront this head-on. Otherwise, it festers. It eats away at you. I'm not letting that happen to her."

"And forcing her into it when she's already exhausted won't make it better!" Gabe's volume rises a level, his frustration seeping through. "She just went through hell, and you want to drag her right back into it? What if she's not ready? Then what?"

Tori groans, rubbing at her temples. "Guys, I—"

"She won't," I snap, fists clenched. "She's Tori. She's strong."

Gabe exhales sharply. "You don't get to decide that for her, Blaze."

"And you do?" My voice is sharp, edged with the kind of protective fury that's been boiling in my chest all damn night.

Tori suddenly slams her hands against the dashboard. "Enough! Both of you!"

Silence crashes over the car, leaving remnants of frustration and rage in the air.

I turn to look at her, and so does Gabe. Her face is flushed, her hands clenched into fists, and her breathing is shallow, like she's been holding everything in and just hit her limit.

Her eyes flick between us, dark and stormy. "I swear to God, I will throw myself out of this moving car if you two don't shut the hell up."

Gabe and I exchange a glance, our argument momentarily forgotten. Neither of us speaks.

She exhales sharply, then shakes her head. "You're both wrong and right at the same time. Now both of you be quiet."

There's a beat of silence. Then we both turn to look at each other, our expressions mirroring the exact same look of irritated disbelief.

I scowl, turning back to the road. "Whatever."

Gabe doesn't say anything, but I can feel his stare burning into the side of my head, like he's just as thrown off by it as I am. I ignore him, focusing on the road ahead as we pull onto our street.

Tori sits up straighter when the house comes into view, her fingers flexing against her thighs. The tension in her shoulders spikes, her breath coming just a little quicker.

I reach over, brushing my knuckles against hers. "It's going to be okay," I murmur.

She nods but doesn't say anything as I pull into the driveway.

I park, cutting the engine, and for a long moment, none of us move.

"Ryder's inside," I say finally, my voice low. "And it doesn't seem as if Thorne's home since we're still short a car in the driveway."

Tori's fingers tighten against her seatbelt, but she doesn't make a move to get out of the car.

Gabe is the first to open his door, stepping out and stretching his arms like this is just another day. Like this isn't some fucked-up, emotional battlefield we're about to walk into. I glare at him, irritated by how unaffected he seems, but don't say anything as I shift to look at Tori.

She's still staring at the house, unmoving.

"Tori."

Her throat bobs. "I can't."

I reach over, unbuckling her seatbelt for her. "Yes, you can."

She turns to me, her expression raw. "What if I go in there and he looks at me like *I'm* the problem? Like he doesn't love me anymore?"

Rage burns through me. I lean in, cupping her chin between my fingers, forcing her to meet my gaze. "Then I'll knock his fucking teeth out."

A small, shaky breath leaves her lips. "That's not an actual solution."

"Sure it is."

A weak laugh escapes her, but it fades just as quickly as it came. She hesitates for another beat, then finally, slowly, nods. "Okay."

I don't let go of her until she moves to open the door. I step out too, keeping my pace slow, waiting for her to fall into step beside me.

Gabe walks ahead, his body moving like he's preparing for something. Like he's expecting a fight.

That makes two of us.

We reach the porch, and I pause, glancing at Tori one last time before pushing the door open.

Silence greets us.

The house is eerily still, the air heavy. It's dark, but there's a faint glow from the lamp in the living room, casting long shadows across the walls.

I step inside first, scanning the space, my muscles tensing. There's no one, nothing but stillness and quiet air. We venture further in, half-expecting to find Ryder in the kitchen for a late-night snack. But he's nowhere downstairs.

He can't still be sleeping, can he?

"Ryder should be upstairs." I finally make mention of it, suggesting we head up to find him.

Tori hesitates behind me. "I don't know if I can face what we'll find behind his door."

I turn back to her, watching the way she shifts on her feet, arms wrapping around herself. She looks smaller somehow. Like she's trying to make herself disappear.

I step closer, lowering my voice. "Tori, no matter what's behind that door, you won't be facing it alone. You hear me?"

Her lips press together, and she gives a slow nod, but I can tell she's still battling with herself. I reach out, my thumb brushing over the back of her hand. "You're not alone in this."

She lets out a breath, something indecipherable flickering in her expression. Then, finally, she gives me a shaky nod. "Okay."

Just as she takes a step forward, the front door swings open behind us. We all spin around, muscles tensing, hearts slamming into our ribs as the tension coils like a spring. And there, standing in the doorway, looking like he just crawled through hell and back, is Thorne.

His shirt is torn, his knuckles bruised and bleeding. His hair is a mess, his face drawn tight with exhaustion and something else—something desperate.

His eyes land on Tori, and relief floods his face like he's just found the only thing keeping him tethered to the world.

But before he can say a word—I punch him.

Hard.

17: THORNE

Earlier that day

Leaving Tori is always the worst part of my day, especially considering how I'm always stuck with Mia. Never once can I just do something on my own.

And that's probably the point.

Diablo doesn't trust us, so he has these *assistants* do every task with us. They're his spies, I know that much, but I also know that Mia isn't a bad person...or so I hope.

We're back to the warehouse today, double-checking crates. Since we didn't see anything at our useless stakeout, Diablo wanted us to check the crates and see if they were messed with, too. This would at least help narrow down the areas where the crates are being changed.

If it doesn't happen at the warehouse, then it happens before that. I'm sure after this, he'll have us follow that trail too.

What I'm learning from Diablo is that once you're the leader, you delegate everything you can. Maybe he already knows the answers. Perhaps he even knows the culprit. More than likely, all this is some twisted game he's put on for us.

"Hand me the crowbar." I hold my hand out toward Mia, who quickly places the cold metal in my hand. With a grunt and a lot of upper body strength, I pry it open and check it. "Yeah, this one was changed, too," I confirm, closing it back up and setting the crowbar down.

I sigh, staring up at the ceiling, so exhausted from all of this. Vic means everything to me, so I will do literally anything she asks of me, but it doesn't mean I'll enjoy it. She wanted to get to know her dad, and I sure as hell am not going to complain to her about this shit.

I want her to keep wanting to get to know him. I want her to form a relationship, even if the guy is a dick to me. He's her father, and I've heard her drone on enough about meeting her parents one day that I won't ruin this for her.

"You okay?" Mia asks, her hands tucked behind her back as she leans forward to look up at me.

It makes me think of a small child.

"Yeah. Just tired." I reach for the bar again, but Mia steps in my way.

"It's not good to work this hard all the time, Thorne," she advises, her eyes locked on mine. "You need to take care of yourself."

"Thanks, Mia. I got it," I say, my tone sharp and annoyed. I'm too tired to try and hide it.

"I can help, you know?" She blinks up at me so rapidly, for a moment I think she has something in her eye.

I sigh, sliding my hand down my face. "Mia, you don't have to worry about me. I'm fine."

She steps forward, too close, too in my personal bubble. I'm still half reaching for the crowbar around her when she suddenly leans in and lands her lips on mine.

What the fuck?

What the actual fuck?

My mind is racing, trying to catch up, but my body...oh, it boils with fury.

You can't hurt her.

You can't kill her.

Calm. Be calm, Thorne.

It takes maybe two seconds—two seconds too long—before I push her. I try not to hurt her as I do, worried Diablo would dole out some repercussions if she was hurt because of me. Still, my anger is too much, and my body doesn't know gentle at this setting, so my push is more of a shove that lands her on the ground, and I'm exploding.

"What the fuck is wrong with you?!" I snap, wiping at my mouth like she poured acid over it. "Why the hell would you do that?"

I turn to grab the crowbar and leave, but in the distance I catch the soft waves of Vic's hair disappearing through a door.

She saw that, didn't she?

Oh, God, no.

Mia!

"You did that on purpose didn't you?" My grip tightens on the crowbar, catching Mia's eye as she swallows hard. There's fear in her eyes...as there should be, because it's taking everything inside of me not to just hit her right now.

"I don't have time for this shit."

I need to catch Vic.

I run through the warehouse, searching for her, but when I make it outside, I see her in the passenger seat of the SUV as Gabe drives them off. Her eyes are misted.

Fuck she saw.

Vic, please. I would never hurt you like that.

I'm seething. My ears are pounding, my head is roaring, and my heart is two beats away from shattering. Try as I might, I can't focus. I can't decide what to do now.

How the fuck do I fix this?

There's only one thing my brain keeps yelling at me. *Mia. Get fucking Mia.*

My feet march their way back to where I left her, thudding against the concrete floor as I practically stomp my way there. She hasn't moved from the floor, only now she's curled into a ball, crying.

"Get up!" I yell at her, because she gets absolutely no sympathy from me ever again.

"Thorne, I—"

"I don't want to hear it. You're coming with me." I drag her up by the arm, probably too rough, rough enough to leave a mark. She yelps, but again, I don't care. "You're going to explain to Tori what happened. What the hell you were thinking."

She pulls away as hard as she can, but I don't let her go, dragging her through the warehouse in protest. I throw her into the SUV as gently as a bear trying to catch salmon and make my way toward my seat.

I have no idea where to go from here, but I start driving, looking for their vehicle even though I know I won't find it. My hands burn as I grip the leather steering wheel so tight you can see the whites of my knuckles.

"Start talking!" I demand, cutting the tense silence as I make a left turn.

"I..." she gets quiet after one word.

My hand slams against the dash, so fucking furious I can't contain it. "I said start talking!"

She flinches, looking at me as if she can't recognize me, as if she doesn't know me.

You don't know me, Mia. You don't know me at all. If you did, you wouldn't have done what you did today.

"It's just—," she starts, hanging her head low. "We were told we needed to push harder. That we needed to get some kind of result if I didn't want—" she cuts herself off there, twisting her hands in her lap.

"Didn't what, Mia? If you didn't want what?" I insist, chasing an SUV down only to realize it's not them when I pull up beside it.

Goddammit!

"To stop paying for my mom's treatments."

"Your mom's treatments?"

"She's sick, and insurance won't cover the treatments she needs. She may not have wanted me back after juvie, but my siblings need her, and she's still my mom." She fidgets again, avoiding all eye contact as she stares at her lap. "Diablo heard what was going on from Cassandra and he offered to help me if I helped him."

"So, what? The kiss was your way of stepping it up?" I ask to clarify, because I am really not understanding what anybody would have to gain from this.

"Yes. We're supposed to try to get you to be unfaithful to Tori," she admits, her voice smaller and meeker, like she regrets it all.

Part of me wants to understand, wants to sympathize, but the larger part of me just wants to kick her out of this moving car right now.

"Why?"

"Cass said it's because Diablo doesn't want you guys to be with her. He wants her to have one guy to help take over. Actually, I think he'd rather the guy be the one to run things," she whispers, her eyes finally daring to meet mine. "I don't think he really trusts Tori to take over. I mean, she just kind of popped up."

If he weren't her father...if Tori didn't want him, he'd be a dead man.

I don't care how powerful he thinks he is—get him alone and he's dead.

"He's going to learn the hard way that we're not going anywhere. Tori is ours, and we are hers. And *only* hers." My grip tightens on the steering wheel so hard it strains to keep its form. "When we find Tori, you're telling her everything. You got me?"

She nods, growing silent again.

All I can think about now—all that I can hope—is that Vic will forgive me for ever letting this happen, for ever letting Mia even have the chance to get close enough to my face.

Don't leave me, Vic. I won't live.

It isn't until I've wandered around the city twice that I remember Blaze made us all get that tracking app. *Always ready, that one.* I pull over and open the app, seeing she's at some random house twenty minutes away. I quickly put my phone away and head that way, running a couple red lights that were taking too long to change. *No cops, no problem.*

When we get there, my heart lurches to a stop. The door is broken, furniture tossed around, shards of glass from a tableside lamp scatter the floor. It's a mess, and by the look of these men, Vic put up a bigger fight than they thought—or Gabe did. *For once, I guess I'm glad he's with her...just for these moments.*

They're all huddled together, wounds mended and faces scowling. They're on the phone, focused on the voice on the speaker when I enter. I gesture to Mia to stay back—because I don't need her getting in my way—and let that anger in me come to the surface. The aura I'm putting out must be murderous, because despite not making a sound, they all suddenly turn to face me. The phone drops, a woman's voice echoing in the silence. "We'll try again tomorrow."

"Did you hurt her?" are the first words to come out of my mouth, dark, sinister. They narrow their eyes, sizing me up from head to toe.

I'm tall, and lean, but these guys are bigger, and because there's three of them, they're thinking they have the upper hand. "I asked you a question. Did you hurt her?!" I enunciate each word loud and clear, raising my voice with each syllable.

The leader of the group, I'm assuming, lets out a chuckle as he stares down at me. "I don't think you understand the situation you're in. You should turn around and walk away while you still can," he tries to warn me, crossing his arms and flexing his biceps to try and intimidate me.

"Clearly, you underestimate me."

I don't wait any longer, pulling my gun out and shooting the man to his left in the knee. He goes down with a shout, cradling his leg to his chest as he groans in pain. The other two leap forward, taking their chances on closing the distance before I can fire again. Too bad for them, I'm a quick shot. I clip the man on his right thigh, making sure he can't get back up. All that's left is the leader, who's exactly the man I want.

His fist rounds forward, aiming right for my jaw, but I duck fast enough, wrapping my arms around his chest and pushing him back to the floor. The gun is knocked out of my hands beneath him, and he reaches for it immediately. Somehow, I manage to kick it away from him and toward Mia.

"Pick it up. Shoot anyone that stands," I order her, and surprisingly she doesn't freeze. Her hands shake and her breathing is panicked as hell.

Idiot. She's scared of guns.

Thankfully, these guys don't know that, and as such, they'll just continue to nurse their wounds rather than try to get up. Leader man and I are tumbling around the floor, throwing punches, which for the most part he misses. He gets me a couple of times in the ribs, but not hard enough to knock the wind out of me.

He breaks away and we're left out of breath and staring at one another. I take the opportunity to slip on my brass knuckles, seeing his eyes twitch as he watches me. He knows this isn't going his way, and by the way his eyes keep darting toward the door, I think he just might bolt and leave these two behind.

"Now, I asked you a question. Did you hurt her?" I ask, keeping my attention on my knuckles as I open and close my hands. After a second, I stare at the man, showing him there's not a single shred of fear in my eyes. His jaw tightens and his teeth grind, but finally he answers.

"Not really. Maybe scrapes and bruises because she put up a fight. But no, we didn't hurt her exactly," he responds, his back hunched, his arms stretched out like he's ready to catch me in a hold if I lunge for him.

"That wasn't very smart of you." I close my fists shut, and I know my monster has come out to play. I can feel it showing by the way my mouth curves into that sinister grin. "Victoria Reyes is my woman, and no one ever lives when they hurt what's mine."

The room grows silent, the air so still, like it too is waiting for something to happen. And then it all snaps, as he decides to make the first move. He's on me in seconds, but these knuckles don't play. They're sharp enough to be considered blades on the other side.

My fists land on his side, punching repeatedly over and over, taking small pieces of flesh and blood with it every time I pull away. He's groaning, mouth shut as he tries to keep himself from yelling. Finally, I land a blow to his head hard enough to make him take a step back. I use that moment of disorientation to tackle him to the floor and beat his face in.

I don't stop.

Not when I hear my name. Not when he stops moving. Not even when he stops breathing.

It isn't until Mia very gently places her shaking hand on my shoulder that I snap to my senses. I take the gun from her hand and shoot the other guys right in the head. Then I find the phone they dropped earlier and pick it up, slipping it into my pocket for later.

Mia's watching me in shock, like she had no idea I could be this dark. There's not a shred of remorse in me for these three. They went after her, and after Nico, I won't stand for anyone who wants to take her from me to breathe another second of air.

I check my phone again, finding Vic is back home, but this time, she's with Blaze and Ryder.

She's safe.

"Let's go," I tell her, walking out like nothing happened. "Call someone to clean up this mess while I drive."

She nods and is on her phone typing away while I speed through town, back to the estate. My heart is hammering, all the anger fading from my body as we get closer. I can't describe this feeling, the ache I feel at knowing I caused her pain. The need I feel to have her in my arms. The absolute fear that's gnawing at me at the chance that she won't forgive me even after Mia tells her what's going on.

When we pull into the driveway, I park the car as quickly as possible, running toward the door without checking to see if Mia is following. There's blood splattered on my shirt, on my knuckles and hands, my hair is pulled in different directions from the fight, but none of that matters—not when I know she's on the other side of this door.

The moment I enter, my eyes land on her and my heart tears wide open. *She's been crying. She's been crying because of **me**.*

I see Blaze coming, and I know he's going to deck me, so I let him, because I deserve it. We both know I do. He doesn't hold back, not an ounce, as I fall back onto the floor.

"What the fuck is wrong with you?" he yells. I don't think I've ever seen Blaze this angry, not even with Nico. "How could you hurt her like that?"

"Tori, I—"

"No! You don't get to talk to her! She saw you kissing her, Thorne!" Blaze interrupts, his anger erupting like Mount Vesuvius.

I ignore him, because yes, he's right. I fucked up, but like hell am I going to let him keep me from talking to Vic.

Her eyes lock onto me with a plea. She wants me to give her something, anything, some way that she can forgive me, and that alone tells me I have a chance. And then at the worst possible fucking moment, Mia walks in.

Vic is vicious, her eyes locking on Mia with a murderous intent. We all see it, but the one to hold her back is Gabe. Vic lunges for

Mia, metaphorical claws out and all, but Gabe wraps his arm around her waist, hoists her up in the air, and keeps her there.

"Calm down, Tori. Listen to what they have to say. Remember what I told you about your father," he whispers, and now I'm curious about what he said. Maybe she knows what Mia is about to tell her.

Vic's nostrils stay flared as she glares at Mia, as if her eyes alone could kill the girl. They very well could, with how badly Mia is shaking. She might just have a heart attack.

"Start talking. Both of you!" Vic demands.

"It was my fault. Your father ordered us girls to be more aggressive and get your guys to be unfaithful to you. I took my chance and kissed him, but he—"

"Why didn't you push her away immediately?" Those beautiful brown eyes are on me, demanding an explanation, not caring for a single word Mia said.

"I did push her away, but you're right...it wasn't immediately," I admit, getting off the floor and walking toward her. Blaze is tense. I can tell he wants to stop me, but he holds himself back. When I get to her, I don't hold her like I want to. I don't grab her hand like I desperately need to. No. Instead, I kneel in front of her, because she's my goddess, my queen, my love, and I hurt her today. "Please forgive me, Vic. I should have never given her the chance to kiss me. I promise that my reason for not pushing her away instantly wasn't romantic. More like I didn't want to end up hurting her too badly when I did. I couldn't get my anger under control." I look down at her feet, fear creeping into my soul. *Can she forgive me?* "I swear to you, Vic. You're my whole heart—all of it. There is no world in which I could love anyone else, need anyone else, the way I do you. You have me, Victoria Reyes. All of me. Please," my voice shakes, and for the first time in a long time, I feel ready to burst to tears. *It doesn't happen often. Hell, it practically never happens. But Vic somehow always brings out this softer side of me.* "Forgive me."

There's silence, utter and complete silence. The seconds that tick away feel like millennia as I wait for her response, too scared to look up. It isn't until she kneels in front of me, until her hand gently lifts my chin that I fall into the depths of her brown eyes.

"You're my everything, Thorne. When I saw her kissing you today, when you didn't push her away, I..." she trails off, her voice shaking now too. Her eyes mist and I can't help but wrap my arms around her and pull her into me. "I thought you didn't love me anymore. That maybe you started to have feelings for Mia."

"Never. No one could ever come close to you, Victoria. Absolutely no one." I bury my face into her neck, finding comfort in her sweet scent. We hold each other for a long time before Vic pulls away.

She stands slowly, leaving me where I kneel as she adjusts her clothes and very casually marches up to Mia. It's strange how calm Vic seems as she stands before the girl she seemed ready to murder when she walked in. Vic takes a deep breath, stares Mia right in the eye, and then decks her so hard Mia's nose starts to gush.

I think she just broke it.

I want to laugh. I want to laugh so hard, but I hold it in.

"Don't you fucking dare touch him again. Don't even look at him. You're not his assistant anymore. Don't ever cross my path, Mia, because you might not survive."

Gabe is suddenly at her side.

"Tori stop. It's not her fault."

Oh fuck. She's pissed now.

Vic turns her gaze towards him. "Excuse me?"

"This is all your father. She was just following orders, trying to help her family. Please, she can't just leave. Diablo would kill her."

"Good," Vic spouts, her anger clouding her compassion.

"You don't mean that," Gabe insists, as if he knows her so well. He may have been with her every day since we got here, but it doesn't give him the right to feel so close to her.

She's ours, not yours.

"Maybe I do," Vic retorts, crossing her arms, but by the way she's biting her lip, I think Gabe got to her—and somehow that pisses me off more.

"No, you don't. So how about we sit and hear her all the way out?"

Vic rolls her eyes, looking at me over her shoulder. "Fine, but if she goes anywhere near Thorne, I'm not liable for my actions."

Gabe nods and then leads Mia toward the living room. I finally get off the floor, but Blaze is still pissed. And he won't be done being pissed at me for a while.

He should be. Hell, I'm mad at myself, too.

"That's one down, now to talk to Ryder."

"Ryder?" I question, because it finally dawned on me that he's not down here.

Did he let something stupid happen too? Did we both unintentionally hurt Vic?

Before anyone can answer me, a body thuds down the stairs, rolling off each step until it lands on the ground before us.

18: Tori

Ryder takes the stairs like a ragdoll tossed by a pissed-off toddler, his body hitting the ground with a gut-wrenching *thud* that reverberates through the floorboards.

My stomach twists into knots so tight I might as well be a balloon animal.

For a second, my brain refuses to process what just happened. Like if I don't move, don't acknowledge it, then maybe it didn't happen at all.

You're delusional, as usual.

Blaze and Thorne move, but I'm already there, dropping to my knees beside Ryder. He groans, his eyes fluttering open like he's struggling to find his grip on reality.

"Shit," he mutters, trying to push himself up. His arms shake violently, like a newborn deer on ice, before giving out. "Okay. Ow. That was stupid."

A breath rattles in my chest, something between a sob and a growl, and I grab his face, forcing him to look at me.

"Ryder, what the hell happened? Are you hurt?"

His pupils are too wide, his eyelids heavy, like he's barely clinging to consciousness. His whole body is slack, wrong. A rush of something ugly and cold slams into my ribs, sending my pulse into overdrive.

Blaze crouches beside me, his entire body coiled so tight it's like he's trying to hold himself together by sheer will alone. His jaw is so locked, I can hear his teeth grind.

Not good.

"He must have been drugged," Blaze says, his voice like a blade gliding over glass. "I thought it was weird that he was sleeping when I got home, but I didn't think much of it. Or about his open window, or even his..." He stops, staring at Ryder, and what I see in Blaze's face makes my stomach drop.

Pain. Guilt. A rage so sharp it looks like it's cutting him from the inside out.

"I didn't think about his pants being half off."

The words detonate in my chest and everything inside me just stops.

Then, a second later, the world slams back into motion—only it's different now. *Worse.* My breath is gone. My heartbeat is a sledgehammer in my throat.

I thought he had betrayed me. I had assumed the worst. And all that time—Lila drugged him.

He needed me, and I ran the other way.

He needed me, and I didn't help.

*He needed me, and I left him alone...with **her**.*

A part of me wants to break, to sink into the shame, the horror, the fucking *guilt*. It chews at me, digs its claws deep, whispering that I let this happen. That I should have known. That I should have been there.

I shove it down and force my body to move, knowing Ryder needs us right now. "We need to get him upstairs."

Blaze doesn't hesitate. He scoops Ryder up effortlessly, like he's made of nothing, and I don't even think Ryder notices. His head lolls against Blaze's shoulder, his entire body limp.

Thorne's at his side, fists clenching so hard I swear I hear his knuckles pop. He hasn't said a word, but the silence is deceptive—it's the eye of the storm.

And when it breaks, it's going to be brutal.

The rage rolling off them is palpable, so thick it clogs my throat. It's suffocating, but it's nothing compared to what's brewing inside me.

Because Lila did this.

And I'm going to end her for it.

How far did she get? What did she do to him before Blaze got home?

The thought sinks its teeth into me, and I feel something inside me *shift*. It's slow, like a door cracking open to a part of me I've been keeping locked away. The part that didn't flinch when I killed Nico. The part that didn't hesitate when blood was on my hands.

I don't just want revenge.

I want retribution.

The door to my bedroom swings open with a force that rattles the hinges as Blaze shoulders his way inside, his grip on Ryder tight—but I see the strain in his arms, the white-knuckled grip that betrays the anger barely held at bay. Thorne follows close behind, his posture rigid, fists clenching and unclenching at his sides, like he's already picturing what he's going to do to Lila when he gets his hands on her.

Blaze lowers Ryder onto the mattress with more gentleness than I expect, but the second Ryder's weight is off him, he steps back, running both hands through his hair.

Thorne hovers near the doorway, shifting his weight, tension vibrating off him in waves. His fingers flex like he's holding himself back from breaking something—someone.

I drop onto the edge of the bed, my hands framing Ryder's face, forcing him to look at me again. His skin is too warm, his eyelids heavy, and his pupils are still too damn wide.

"Ryder, hey, stay with me," I murmur, brushing damp hair from his forehead. He feels wrong—clammy, burning up and too slack in my grip. Too unlike him.

His lashes flicker, unfocused blue meeting mine as a sluggish, lazy grin tugs at his lips. "Sh, 'm fine, KittyKat. Jus' a lil' sleepy."

My throat tightens, a sharp sting burning behind my eyes. "You were drugged, dumbass. You're definitely not fine."

His chuckle is barely there, weak and slurred, but it's him, and that makes my chest ache more than anything else. "Well, that 'splains why I feel like I got hit by a truck."

Blaze lets out a sharp breath, pacing toward the window, staring out into the night like he's daring Lila to show her face again. Thorne moves to the dresser, arms crossed so tight against his chest I swear he might crack his own ribs. But they both stay silent and let me do all the talking.

I clutch the sheets beneath me, grounding myself before I fall apart. "Lila did this to you. She—she—"

I can't say it. The words lodge in my throat like barbed wire, burning, choking. Saying them makes it *real*.

Ryder's grin falters, something flickering through the haze in his eyes, a moment of clarity breaking through the fog. "She didn't. Blaze—Blaze got home b'fore she could. She got scared, left through th' window."

A breath stutters out of me, but there's no relief. Just something heavier, something darker, wrapping tight around my ribs and squeezing.

I drop my forehead against his, my hands trembling against his cheeks, my thumbs brushing over the stubble along his jaw. "I thought—" My voice breaks. I swallow hard, but the words still come out raw. "I thought you were cheating on me. I thought you wanted her. I thought—" My throat closes as I choke on my guilt. "I didn't help you."

Behind me, Blaze's pacing stops. The air shifts, thickening with a rage that isn't mine. Thorne exhales sharply, a quiet sound, but I can feel the fury in it.

They probably hadn't realized how guilty I feel over this.

Ryder's fingers twitch, weak, but still him as they brush against my wrist, grounding me before I spiral too far. "Don't—" His voice is hoarse, slurred, but certain in a way that feels more real than anything else in this moment. "Don't do that. Don't make this y'r fault."

I shake my head, my breath coming too fast, too uneven. "How can I not? I should've known something was wrong. I should've been here. I should've—"

Before I can drown in the guilt, he stops me.

His lips press against my forehead, soft, lingering, stopping my thoughts before they can take me under. "You're here now." The words are barely above a whisper, but they shatter me all the same. "Tha's wha' matters."

Behind me, Blaze turns away from the window, his shoulders rising and falling like he's trying to keep himself from losing it completely. Thorne exhales again, quieter this time.

A ragged breath hitches in my throat, but I don't pull away. I don't argue. I just stay curled up with him.

Because I need to hold onto him.

The weight of exhaustion presses against me, but I refuse to move, refuse to let go of Ryder even as his breathing evens out, slow and steady. His body sinks into the mattress, his warmth bleeding into me as I shift, wrapping myself around him like some kind of protective shield. My arms tighten, one hand smoothing over his hair, brushing damp strands away from his forehead as he lets out a quiet sigh.

Blaze and Thorne remain in the room, lingering, a silent promise that they won't let this slide. I don't need to look at them to know they're still wound tight, their bodies coiled like they're barely holding back the need to do something. But right now, Ryder is what matters.

The door creaks open, and my head snaps up as Gabe steps inside, his usually unreadable face carrying the weight of quiet exhaustion. He doesn't say anything at first, just lets his gaze sweep over Ryder before flicking to the rest of us.

"I sent Mia home," he finally says, voice low...careful. "She'll talk to you when you're ready. But she's done here for tonight."

Blaze exhales sharply, dragging a hand through his hair. "And you trust her to just go home?"

"She's not a threat," Gabe replies evenly, leaning against the doorframe. "She was never one to begin with."

Thorne folds his arms, exhaling slowly like he wants to argue but can't find a good enough reason.

"I also called a doctor," Gabe adds, shifting his gaze to me. "Someone who doesn't work for Diablo. Someone I trust. He'll be here soon to check on Ryder."

Blaze and Thorne exchange glances, and even though the tension in the room doesn't lessen, there's a flicker of something else beneath it. Appreciation... maybe? A reluctant one, but it's there.

Still, it's *me* who finally says it.

"Thank you, Gabe."

His eyes meet mine, steadfast and searching, before he nods once. "Get some rest, Tori. You need it."

I don't answer. Instead, I glance back down at Ryder, his lips slack, his breath fanning against my collarbone, his body heavy against mine.

I feel the way Gabe lingers, watching us. And for a moment, an odd thought takes root in my mind—he fits. Like a missing puzzle piece, someone who wasn't supposed to be here but somehow belongs anyway. Like an older brother I never had, someone who's looked out for me from the moment I entered his life. Maybe it's because he's older, the anchor that offsets the storm.

But it's a fleeting thought, one I don't have the energy to examine right now. Not when Ryder stirs, pressing closer in his sleep.

Blaze steps forward, squeezing my shoulder, pulling me back to reality. "We'll be right back. Just rest with him."

Thorne doesn't say anything, but when I glance up, his gaze is softer than it was before. They know I won't leave Ryder's side.

I nod, curling in tighter against Ryder as the guys slip out of the room, their footsteps fading down the hall. The front door slams before the house settles into silence again.

Minutes pass, maybe longer. I don't move, just listen to the constant rhythm of Ryder's breathing, the occasional twitch of his fingers against my arm. My own eyes start to drift closed when I feel him shift.

"Y'know," his voice rasps against my skin, still groggy but no longer slurred. "If I ever end up in a coma, just make sure no one gives me a sponge bath. E'cept for you. You can do whatever you like to me."

My heart stutters before relief slams into me so hard I almost laugh. But instead, I pinch his side lightly. "Duly noted. But don't count on it. Blaze would probably sign you up for a full-body scrub just to mess with you."

He huffs a weak laugh, but it's shorter than usual, and when I pull back enough to see his face, there's something guarded there.

"She really drugged me, huh?" He sounds so small as he asks, even though he's trying to play it off.

"It seems that way."

"So," he says, stretching a little, wincing as his body protests. "On a scale from 'the guys are going to chop my balls off for letting myself get drugged' to 'they already took them while I was out,' where are we at?"

I stiffen. The joke shouldn't bother me. *This is Ryder.* He makes light of everything, *even his own trauma.* But this? *This isn't funny.*

"Are you seriously cracking jokes about this?" My voice comes out sharper than I intend, but I don't regret it. "Ryder, she drugged you. That's not— That's not something you just—"

I break off, my throat closing, and for the first time since he woke up, his face shifts.

His easygoing mask falters, just for a second. "Tori—"

"No, don't *'Tori'* me," I snap, sitting up just a bit, my fingers still threading through his hair. "You almost—If Blaze hadn't come home—" My voice cracks, and I hate that it does, but there's nothing I can do to stop it. "You *know* what almost happened. And you're sitting here trying to joke about it like it's nothing."

A long silence stretches between us. *Too long.*

Then, finally, Ryder sighs, his fingers brushing against my wrist. "I don't know how else to talk about it."

I freeze.

His voice is quieter now, more honest than I think I've ever heard it. "I make jokes. That's just...what I do. It's easier than dealing with shit. Easier than—" He exhales, his gaze flickering away before finding mine again. "It's easier than feeling like a victim."

The breath in my lungs shudders. I know what he means. I understand it more than I ever wanted to.

I swallow hard, shifting so I can press my forehead against his again. "Being a victim doesn't make you weak," I whisper. "Not to me. Not ever."

His fingers curl against my arm, and I feel something crack inside him. The walls he keeps up, the ones he thinks protect him but really just keep him caged.

"Ryder," I say, soft but firm, my fingers brushing against his cheek. "This doesn't make you weak. It doesn't make you any less you."

He doesn't say anything. Just breathes, slow and even, his body relaxing—really relaxing.

"I just—I don't know how to process this," he admits, voice barely above a whisper. "I never thought...I mean, shit, I never thought someone would even try to—" He stops himself, shaking his head like the words are poison.

I hold him tighter, not pushing, just letting him be.

"Ryder, listen to me." I tilt his chin until he meets my gaze. "What happened wasn't your fault. It doesn't take away who you are."

He swallows hard. "I just...don't want you to look at me differently."

I shake my head, fierce and unrelenting. "I don't. I never will. If anything, I look at you now and see how strong you are. You're still you, Ryder. And I still love you."

His breath shudders out of him, and for the first time since waking up, the tension in his body *truly* melts away.

I brush my fingers through his hair again, gentle, soothing, and he leans into the touch like he needs it more than air.

I won't let him carry this alone.

Not now.

Not ever.

Before either of us can say anything more, there's a knock on the door, sharp and precise. Ryder tenses beneath me, his fingers twitching lightly over my skin. I barely lift my head from where I'm curled around him.

"Come in," I say softly, my voice raw from everything tonight has thrown at us.

The door creaks open and a man strides in, clean-cut, dressed in dark slacks and a button-down. His calm expression screams he's seen worse than this.

"This is Dr. Langley," Gabe introduces from the doorway, arms crossed. "He's going to check on Ryder now."

Langley nods once, setting down a small medical bag and rolling up his sleeves. "Vitals first."

I sit up reluctantly but keep my hand on Ryder's chest as the doctor pulls out a stethoscope, pressing it against his back, then his chest. Ryder exhales sharply, his muscles coiling like he's preparing for something worse than just a cold metal disk against his skin.

"Relax, kid," Langley murmurs, clinically detached. "Not here to make things worse."

Ryder snorts, though there's no humor in it. "Would be impressive if you could."

Langley doesn't rise to the bait, just checks his pulse and then tilts Ryder's chin to examine his pupils. The flashlight flickers between his eyes, and Ryder grimaces, squeezing them shut before groaning. "Okay, yeah. Not a fan of that."

Langley hums under his breath. "Tell me what happened."

I exhale slowly. "He was drugged. Something strong enough to knock him out but not keep him under."

I know Ryder is more than capable of answering for himself, but why should he have to?

Langley nods, already pulling out a small vial and syringe. "From the way he's responding, I'd bet it's Flunitrazepam. Commonly known as Rohypnol. Fast-acting, metabolizes quickly, leaves you disoriented but functional once it starts wearing off. Drowsiness, confusion, memory gaps." He flicks the syringe, then presses it lightly against Ryder's arm. "This is just fluids to help flush it out. He needs water, rest, and no alcohol for at least seventy-two hours."

Ryder hisses as the needle pierces his skin, flexing his fingers like he's fighting the urge to yank his arm away. "Yeah, well, I wasn't planning on doing shots tonight anyway."

Langley arches a brow, unimpressed. "No permanent damage," he continues, ignoring Ryder's usual deflections. "But the mental effects? That's up to you."

Ryder stiffens beside me, his grip on my wrist tightening briefly. "Thanks for that, Doc. Real sage advice."

Langley looks at him, and for the first time, there's something like understanding in his gaze. "Pretending won't change the fact that it happened."

Something shifts in Ryder's expression. A flicker of something raw before he rolls his eyes, pushing out a heavy breath.

Langley snaps his bag shut. "I'll leave my number with Gabe in case anything changes. But he'll be fine. Just keep him hydrated and let him sleep."

Gabe sees him out, the door clicking shut behind them as silence fills the air. I run my fingers through Ryder's hair again, his body still tense beneath my touch.

"You okay?" I ask softly.

He cracks one eye open, his smirk faint but there. "Well, I'm not dead, so that's a plus."

I huff a quiet laugh, shaking my head. "Always aiming high."

His smirk fades a bit, his gaze searching mine. "You're not gonna—like, sit there and stare at me all night, are you?" He tries to make it sound teasing, but there's something vulnerable beneath it. Like he already knows the answer and doesn't quite know how to feel about it.

I press a kiss to his temple, my voice firm. "Yeah, I am. And you're just gonna have to deal with it."

His breathing evens out, his weight sinking into me fully. I hold him a little tighter, letting my own exhaustion creep in.

I press my lips together, voice barely above a whisper as I say, "You've always been like fire, Ryder. And fire isn't meant to burn alone. So let me be here to fan your flames when they start to get small."

"Real poetic there, Sprout. " He shakes his head like he's disappointed with my cringiness, but I see the way the corner of his lips tug, trying not to smile.

"I love you, Ryder."

"I love you, too, Victoria."

19: Tori

Sleep is a luxury I don't seem to get often. It barely clings to me before it's ripped away.

A hand brushes my shoulder, firm but careful, the touch bringing me just to the edge of consciousness. My body reacts before my brain does—muscles tensing, breath hitching.

Ryder.

Oh my God, Ryder.

I glance at Ryder. He's still out, his breath even.

Good. He should be resting.

My pulse kicks up, the last fog of sleep fading with each blink. Before I can jolt upright, a shadow looms over me.

Thorne.

He crouches beside the bed, face dimly lit by the sliver of moonlight cutting through the blinds. One finger lifts to his lips—a silent command. *'Stay quiet.'*

My brain scrambles for a reason why Thorne is waking me like this. I flick my gaze behind him and spot Blaze standing near the doorway, arms crossed, posture rigid.

Something's happened. Something bad.

What now?

I push myself up, careful not to wake Ryder, swallowing the hoarseness from my voice. "What is it?"

Thorne doesn't answer right away. Instead, he stands, offering his hand. I take it without question.

"Come with us," Blaze murmurs, keeping his voice low. "We need you."

Can't exactly say no to that.

I follow them out of the room, my bare feet padding against the cool tile as we move down the hallway, then through the kitchen. Gabe is at the back door, leaning against the frame. He doesn't speak, just nods once, like he already knows what's about to happen.

Blaze steps ahead and pulls open the door, the night air rushing in. It's crisp, thick with the lingering scent of blood.

My stomach tightens.

"Where are we going?" I ask as I step outside, my voice steady despite the way my pulse pounds in my ears.

Thorne walks beside me, matching my pace. "The shed at the edge of the property."

My brows knit together. "The one the gardener uses?"

Blaze nods. "That's the one. Thought it would have some useful tools."

That's when it clicks.

I know who's inside before they even say her name. The way they woke me without waking Ryder, the vengeance charging the air around them.

Lila.

Adrenaline shoots through my limbs, igniting something deep, something primal. My hands curl into fists, nails biting into my palms.

Lila drugged Ryder. She tried to take something from him.

Now I'm going to take everything from her.

We move through the backyard in silence, the grass damp beneath my feet. The shed looms ahead, a small, quaint thing. All too normal for what's about to happen inside.

Blaze reaches the door first, pulling it open without hesitation. The scent hits me instantly. Metallic and thick, the sharp tang of blood mingled with fear.

Inside, the single overhead light flickers, casting shadows against the walls. And in the center of the room is Lila. Tied to a chair. Bruised. Bloody. Broken.

They started without me.

How rude.

Her head lolls forward, hair matted against her face. Blood crusts at her temple, a fresh cut splitting her bottom lip.

I step inside, my breath measured, my hands at my sides. I don't look at Blaze or Thorne—I don't need to. I keep my gaze on *her*.

Blaze closes the door behind us, the soft click echoing in the otherwise quiet space. Lila stirs, her body tensing before her swollen eyes crack open. At first, there's confusion—then recognition. Then? Panic.

I tilt my head, voice smooth. "Rough night?"

She exhales sharply through her nose, struggling against the restraints. "Just having some fun with your guys—"

A laugh I don't even recognize escapes me, a singular dark scoff. "Oh, please. Don't strain yourself, Lila. You're gonna need your strength to get through having 'fun' with me."

She shifts in the chair, trying to pretend like she isn't afraid.

"Not much strength needed for that," she spits back, voice hoarse. "You're not cut out for this."

I smile—not a kind one, but an 'I'm about to enjoy what I'm going to do to you' type.

Blaze speaks from behind me, voice like crushed gravel. "You'd be very wrong to assume so, Lila. The reason you're still breathing is for Tori to get to do what she wants to you."

I glance at him, at Thorne, at the way they are encouraging me. I turn back to Lila, slowly rolling my shoulders, shaking out my fingers.

"And oh boy do I have some plans," I murmur, leaning in, my voice dropping to something dark and final. "You should've never touched Ryder."

Her pupils dilate.

She finally understands.

Her fate was sealed the moment she drugged my Ryder.

Lila shifts against the ropes binding her, creaking under the pressure of her weak, pointless resistance. Her swollen eye barely opens as she watches me step forward, my shadow stretching across the concrete floor like it's reaching for her.

*She **should** be afraid.*

The dim overhead light casts fractured shadows over her battered face. I crouch in front of her, tilting my head as I take in the damage. Blaze and Thorne didn't go easy on her—not that she deserved it. But they left enough untouched for me.

They left the rest to me.

"You like being the center of attention, don't you, Lila?" My voice is almost conversational, almost friendly. "Well, guess what? Tonight's your night."

She swallows, but her throat is dry. I can hear it. The scratch, the effort.

"Tori—"

I press a single finger against her lips, the gentleness of it mocking the brutality waiting in my hands. "Don't call me Tori. You don't get to speak my name as if we're friends. We're far from it."

I stand, stepping behind her and dragging my fingers along the back of the chair, the wooden surface worn and splintered.

My hand finds the knife resting on the nearby table, cold and daunting. I twirl it once before pressing the tip against the soft flesh behind her ear, just enough to make her hold still.

"You know something, Lila? I've been wanting to hurt you for a while now." I hum, tracing a slow line down her jaw with the blade. "You're so goddamn disrespectful. The way you flirt with Ryder, touching him like you think he belongs to you, even in front of me."

She doesn't answer. She's at least smart enough to realize I'd cut her tongue if she did.

"You really thought you could take something that wasn't yours." I dance the blade down her neck and over her shoulder, digging it in just enough to break the skin, a bead of red blooming beneath the pressure.

Her breath stutters, and I drink it in. The anticipation. The terror that takes the place of the bravado she was desperately holding onto.

It's a rush.

Jesus, Tori. When did you start enjoying this shit?

"You made a mistake, Lila." I twist a strand of her blood-matted hair between my fingers. "But don't worry, I'm going to help you make it right. I'll accept your blood as payment. Screams are a bonus. Ooo, and if you beg enough, maybe I'll end it all faster for you."

The scream she lets out when the knife bites deeper into her shoulder is just the beginning. "That's perfect, Lila. Just like that."

The first cut is just deep enough to sting but not seriously injure.

"Hurts, doesn't it?" I murmur, tilting my head. "It's funny. I wonder if Ryder felt like this after you drugged him—trapped, helpless."

Her breath is shallow, ragged, but she keeps her lips pressed together, refusing to beg. *For now.*

I press the blade lower, just above her sternum. "The thing is, Lila, I could kill you fast. A quick slice—right here—and you'd bleed out in minutes. But where's the lesson in that?"

I drag the knife slowly down, tearing fabric, not flesh. *Not yet.* Her blouse splits, revealing pale, trembling skin beneath.

"I'd rather take my time," I whisper. "Make sure you really understand how badly you fucked up. Contemplate those life choices, Lila. You're going to be here a while."

Her body jerks violently against the restraints, her breath coming in sharp, terrified gasps.

It's useless, bitch. You're not going anywhere.

"Struggling won't save you," I say, pressing a finger into the first shallow cut on her shoulder, feeling the warmth of her blood coat my skin.

Blaze exhales from where he leans against the wall, arms crossed, his eyes unreadable. "I don't think she realizes that Thorne and I aren't the ones she should be scared of. Her nightmare is just starting, isn't it, Doll?"

Lila's lip trembles, her gaze darting toward him, then to Thorne, who stands silent, watchful.

"Truer words have never been spoken," I respond, stepping around her, dragging my nails along her skin just to watch her flinch. "I bet you thought because you had a pretty face and a few well-placed smiles, you could get away with anything. But this is the real world, and when you touch what isn't yours..." I lean in, voice a whisper against her ear. "You get your fingers cut off."

I press the knife between her index and middle finger with just enough pressure to make her believe I would cut one right off.

Thorne finally speaks, his voice dark and menacing. "She's shaking now. Took long enough."

I don't look away from Lila. "She's realizing just how much pain she's going to be in."

The blade drags, a thin red line appearing against her trembling skin. I kneel in front of her again, lifting her chin with the edge of the knife, forcing her to meet my gaze. "Do you want me to stop, Lila?" My voice is sweet, almost pitying.

She nods, tears finally spilling over.

I'm a little scared by the way my body hums in pleasure at the sight of her tears, a rush of power running through me like a tidal wave.

"Say it."

She swallows hard. "P-please."

I tilt my head. "Please what?"

"Please stop," she gasps, voice barely above a whisper. "I was wrong. I—please."

"Hey, Blaze?" I call for him over my shoulder, but my eyes never stray away from Lila. "Could you hear that from over there?"

"Nope. Couldn't hear a damn thing," he responds, his voice full of amusement as he plays along with me.

I think he and Thorne might be enjoying watching me hurt Lila more than the fact that Lila is being hurt.

"Yeah, I didn't think so." I tsk my tongue at her, holding the knife above her thighs. "Too bad, guess we have to keep going."

Lila's eyes widen so much, I think they'll pop right out of her head. I almost laugh at the sight, but I bite it back.

"No, please!" She quickly pleads as tears well in her eyes.

"Shh. Shh. Shh." I press the blade against her lips. "The time for begging is over. Now it's time to play. You like games, Lila, don't you? I can only assume so, since you've been playing them this entire time."

I twirl the knife idly, enthralled by the reflective silver surface. "I think playing with me seems only fitting. It's a very simple game. I'll blindfold you, so you can feel just as helpless as Ryder did. Once you're blindfolded, I'll place a paper in front of your hand. You get to point to a word. If it's a body part, I get to cut it. If you point to a word that isn't a body part, I won't cut you that round."

I place the blade on the nearby work table, and grab a red, grease-stained rag. When I turn toward Lila, seeing her weave her head around to try and avoid the blindfold. Blaze steps forward, holding her face still, long enough for me to tie the rag tightly against her face and then steps away as if he was never there.

I grab a paper and begin scribbling words, parts of her body I really want to cut into, parts I'd like to set on fire, then I add tools I could use as weapons that I see around the shed. "I'm going to be honest with you, Lila. Most of these are body parts, but about five of them aren't. Those five are times when I'll switch your instrument of torture. Would you like to know what they are?"

I'm having too much fun with this.

Lila shakes her head, her teeth clenched as tight as her fists. "That's too bad, I'm going to read them to you anyway. Suspense is the best thing in a game."

"Just stop," Lila finally speaks, her entire body shaking as tears stream down her cheeks. "I get it. I know I messed up. Please. You don't have to do this."

I ignore her pleas, even though I'm enjoying the begging, and start reading the list. "I have every body part imaginable on this list, but the weapons are the rusty garden scissors, the hatchet in the corner, nails and a hammer, the knife I've been using already, and some random bent lawnmower blade. Isn't that just so exciting?"

I smile as if it's just another board game and not a sick way of keeping her scared while also hurting her.

"Please, Tor—" I punch her in the mouth, cutting her off before she can finish my name.

"I told you not to call me that." My smirk fades, all the twisted playfulness disappearing from my tone as a voice so menacing takes over. "Now, just like Ryder, you don't get to speak. Thorne, do you have something I can gag her with?"

Thorne reaches into his jacket pocket, pulling out a silk handkerchief—jet black, smooth, elegant. "It's nothing special."

"Oh great. Just like her."

I take it from him, letting the silk slip between my fingers before turning back to Lila. Her breath comes in shallow gasps, her swollen lips parting, maybe to beg, maybe to curse me—doesn't matter. I grip her chin, nails pressing into her clammy skin, forcing her to look at me.

"Open up," I murmur, my voice dripping with mock sweetness.

She shakes her head violently, muffled protests bubbling in her throat.

"Wrong answer."

I squeeze her cheeks hard enough to make her yelp, her jaw popping open. Before she can snap it shut, I shove the silk between her teeth, pressing it deep until it muffles whatever pathetic words she might try to spit out.

"Better," I hum, stepping back to admire the effect. "Now you don't get to ruin the moment with your words."

Blaze exhales a quiet chuckle from his spot against the wall, arms crossed, eyes gleaming with dark amusement. "She sounds better like that."

"Let's go ahead and start our game. Remember, Lila, you're the one picking where I'm cutting you." I pick the paper up, waving it around so she can hear it, before I put it close to her hand. "Now point, and let me add that if you don't pick, Thorne or Blaze will pick, and I am sure they won't be kind."

Her entire body trembles, the chair beneath her creaking from the force of her shaking.

You deserve so much worse for what you did to Ryder.

She flinches hard as the paper touches her, a muffled squeal vibrating through the silk. Her hands stay clenched in tight fists rather than following instructions.

"Come on, Lila," I sigh. "Do you really want the first place I cut deep to be your tits or your face? Cause I'm sure that's what they'll pick."

Her hand slowly unravels, realizing her chances are better with the paper than with the two radiating murder vibes behind me.

I mean, she's wrong, but I won't tell her that.

Her index finger slowly extends until it touches the paper right where I want.

No one said this game would be fair.

No one said it wouldn't be rigged.

"Oh, ouch. The soles of your feet," I pretend to wince, like hurting her is going to hurt me.

As if.

"That's okay, though," I continue, setting the paper down to pick the knife back up. "You won't be using that part of your body for a while. There's no running away from here."

Lila's muffled screams get louder as she feels me approach, her senses sharper now that she can't see. She's kicking her legs, doing what she can to keep this from happening, but what she doesn't realize is that there's nothing she can do.

*I'm going to cut her... **a lot**.*

Thorne steps forward, gripping Lila's ankles and lifting them up so I can get to the bottoms of her feet. I smile like he's done the most romantic thing as I kneel in front of him, knife gripped tight, and begin to carve 'rapist' into her skin.

She thrashes, screaming bloody murder, but Thorne does a good job of holding her down and in place. When I'm done, I admire my handiwork for a second before standing back up.

Thorne lets Lila's feet drop with a heavy thud and another painful scream. He grips the handle of the knife in my hand and meets my gaze, expression masked. "You done?"

I hum, dragging my fingers over her arm, enjoying the way Lila's body locks up at the mere touch. "Not yet. It's not nearly enough."

I think about the way Ryder is feeling, how broken she made him feel, and the anger in me bubbles back up. It demands blood. *It demands it now!*

Thorne doesn't say anything, but he steps back, arms crossed, letting me continue.

There's a wicked smirk across my lips as I stare down at Lila, tilting my head. "Let's play again. Maybe this time you'll get lucky."

She shakes her head, her body spent as her feet slide around in the blood pooling beneath her. Her hands are balled up again, and I know if I want to keep playing, I need to give her a false sense of hope.

"I'll make you a deal. I'll add a word to the list. Freedom," I whisper into her ear before standing straight again. "If your finger lands on freedom, I'll untie you and let you drag yourself out of here."

Her hands are still fisted, but they loosen just enough to let me know she's buying it. "And for every time you point to a word that isn't a part of your body, like one of the weapons, I'll add another freedom to the paper."

All lies, Lila.

I won't even write the word once.

She takes a deep breath, pulling herself back together to try and sit up. Her mouth is still gagged so she can't vocalize her answer, but when her finger extends, I know she's ready.

"Excellent. Let's continue our game. Who knows, maybe you'll get lucky and it'll end this round," I suggest, throwing in more false hope. *Because why not?*

I take my time as we play, cutting her in places that won't kill her—small, shallow wounds in the places she points to that sting but won't send her into shock. Every new slice earns another choked whimper, another broken sob. And I *love* it.

Not just because she deserves this. Not just because of what she did to Ryder. But because it feels good.

The power, the control, the justice. It burns inside me, a dark, thrumming satisfaction.

I'm fucking embracing it.

I've changed weapons twice, working with the rusted scissors now. They help me not cut so deep, since they're dull. She's shaking violently, blood trickling down her torso, her leg, her arms, her...everywhere. It's pooling beneath her chair in a puddle that looks deep enough to swim.

"No luck, Lila," I say, stepping back, flexing my fingers, as if shaking off the adrenaline. "Seems you couldn't get the word freedom. But that's not surprising, seeing how easily you took Ryder's freedom away. The word seems to elude you. But you know what, Lila? I think I'm done."

Blaze watches me carefully, his expression impassive. Thorne, though—his gaze flickers between me and Lila like he's trying to decide if he should have stepped in earlier.

Lila moans weakly, slumping against the restraints, and I tilt my head at her. "How does it feel being at someone else's mercy? Not fun when you're not the one in control, huh?"

She doesn't answer. She can't.

I turn to Thorne and Blaze. "She's all yours."

Blaze pushes off the wall, rolling his shoulders. "I was hoping you'd say that."

I don't watch what happens next. I don't need to. I know whatever they're going to do to her will be well-deserved.

I head for the door, stepping outside into the morning air. The darkness I'd been keeping at bay for so long? I don't feel like fighting it anymore.

I want to welcome it.

20: BLAZE

I haven't slept. None of us have. Except maybe Ryder, but that wasn't necessarily by choice.

Ryder's been knocked out in Tori's bed, curled up like she's his anchor. And she is. Always has been.

Thorne and I left them alone, gave them space. Not like we had a choice. We had business to handle.

Lila.

She's back where she belongs—bloodied, broken, and dumped at Diablo's feet.

We didn't kill her. *Could have. Should have.* But a bullet would've been a kindness, and Lila didn't deserve kindness.

We made sure she understood that. Made her feel every ounce of the fear she tried to force on Ryder.

By the time we left her, there was nothing left of the smug, overconfident woman who thought she could play with our lives. Just a beaten, whimpering mess Diablo wouldn't even recognize as useful.

He'll see her for what she is now. A failure. A liability. A reminder.

I don't regret it. *Not for a second.*

What Tori did to Lila did something to me. I'd always known she was strong—always known she had the fire to stand in our world—but I hadn't expected that. Hadn't expected her to take to it like she did. *Like she was made for it.*

She didn't just handle Lila. She owned her. And the way she did it? It was for Ryder.

That's what hit me the most—the love behind it. The lengths she'd go to for him, the fury she had in her for what had been done to him. It was ruthless. And it was damn near beautiful.

But the moment we walked back through our door, I knew—we weren't done.

The living room is dim, the kind of lighting that makes it feel smaller. Tori's perched on the arm of the couch, fingers tapping against her knee like she's two seconds from blowing something up.

Gabe leans against the wall, arms crossed, quietly watching. But after tonight, he's not an outsider anymore.

Thorne walks toward the fireplace, tense, still thinking through everything. He has a tendency to replay things in his head in excruciating detail.

And Ryder—finally awake—sits up, looking like hell. But he's here. And whatever he's about to say is going to matter.

I crack my knuckles, shifting forward. "Alright. Let's hear it."

Ryder runs a hand through his tangled hair, the bruises on his face from his tumble down the stairs still too fresh. *He looks like shit.* But his voice is steady.

"I got some information before Lila drugged me. In the bathroom, with an informant." His jaw tightens, and Tori tenses at the mention of Lila. "I managed to get a name from him."

I meet his gaze, doing my best to keep his focus on the informant and that little bitch. "Who?"

Ryder's eyes flick to mine, too seriously for him. "Cass."

Thorne is the first to speak again, exhaling sharply, like he's piecing something together. "When I was looking for Tori, I ran into some guys who had tried to take her. They were on a call with a woman. She was giving orders." His lips press into a thin line. "Didn't think much of it at the time. But now—"

"Now we know it wasn't just some random woman," I finish, feeling like an idiot for how stupidly we've been played by everyone since we got here. Gabe. Diablo. Now her. "It was Cassandra."

Tori's hands tighten into fists. "You've got to be kidding me." She shakes her head, not because she doesn't believe us, but because she can't handle what it means. "That's it. I'm not allowed to pick my friends anymore. My she's-out-to-get-you radar is clearly broken."

Gabe finally speaks, voice low, ignoring Tori's comment completely. I don't blame him. He has no idea what she's talking about, the kind of betrayal she's experienced. "Makes sense. Cassandra's always been looking for an opening."

I glance at him, studying him for a moment before asking, "And you know this how?"

He doesn't hesitate, answering immediately. "Because Diablo had me watching her when I first started working for him."

Tori raises an eyebrow. "Why?"

Gabe exhales. "He's never fully trusted her, but she's ambitious, cutthroat, and has connections that have proven useful to him. But she's reckless. She's been making moves that haven't added up. At first, I thought she was just trying to prove herself. Now—"

"Now we know she's trying to take Diablo out," Thorne mutters. "And she sees Tori as a problem."

Ryder drags a hand down his face. "Which means she's not just following orders. She has her own endgame. And our girl is at the center of it again."

Tori exhales, pressing her hand to her forehead like she can't stand the thought. "Great. Just great. I so love this for me." She rolls her eyes, sarcasm high as always. But then she shifts, taking a breath and sitting straight. "Fuck this! We're not losing. We didn't last time, and we won't this time."

We aren't just dealing with Diablo anymore. We have another enemy. One who's been right in front of us the whole time. But she's right, we're not going down without putting up a fight.

Gabe pushes off the wall, stepping forward. "If we're doing this, we need a plan."

I nod. "Agreed. And I think I know exactly how to play it."

Thorne meets my gaze, dark eyes sparkling with excitement. He's got some pent-up anger he'd like to release on these sorry fuckers after everything that's happened. And I'm right there with him. "A setup," he suggests with a twitch of his lip.

Ryder smirks, though it's tight. Strained. "The best kind."

He's still not fully himself.

Tori leans back, eyes flicking between all of us. "Then let's make it perfect, because nobody is getting hurt this time."

It's silent enough that Ryder's leg twitching sounds like bricks falling. He's been left to think too long, and I'm sure his mind is running to places it shouldn't. We've all been silently plotting, trying to come up with the best set up, but everything feels wrong.

Thorne finally breaks the silence, crossing his arms. "Cassandra's got a network of people we don't know. But she's also got people tied to Diablo. Someone in that mix has to be questioning whether or not she can take control of The Diablos, and that's the person we need to take advantage of."

Gabe speaks up, his voice measured. "Juan."

Tori raises an eyebrow. "Juan? As in right-hand-man Juan?"

"He's been with Diablo for years, but he's not blindly loyal. He has values, and as of late Diablo has been crossing them. Cassandra knows that, and I'm sure she's approached Juan already, getting him on her side. But considering the way Cassandra has been handling things with Tori, I'm sure Juan isn't agreeing with her methods either. Surprisingly, Juan seems to have a soft spot for Tori."

Tori smiles, clearly liking the fact, probably because she's got a soft spot for him too after he helped last time. "Then let's see if we can't flip him to our side."

"It shouldn't be too hard," Ryder adds, gaining all our attention. "I think he's already halfway there. He slipped me a warning before I met with that informant, a whole fucking file on us. His way of looking out, I guess."

I nod, trying not to question this further, because I know Ryder can't handle an interrogation or even some light scolding on my part. For now, I'll just take it as a good sign and move on. And it seems, I'm not the only one with that plan as no one else speaks on the topic.

We lay out the best plan we can. Hours of breaking it down, picking it apart, and putting it back together. Every angle covered. Every outcome considered. And when it's done, I sit back and look at it—the most elaborate plan we've ever put together. A setup so seamless it keeps our hands mostly clean, keeps us out of the fight for the most part. It's something I've learned from my failures with Nico.

I should feel relieved. Maybe even satisfied. Instead, my blood is still running hot, my mind still stuck on the way Tori handled Lila, the fire in her eyes, the vicious, unrelenting strength in her. I knew she had it in her, but seeing it? That was something else.

Something intoxicating.

Thorne helps Ryder upstairs, his arm slung over his shoulder as he mutters something low to him, reassuring. Tori stands in the middle of the living room, watching them go, her body still tense from the weight of the night, from everything she's learned...from what she's done.

I move behind her, letting my fingers brush over her shoulder as I sweep her hair aside, exposing the smooth line of her neck. My lips follow immediately after, pressing against her pulse point, feeling the wild thrum beneath my mouth.

"You're incredible," I murmur against her skin.

She lets out a slow breath, but she doesn't pull away. Instead, she leans into me, just slightly, like she needs the contact as much as I do.

"I mean it," I continue, my hand trailing lower, resting against her waist, pulling her back into me. "Watching you handle Lila? Watching you take control like that?" I exhale a quiet laugh. "Fucking mesmerizing."

She tilts her head, just enough to let me deepen my kiss along the curve of her throat. My hand slides over her stomach, then up, palming her breast through her shirt.

Soft. Fuller than usual. A thought flickers at the back of my mind, but then she exhales sharply, her body reacting to my touch, and I lose the thread of whatever it was.

A sharp inhale from across the room reminds me we aren't alone.

Gabe is still leaning against the wall, watching. His eyes dart to the floor, then back up again like he's debating saying something.

I brush my nose against Tori's skin, squeezing her breast just enough to make her gasp. "You gonna stand there all night?" I ask, my voice slow, taunting.

Gabe clears his throat, shifting uncomfortably. "I, uh—I should go check on Mia, make sure she hasn't said anything to Diablo or Cass."

I don't respond. I don't need to. I'm too busy watching him turn on his heel and practically bolt from the room, and the satisfaction that comes with it is instant.

Tori lets out a breathy laugh. "Did you do that on purpose?"

"Maybe." I roll her nipple between my fingers, relishing the way she trembles against me. "Not my fault he doesn't know when to make himself scarce."

She twists in my hold, looking up at me with dark, hooded eyes. "And what exactly do you plan on doing now that he's gone?"

I let my hands roam, sliding under her shirt, feeling the warm, soft curves of her body. My fingers brush over her bare skin, heat spreading where I touch. Her breath hitches as I trace a slow line up her spine, dragging my fingertips just lightly enough to make her shiver.

"Whatever the hell I want."

She swallows hard, eyes locked on mine, pupils blown wide with want. "Yeah?"

"Yeah."

I grip her hips, turning her around to face me fully. She stumbles a bit, but I steady her, pressing her against the edge of the couch, trapping her between it and me. My mouth is on hers before she can say another word, swallowing the small gasp that slips from her lips as I take exactly what I want.

She tastes like adrenaline and something sweeter, something distinctly her. I press closer, deepening the kiss, my hands gripping her waist, her ribs, her back, like I need to feel all of her at once. Her fingers dig into my shoulders, nails scraping against my skin, and fuck, if that doesn't make me even hungrier for her.

I break the kiss just long enough to murmur against her lips, "Tell me you want this."

Her breath is ragged, her body already moving with mine. "You know I do."

That's all I need.

I grab the hem of her shirt and pull it over her head, tossing it aside. My eyes roam over her bare skin, the soft curves that are all mine to touch, to take. My hands follow, palming her breasts, thumbs brushing over her already pebbled nipples.

"Fuck," I breathe, voice rough. "You feel so damn good."

She arches into my touch, biting her lip, her eyes dark with need.

"Then don't stop."

I don't plan to.

I trail my mouth lower, kissing down her jaw, her neck, and further. I take my time, savoring the heat of her skin under my tongue, the way she gasps and writhes beneath my touch. Her fingers tangle in my hair, urging me on, and I let her guide me—just a little—before I take control again, keeping her pinned against the couch as I nip at the delicate skin of her collarbone.

"You drive me fucking crazy," I murmur, my hands sliding down to grip her hips. "You know that?"

She exhales a breathless laugh, but it turns into a moan as I drag my teeth over her sensitive skin. "I should be telling you that."

I press a knee between her legs, spreading them enough to make her squirm against me. "You like it when I take my time?"

She swallows hard. "Blaze—"

I silence whatever she's about to say with another deep, consuming kiss, one that makes her body go lax against me, giving in completely.

This? This is mine. Every breathless sound, every desperate movement, every inch of her. And tonight, I plan on taking my time proving that to her.

Tori's body trembles beneath me, her breath catching as I slide my hands down her sides, slow, possessive. I don't rush. I want her to feel every inch of this, to know she's mine, completely and utterly.

The weight of everything we've done, everything we've endured, hangs between us like a taut wire. And she wants this—needs this—to snap the tension, to lose herself in something else, something that isn't betrayal or bloodshed. Something to make her forget the misplaced guilt she's feeling for Ryder.

She whimpers as I bite down on her neck, dragging my tongue over the mark immediately after, soothing it before doing it again. Her hands claw at my shoulders, desperate, restless. I love her like this—wild, insatiable, pushing back against me for more. I always give it to her, but tonight, I'm taking, too.

"Blaze," she gasps, arching into me, her fingers curling into my hair. "I need more."

A dark chuckle rumbles from my chest. "That ready for me, huh?"

Her only answer is another breathy moan as she presses against me.

My grip tightens around her waist, and I flip her effortlessly, pressing her face down against the couch. She barely has time to suck in a breath before I'm pinning her there, my mouth at her ear, my body covering hers.

"Like this?" My voice is low, dangerous, the edge of command lacing it.

She shudders, her breath coming out in a desperate little whine. "More."

I fist a handful of her hair, tilting her head to see the side of her face. The need in her eyes is enough to wreck me. I swear I could make her come from my voice alone if I wanted to.

"You need this, don't you?" I murmur, dragging my free hand down her back, feeling the tension rippling through her muscles. "You want me to take you so hard you forget everything else?"

She nods frantically, a whimper slipping past her lips.

"Use your words, Tori."

"I need it," she breathes, barely getting the words out before I bite down on her shoulder, eliciting another moan. "I need you, Blaze."

That's all I need to hear, Doll.

I release her hair and let my hands roam, sliding the rest of her clothes off—admiring her bent over the arm of the couch like this for me—before I shimmy my pants down enough to release my throbbing cock. My fingers dig into her skin as I grip her hips and pull her back against me, placing her exactly where I want her. She gasps, shuddering as I press a hand against her spine, keeping her in place, making sure she knows she isn't going anywhere until I say so.

I grind against her slowly, making her feel everything, teasing her, dragging this moment out until she's shaking with need. I want her desperate, ruined by the time I give her what she wants.

She cries out in frustration, pushing back against me, nails digging into the cushions. "Blaze, please—"

I chuckle darkly, pressing my lips to the back of her neck. "I love hearing you beg."

"Dammit, Blaze," she gasps. "Just—just give me more."

I lean over her, my lips right against her ear. "You're already mine, Tori. But tonight? I want you to scream it."

She moans at that, and I feel her body give in completely—no more teasing, no more barriers. Just us, lost in each other, drowning in the fire that only we can make burn this hot.

I move lower, dragging my tongue along the line of her spine, tracing every dip, every curve that belongs to me. She's trembling beneath me, breathless and undone. My hands grip her thighs, squeezing, spreading her open for me, and she gasps at the possessive hold.

"You take everything I give you," I murmur against her skin, voice rough, threaded with restraint I'm close to losing. "Always so fucking perfect for me."

She whimpers, pressing herself against me, chasing every touch, every bit of friction. "I want all of it."

I nip at the sensitive spot where her neck meets her shoulder. "You think you can handle all of it?"

She nods frantically, her hands clawing at the fabric beneath her. "I can."

I whisper dark promises that send a full-body shudder through her. "Then let me wreck you, Doll."

And I do.

I slide into her, inch by inch, encircled by her warmth. It's almost too much, too overwhelming, but I manage to hold myself together. I take my time, dragging her into sensation so deep she can't breathe, can't think of anything but the way I'm consuming her, the way she's unraveling beneath me.

My name spills from her lips like a plea, like a prayer, and I give her everything she asks for—harder, deeper, more, more, more—until she's shaking, until she's clawing at me, until she's gone, lost to the overwhelming force of us.

I don't stop.

I push her past that edge again and again, watching as she falls apart only to pull her back together, only to do it all over again. My control is razor-thin, held together only by the need to watch her come undone for me.

Her cries grow louder, needier, the tension building so sharp I can feel it radiating off her in waves. I can't take my eyes off her—her body, her face, the raw desperation in her as she looks back at me, silently begging me to end her, to give her that last, final push.

I wrap my hand around her hair, tugging it so that she has to hold my gaze from the corner of her eye. "Let go."

And she does.

She shatters against me, a broken, beautiful mess, and I follow right after, growling her name as I bury myself deep, as I claim every last piece of her all over again.

For a long moment, neither of us moves, our bodies still tangled, breath ragged, nothing but the sound of us.

Then she exhales a soft, contented sigh and shifts onto her side, resting her forehead against my chest as I turn to face her, lying beside her. I tighten my arms around her, holding her close, letting the silence settle around us like a blanket.

Her fingers trail lazily down my spine. She smirks, but there's something else in her expression—something softer, more vulnerable. I brush my fingers over her jaw, tilting her face up to mine. "You okay?"

She nods, but her voice is quieter when she speaks. "I needed that."

I study her, knowing exactly what she means. I felt it, too. This wasn't just sex. It was something else, something deeper. A way to take back control. A way to remind ourselves that after everything, we're still here. We still have each other.

I press my lips to her forehead, lingering there. "Yeah. Me too."

21: GABE

Years. I've lived in the dark for years, convinced the light wasn't meant for me anymore. That I'd accepted my role, accepted that some people aren't meant to feel warmth again. But then Diablo said, *'Guard my daughter,'* and in walked a 5'5" ball of attitude with a fire so bright, I had to shield my damn eyes.

Tori was nothing like I expected her to be. She had sharp edges but a soft heart, a walking contradiction that made no damn sense and yet—somehow—fit perfectly. She had no reason to, but she stuck up for me. Called off her wolves—Blaze, Ryder, and Thorne—even though she wasn't sure if I was a threat. She teased me, taunted me, made me laugh when I'd long forgotten how...*even if most of the laughter was internal.* She cracked something open inside me.

She reminded me what warmth felt like.

The military changed me. As it does everyone. But coming back? That was worse. I had siblings to take care of, and I knew damn well I wasn't the kind of man who should be raising kids with the amount of baggage I was hauling. So I left them with someone better. Someone not like me. And I thought that meant I was done feeling, that I'd buried whatever softness was left.

Then she walked in, and I don't plan to let go of that light again.

Tori isn't mine. She never was. And after today, I'm almost sure I won't even be allowed near her. She's taking down her father, and I'll be right beside her, making sure it happens. I'll be whatever she needs—her right-hand man, her stepping stone, her weapon. If she needs to walk over me to get to her goal, I'll lay myself flat on the floor.

I watch her now, seated at the table across from her father, not an inch of fear in her. She doesn't fidget. Doesn't blink. Her shoulders square up, her chin high—she looks like she already owns the damn room.

Diablo doesn't see it. He sees his *daughter*, the one he thinks he can still mold into the perfect heir. He has no clue he's already lost.

The door opens, and Juan walks in. His usual confidence is toned down, just a fraction, but I catch it. He knows what's about to happen. We both do. Our eyes meet, and he tilts his head subtly—a question, a hesitation.

I give a slow nod. *We're good. For now.*

The conversation swirls around us, sharp words laced with polite edges, business disguised as civility. Diablo thinks he's maneuvering the board, thinks he's still holding the reins. Cassandra sits off to the side, swirling her drink like she's a cat holding a mouse, completely blind to the knife at her back.

Tori shifts—just a flick of her fingers, so subtle. But I see it. I always do.

That's my cue.

I lean toward Juan, voice low. "Let's see who loses their cool first."

He exhales through his nose, almost amused, then nods.

Let's get this show on the road.

The meeting starts slow, the way all power plays do. Diablo speaks first, voice smooth and even, like he hasn't spent years shaping his empire through blood and betrayal. I keep my expression blank, my posture relaxed, but my mind is tracking every detail. Every flicker of movement, every stray glance exchanged between the people at this table.

Juan settles into his seat. He knows the pieces are moving. Knows that this ship is about to go down, and if he isn't careful, he might go down with it.

Tori, though—Tori looks completely at ease. Like she's playing a game she's already won. She doesn't rush to fill the silence, doesn't shift under her father's scrutiny.

"You've been adjusting well," he says, watching her like she's an unpredictable animal. "I knew you had it in you."

Tori cocks her head, a flicker of amusement in her eyes. "You knew?" She leans forward, resting her arms on the table. "Funny. I didn't really get that notion when you asked Mia, Lila, and Eve to work for you."

The air between them tightens, like a rope being pulled at both ends. Diablo doesn't react right away, and that's how I know she's rattled him. He expected her to resist, but he didn't expect her to be so damn confident while doing it.

Juan shifts beside me, just enough that I notice, his fingers tapping out a slow rhythm on the table. He's waiting for the right moment to interject.

I don't move, don't speak. This part isn't mine to play. I'm just watching, listening, like I always do. And I know the second Diablo starts talking again, the ground beneath him is going to crack.

"I wanted to make sure you weren't distracted," he finally says, voice quieter now, like he's trying to remind her. Trying to claim credit for the woman in front of him. "I wanted to give you the chance to see what your *men* are really like."

Tori leans forward towards Diablo, eyes sharp and unyielding as she stares him down. "No. You tried to break us. We did fine in *spite* of it."

Diablo exhales through his nose, a quiet laugh, but his fingers curl noticeably against the table. Frustration. He's losing control of this conversation, and he hates it.

She leans back, crossing one leg over the other, her tone shifting into something more casual, almost mocking. "In fact, what's going on with Lila?"

Diablo's fingers tense, just barely. "What about her?"

Tori shrugs. "I heard she got hurt, didn't she? Considering she's *your* employee, I'd think you'd be more concerned."

His gaze sharpens, flicking between her and me, like he's trying to decide whether this is bait. He settles for a half-truth. "She's no longer my problem. I have no use for failures."

Tori hums, sounding as indifferent to his answer as she can, considering she's seething inside. "Good to know."

That's it. That's all she gives him, but it's enough. Diablo may be a bastard, but he's not stupid. He knows it was her, that it was Blaze and Thorne who left Lila on his doorstep. They both know what they're really saying, but neither of them is willing to admit it to the other.

Juan clears his throat, shifting the energy. "Should we get to business?" he says, voice neutral.

Diablo takes the out, leaning back in his chair. "Of course." He gestures toward Cassandra, who's been quiet up until now. "We have pressing matters."

Cassandra sits up straighter, eyes flicking briefly to Tori before she starts speaking. She's good at this. At looking composed. But I see the tension in her shoulders. The way she avoids looking at Diablo for too long. She's nervous.

She should be.

Tori doesn't even glance in her direction. She keeps her focus on her father, watching him like she's memorizing every breath he takes. Like she's waiting for him to make his final mistake.

She's so powerful.

Cassandra clears her throat. "There have been...issues," she begins, her voice crisp but laced with hesitation. "Certain shipments have been delayed. Others have been intercepted. We need to discuss how to secure our supply lines."

Diablo barely spares her a glance, his focus still locked on Tori. "You should have handled that already. Why are you bringing it to me?"

Cassandra falters, barely, but I catch it. "Because whoever's interfering knows our routes. Our operations. We must have a leak."

Juan leans forward, interest piqued. "And you think it's someone inside?"

"I don't think. I know," Cassandra replies, her tone more certain now, her eyes continuing to shift toward Tori. "This isn't just random attacks. Someone is feeding them information."

Tori finally moves, reclining in her chair, her expression unreadable. "Then maybe you should be asking yourself who has the most to gain from those attacks."

Cassandra stiffens, but she doesn't flinch. She's smarter than that. "Funny. That's exactly what I've been asking myself." Her gaze drifts over to me, then flickers to Juan before settling on Tori. "Someone's been conveniently in the right places at the right times. The kind of access only someone with *inside* knowledge would have."

I see what she's doing. Twisting it. Trying to make the pieces fit a different puzzle.

Diablo finally turns to fully look at her, his patience wearing thin. "If there's a traitor, you find them. You handle them. That's why I keep you around."

For the first time, a flicker of panic crosses Cassandra's face. "I will. But I need resources—"

"No excuses," Diablo cuts her off. "I want names. Soon. Or I'll assume you're protecting someone."

Tori angles her head to the right, studying Cassandra the way a cat watches a mouse right before the pounce. "You sound nervous, Cassandra. Almost like you're trying to shift blame."

Cassandra lets out a tight laugh, but it doesn't reach her eyes. "I just find it interesting that things started falling apart right around the time you and your men showed up."

Diablo's eyes narrow. He's listening now.

Tori smiles, slow and sharp. "Then you're not as smart as I gave you credit for."

The tension is suffocating. Cassandra nods, but I can tell she's already running through every way out she has left.

Silence stretches across the room like a rubber band pulled too tight, waiting for someone to let go and snap it across the wrist. Cassandra keeps her face still, carefully blank, but I see the tension in her shoulders, the flicker of calculation in her eyes. She's cornered, and she knows it.

Which means she's about to do something really fucking stupid.

Diablo exhales slowly, fingers drumming against the armrest like he's contemplating a firing squad.

That's not an exaggeration. I've only seen him go this quiet right before wiping a man off the map.

"Don't imply, Cass," Diablo finally says, smooth as silk but sharp as a blade. "I don't care to hear your speculations. Find the leak. End it."

Cassandra nods, but there's something tight in her expression, like she's swallowing glass. She knows the margin for error just shrunk to nothing.

Tori, on the other hand, looks like she's enjoying herself. Her fingers tap a slow rhythm against the table, not rushed, not nervous—just...waiting. I recognize the patience of someone who already knows how the game ends. She doesn't even spare Cassandra a glance, just keeps her focus on Diablo like she's waiting for him to step into a trap he hasn't noticed yet.

I always thought power belonged to the biggest, baddest bastard in the room. The one who could break a man's jaw with a glance, who commanded respect by sheer brutality. But watching Tori, I realize I had it wrong. Power is control. Owning the space without lifting a finger. Making every other person in the room adjust to your presence instead of the other way around.

And right now? This room belongs to her.

Juan leans back beside me, grinning like he's watching a car wreck in slow motion. He hasn't officially chosen a side yet, but he's been playing this game long enough to know which horse to bet on. And it's sure as hell not Cassandra.

Tori, ever the patient predator, shifts gears. "I have an idea."

Diablo raises a brow, intrigued despite himself. "Do you, now?"

"Cassandra should handle the next shipment personally," Tori suggests, leaning back like she's just tossing out an idea instead of setting the stage for a masterstroke. "It would be the best way for her to find the leak. She can see at exactly what point it goes wrong and who she gave that information to."

Cassandra stiffens. Not enough for the untrained eye to catch, but I see it. Juan sees it too.

She knows we're up to something, but before she can figure it out, it'll be too late.

Diablo takes a moment, his breathing even, his fingers pressed together as he contemplates Tori's suggestion.

"Juan will join her in overseeing the shipment," he finally responds, gesturing for Juan to join Cass and leave.

It's a simple order, but it derails our plans. Everything now rests on Tori and her ability to sway Juan to her side. If she can get him to back her one-hundred percent, then we have this in the bag.

Juan stands, scratching the floor with the back legs of his chair as he pushes away from the table in a huff. It's clear he's unhappy about the situation, but I'm not sure if it's toward Tori who suggested the plan or toward Cassandra who's causing the problem.

"We'll meet again tomorrow. I expect to see results."

With that, Cassandra follows Juan out, the two of them bickering as they exit the room. Their voices muffle when the door clicks shut behind them, and my attention snaps right back to the man I'm meant to be loyal to.

"Now, mija. We need to talk." His voice drops a chilling octave, and my body tenses instinctively, ready to jump into action if needed. "I heard what happened between Mia and Thorne. It's to be expected, given the kind of relationship you have. You can't expect a man to be faithful when you're not giving him the same courtesy."

Tori bristles under his comment, and part of me wants to snap at him for her. Neither of us do, though. It's obvious he's trying to get a rise out of her. With a long exhale, Tori's fists loosen under the table.

"Funny you should say that." She tilts her head ever so slightly. "We're actually going to get married."

I have to restrain my laughter, biting my cheek to keep from snickering. Diablo's face is hard to describe, but it's as if someone stuck a cold rod up his ass and it got stuck to his skin on the way in.

"A second wedding, Victoria? Will that be two failed marriages then?"

This. This comment is what sets Tori off. Her chair falls to floor behind her, thrown down from the force as she stands so quickly she's almost a blur. Her hands grip the edge of the table so tight you can hear the wood creak in protest beneath her palms.

"Don't you dare throw that in my face. A marriage under duress to a kidnapper does not count and you know it." Tori's eyes may be dark, but right now they're shining bright with the fire burning inside her. "Let me make one thing clear, *Father:* Thorne, Blaze, and Ryder aren't going anywhere. They're not unfaithful despite the many tricks you throw their way. They are *mine*. And if you keep trying to take them, you'll regret it."

Her shoulders rise and fall in uneven breaths as she struggles to calm herself. Yet there's a power radiating off her that could draw a moth to a flame.

"Now, if that's all, Gabe and I will be leaving. I need to go check on those guys you hate so much." She pushes herself off the table, standing so straight she could pass for being an inch taller than she normally is. Her hand is on the doorknob when she turns to look at Diablo one last time. "Oh, and Mia, Eve, and Lila are officially fired. If I see any of them, you'll be short an employee."

The threat is obvious, and the fury in her eyes tells me she means it. She'll kill them.

Diablo says nothing, his fingers twitching at his sides as he watches Tori. It's not often Diablo does not get the last word in, but it's clear he's too angry to think straight. Rather than say something stupid, he bites his tongue.

I hurry after Tori, closing the door on Diablo in a way that feels all too permanent. *Sorry, sir, but I'm following your daughter now.*

"Are you really marrying Thorne?" I whisper as I catch up, matching her stride toward the front door.

"No. Yes. Maybe. I don't fucking know." She's huffing, her anger still high as her Converse hit the earth like they're trying to tear it apart with each stomp.

"That clears that up." I shake my head, opening the door to the bright afternoon sun.

She freezes, eyes wide and on me. "Did you—" she pauses, finger pointed at me. "Did you just crack a joke?"

I smirk at her as I take the first step out, leading us to the car.

"Oh my God. I'm rubbing off on you, aren't I?" She laughs, smiling so proudly as she follows closely behind.

"Sure. You can tell yourself that." I pat her on the head before opening the door and gesturing her into her seat.

"Oh, I definitely will."

Her smile is wide, her anger faded, and my job done.

I know Tori can never be mine, not in the way I really want her, but she can still be the light in my darkness. I will keep her safe. I will keep her protected. I will keep her smiling, even if I can't have her.

I walk around the car and take my place behind the wheel, turning the ignition with a silent hum. "Okay, step one complete, Killer Queen. Now, on to step two. Ready?"

"As I'll ever be. But we need to work on your nicknames," she laughs, shaking her head at me as I start to drive us to the estate.

"It's not any worse than KitKat."

Her laughter rings in my ear, and I swear that with each giggle, she erases a little piece of the horrors I've lived through.

"I'll have you know I've grown fond of KitKat. But never tell Ryder that."

"My lips are sealed."

The rest of the ride is a mixture of her singing along to her crazy music or her taking a jab at me to get me to crack another joke or say another witty comment. I think she's made it her mission to hear me laugh hard, and I'm sure she'll soon succeed.

I'll love you from a distance, Tori. And if these three ever fuck up, I won't give them a chance to make it up to you.

I'll take you away.

22: RYDER

I adjust my collar as we pull into Juan's driveway, rolling my shoulders, hating the way my skin still feels wrong, like Lila left something on me I can't scrub off. I need to burn this fucking suit. I need to burn the memory of that night straight out of my head.

But I can't.

I stare out the window, drumming my fingers on my thigh. I should be thinking about Juan, about what we need to say to bring him over to our side. Instead, all I can hear is Lila's voice whispering bullshit in my ear, her nails dragging down my chest like she has some kind of claim to me. My jaw clenches so hard it clicks.

Control.

I need to take it back. Over myself, over my life, over what happens next. And that starts with making sure Diablo burns for every last thing he's done.

Blaze is driving, his grip tight on the wheel, his whole body radiating that tension I know has his asshole puckered. Thorne sits beside him, arms crossed, too quiet, too in his head. Meanwhile, I'm in the back, trying to pretend I'm fine.

Everything is just peachy over here.

"So, what's the plan if Juan doesn't go for it?" I ask, because talking is better than thinking.

"He will," Blaze says without looking at me.

Some optimism.

Thorne glances at me in the rearview mirror, eyes sharp, staring right into my fucking soul. *How the hell does he do that?* "But if he doesn't, we improvise."

I huff a laugh, leaning back. "Improvise. Right. Because that always goes well."

Blaze shoots me a look like he's considering whether murder is still illegal if it's between friends. I hold my hands up in mock surrender. "Kidding. Mostly."

Truth is, Juan isn't the problem. The guy's been playing the long game, waiting for his moment to cut the leash Diablo keeps wrapped around his throat. Or so Gabe tells us. We just have to convince Juan that moment is now. That we're his best shot.

And if he says no? Well. I've always wanted to know what a mutiny looks like up close.

Long live KitKat!

We pull up to the house, and Juan is already waiting outside, his arms crossed, expression stoic.

Such a warm welcome, Juany.

I step out first, adjusting my cuffs like this just an afternoon chat amongst colleagues. "Juan, my favorite morally gray businessman."

Juan's lips twitch, but he doesn't smile. "You have something to say, Ryder, or did you come just because you missed me?"

"Me? Miss you?" I shake my head as I point between us. "In your dreams, Juany. I don't roll that way." I wink at him which only gets me an exasperated eye roll.

Eh. He can pretend, but I know he loves it.

The atmosphere changes as Blaze and Thorne step up beside me. No more jokes. No more bullshit.

Tori should be the one handling this, but she's got bigger things to worry about right now. So it's on us.

On me.

"We're taking Diablo down," I say simply. "And we want you on our side when it happens."

Juan doesn't react. Doesn't flinch. Just tilts his head, studying us like he's trying to figure out if he can really trust us. Or if we're just bullshitting him and this is all one of those diabolical Diablo plans. *Maybe that's why he calls himself Diablo?*

"And what makes you think you can?" he finally asks, voice even.

Blaze steps forward, voice low, measured. "Because we already have everything we need. We can prove Cassandra is the leak. Diablo just needs to see it with his own eyes."

Juan raises a brow. "And after that?"

Thorne smirks, rolling his shoulders like he's been waiting for this. "After that, he'll be too busy cleaning up the mess to notice us coming. And just when he thinks he's regained control—"

"We take it from him," Blaze finishes, his voice dark with finality.

Juan exhales, running a hand over his jaw. "And what happens to his empire?"

"Tori takes over," I say, because there's no other answer. "With your help. With Gabe's. You two can help her run things until she's ready. Having you both would help ease the transition better than having us at her side."

He laughs, shaking his head. "That girl is a wildfire waiting to spread. She's still young. Still reckless. You really think she can do this?"

"She can do it with all of us at her side," Blaze says. "She won't be alone."

Juan studies each of us in turn, weighing, measuring. Then, slowly, he nods. "I want to believe in Tori. But I hope you know this isn't going to be easy."

Relief washes through me, but I don't let it show. Instead, I nod. "Easy? I wouldn't dream of it."

Juan scoffs. "Yeah, knowing you three, you'll make this a million times more difficult than it needs to be."

"Hey! I take offense to that," I joke, crossing my arms with a light pout. "I make things a million times more fun, even if it means complicating them."

"Thank you for proving my point." He shakes his head with disapproval but I see the smirk on his lips.

Already falling for my charms, aren't you, Juany?

Blaze leans in, eyes locked on Juan's. "You've worked under Diablo for years. What's his biggest weakness?"

Juan shakes his head. "His ego. He thinks he's untouchable. You make him feel like he's still in control, and he won't suspect a thing."

Thorne nods. "So we keep him busy with Cassandra's mess, make him believe he's putting his house back in order, and right when he feels secure—"

Blaze's voice drops, lethal. "We show him just how *not* in charge he actually is."

"Would you stop that?!" Thorne snaps at Blaze, rolling his eyes.

"You're stealing his thunder," I add in a lightly scolding manner, holding in my laughter. They both glare at each other for a moment before staring my way casually, and I realize they're putting on a show for me.

What are friends for if not to help you forget your traumatic life events?

"That's my job," I add, draping my arm over Thorne and holding him close.

"Yeah, yeah." Thorne rolls his eyes, but his arm comes up over mine as he pulls me into his side. "Don't worry, Ryder. You're definitely center stage."

"And you want me to put my faith in you all." Juan interjects, breaking the brotherly moment with a shake of his head.

"Don't worry, Juan. You'll be the Daddy. I'll let you ground me, and if you do a good job, I might even let you spank me." I throw a wink his way for dramatics.

Juan goes still, his face morphing into disgust and we all laugh. Juan included.

"Alright, alright. Let's get serious." Juan strokes his stubble thoughtfully. "You're going to need more than just evidence against Cassandra. Diablo's not the type to make a move based on logic alone. He needs to feel like he's personally been wronged. If you can make him feel betrayed, like Cassandra has been playing him for a fool..."

I snap my fingers. "Then he'll gut her himself."

Juan nods. "Exactly."

Blaze's jaw tightens. "We've already put Cassandra in a position where she'll be caught red-handed with this new shipment she's in charge of. Diablo will have no choice but to act."

Thorne cracks his knuckles, his grin all teeth. "We're better prepared for this than you might think."

I hook my arms over Blaze and Thorne's necks and pull them to my chest. "We've got this. No problem."

Juan watches us for a long moment, as if he's studying the four of us. "You're all crazy. But I like it."

Blaze smirks. "Good. Because this is just the beginning. We're going to be working together for years to come."

Juan shakes his head, laughing under his breath. "I'll start pulling the strings on my end. I'll make sure Diablo sees it the way you need him to. But if this goes sideways—"

"It won't," Blaze assures him.

Juan exhales, eyeing us like we're a goddamn hurricane about to rip through everything he knows. "Then let's take Diablo down to hell where he belongs."

Damn fucking straight!

Juan's message comes through just as we're finishing up plans at the estate. My phone vibrates on the table, and when I check it, the message is short and to the point:

Juan: Warehouse. Now. She's here.

That's all we need. Within minutes, we're in the car, speeding through the city under the cover of night. The ride is quiet, tense. No music, no joking around. Just the hum of the engine and the weight of what's about to go down.

Thorne's driving, Gabe at his side and Tori's sandwiched between Blaze and me in the backseat, arms crossed, foot bouncing like she's trying to shake off some invisible weight. As we near the warehouse, she wrinkles her nose and mutters, "Jesus Christ, it smells like rotting asshole in here. What the fuck are they storing? Corpses?"

Blaze doesn't look away from the windshield. "Wouldn't put it past them."

She wrinkles her nose like she can't bear to take another breath. The smell isn't exactly pleasant, but then again, maybe I'm not smelling what she is, judging by her dramatic reaction.

We park down the street, slipping into the shadows like we're trying to be ghosts, undetected until we spot Juan. He stands tall and unbothered, like the entire plan unfolding isn't even a blip on his radar.

Probably because he's not the one doing the hard part.

He spots us, tilting his head in a silent command for us to go around the side, pushing us along until we're huddled down looking like kids sneaking around at school.

"Are you sure this is going to go the way you planned?" he asks, his brows furrowed in that serious way of his that says he's not buying it.

Oh, ye of little faith.

"Of course it is, bud." I clap his back, the gesture friendly enough, but it only seems to annoy him more.

"We've got it handled, trust me," Gabe adds, his voice smooth and confident, instantly putting some ease into Juan's tense posture.

Juan nods, his focus shifting solely to Gabe now, his attention sharp. "She told me she had this covered, rushed me home saying she'd handle the rest. So I'm sure she's messing with the crates by now."

"Got it. Leave the rest to us. We'll send you the video once it's done," Gabe reassures him, clasping hands with the big man in a way that feels like some kind of pact we're not meant to understand.

Juan leads us to a side entrance he left open for us, and we slide right on in. Inside, the air is stale, thick with the scent of oil, metal, and something that has Tori gagging.

"Okay, I take it back. Whatever that smell is, it's demonic," she whispers, shuddering. "That is the scent of actual death. I'm convinced."

"Noted. I'll get you a candle," I whisper back. "Maybe 'Warehouse Rot'—limited edition."

She shoots me a look but doesn't say anything.

We crouch low behind a stack of crates, peering through the gaps. Cassandra is at the far end, shifting boxes, her phone tucked between her ear and shoulder as she barks orders to someone.

"Don't worry. I have it handled. Just do what I said, and get me what I asked for."

Bingo.

Blaze taps his phone, recording. Thorne shifts beside me, eyes locked on the scene like he's committing every detail to memory. Tori watches too, her jaw tight, her fingers twitching like she's itching to end this herself.

I get it. I want to end her too.

Cass is the reason Mia and Lila did what they did.

My foot inches forward, wanting to march right out and punch the bitch myself, but then, right on cue, Juan's message pops up.

Juan: Got it. Sending to Diablo now.

As we wait, we listen in to her conversation, hoping to hear something about her plans. I'm almost certain that she knows this is a set up, and she's walked into it a little too easily.

Somethings gotta be up.

"I need it now if this is going to work," she argues into her phone, her hands deep inside a crate. Part of me wants to run behind her and push her in, closing the lid tight and shipping her off. "Don't give me that shit! Find a way!"

We watch her carefully as she closes the crate and then abruptly hangs up the phone. She taps something onto her screen and then pockets the device with a look that has my skin crawling.

She's confident.

No.

She's smug.

We barely have time to get comfortable before we hear the roar of an engine outside, headlights slicing through the dark. The ground rumbles as an SUV skids to a stop, tires screeching against pavement. Doors slam open, and a handful of men, including Juan, flood the entrance like a goddamn execution squad.

Diablo doesn't just send men. He comes himself.

"Showtime," I mutter, shifting my stance.

Cassandra hears the engine, too. Her head snaps up, eyes darting to the doors just as they swing open. Diablo strides in like the goddamn Grim Reaper, his men fanning out behind him.

For a second, no one moves. No one speaks. Then Cassandra lifts her chin, and I swear to God, she *smiles*.

"This should be good," Tori whispers, voice dripping with sarcasm.

Blaze elbows her lightly, but even he's watching with sharp interest.

Diablo steps forward like he owns the place, the whole damn room. "Tell me, Cassandra," he says, voice deceptively smooth. "How long have you been betraying me?"

Cassandra doesn't even blink. She lifts her chin, maintaining that calm, innocent expression, her hands folded neatly in front of her. "Betraying you?" she repeats, her voice smooth, almost confused, like she's genuinely trying to comprehend what he's implying. "I've done nothing but follow orders, Diablo. You know that."

She pauses, letting her words hang in the air for a moment. "But there are others, others who would rather see you fall. You've been too busy with your daughter to notice, but I've been trying to find the real threats. The ones working behind your back."

I can't help but roll my eyes. She's laying it on thick, playing the innocent victim to the hilt.

Diablo steps closer, his men flanking around him but keeping their distance, allowing him to press Cassandra with his intimidating aura. He narrows his dark eyes before letting out a singular laugh full of scrutiny.

"You take me for a fool, Cass?"

"No, of course not!" She taps her phone screen and holds it out to Diablo. "I have footage of Thorne opening one of the crates last night. I thought you'd want to see it, since it's clear no one else is being honest with you."

Diablo takes the phone from her, his expression guarded as he watches the video. I don't need to watch it to know what's on it. It's probably doctored so that Diablo sees exactly what she wants him to see. Which is apparently Thorne at a warehouse opening some crates.

Not hard to find footage like that, seeing as his task with Mia mainly consisted of checking the crates—which means opening them.

This bitch is worse than a roach.

Blaze shifts beside me, barely containing his frustration. We're all ready to jump in, but the plan was for us to come out of this with our hands generally clean. If we step out now, I'm not sure we'll be able to keep that objective. And I know more than anyone how badly we want to keep Tori from having to kill someone else, especially not someone she thought was a friend, or even her own father.

Man, we wanted Cass and Diablo to take each other out. What utter bullshit is this?

Diablo watches the footage for a moment, the silence in the room stretching so thick I can almost hear his mind working. His lips tighten into a thin line, and I can see the wheels turning. He's thinking—and that's where we need to be careful.

"Thorne," Diablo murmurs, his voice low. "You expect me to believe he was the one to mess with my shipments when this problem began before he even arrived?"

"Well, no," Cassandra says, her tone still calm, too calm. She doesn't even flinch under Diablo's scrutiny. "Didn't Juan help Tori and her guys with the whole Nico fiasco? Wouldn't it make sense that they formed a bond, or even a plan back then? That they'd join forces to take down—" She pauses for effect, letting the words hang in the air, "—to take your kingdom over?"

I don't like where this is going.

Juan's voice cuts through the air, furious and sharp. "Bullshit!" he spits, stepping forward so abruptly that his anger almost radiates off him like heat from a furnace. "My leg was shot. I was on the mend for at least a month. *Jefe*, you know that! I was with you for most of it!"

Diablo's head snaps toward Juan, his eyes narrowing dangerously as if deciding whether or not to believe the man he's called his right hand for so long.

Cassandra doesn't even blink, though. She keeps her calm, keeping the pressure measured. "You were with him, sure, but how much of that time was really spent watching?"

Juan's face flushes with anger, his hand reaching for the grip of his gun, but Diablo holds up a hand to stop him, his gaze never leaving Cassandra.

"What exactly are you saying?" Diablo's voice lowers, his tone now all business, cold and calculated. "You're telling me Juan, my most trusted man, is in on this with them?"

Cassandra doesn't back down. "I'm not saying Juan's *in* on it, Diablo. I'm saying he *could* be. I'm saying he's been too close, too involved with Tori and the others to be clean. All the pieces are here, Diablo. It's all starting to come together."

I almost choke on the disgust rising in my throat. She's feeding him lies—she's twisting everything to make it sound like we're the enemy. But what makes it worse is that Diablo is listening. He's actually considering it.

I glance at the others, and I can tell they're feeling the same thing. We can't let this drag on any longer. It's time to step out. Time to put an end to this once and for all.

Tori—*as usual*—doesn't hesitate, doesn't even wait a second longer. She's stepping out, shoulders squared, head held high, and fists of fury at her sides. She doesn't even look at us as she crosses the room, making her presence known.

"The only thing that's coming together is your downfall, *Cass*," Tori's voice drops with venom as she says her name—feelings of rage, of betrayal chiming in. "You really think you can play everyone, twist the truth like this? You're not as clever as you think you are."

Cassandra's eyes dart to Tori, and for a fraction of a second, I see the panic flash in her eyes before she masks it again. She knows she's been caught, but she's not ready to admit it.

"You—" Cassandra starts, but she's cut off by Tori before she can even start.

Tori's voice rings out, loud and cutting, as her gaze locks onto Cassandra with the fury of someone who's finally had enough. "You act like you're some amazing female in power that I should follow and listen to, but you're no better than the rats scurrying along this warehouse," she spits, her words sharp, her breath coming in quick bursts. "I thought I could trust you when really you were plotting, ready to stab me in the back at your earliest convenience. *Fuck you, Cass!*" Her voice is trembling, not from fear, but from the raw anger that she can't contain anymore.

Gabe places himself between Diablo and Tori, covering her back to keep her safe. She seems to have forgotten the biggest threat isn't Cass, but her father. "You have the footage of Cassandra messing with the crates tonight. There's no denying that, so why are you even entertaining the notion that it could be us?" His voice is leveled, his gaze hard. He's not about to let Diablo buy Cassandra's lies.

"He's right," he says, the words forced but necessary. "Open the crate and see for yourself. There's nothing to hide."

The tension in the room rises, every eye turning toward Diablo as his men move to the crate. Cassandra's eyes widen, but she doesn't speak, her lips pressing together in a tight line.

The guard opens the crate carefully, and the lid creaks as it's pulled back. Diablo steps forward, his eyes locked on the contents, watching closely for any signs of tampering.

The seconds stretch into eternity as the lid fully opens. Silence settles over the room like a heavy weight.

Inside? Just the usual. Nothing out of place. No sign of tampering, no hidden surprises. It's exactly what it should be.

This bitch is too good.

Like I want to commend her, but also just kind of stab her in the temple.

Diablo stands there, staring into the crate, his expression unreadable. His eyes flickering toward Cassandra, who straightens up, her shoulders back, her lips curling into that smug little smile of hers.

"See?" she says, voice sweet, like she's won. "Told you it isn't me who's messing with your shipments."

I almost lose it right then and there. But it's Tori who moves first, and the explosion of anger that follows is impossible to ignore.

Without warning, Tori strides forward, her face twisted in pure fury. Her voice rings out, cutting through the tense silence like a whip. "The only thing that's not messed with here is your damn face, Cass."

Cassandra's smug expression doesn't falter, but there's a glint of something darker in her eyes now. She's still playing the game, but I can see the flicker of doubt beneath the surface, like she knows she's losing balance on the tight rope she's walking.

Tori doesn't wait. She's done with pretending, done with keeping her cool. "You think you've been so clever, huh? Playing the hero, acting like you're so innocent, but all you've been doing is sinking your claws into whoever you can." Her voice rises with each word, the anger pouring out in waves. "You used Lila to drug Ryder, you used Mia to get her to kiss Thorne, to get under my skin. You told them you're their mentor, but abandoned them the moment their usefulness was done."

The words spill out, one after another, harsh and cutting, each one a blow aimed straight at Cassandra's carefully crafted persona. Tori steps closer, her hands clenched at her sides, barely able to contain herself. "You've been playing everyone, Cassandra, everyone, and now you're going to pay for it."

Tori moves faster than I can blink. One moment, she's standing there, furious but controlled, and the next, her fist is colliding with Cassandra's face with a sickening crack. The punch is clean, brutal, and Cassandra's body hits the ground hard. She staggers, her hands scrambling to catch herself, but it's too late. She crumples to the floor, completely unprepared for the sheer force behind the blow.

Cassandra lies there for a moment, stunned, her breath coming in ragged gasps as her now broken nose gushes blood. Her face is flushed with the pain of the punch, her pride shattered in the wake of the hit. For the first time in this entire ordeal, Cassandra looks vulnerable. For the first time, she looks like someone who's lost.

Tori stands over her, chest heaving, her body still vibrating with the anger that's now been unleashed. She glares down at Cassandra, her eyes filled with a fury that could burn the world down. "You played with the wrong girl, Cass. And deep down, I think you know that."

Cassandra's eyes are wide, her lips trembling as she tries to push herself up, but Tori doesn't give her the chance. Instead, she pushes her down again.

"Stay on the floor where you belong and watch how things are settled." She turns to her father, arms crossed, eyes blazed in fire. "Call the last number on her phone," she demands, her voice unwavering despite the storm of emotions swirling through her.

Diablo raises an eyebrow, but he doesn't question it. He picks up Cassandra's phone, his fingers tapping across the screen, dialing the last number without hesitation. The phone rings once, twice—each second stretching into an eternity. And then, finally, it picks up.

The voice on the other end is low, almost eager. "Did you get it? Did he believe you?"

Diablo's expression darkens, and he holds the phone up, his eyes never leaving Cassandra. "Who is this?" he asks, his voice cold, commanding.

For a moment, the line crackles with silence. Then the line goes dead with a final click.

The room is deathly silent.

Diablo looks down at the phone, his grip tightening. His gaze flicks from the phone back to Cassandra, and then to the rest of us. The cold fury in his eyes is unmistakable.

Cassandra's face is pale now, her composure slipping completely. *The jig is up.*

Tori stands over her, her hands still clenched at her sides, but the anger in her eyes is starting to fade, replaced by something colder. "You're finished," she says quietly, her voice chilling in its finality.

Cassandra's mouth opens, but no words come out. She can't say anything. The lies have crumbled. Diablo's already made his decision. This is the end for her.

Diablo wastes no time, pulling his gun from his waist and aiming it right at Cassandra's head. She staggers, mouth open, words ready to form, but they don't get the chance to leave her mouth as the gun fires. The sound echoes through the warehouse, loud and final, her body crumpling by Tori's feet.

My KitKat doesn't even flinch. She steps over Cassandra's lifeless body, splattered in the woman's blood, and marches right up to Diablo.

The man still has a gun raised!

"I can't believe you even gave thought to her accusation," she says, sounding disappointed as she shakes her head like he's a small child. "This is why you're losing your edge."

At her words, the men that were flanking Diablo walk around him, taking their spots behind Tori.

"What is this?" Diablo's voice is low, even, but there's something coiled beneath it. He already knows. He just doesn't want to believe it.

Tori tilts her head, giving him a slow roll of her shoulder. "Hostile takeover."

He chuckles.

Fucking chuckles.

"You think you can just take what's mine?" He shakes his head, amused.

Tori doesn't flinch. "I think you underestimate me."

Diablo exhales sharply through his nose, but the amusement is gone. He looks at Juan, waiting, but Juan doesn't move.

Yeah, that's gotta sting.

For the first time since we met the man, I see real anger crack through his exterior. Not the cold, calculated kind that makes him terrifying, but something else. Something more raw.

"You're making a mistake, mija," he warns, voice dropping to something quiet, almost gentle.

Tori lifts a shoulder. "Maybe. But I'd rather make my own mistakes than be made a puppet."

His jaw flexes. "And if I say no?"

She smiles, but there's nothing warm in it. "Then you die here."

The thing is—we all know she doesn't want to kill him. Not really. But if she gives him anything less than an ultimatum, he'll see it as weakness. He'll bide his time, wait for a crack, and strike.

This? This puts him in a corner.

He inhales slowly, looking past her, past all of us. Measuring his options.

I don't dare move. No one does.

23: TORI

Diablo, the goddamn legend, stands before me, an easily manipulated fool. His right-hand man, Juan, has deserted him. Gabe is mine now. All he has left is his name, and I'm about to take that from him, too.

I expect him to lash out, to spit venom, to throw one last desperate punch before the lights go out. Instead, he just...laughs.

That's not ominous at all.

It's a quiet chuckle at first, barely more than a breath. Then it builds, rolling into something low and dark, it's a sound that unnerves me for a second.

"Oh, mija," Diablo murmurs, shaking his head. "what do you think you're doing?"

I arch a brow. "Taking your empire."

His smile doesn't fade. If anything, it sharpens. "You think taking my men, my business, my fucking empire is as easy as making declarations? That my men will fall at your feet just because you said so?"

I tilt my head, feigning boredom. "Worked on Gabe."

That earns me a flicker of something in his eyes—resentment, maybe even betrayal—but it's gone as fast as it appeared. He rolls his shoulders like a man shaking off a weight, even though we both know it's too late.

Just accept defeat.

Don't make this harder.

"My mistake," he says smoothly. "I underestimated how much of me is in you."

The words hit harder than I want to admit. I keep my face blank, refusing to let him see it.

"Hardly. I don't take interest in tearing others apart. Why did you spend so much time trying to turn me against Thorne, Blaze, and Ryder? Why test them at every turn? What the hell was your endgame here?"

Diablo exhales slowly, like he expected this question, like he's been waiting for it. "Because I knew you wouldn't leave them behind willingly."

My stomach tightens, a cold, creeping sensation slithering under my skin.

He's been planning this since I called him to tell him they were coming.

He continues, voice calm, almost too calm. "You say you love them, but I know love, and I know what this world does to it. I needed you to see the truth for yourself. That at the end of the day, power wins. The moment they fucked up," His gaze darkens. "I knew I was right."

I scoff, but it feels forced. "So, you threw a bunch of tests at them, hoping they'd fail?"

"I knew they'd fail." He looks at me, truly looks at me, and for the first time, I see something raw in his expression. "But I needed you to know it, too."

I hate the way his words slither under my skin, like poison I can't purge.

My mind drifts back to Mia's kiss, the way Thorne didn't push her off. Then I remember the way Ryder let Lila outright flirt with him. Blaze was the only one who didn't lean into his assigned girl in some way.

I shake the thought off. I won't let Diablo get into my head. Not now. "But they didn't fail. They're still here, still by my side."

He chuckles, the sound deep and rich, like I just told a joke he found genuinely amusing. He tilts his head, studying me like I'm some puzzle he's finally solved. "But for a moment, they weren't. For an instant, they did fail."

No.

That wasn't their fault.

But the seeds of doubt have been planted, and Diablo fucking *knows* it.

I grit my teeth. "Only because Cassandra played us. She played you just as much. The difference is, I can fix it."

He exhales sharply, and for the first time, his mask cracks. Just for a second.

"Cassandra was always a problem," he mutters, almost to himself. "Too ambitious. Too hungry. I should've dealt with her years ago."

I scoff. "Yeah? And yet, here we are. Your own lieutenant put the knife in your back, and now you're bleeding out in front of me. Poetic."

Diablo's gaze flicks back to mine, and something shifts.

Something cold.

Something *deadly*.

"You still don't understand, do you?" His voice drops, just a fraction, but it carries weight. I don't react, but the atmosphere between us tightens. "I didn't need Mia and Lila to break your men—I only needed you to realize you didn't trust them. And I was right, wasn't I?" His voice is soft now, almost hypnotic. "You doubted them."

A slow smirk curves his lips, dark amusement flickering in his eyes. "That's why you hesitate now. Because you know, deep down, that you're no better than me."

I snap. I grab him by the collar, slamming him back against the wall, my fingers curling into the fabric of his ruined suit. His body jerks from the impact, but he doesn't fight me. He doesn't flinch.

Instead, he just grins.

And I *hate* that for half a second...*I wonder if he's right.*

Yeah, okay, like maybe for a moment I didn't trust them. But I mean, can you really blame me? Mia kissed Thorne. Ryder had Lila pressed against him. What else was I supposed to think?

His confidence digs under my skin like a blade. Deep. Sharp. Irritating the fuck out of me.

I should end this.

But for some reason I don't.

Because despite every instinct screaming at me to finish him, there's something in his eyes. Something calculating, something that tells me that even cornered, even outnumbered, he's still playing the game.

And that's what stops me. Not hesitation. Not fear. But the realization that if I take his place, I become *him*.

That's what he wants. That's what this whole fucking game has been about. Not just breaking me, not just testing me, but *shaping* me—forcing me into a mold until I become the only thing he understands.

Another Diablo.

Fuck that shit.

I came here ready to take everything—his power, his empire, his goddamn throne. I thought that was the only way to win. That I had to *own* his kingdom to destroy him.

But that's how he keeps his legacy alive. Because if I sit in his chair, take his men, wear his crown, then he never really loses.

And that? That pisses me off more than anything.

The way he's waiting for it, the way he's already planning my first war, my first betrayal, my first lesson in the cost of power.

Because that's what power does. It eats at you, wears you down until the person you were is just a ghost haunting the person you had to become.

And maybe that worked for him. But I'm not him. I don't need to take his seat to win. I just need to walk away with everything that matters.

I have my own empire to build. One that *doesn't* wear his name. One that will bury his.

I exhale slowly, then look him dead in the eyes, and lean closer. "You're wrong. I'm nothing like you. That small moment of doubt that you and Cass created made us stronger. I can tell you without a shadow of a doubt that they're never leaving my side, and I'm never leaving theirs. We are, however, leaving *you*. Leaving *here*."

The three of them move around me, taking a small step forward that only I notice. They feel the change, the shift in plans, and they don't seem to mind. They'll do whatever I ask because they love me, because they know I would never do anything to hurt us...*at least not on purpose.*

Diablo's smug expression falters, just barely, but I catch it. "Leaving?"

A noise behind me—a sharp inhale.

Juan.

Even from the distance, I feel the way he tenses, the way his hands twitch at his sides. He agreed to follow us, sure—but he thought we were taking over.

I can almost hear him thinking: That wasn't the deal.

But it is now.

"Yeah." I tilt my head, feigning boredom. "I never came here wanting to take over. I came here to learn, and you've taught me a lot. Mainly what not to do, but there were a few nuggets of wisdom I'll take with me and shine. So thanks for that."

Diablo blinks slowly, like he can't quite comprehend what he's hearing. He stares at me in a sort of blank disbelief. "Then what are you planning, mija?"

I smirk. "We're going back to California. And we're taking some of your best men with us. The ones who see what I already do—that you're done."

Blaze shifts beside me. Not much, but enough. Meanwhile, Thorne's arms stay crossed, his face as serious as ever.

Ryder fucking *whistles*. A low, impressed sound, like he's watching a particularly nasty poker bluff go down at a high-stakes table. "Well, shit," he whispers under his breath, shaking his head.

Diablo exhales slowly, his grin thinning at the edges. "You think they'll follow you?"

I let out a quiet laugh. "I don't *think*. I *know*."

His nostrils flare, but his voice stays steady. *Annoyingly steady.* "And when someone decides to challenge what you've built? You think your pretty little dream of a kingdom will hold?"

I shrug. "If they come, we'll handle it."

A dry chuckle leaves him, like he can't believe what he's hearing. "You sound like me."

I tilt my head. "Then maybe you should've been smarter."

That gets him. His nostrils flare a bit, and I see the moment he realizes I'm not his legacy, but a rival in the making.

And that's what gets to him.

Blaze finally exhales, long and slow, like he's still wrapping his head around it. Thorne just runs a hand through his hair, muttering something too low for me to catch. Ryder just looks amused. And Gabe just stands tall, as serious as ever, with his arms crossed and his gaze focused on our surroundings.

Of course he does.

Juan, though? His hands clench at his sides. He's silent, but his body language isn't.

My bad, bud.

Diablo leans forward, like he needs a second to process. "I underestimated you, mija."

I smile condescendingly. "Yeah. You did."

I take a step back, eyeing him, memorizing him this way—a lesser version of himself—before I turn away.

Diablo calls after me, voice rough. "You know I won't need to come after you. Someone else will get to you before I ever have to lift a finger."

I don't stop walking. "Maybe," I call back. "But I never stay down for long."

That's the difference. I don't let things weigh me down for long. I bounce back stronger and more powerful every time.

Let them come.

Diablo doesn't speak. Staying silent as I'm sure he watches me leave, his gaze burning at my back.

I don't turn around to watch him process it all. I don't need to. I know exactly what's happening behind me—his mind racing, calculating, trying to find a new angle. A way to make me regret leaving him. But there's nothing left for him to twist.

This is checkmate.

And he knows it.

Blaze falls into step beside me, his arms tense like he's waiting for me to change my mind...*again.*

Thorne is a few paces behind, his boots crunching against the bloodstained ground. His eyes are on me, his muscles coiled tight as he tries to psychically make out what I'm thinking.

Ryder, on the other hand, just grins. Like he's enjoying the fucking show, like this is the best plot twist he's ever seen play out.

And Gabe, ever my shadow, is a few paces behind, keeping me guarded as always.

Juan lets out a sharp breath, his shoulders stiff, but he follows behind along with the three others Diablo brought. I'm sure there will be more who'll hear the news and make their way to us by tomorrow. But for now, knowing I'm taking my father's two top guys with me is enough of a victory.

Behind me, I can hear Diablo slowly exhale, slow and measured, like he's trying to keep his composure, but there's a weight to his silence. A grudging acceptance that he can't stop this.

Finally, he chuckles. It's a hollow sound, scraping at the edges of my patience. "You know what I like about you, mija?"

I don't answer.

I've wasted enough of my breath on you.

"You never do what I expect."

I glance over my shoulder, meeting his eyes one last time. "That's because you never knew me."

I don't wait for his response.

Gabe moves beside me, silent, the way he always is. But there's something different in how he carries himself now—less like a man following orders, more like a man who made his choice and knows exactly what it means.

He doesn't look at Diablo, just stares ahead, and for a moment, I swear I can see a flicker of happiness in his deep blue eyes.

Blaze exhales a breath like he's holding something back. I don't know if it's relief or something else, but I feel the weight of it anyway. I see the tension, the unspoken thoughts turning behind his sharp gaze. If anyone is already mapping out our next move, it's him.

Thorne barely makes a sound, but I *know* he's there, absorbing every last word. Always watching me closely, always reading my mind.

Ryder walks beside me like he's walking off a battlefield—which, in a way, he is. His stride is easy, loose, but I don't miss the way he scans the area one last time, like he's committing it to memory.

It smells like victory. Like endings.

But more than that?

It smells like the start of something new.

Metaphorically, anyway, because literally it still smells like shit, and I swear I'm going to hurl.

I walk toward the car, without hesitation, without second-guessing, without even a flicker of doubt.

I'm leaving behind any notion I had of Diablo as a father and walking ahead.

My empire awaits.

24: THORNE

The drive back is quiet. Not tense, not weird—just a lot to process. Oregon's night stretches ahead of us, dark and endless, the headlights cutting through the mist rolling off the roads. The SUV hums beneath my hands, but my grip is tighter than it needs to be.

We should be celebrating. We just walked away from Diablo's crumbling empire, untouched, taking his best men with us. He didn't try to stop us. He couldn't.

And yet, I still feel wired, like we're not out of the fire yet.

Tori sits in the passenger seat, her head tilted against the window, fingers tapping absently against her thigh. She hasn't said much since we left.

Since she flipped the script and changed everything.

I still don't know how to feel about that. We were supposed to stay. To take over. That's what we fought for. Then, in one breath, Tori made the call to leave it behind. And the crazy thing is, she was right.

The moment I heard her say it, I knew. Taking over Diablo's empire would've meant living in his world, fighting his wars, keeping his ghosts alive. And that's not us. It's not her.

California is. That's where we rebuild. That's where we make something bigger. *Ours.*

I pull the SUV into the driveway, cutting the engine. Tori sighs, stretching her arms above her head before pushing open the door.

"Alright," she says, not looking back. "You can chew me out inside. Let's go talk."

Blaze, Ryder, and I exchange a glance before following her inside. Gabe lingers for a second, like he's giving us space even though we know he's not.

Inside, the place is quiet, untouched by everything we just did. Tori drops onto the couch, stretching out like she's the only one who needs to sit. Blaze perches on the arm of the chair next to her, silent, watching. Ryder drops into the seat across from her, spinning a knife between his fingers.

I stay standing. Not because I don't want to sit, but because I need to move.

Blaze exhales. "So." His voice is even, controlled. "You sure about this?"

Tori doesn't hesitate. "Yeah. I am."

Ryder tilts his head, tapping the blade against his knee. "Not gonna lie, KitKat, you threw us for a hell of a loop back there."

Tori snorts. "Yeah? Imagine being me."

Blaze gives her a flat look. "That's not an answer, Doll."

She sighs, rubbing a hand over her face. "Look, I went in there, ready to take it all. Diablo's men, his empire, the whole damn operation. I thought that was the only way to win. But standing there, looking at him, it hit me." She leans forward, elbows on her knees. "I didn't want it. Any of it."

I cross my arms. "What changed?"

She hesitates. Just for a second.

Then, she exhales, and I see it—the moment she settles into her decision, the weight of it fully hers.

"If I took his empire, I'd be stuck in his world," she says. "His enemies, his battles, his rules. It would never really be mine. I'd just be another version of him, wearing his crown." Her gaze sharpens. "And I'd rather burn it to the ground than become him."

Ryder lets out a low whistle. "Damn."

Blaze nods once, a slow, measured thing. I can tell he's still processing, but he gets it.

And yeah. I get it too.

She looks at me, like she's waiting for me to argue, but I don't. Instead, I ask, "And California?"

Tori leans back, smirking. "We take our people, we go home, and we build something bigger."

Gabe steps forward then, voice even. "It's the right call."

Blaze glances at him, brows raised.

Gabe shrugs. "I will talk to Juan. Smooth things over. I'll get him to meet us in California with the other men who are loyal. No stragglers."

Blaze lets out a slow breath, rubbing the back of his neck. "Alright. We do this. We go back." His jaw tightens. "I'll call Marcus. If we're making a move this big, we need him on board."

Tori almost lets out a giggle. "Think he'll be excited?"

Blaze snorts. "I think he'll need a drink."

That settles it. We're doing this. And, if I'm being honest? It feels right.

No second-guessing. No unease in my gut. Just the kind of clarity that doesn't come often.

Tori groans, stretching again. "I swear to God, I still smell like blood and gunpowder." She wrinkles her nose. "I'm showering before I start feeling like a crime scene."

She stands, already heading for the hallway. I don't think about it. I just move. And so do Blaze and Ryder.

She slows when she notices all three of us trailing her, glancing back with an arched brow. "What, you think I need supervision now?"

Ryder grins. "Nah, baby. Just making sure you get real *clean*."

Blaze shakes his head, muttering something under his breath, but he doesn't stop walking.

Neither do I. We're going home. But right now?

Tori comes first.

Tori doesn't stop walking. She doesn't speed up either. Just keeps moving, her pace measured, but I see it—the way her shoulders tense, the way her fingers twitch like she wants to reach for something, like she's already bracing herself for us.

She knows what's coming.

She wants it.

I can feel it in the way her breath hitches, the way her heartbeat isn't slow, isn't calm.

We follow her through the hallway, the air thick with something more than just post-battle adrenaline. It's need. It's the unspoken truth that we made it out of that war alive, together, and now we need to remind ourselves—physically, thoroughly, deeply—that we still have each other.

Tori reaches the bathroom and flicks on the light, the brightness spilling into the dim hallway, casting sharp shadows against the walls. She moves to the tub, turns the faucet, lets the water run.

I close the door behind us, locking it. All the while, she watches me in the mirror, her lips parting slightly, her eyes dark and knowing.

Ryder's the first to move, his hands firm on her hips as he presses against her. His voice is low, teasing, but there's heat beneath it, a dark edge of possession. "Are you up for some company, KitKat?"

Tori's grin is sharp, a challenge in itself. "I let you follow me in here, didn't I?"

Ryder smiles against her neck, nipping at her skin. "Yeah. You did."

I'm next, my fingers trailing up her arm, my touch barely there but enough to send a shiver down her spine. My lips brush just below her ear. "You still smell like blood."

Tori exhales, letting her head hang as she starts to unwind. "Then clean me up."

She barely has time to react before I grip her chin, tilting her head toward me as I crash my mouth against hers. She opens for me instantly, her fingers sliding into my hair, gripping, holding on. Her breath catches sharply, a tiny gasp escaping between our lips.

Ryder tears her away from me, turning her as he palms the back of her thighs and lifts her onto the counter in one smooth motion, knowing exactly what she needs. He leans in, teeth grazing along her collarbone, leaving a trail that makes her shiver.

Tori's eyes are hooded and heavy, a soft sigh slipping through her parted lips. Ryder doesn't waste the invitation, his mouth brushing against her exposed neck, leaving a slow, teasing trail of kisses along her skin.

"I think I like this new strategy of yours," Ryder murmurs against her skin, pure amusement coloring his voice. "You know, taking down crime lords, stealing their armies. Sexy as hell, KitKat."

She rolls her eyes but leans into him anyway, fingers brushing absently over his forearm. "Glad you approve."

Blaze moves quietly as he sets his gun down on the counter with a soft click before heading to the tub to shut the water off. He shifts closer, his eyes dark and intense, studying her in a way that screams he wants to pleasure her just right.

He steps in closer, positioning himself to the right of Ryder. His fingers slide beneath the hem of her shirt, dragging it upward inch by slow inch. Tori lifts her arms without protest, the fabric hitting the floor beside us. Ryder's hands instantly slip over the exposed skin of her waist, teasing her in a way he knows will drive her fucking crazy.

"Impatient, Ryder?" Blaze murmurs, voice low, amused, eyes locked on Tori's flushed face.

Ryder shrugs, eyes shimmering with mischief. "Just trying to help her unwind. It's been a stressful day and all, you know?"

She snorts softly. "Understatement of the year."

My fingers brush along her jaw, thumb trailing across her lower lip. She tilts her chin up to meet my gaze, her eyes still lit with fire. "You know," I murmur quietly, "you might be the first person ever to walk out on Diablo and leave him speechless."

"Yeah, well, he thinks too highly of himself," she whispers back. "One of us had to show him he was wrong."

I lean in closer, voice dropping lower. "And you did it beautifully, Vic."

Ryder makes a disgusted noise along her neck. "Can we not bring up her dad before we're about to fuck? I'd like to stay rock hard."

Blaze shakes his head, mouth twitching into a half-smile. "And here I thought your erectile dysfunction wouldn't start till later in life."

Tori chuckles softly, relaxing more into Ryder's embrace.

"Woah, you and I both know that's never going to be a thing I suffer from," Ryder mutters, somewhat offended despite the teasing way Blaze said it.

Tori reaches back, threading her fingers through Ryder's hair, gripping tightly enough to shift his focus back to her. "Shut up and kiss me already."

"Your wish is my command," Ryder murmurs, his mouth capturing hers without hesitation.

She melts against him instantly. Blaze and I exchange a glance, heat sparking between us, familiar and addictive. My heart pounds harder in my chest, adrenaline fading into something else entirely.

Desire. Need.

Blaze's hand slides along her spine, slowly unhooking her bra as Ryder deepens the kiss. Tori breaks away briefly, breathless. "Are we really doing this in the bathroom again?"

Ryder chuckles. "Come on, KitKat. We're traditionalists at this point."

Blaze's brow arches. "Four times makes a tradition?"

"Sure as hell does." Ryder's voice dips low, mischievous as always. "Besides, bathrooms are basically our brand now. You wanna disappoint the fans?"

Tori laughs quietly, rolling her eyes as she reaches for Blaze's shirt, tugging him close. "What fans?"

Blaze doesn't wait. He claims her lips fiercely, cutting her off. My pulse spikes again at the sight. God, I'll never get tired of watching her like this—how completely she gives herself over to us, trusts us, loves us.

Loves us enough to walk away from Diablo's power to build our own.

My hands settle on her waist, tracing the curves of her hips. She shivers beneath my touch, heat rolling off her in waves.

"You sure about leaving it all behind?" I murmur against her shoulder, my lips brushing lightly against her skin. "It was all yours."

She leans her head back against the mirror, eyes half-closed, breaths coming faster. "I don't want his scraps. We'll make our own empire. Better. Stronger."

Ryder smirks as always, but there's something new dancing in his gaze. "You sure you're not quoting some cheesy movie now?"

"Oh hush," she murmurs, pulling back just enough to glare at him. "I most definitely am not."

Blaze inches forward, leaning in until his lips brush against her jawline. "Trust me, Doll, we'll make sure he shuts up."

Ryder grins wickedly. "Promises, promises."

Tori eyes each of us one by one with a challenge in her eyes. "Great. So how about less talking, and more doing."

She's fucking perfect.

Blaze's eyes darken dangerously. "Whatever you say, Doll."

Her legs hook around Ryder's waist, pulling him even closer. He moves his mouth to her collarbone, grazing it softly with his teeth. Her eyes flutter shut briefly, her pulse hammering visibly at her throat. When she opens them again, her gaze locks onto mine—fierce, defiant, hungry.

"Are you just gonna watch, Thorne?" she challenges softly.

I lean in, my lips brushing lightly against her ear. "Maybe I like the view."

She scoffs, fingers gripping my shirt and pulling me closer. "Join in, asshole."

I grin, sliding my hand into her hair, gripping gently to tilt her head back toward mine. "Careful what you ask for, Vic."

Her lips curve slowly, wickedly, irresistibly. "I'm not asking. I'm demanding."

And fuck if that isn't the hottest thing she's ever said.

Blaze lets out a low chuckle, his voice rough, amused. "Didn't we already learn that Tori always gets what she wants?"

"Smart man," she says, hooking her legs tighter around Ryder's hips, pulling him even closer. Ryder doesn't resist, pressing forward, his mouth claiming hers fiercely. She sighs into the kiss, fingers curling into his shirt like she's never letting go.

Ryder breaks the kiss long enough to tug at her pants, helping her slide them down her legs, revealing smooth skin and leaving her clad only in panties. She huffs impatiently, kicking the fabric aside as Ryder's lips return to her throat, teasing and nibbling softly.

Blaze moves closer to Ryder's right, his hand tracing possessively over her thigh, fingertips grazing slowly upward, teasing along the soft skin at her hip. Her body trembles under his touch, hips shifting restlessly.

I step closer to Ryder's left, tracing my fingers gently along the inside of her thigh. Her skin is warm, silky beneath my touch, and

I watch the instant reaction—the way her breath catches, her body tensing and moving subconsciously toward my fingers.

Her eyes flutter open again, meeting mine with that fierce heat, a spark that never fades no matter how many times we find ourselves here.

"You good, Vic?" I murmur softly as my fingers slide higher, brushing lightly over the sensitive skin near her center.

She narrows her eyes at me, defiant even now. "Are you?"

"Always," I whisper, letting my fingers glide gently over her covered heat, teasing her slowly, deliberately, drawing a quiet gasp from her as her grip tightens on Ryder's shoulders. She arches against him, hips pressing eagerly forward.

Ryder inhales against her throat. "Drop the tough-girl act, KitKat. You love when we drive you crazy."

She laughs breathlessly, her gaze stubbornly challenging despite the way she squirms. "You know what I'd love even more? If you all would stop playing and actually do something."

Blaze's expression darkens with desire, his fingers hooking into the edge of her panties, slowly drawing them down her hips and thighs. She shifts impatiently, hips lifting to help him discard them completely.

"You're impatient tonight, Doll," Blaze murmurs huskily, his voice teasing and deep. "Did taking down Diablo leave you worked up?"

"For God's sake," she groans, one hand reaching out to grip my shirt, pulling me closer. "Less teasing, more doing."

Ryder chuckles deeply, gently biting her shoulder. "Whatever you say, KitKat."

My fingers slip back between her thighs, finally stroking her bare skin, feeling her warmth and wetness as she moans softly. Her head falls back, eyes closing as I slide a finger inside her, teasingly slow.

She gasps sharply, hips pressing down against my hand, craving more. I ease the rhythm, deliberately slow, watching as frustration and pleasure battle across her beautiful features.

Her fingers tighten around the hem of my shirt, and she jerks me toward her, our lips meeting in a rough kiss. It's hungry and fierce and full of fire. I slide another finger inside her, her body responding instantly, clenching tight around me. She moans, her nails scraping lightly against the skin of my stomach where she's bunched up my shirt, her breath hitching and her lips trembling against mine.

Blaze's fingers curl tightly around her hips, and he moves close, his breath hot against her throat. He presses kisses against her heated skin, moving slowly down her neck, over her shoulder, his fingers teasing up her inner thigh.

I feel Ryder shift in front of her, his own lips brushing against her breasts. She shivers, and her hips roll, her body pressing back against the mirror and then forward toward me.

I smile, leaning closer, kissing her again, harder, hungrier. She kisses back fiercely, her lips moving against mine with a desperate passion, and I can't get enough of her. My thumb brushes over her clit, and she moans sharply, her body writhing in their arms, so much need and desire.

I work her up, getting her closer and closer, but never there, easing the movement of my fingers when I feel her right on the edge of coming.

"Don't tease," she groans.

"But you love when we do," Blaze murmurs, his hand sliding between her thighs, grazing against my own as I pump my fingers in and out of her again.

"Not tonight," she pants, her head falling back once more, her breathing ragged. "Please."

"You want it rough tonight?" Ryder asks, confidence thick in his tone.

"Yes," she hisses, her hips rocking against my hand, a desperate plea. "Now."

"So bossy. So fucking sexy," Blaze mutters, a smirk curling the corner of his mouth.

"God, you're beautiful, Vic," I murmur, watching as Ryder moves back, just enough to give me room.

"She's perfect," Ryder whispers, his voice husky.

"Fucking perfection," Blaze growls.

Her eyes lock onto mine, dark, unyielding, a challenge.

I slide another finger inside her, curling them, stroking her.

She arches her back, her eyes fluttering closed. "Thorne."

"Come for us, princess," I whisper, my thumb circling her clit, teasing her, drawing her closer to that high.

Her fingers curl around the edges of the counter, knuckles white, her breath coming faster, the pleasure building, rising.

I lean in, my breath feather-light against her ear. "Come for me."

The order comes out a command, a demand, and it sends her over the edge. She gasps, her entire body shaking, her hips rocking against my hand. I keep going, letting her ride out the wave, her pleasure crashing over her in waves.

She slumps back against the mirror, breathing hard, eyes closed, her skin flushed.

25: TORI

The counter is freezing against my bare thighs, but I won't complain, not when all three of them are eyeing me like that. Like I'm some kind of delicious dessert they've never had the pleasure of tasting. Only they have. Every time we do this, they act like it's the first time.

The last couple of times I've noticed how they don't seem to care which one of them is inside me as long as they're all present. It's almost as if they get off watching each other be with me. The thought ignites another, imagining them having a moment. But the daydream is quickly washed away, picturing Thorne's grumpy expression when Ryder starts to laugh instead of kiss him.

I could just imagine the whole thing and half of me kind of wants to see it. Maybe one day. My full attention snaps back to the bathroom when Thorne flicks my clit and I yelp. He arches a brow as one corner of his lips lifts into an arrogant smile.

"Where'd you go?"

"You really wanna know?"

"Always," Ryder answers.

I give him a wink.

"Go on, then. We're listening," Thorne encourages, his tone light, his eyes still holding a little worry.

I shrug. "Just got caught up in a daydream."

"Ooo! A daydream. Go on, KitKat, share with the class," Ryder encourages.

Blaze gives me a look and a head tilt. "Spill it, Doll."

"Ugh, fine," I groan, because I would really rather not tell them, but part of me hopes they'll hear about it and start imagining it themselves, too. "I was just thinking about Thorne and Ryder kissing, and how that all would play out."

Ryder's face is nothing short of an overly confident, self-assured smirk and he leans in closer. "Oh, yeah, KitKat, I've had that daydream before, too."

Holy shit balls, actually?

Ryder?

***The** Ryder?!*

The same Ryder who swore he wasn't in a relationship with these two assholes, is sitting here confessing that he's imagined kissing Thorne.

That's it. I can die now.

"You've had what now?" Thorne asks, eyes narrowing at the man he claims is like a brother.

"The one where you and I are kissing and KitKat likes it," he tells him. "And then I imagine it's her and Blaze, and the whole thing ends with her sitting on my face."

"What?" Blaze and I say in unison.

"Yeah," he shrugs. "It's a good daydream."

Thorne's hand slips from my clit and moves down, dipping into my slit. I suck in a breath, arching my back a little.

"So, you wanna?" Ryder leans forward, cupping the side of Thorne's face.

I can feel Thorne's finger inside of me move a little more, and I know it's just the beginning of his torture.

"Thought you'd never ask," Thorne whispers, leaning forward. Their lips are an inch apart when they suddenly stop. Ryder rests his forehead against Thorne's, both of them turning to look my way with shit-eating grins.

"Nah," Ryder says, his blue eyes shimmering with mischief.

"Not yet," Thorne adds. "We gotta save something for the honeymoon, right?"

Honeymoon? What honeymoon?

Oh! They're joking.

Ha ha, very funny.

"I hate you both," I grit out, rolling my eyes so hard they might just pop out of my head. They don't get what they just did to my heart, to my insides...I'm burning up. I'm sure Thorne can tell. His finger is still deep inside me, slicked in my undeniable want for this—for them.

"You love us," Thorne says, pushing his finger deeper inside.

"So much, Doll," Blaze echoes, brushing my hair from my neck, placing a gentle kiss.

"So, so, so much, KitKat," Ryder adds.

"I really don't." They're right though, I do love them, so, so, so fucking much. It's really not fair.

"That's okay, Vic. We love you so, so much, too." Thorne turns back to Ryder and my heart stops.

Ryder is smiling wide, eyes alight, and just when I think Thorne is going to kiss him, he fools me for a second time. I don't even have time to think, and when his lips connect with mine, his finger slides from my slit to my ass, and he presses.

Hard.

And then everything goes white.

"Come for us, Doll," Blaze whispers into my ear.

And I do.

Not five seconds later, as I'm still coming down from my high, Ryder whispers in my ear.

"So, KitKat, do I get to come inside you again? I love to see my cum dripping out of your beautiful little cunt." His fingers dance over my thighs in small circles as his lips brush against my jaw.

"If you want entry, I demand a kiss." I cross my arms, pretending like I could actually hold out on sex with them.

As if.

Thorne steps forward, cupping my cheek, and his lips press gently against mine. It's soft, loving, and sweet. His thumb rubs against my skin as he pulls away and smiles down at me.

"That's not the kiss I meant, and you know it." My eyes light with fire, begging, needing them to fulfill my fantasy. I mean, it's one little kiss between them.

They can do that for me, right?

Just once.

I bite my lip and wait, hoping they don't catch my bluff.

Thorne and Ryder eye each other, as if telepathically communicating with one another.

Oh my gosh, are they going to do it? Will they kiss each other for me?

Thorne turns toward Ryder and he gives me the biggest, sexiest smirk, and then shakes his head.

"No," he says with a wink.

"What? No? What do you mean, 'no?'"

Thorne shrugs, leaning back to get a better view of me.

"Yep. That's a big no," Blaze chimes in, stepping up next to me, his fingers wrapping around the back of my neck, pulling me in closer. His mouth is so close I can almost taste him, but he pauses, waiting for the rest.

"Yeah, that's a hard no, KitKat." Ryder's voice sounds next, and then his lips are on my shoulder. "Now let me fuck you already."

Blaze closes the distance, pressing his mouth against mine. He's not gentle or soft, but hard and demanding. And I love it.

His hand slides from the back of my neck around to my front, cupping my breast with a firm squeeze, his thumb brushing over my nipple just enough to send a jolt of heat cascading down my spine.

"Mmm," I moan softly into his mouth, arching into his touch, and almost instantly feel Ryder's warm breath tickle the skin just behind my ear. My entire body shivers, hyper-aware of every sensation, every small movement.

"Get her legs," Ryder orders roughly, and honestly, I don't even care what they're plotting next. At this point, I just know I want them. All of them.

Dammit. They knew I was bluffing. They always do. It's infuriating. I'd pout about it if I weren't currently losing my mind with how turned on I am. I swear, lately it feels like I'm hornier than usual—which is saying something, considering the company I keep. Right now, this moment is purely selfish, purely about me getting what I need.

My fingers grip tighter onto the cold countertop, my breath quickening as Ryder steps back, holding my gaze as he undoes his jeans and frees his cock. My mouth waters at the sight—thick, pierced, and ready for me. The gleam of those piercings under the harsh bathroom lights sends a thrill straight between my thighs. Anticipation pools hot and slick inside me, leaving me aching, desperate to feel him buried deep.

I lift my hips instinctively, inviting, needing, and Ryder doesn't hesitate. He steps in close, spreading me wide open, fingers slipping down to tease my clit before sliding further back, lingering briefly around my sensitive ass.

"Fuck," Ryder groans deeply, his teeth digging into his bottom lip, eyes darkening with lust. "You're always so damn tight."

"Maybe you're just too fucking big," I retort breathlessly, trying to sound witty, but it comes out needy, raw, desperate.

Pressing one hand firmly against the mirror to steady myself, I brace for him, heart pounding wildly in my chest. Ryder eases into me slowly, deliberately, each piercing slipping inside rung by rung, stretching me deliciously. It's nearly overwhelming, toeing that addictive line between pleasure and pain, pushing me closer to the edge with every slow, measured thrust.

I catch Blaze's dark gaze, locked on me. His cock is in his hand, hard and heavy as he strokes himself, captivated by the sight of Ryder moving inside me. He steps closer, his free hand reaching out to grip my breast roughly, tugging and rolling my nipple between his fingers in a way that makes me arch further off the counter.

"Harder," I beg shamelessly, rocking my hips desperately against Ryder, needing more, needing everything.

Ryder growls lowly, gripping my waist tighter, digging his fingertips into my skin. Thorne moves into view, his gaze hungry, practically devouring me as his hand moves up and down his cock, matching Ryder's rhythm in a way that makes my thighs clench tighter around Ryder's hips.

"Pick her up," Thorne commands roughly, his tone leaving no room for argument.

Ryder obeys instantly, gripping my thighs and lifting me effortlessly. My legs wrap firmly around him, driving him even deeper, making me gasp as every piercing sends delicious sparks ricocheting through my nerves. My fingers dig into Ryder's shoulders, clinging desperately as Thorne steps behind me, his cock pressing insistently against my ass.

"Oil," Thorne demands.

Blaze quickly pours some into Thorne's waiting hand. The cool slickness feels perfect against my overheated skin, Thorne's fingers sliding easily down, pressing against the tight ring of muscle before carefully slipping inside.

My body instantly goes taut, pulled between the sensation of Ryder filling me completely and Thorne slowly preparing my ass. My breath escapes in tiny gasps, every nerve stretched taut, ready to snap. Thorne adds a second finger, and a moan tears from my throat as he stretches me further, pressing closer to Ryder inside me.

"Fuck, Thorne," Ryder growls, his hips jerking slightly. He clenches his jaw, clearly fighting for control.

"Don't come yet," Thorne orders firmly.

"Don't make me," Ryder fires back, voice strained.

Before I can even react, Blaze's hand slips between Ryder and me, his fingers immediately circling my clit with just the right pressure, just the right rhythm. My orgasm rises dangerously fast, uncontrollable, unstoppable.

"Shit," Ryder groans, eyes squeezed shut, his breathing ragged. "She's gonna come."

Thorne's voice is rough, dominant, almost daring. "Hold it."

"Fuck—" Ryder hisses, clearly struggling.

Blaze rubs harder, faster, refusing to relent, pushing me ruthlessly over the edge. "Fuck, I'm coming!" I cry out, clenching uncontrollably around Ryder, my entire body shaking violently.

Blaze withdraws his hand, and my pussy pulses frantically, clenching Ryder's cock even tighter. Ryder's restraint is paper-thin, his teeth sinking possessively into my shoulder as he battles to hold on, breath hot and ragged against my skin.

"Fuck, fuck, fuck," he mumbles over and over, his entire frame trembling beneath me.

Thorne withdraws his fingers, gripping my ass firmly, spreading me open wide as he positions himself carefully. His cock presses against my asshole, thick and intimidating, slowly—agonizingly slowly—stretching me open as he eases himself inside.

"Shit," I gasp, the pressure intense, almost overwhelming.

"Breathe, Vic," Thorne murmurs soothingly against my ear, his chest pressed against my back, arms wrapped tightly around my waist. Blaze cups my jaw, forcing me to meet his eyes, dark and intense.

"Breathe, Doll," he repeats gently, leaning in, his lips claiming mine in a searing kiss.

I exhale shakily into his mouth, forcing myself to relax as Thorne's cock slowly pushes deeper, the pressure shifting from painful to deliciously full.

"God, she's so fucking tight," Thorne growls, voice thick with pleasure.

"I can feel you," Ryder groans, clearly affected, eyes squeezed shut as he struggles for control.

For one delirious second, I almost think they'll kiss. God knows Ryder looks turned on enough by the idea right now. I watch him intently, loving the pleasure that dances openly across his face, the desperation clear as Thorne moves slowly behind me, separated by just a thin wall of my own body.

"Move," I plead, squirming between them, unable to bear it any longer.

The three of them curse simultaneously, voices rough with need. Thorne grips my hip possessively, his eyes locked onto mine through the reflection in the mirror, heated, commanding.

Slowly—torturously—he begins to move, and the friction, the fullness, the intense sensation of being completely claimed by them pushes me toward another peak.

I let go of everything, surrendering completely, lost to them—and God, it feels so fucking perfect.

Blaze adds more oil to his hand, slicking it along his thick cock, his eyes locked onto mine the entire time, careful to ensure I don't feel even a hint of discomfort. My heart thuds violently in my chest, my breath catching as I watch him pump himself with deliberate, slow strokes. His free hand reaches out, sliding possessively across my skin, exploring every inch he can reach—my breasts, my waist, my thighs—as he trails heated kisses across my jaw, my neck, my shoulders, each touch igniting sparks across my skin.

My moans build steadily, growing louder and more desperate with each thrust Thorne makes behind me, every deep stroke Ryder delivers in front. Thorne's grip tightens around my hips, holding me securely, his ragged breath hot against my neck as he buries his face there.

"Come on, Vic," he rasps against my skin, his voice a deep, rumbling command. "Ride us."

A thrill rushes through me at his demand, and I give in eagerly. I rock my hips, moving as much as their hold allows, chasing the intense friction that builds rapidly within me. I bounce, rolling my hips and meeting their thrusts, desperate for more, for everything they're willing to give me. But it still isn't enough—I crave more, always more.

My eyes lock onto Blaze again, heat pooling low in my belly as his hand moves faster along his shaft, his eyes dark and hungry as they devour the sight of me being taken by the others. My tongue darts out to wet my lips, the craving for his taste overwhelming every other thought in my head.

"Don't come," I warn him breathlessly. "When I'm done with these two, I want that"—I nod pointedly toward his cock—"in my mouth."

Blaze's breath catches, his jaw tightening visibly. "Fuck, Doll. You're killing me."

My eyes slam shut, my head spinning faster than my pulse.

God, they're so damn good at this.

Ryder softens immediately, leaning in to kiss below my ear. "Come on, KitKat," he whispers soothingly, his voice dropping low, coaxing. "We'll be good. Just keep bouncing like that. Just like that, beautiful."

And fuck, I listen, helpless to do anything else.

I move with abandon, riding the wave of sensations as their cocks fill me, stretching and claiming every inch. The building tension spirals higher, tighter, threatening to unravel completely. My breathing is ragged, uneven, punctuated by desperate gasps and moans that echo off the bathroom walls. It's not long before the pressure becomes unbearable, and I'm falling apart again.

My orgasm tears through me, raw and powerful, consuming every thought, every nerve-ending igniting simultaneously. Pleasure crashes through me violently, overwhelming in its intensity.

"Shit, shit, shit," Thorne groans, his voice breaking, his cock pulsing deep inside me as he fills my ass with his release.

"Fuck—oh, fuck," Ryder gasps desperately, hips jerking, his cock throbbing inside my pussy, his teeth sinking sharply into my shoulder, marking me possessively as his cum spills hot and thick.

"Oh fuck, Doll, you look so hot right now," Blaze rasps, hand still wrapped tight around himself, pumping furiously, his breathing shallow. "Your face glowing, so goddamn beautiful."

His voice cracks slightly, his movements stuttering, and I see he's dangerously close to coming undone. I point at him, breathless but determined. "Don't you dare come, Blaze."

Before they can stop me, I gently lift myself from Thorne and Ryder, feeling their softened cocks slip free. My legs wobble as they lower me down, but determination fuels me as I drop gracefully to my knees in front of Blaze.

My tongue slips out instinctively, waiting hungrily, mouth open and eyes wide with expectation. Blaze threads his fingers into my hair, holding me firmly but tenderly, his cock hard and throbbing inches from my lips.

"You look so fucking good on your knees, Doll," he whispers hoarsely, his hand tightening as his breathing quickens further. His eyes glaze over, muscles tensing visibly as his hand moves quicker, nearing the edge of control.

"Come in my mouth," I demand softly, voice full of desire. "I want to taste you."

"Fuck, yes," Blaze gasps, hips thrusting forward involuntarily, his cock pulsing as he finally spills into my mouth. Warm, salty, addictive—I swallow eagerly, savoring him completely. My finger catches the excess along my lips, sliding it seductively into my mouth and licking it clean, relishing how his heated gaze follows every move.

Blaze shudders, his hand loosening from my hair as his entire body relaxes. I smile triumphantly as he sinks slowly down beside me, clearly spent.

"So good, Doll," he murmurs softly, eyes closing briefly in blissful exhaustion. "You're fucking perfect."

I glance over my shoulder at Thorne and Ryder, still catching their breaths but watching me intently, matching satisfied, lovesick grins on both their faces. The silence stretches pleasantly, contentedly, until Ryder finally speaks.

"We should probably get you cleaned up now," he says gently, eyes softening with warmth.

"Mhm," I hum lazily, my limbs feeling heavy and languid in the aftermath.

Thorne steps forward, offering his hand to help me up. "Come on, princess. We'll get you taken care of."

I accept gratefully, and in an effortless motion, Thorne lifts me gently into his arms, carrying me toward the shower. The water feels heavenly on my skin, but even better is the gentle attention of three pairs of hands washing me, caressing me, pampering me, treating every inch of my body like something precious, something treasured.

And as they surround me with love, affection, and care, I decide right then and there—this is the best damn feeling in the world.

26: Tori

I wake to the rustling of a bag near my ear. The bed is surprisingly empty, which only makes me feel worse. Nausea rolls through my stomach, probably from all the fucking semen I swallowed last night. We didn't exactly stop after the bathroom. I couldn't tell you how many times I came; at one point I think I blacked out a little. We finally stopped, only because Blaze, ever the voice of reason, reminded everyone that as much as we enjoy marathon sex, sleep is still required.

"What are you doing?" I groan, prying an eye open to find Thorne standing by the bed, pulling something out of a gray plastic bag with a bright red W. Squinting, I watch him set something rectangular on the nightstand. My brows furrow as I slowly recognize the box.

Early detection pregnancy test.

And just like that, I'm wide-fucking-awake.

I sit up so fast the entire room spins violently, my stomach lurching from a gentle roll to a tsunami about to break. Throwing the sheets off, I leap from the bed—at least, that's the plan. Instead, my foot tangles in the fabric, nearly sending me face-first into the floor. Cursing under my breath, I barely manage to kick free and stumble to the bathroom, my knees slamming onto the tile floor just in time to empty what little is in my stomach into the porcelain bowl.

Fuck.

This is morning sickness, isn't it? Not the aftereffects of a night of endless orgasms or Ryder's relentless stamina, but honest-to-God pregnancy nausea.

A cold wash of reality slaps me hard, sobering my swirling thoughts.

A kid.

Me, Tori—sarcastic, stubborn, damaged-as-hell Tori—bringing a life into this world.

I grip the edges of the toilet seat, heart hammering, panic squeezing my chest so tight I can barely breathe. I'm on the verge of puking again, but this time for completely different reasons. Fear. Doubt. The thought of being responsible for another human being. God, I can barely keep my own shit together half the time. I have absolutely no business trying to parent. The word 'mom' tastes strange on my tongue, foreign, heavy with responsibilities I don't think I'm qualified for.

But then, Thorne's large, comforting hand slides gently along my spine, rubbing small, soothing circles. Blaze appears beside me, quietly gathering my tangled mess of hair in his hands to keep it away from my face, whispering softly, telling me to breathe. Ryder leans casually against the doorframe, his blue eyes sparkling with the kind of mischief only he can manage in a situation like this. He looks utterly thrilled, his grin stretching wider than the fucking state of Texas.

And suddenly, I remember—I'm not alone.

I've never been alone, not really, not since these three idiots barged their way into my life. Sure, they drove me crazy at first, bullied me, tormented me, confused me—but now, they're the air I breathe. They're my entire world. And a kid, our kid, would have the kind of love and protection I never got to have. We're all damaged, sure. Each of us fucked up in our own way, carrying scars from shitty childhoods. But maybe that's exactly why we'll be good at this.

We know exactly what not to do.

One of them is the father—though, let's be real, if I had to place bets, it's Ryder. That asshole has been coming inside me repeatedly without even pretending to pull out. He totally knew what he was doing. I'm sure of it now.

My eyes narrow playfully, locking onto him. "Ryder Hayes, did you fucking baby trap me?"

Ryder's smirk shifts into an outright laugh, completely unashamed. "Maybe a little. Can't blame a guy for securing his place, KitKat."

Thorne snorts softly, trying—and failing—to hide his amusement, while Blaze merely shakes his head, the corner of his lips quirking up in that rare, genuine smile he reserves for moments like this. Moments when we're messy and complicated and terrified, yet somehow still perfect together.

"You okay, Vic?" Thorne murmurs gently, leaning closer and brushing his lips across my temple, his voice soft and careful.

I nod slowly, swallowing down the remaining nausea, letting the warmth of their presence settle my racing pulse. "Honestly? I have no idea. Terrified, excited, nauseous as fuck? Probably about to panic again any second. Take your pick."

"You're gonna be an amazing mom," Blaze reassures me quietly, his voice so certain that my throat tightens unexpectedly.

"And the kid is definitely mine," Ryder adds with absolute confidence, not an ounce of doubt in his voice, eyes gleaming mischievously.

Blaze rolls his eyes, throwing a pointed look at Ryder. "Statistically speaking, sure. But let's face it—any kid raised by the four of us is gonna end up sarcastic, reckless, and probably banned from at least three countries before they hit puberty."

"Sounds about right," Thorne mutters with amusement, pressing another soft kiss to my hair.

The image makes me laugh, genuine and deep, cutting through the tension still lingering in my stomach. Suddenly, the panic eases slightly, replaced by something else—a warm, hopeful feeling that maybe, just maybe, this can actually work. We're not exactly traditional parents, but we have something stronger than that. Love, and a fierce determination to do better for our child than what was done to us.

"I'm still freaking out, though," I admit softly, looking up into their faces. "We don't exactly scream 'normal family,' you know?"

Ryder shrugs easily, still grinning. "KitKat, what's normal anyway? You think anyone else out there has the kind of badass mom who's taken down crime lords or three dads who are basically superheroes in bed?"

I laugh despite myself. "You're an idiot."

"Yeah, but I'm your idiot," he reminds me, blue eyes full of warmth. "And now you're stuck with us."

Forever. A family. It's not perfect, it's definitely not conventional, but it's ours. A rush of warmth floods through me, spreading to my chest, my heart swelling with a powerful certainty.

I take a deep breath, nodding slowly, gripping Thorne's hand tight in mine. "We can do this, right?"

Thorne gives my hand a gentle squeeze, his thumb stroking softly against my knuckles in silent reassurance. Blaze nods, the usual quiet intensity in his eyes softening into something reassuring, certain, unwavering. Ryder's grin fades, transforming into a look so unexpectedly tender my heart nearly stalls out in my chest.

Blaze clears his throat gently, breaking the tender silence. "Maybe we should actually confirm you're pregnant before we start picking baby names and nursery themes?"

"He's got a point," Ryder agrees quickly, pushing off the doorframe. "I mean, I'd hate to waste all this stellar baby trapping I've clearly mastered."

I roll my eyes, shaking my head as Ryder heads out to the bedroom, grabs the box, and strolls back in like he's delivering the crown jewels. He hands it off ceremoniously to Blaze, who then passes it to me, his expression soft and carefully composed—almost as if he's bracing for impact.

"Here you go, Doll," he murmurs softly, holding my gaze. "Moment of truth."

My pulse quickens as my fingers close around the thin cardboard. My heart pounds, my stomach knots, but my mind is at ease knowing three possessive, protective men are by my side.

I take the box in shaky fingers, feeling suddenly like the flimsy cardboard weighs a thousand pounds. Blaze's hand slides over my shoulder, giving a gentle squeeze. I glance at him, his dark eyes calming me.

"You good, Doll?"

I nod once, swallowing thickly. "Yeah. Fine. Totally cool. Just casually peeing on a stick to find out if one of you knocked me up. Typical Tuesday."

Ryder snorts softly, leaning against the counter now. "Just for the record, if it's positive, we're naming it Ryder Junior. No negotiations."

Thorne shoots him a look. "Absolutely not."

Ryder gasps dramatically, pressing a hand to his chest. "You wound me, Thorne."

"Keep talking and I'll make it literal," Thorne replies dryly, but his eyes twinkle, the warmth behind his harsh tone reassuring me more than anything.

Blaze gently nudges me toward the toilet. "Ignore them."

"I know you've seen me naked and all, but could you guys maybe not watch me pee?" I arch a brow, wondering when exactly they plan to leave the bathroom to let me pee. They stare at me blankly, as if

I've just asked them to chop their hands off and they're waiting for me to say 'haha, just kidding.'

"Come on," Thorne sighs, pushing the other two out, and closing the door behind him. I can hear Ryder protesting but I block it out as I sit on the toilet, tearing open the box, my fingers trembling. My mind races a mile a minute. *What if I am pregnant? What if I'm not? Do I even know what outcome I want?*

I pee, missing at first because I've never had to pee on something before. When I finish, I set the test on the counter, wash my hands, and then open the door. Three pairs of eyes snap toward me instantly, each filled with varying shades of anticipation and barely restrained nerves.

God, they're beautiful idiots. How did I get so damn lucky?

"How long?" Ryder asks, impatiently tapping his fingers against his thigh. "Feels like forever."

"It's literally been ten seconds," Blaze points out dryly.

"Longest ten seconds of my life," Ryder mutters.

Thorne steps forward, gently cupping my cheek, his thumb stroking tenderly across my skin. "You okay, Vic?"

I hesitate, biting my lip as I look into his eyes. "I think so. I just...what if we're terrible at this? What if we screw everything up?"

"You kidding me?" Ryder cuts in, instantly serious, his voice soft and deep, holding a vulnerability I rarely hear from him. "KitKat, I grew up with everything except love. Money, reputation, prestige—none of it made me happy. None of it made me feel wanted. But here? With you three? I feel more loved than I ever thought possible. If that's all we give this kid, that's more than enough."

My throat tightens unexpectedly, and Blaze's warm hand lands on my shoulder. "I spent my whole life trying to please a man who was never proud of me, no matter how perfect I tried to be. But here, with you? I'm good enough, Doll. We're good enough. Our kid won't know what that feels like. We'll make damn sure of it."

I blink back the tears that suddenly blur my vision, looking up at Thorne, who gives me a soft, almost hesitant smile.

"My dad hated me. You know that better than anyone," Thorne says quietly. "He blamed me for everything wrong in his life, and for a long time, I believed him. But then you came along, Vic. You saw through all the damage, all the broken pieces, and decided they were worth loving anyway. I might not know shit about being a dad, but I know you've already shown me what unconditional love looks like. Our kid's gonna have that. And I think that makes us pretty fucking unstoppable."

A breath leaves me in a shaky rush, relief and love washing through me so strongly it steals my words. "Dammit, you guys are making me emotional."

Ryder breaks the tension with a wink. "That's pregnancy hormones, baby mama."

I swat at him, laughing despite myself. "Don't start."

"Too late. Ryder Junior is incoming," Ryder singsongs, wiggling his eyebrows.

"God, I hope it's Blaze's," Thorne deadpans.

"Same," Blaze mutters. "At least the kid would have some sense."

Ryder shrugs, entirely unfazed. "Nah, it's mine. Strong swimmers, remember?"

I roll my eyes, shaking my head at their antics, but loving them all the same. They're idiots, absolute idiots, but they're my idiots. The anxiety loosens its grip just a bit, replaced by warmth, by certainty, by an overwhelming sense of belonging.

"Time's up, Doll," Blaze says quietly, nodding to the test still face-down on the counter. My heart pounds in my chest like it's trying to break free.

This is it. Moment of truth.

Sucking in a deep breath, I step forward, reaching out to grab the test. My fingers tremble as I flip it over.

Two pink lines.
Holy fucking shit.

Two lines stare back at me, vibrant, undeniable. My heart thunders in my chest, louder than any drumbeat. I turn slowly, meeting three pairs of eyes watching me, holding their breath. The entire bathroom is thick with tension, expectation, hope.

"So?" Ryder whispers, finally breaking the silence, his voice barely audible, almost afraid of the answer.

I swallow past the lump in my throat, holding up the test, hands still shaking. "Positive."

The silence that follows is the loudest sound in the world. Then suddenly, chaos erupts.

Ryder lets out a whoop, a huge, idiotic grin splitting his face as he practically leaps across the bathroom to reach me. Thorne exhales sharply, tension draining from his shoulders before he steps closer, wrapping a protective arm around my waist. Blaze is quiet at first, his eyes widening slightly before they soften, his entire expression melting into something I've never quite seen on him before—pure, unfiltered joy.

Before I can say anything else, Ryder's strong hands are around my waist, lifting me effortlessly into the air. He spins me around, laughter spilling from his lips, contagious and genuine, filling the room with warmth. I can't help but laugh, clinging to him, feeling lighter than air.

"I knew it!" Ryder cheers, setting me back down carefully, eyes shining brighter than ever. "Told you. Strong swimmers, baby."

I swat at him playfully, but there's no real annoyance in me—just a dizzying kind of happiness that leaves me breathless. "You're impossible."

"You love it." He kisses me firmly, his lips tender, his usual playful energy tempered with something deeper, more meaningful. "And I love you. We're really doing this."

"Yeah," I whisper, voice catching. "We really are."

Blaze steps closer next, his dark eyes searching my face intently before he wraps me up in his strong arms. He presses his lips softly against my temple, holding me gently but firmly, protective as always.

"You okay, Doll?" His voice is steady, calm, grounding me instantly. "I mean, really okay?"

I hesitate, biting my lip. "Honestly? I don't know. Excited, terrified...maybe a little in shock."

He nods slowly, pulling back just enough to meet my eyes. "Yeah, I feel that too. But we've faced worse, right? We got this."

I breathe in slowly, taking comfort from his steadiness. "Yeah, we do."

When Blaze steps aside, Thorne finally moves toward me. There's a strange hesitation in his steps, a tension radiating from him that coils around my chest, making my heart ache. Thorne, my rock, looks vulnerable as hell right now, his dark eyes shadowed, fear flickering beneath the surface.

"Thorne?" I reach for him, gently threading my fingers through his. "You okay?"

He swallows hard, his throat working. "Are you okay, Vic? Really? Any nausea? Pain?"

His eyes scan me critically, almost frantically, looking for something wrong. It hits me hard, understanding slamming into me so suddenly I nearly gasp.

He's terrified.

Because his mother didn't make it.

My chest squeezes painfully. I cup his jaw, forcing him to look at me. "I'm okay, Thorne. I promise."

He exhales shakily, pulling me tightly against him. "We're going to the doctor first thing tomorrow," he says firmly. "You're getting a full checkup, blood tests, vitamins—the whole damn thing."

Ryder arches a brow, clearly amused by Thorne's sudden shift into health-nut mode. "Looks like Dr. Google just got promoted."

Blaze chuckles softly, shaking his head. "You realize he's going to read every pregnancy book in existence now, right?"

Thorne doesn't even crack a smile. His teeth clench, stubborn determination settling in. "You're damn right I am. We're doing everything by the book. No exceptions."

My heart twists at the unspoken fear lacing his words. I stroke his cheek gently, my voice softening. "I'm not going anywhere, Thorne."

He leans into my touch, exhaling slowly, the tightness in his shoulders easing subtly. "I can't lose you, Vic. Not like—" He cuts himself off, swallowing hard. "I'm just not losing you."

"You won't," I promise quietly, my voice fierce, absolute. "I'm right here, and I'll do whatever ridiculous, overly-cautious thing you need me to do to prove it."

He finally cracks a small smile, pressing his forehead against mine. "Good. Because you're eating healthy, resting, and you're definitely not doing anything stupid for the next nine months."

I roll my eyes, but secretly, the intensity of his protectiveness warms me from the inside out. "Yes, sir."

"You guys realize this means we're officially a family now, right?" Ryder interrupts gently, unable to keep the beaming happiness off his face, clearly loving the idea of the word family rolling off his tongue. "The four of us—and now baby Ryder."

I roll my eyes again, but I laugh softly. "Nope. No Ryder Junior. You're vetoed."

"Vic Junior?" Thorne teases, chuckling when I shoot him a playful glare. "Okay, maybe not."

"We'll find a perfect name," Blaze assures me quietly, already taking charge of this zoo. "We'll figure everything out."

I bite my lip, my heart thudding with excitement and nervousness all at once. "About that. If we're really going back to California, how is this baby going to fit into everything?"

Ryder shrugs, completely unfazed, his confidence unwavering. "We build something better than Diablo ever had. Stronger, safer...legal. Something we can pass on to our kid one day—something worth having."

Blaze nods his agreement, his eyes soft on me. "And we'll make sure it's safe. Legit. Something we're all proud of."

Thorne's grip tightens around my hand again, his voice quieter, serious. "We do this our way, Vic. A life our kid deserves."

My heart swells, my chest tight with emotion as their words settle around me. I never knew family, not really, but standing here, surrounded by these three men who've fought to hell and back for me, for us, it's impossible not to feel how deeply we're already a family.

"This isn't gonna be easy," I murmur softly, my voice cracking slightly. "We didn't exactly have stellar parents ourselves."

Blaze smiles softly, his expression tender. "That's exactly why we'll be good at this, Doll. We already know how not to be shitty parents."

Ryder's playfulness softens into something deeper, surprisingly gentle. "And as fucked up as we all are, we're pretty great at loving each other. That counts for something."

Thorne cups my face gently, his eyes warm, vulnerable, determined. "And I'll spend every second of every day making sure you're okay. Both of you."

I let out a breath, my eyes stinging as tears threaten to well up. "Dammit, stop making me emotional."

Ryder chuckles quietly, reaching out to press a kiss to my temple. "Too late, baby mama."

"You're an idiot," I say again.

Blaze leans in, pressing a tender kiss to my other temple. "But he's your idiot, right?"

I sigh dramatically, smiling despite myself. "Unfortunately, yes."

Thorne's arms wrap around me, holding me protectively. He kisses my forehead softly, breathing me in, calming himself as much as he's reassuring me.

"Whatever happens," Thorne murmurs softly, sincerity coating every word, "We're in this together."

"Together," Blaze echoes quietly.

Ryder nods firmly, his gaze serious despite the gentle smile on his lips. "Always."

A sense of peace I've never felt before spreads slowly through me, calming my heartbeat, quieting my doubts. It doesn't matter that our pasts are filled with trauma, that we're flawed and damaged in ways most people can't even imagine. What matters is right here, right now.

"Okay," I whisper softly, leaning into their warmth. "Let's do this."

They hold me tighter, like they can't bear the thought of ever letting me go.

No matter how terrified Thorne is, no matter how uncertain any of us feel, we're choosing each other.

And really, that's *all* that matters.

27: Tori

We cross the California state line like we're goddamn conquering heroes. Ryder's practically hanging out the window, the wind whipping through his hair, his grin so wide it might split his face in half.

"Careful, Ryder. You swallow a bug, I'm not performing CPR," Blaze says dryly, glancing at Ryder from the rearview mirror.

Ryder scoffs dramatically, pulling himself back inside. "A bug wouldn't dare enter this mouth uninvited. I have standards."

"You have zero standards," Thorne mutters from beside me, but even he's got a quiet smile on his face. He hasn't let go of my hand the entire drive—like if he lets me go for even a second, I'll vanish.

Not a chance, big guy. You're stuck with me.

I squeeze his hand reassuringly. He gives me a look that softens the hard lines of his face just enough to make my heart trip.

Okay, hormones, settle down.

Blaze shifts his attention briefly back to Gabe, who's been suspiciously quiet in the passenger seat. "You good, Gabe?"

Gabe nods once, eyes focused on the road ahead. "Just wondering if your California guys are gonna be as friendly as you say. This isn't exactly a small crew."

I glance in the side mirror, spotting Juan riding shotgun in the second car, with Diablo's men filling several vehicles behind us. It's an intimidating parade of muscle and menace.

Honestly, it's a miracle we haven't attracted half the cops in the state.

"Marcus knows we're coming," Blaze says simply, his grip tightening on the wheel. "We should be fine."

"Fine is good," Gabe says, his voice level, if skeptical. "But fine would also be a first."

I lean forward, gesturing out towards the view like I'm some sort of stewardess. "Welcome to California, Gabe. The land of sunshine, beaches, and impending chaos."

Ryder laughs, nodding enthusiastically. "Oh, Gabe's gonna love it here. He already has resting *'I hate everyone'* face down perfectly."

Gabe just sighs. "Thanks, Ryder. Glad I fit in already."

"Anytime, man," Ryder beams.

We finally turn onto our familiar street, and something in my chest loosens. My muscles relax, tension melting away as the iron gates of our mansion swing open. The sprawling driveway is lined with familiar vehicles and faces.

And one not-so-expected face lounging casually on our porch steps.

I blink, certain I'm hallucinating. "Is that Keagan?"

Blaze pulls up slowly, expression caught between confusion and irritation. "You gotta be fucking kidding me."

Ryder bursts out laughing. "Keagan? Our Keagan? He's still here?"

Thorne pinches the bridge of his nose, groaning softly. "Please, someone tell me he's not staying in our house."

Keagan pushes up off the steps, arms spread wide as we exit the car. "Well, if it isn't my favorite criminal empire! Miss me?"

"Define miss," Blaze deadpans, stepping out to give him a grudging handshake.

Keagan snorts, slapping Blaze's shoulder a little too enthusiastically. "Aw, come on, Blaze. I know you cried yourself to sleep every night without me."

"Pretty sure I slept better," Blaze replies, expression flat, but there's amusement lurking behind those dark eyes.

"Denial doesn't look good on you, buddy," Keagan smirks, turning his attention to Ryder, who's already grinning like an idiot.

Ryder slings an arm around Keagan's neck, pulling him into an obnoxiously tight hug. "I missed your annoying ass! Who else am I supposed to torment when Thorne and Blaze get moody?"

"I am not moody," Blaze protests.

"Of course not, you're a beacon of positivity," Keagan quips, pushing Ryder away gently. He turns toward Thorne, who just narrows his eyes suspiciously. "What, no hug, big guy?"

"Not a chance," Thorne says dryly. "I prefer my personal space uninvaded."

Keagan shrugs, unbothered, before his gaze finally lands on me. A warm smile tugs at his lips as he steps forward. "And there's our fearless queen. Please tell me you've finally come to your senses and dumped these idiots."

I snort, crossing my arms. "Sadly, I've become attached."

"Stockholm syndrome, got it," Keagan teases. He glances behind me, noticing Gabe leaning against the car, silent and imposing as ever. Keagan's brows lift in curiosity. "And who's tall, dark, and brooding back there?"

"Oh," Ryder announces brightly, a mischievous glint lighting his eyes. "You haven't met our new bestie yet. Keagan, meet Gabe. Gabe, meet Keagan. Try not to kill each other—we just got home."

Gabe's mouth twitches downward, giving Ryder a look that promises retribution later. But he pushes off the car anyway, moving forward with slow, cautious steps. He extends his hand toward Keagan. "Gabriel Morales."

Keagan eyes Gabe's outstretched hand skeptically before taking it, shaking briefly. "Keagan Hart. You must be the new babysitter."

Gabe arches a brow coolly, withdrawing his hand. "If by babysitter, you mean the only adult present, then sure."

"Ouch," Keagan chuckles, feigning hurt. "Snarky and serious. You and Blaze must be real fun at parties."

Blaze shoots him a glare, clearly not appreciating the comparison.

Ryder elbows Keagan playfully, chuckling. "Careful. Gabe's a real badass. Probably knows a dozen ways to kill you with his pinky."

Keagan gives Gabe a skeptical glance. "He looks more like a knife-and-fork kinda guy to me. Proper. Polished."

Gabe stares flatly. "And you look like the guy who eats cereal straight from the box."

Keagan blinks, clearly caught off guard by Gabe's quick comeback, before letting out a chuckle. "Actually, I use a bowl like a civilized person, but I appreciate the judgment."

Ryder chuckles, leaning in toward me. "Is it just me, or do we have a bromance brewing already?"

"Don't push your luck, Ryder," Gabe warns, though I notice the faintest hint of amusement behind his guarded expression. He eyes Keagan critically. "Are you here to cause trouble, or just annoy the shit out of everyone?"

"Can't I do both?" Keagan counters, entirely too cheerful.

Blaze sighs deeply. "Unfortunately, yes."

"So, are you sticking around longer?" Thorne asks, clearly trying to sound indifferent but failing miserably. We all know Thorne secretly enjoys Keagan's chaotic energy—even if he'd never admit it.

Keagan shrugs easily, shoving his hands into his pockets. "Depends. I've been pretty busy, actually. While you four were off playing gangster politics, Marcus and I got shit done around here. Speaking of which—"

As if on cue, Marcus emerges from the house, calmly making his way toward us, looking as cool and collected as ever. His eyes immediately find Blaze, relief flickering in his expression for just a second before he smooths it away.

"You finally decided to grace us with your presence, brother," Marcus greets, stepping forward and clasping Blaze's hand firmly before pulling him into a quick hug. Blaze stiffens momentarily but relaxes into it, patting Marcus on the back before pulling away.

"Glad to see you survived without me," Blaze says softly, genuine warmth lighting his dark eyes.

Marcus' mouth twitches. "Barely."

Keagan rolls his eyes dramatically, nudging Marcus. "Don't act like you didn't love having me around, keeping you on your toes."

Marcus sighs heavily, clearly resisting the urge to strangle Keagan. "Oh, yes. Loved every minute."

I watch their easy exchange, my heart warming. It feels good to be back, to see Marcus and Keagan so effortlessly integrated into the family we've somehow built. But even better, there's an undeniable air of optimism here, a sense that we might finally have found our place.

Ryder interrupts my internal monologue, draping an arm around my shoulders. "So, KitKat, wanna bet on how long it'll take before Gabe strangles Keagan?"

"I give it two days, tops," I reply dryly.

Gabe rolls his eyes, but Keagan smirks at me, utterly unfazed. "Aw, come on, Tori. You know you missed me too."

"Like a root canal," I quip, almost smiling too wide.

Keagan pretends to clutch his chest, wounded. "Ouch. Harsh."

Thorne interrupts, nudging my side softly. "If we're done with reunions, we should let them know why there's an army of men standing around, waiting for orders."

We glance around simultaneously, remembering a few of Diablo's former crew is loitering uneasily around the driveway, eyeing the house—and Marcus—with open curiosity.

Marcus tilts his head, sizing them up, then glances back at Blaze, eyes questioning. "Care to explain why it looks like you stole Diablo's best men?"

Blaze shrugs casually, barely hiding a smirk. "Technically, they volunteered."

Juan steps forward cautiously, his presence solid and unwavering, eyes respectfully trained on Marcus. "We're here because we chose loyalty to Tori. Diablo no longer calls the shots. She does."

Marcus' gaze snaps sharply to mine, brows lifting in surprise. "Taking over the world, Tori?"

I loop my arm through Ryder's, leaning comfortably against him. "Nah, just changing the game."

Marcus looks amused, shaking his head subtly. "Well, if anyone could do it, I suppose it'd be you."

Gabe clears his throat, clearly done with pleasantries. "We should probably get inside and actually plan out what comes next. As entertaining as this reunion has been, we need to discuss our future."

Marcus nods, already turning toward the house. "Agreed. And someone get Keagan a babysitter so he doesn't cause trouble during the grown-up meeting."

Keagan feigns outrage. "Excuse you, I am the grown-up."

Marcus snorts quietly. "Sure you are."

Gabe steps past Keagan, pausing just long enough to offer a sardonic smile. "I'm guessing they keep you around for comedic relief."

"Oh, this is fun," Ryder whispers loudly, watching Keagan's eyes narrow at Gabe's back.

"Careful," Keagan calls after him. "This 'comedic relief' bites."

Gabe merely lifts his hand, dismissing Keagan without a backward glance.

I almost laugh, turning back toward Thorne, Blaze, and Ryder. "See? We're home for five minutes, and everything's already chaos."

"Did you expect anything else?" Blaze murmurs, nudging my shoulder affectionately.

I laugh softly, watching our makeshift family head toward the house—this mismatched group of dangerous men and dysfunctional personalities who, somehow, make perfect sense together.

Home sweet home, indeed.

We make our way inside, the familiar house wrapping around me like a warm embrace. It's crazy how much can happen in such a short amount of time, how everything feels the same yet completely different. My stomach twists a bit, a weird mixture of nerves and excitement. I glance at Thorne, noticing how his fingers tighten around mine the closer we get to the main sitting room. He's quiet, but then again, Thorne's always quiet when his brain's working overtime.

"You good?" I whisper softly, bumping my shoulder gently into his side.

His dark eyes soften slightly, the corners of his mouth tilting upward. "Yeah, Vic. Just...a lot to process."

"You mean the army we accidentally stole from Diablo or the baby growing inside me?" I tease, trying to keep it light even though I know exactly why his expression holds that tinge of worry.

His jaw clenches subtly, eyes darkening with barely concealed anxiety. "Both. Everything."

I reach up, cupping his cheek, forcing him to meet my eyes fully. "Hey, we got this. You're not alone, remember? We're all gonna figure it out together. Plus, you're gonna read so many damn parenting books, I'll probably go insane. You'll be the world's most annoyingly knowledgeable dad."

He chuckles softly, leaning his forehead against mine for a moment. "Damn right, I will."

Ryder bursts into the sitting room ahead of us, sprawling across one of the sofas with dramatic flair. "Ah, home sweet home! Still smells like trouble, questionable life choices, and Keagan's body spray."

Keagan snorts from the doorway. "Says the guy who smells like cheap cologne and regret."

"Correction, expensive cologne and zero regrets," Ryder fires back, grinning widely.

Blaze clears his throat loudly, drawing our attention as he moves toward the center of the room, his presence naturally commanding. "Alright, enough bickering. We need to focus."

Marcus settles into a seat across from Blaze, posture straight, expression serious. "Agreed. You brought back Diablo's men—what's the plan here? We're not equipped to handle open warfare if Diablo retaliates."

"That won't happen," Gabe interjects calmly, stepping forward. "Diablo isn't interested in retaliation, and Tori made it clear we're done fighting his battles. They chose to come with her, and they'll follow her lead."

Marcus studies Gabe carefully, assessing his sincerity, then nods slowly. "Alright. Let's assume for now that's true. What exactly are we going to do with all these new men? We can't exactly keep operating as gangs. That's too much heat, especially now."

Blaze shifts his stance, arms folded firmly across his chest, brows tight in thought. "We've talked about it some. If we're truly going legit, we need something that suits our strengths. Something legal but useful."

"I'm sorry, legit?" Keagan cuts in incredulously, looking around the room like he's stepped into some alternate dimension. "Did I miss a memo?"

I roll my eyes at him. "Yeah, apparently you weren't on the mailing list."

Ryder leans in, another smart remark ready. "Maybe check your spam folder."

"Ha ha, hilarious." Keagan folds his arms, leaning against the doorway with an annoyed huff. "So what exactly does 'legit' look like for people like us? A bakery? A coffee shop called Crime and Grind?"

Ryder's eyes widen, finger snapping. "Wait, actually—"

"No," Blaze interrupts firmly, glaring daggers at Ryder. "Absolutely fucking not."

Ryder slumps back with exaggerated disappointment. "You never support my dreams."

Blaze rubs his temple, clearly resisting the urge to strangle him, and Marcus smoothly intervenes. "How about we pick something that actually uses our skills? Something with minimal questions, good money, and perfectly legal."

"Private security," Gabe states simply, arms crossed, confidence radiating from every inch of him. "We have muscle, strategy, and more than enough firepower. High-profile clients always need protection, and honestly, it's not that different from what we already know how to do."

Thorne tilts his head thoughtfully, his dark gaze considering Gabe's suggestion. "It makes sense. We can leverage the loyalty and trust we've already built. The guys from Diablo's crew won't object—they already respect strength, and protection comes naturally."

Blaze nods slowly, clearly seeing the logic. "I agree. It gives everyone a job, keeps them busy, and keeps us off the radar."

Marcus looks intrigued. "We'd need licenses, permits, proper training certifications—"

"We have enough money and resources for all that," Blaze counters smoothly. "Diablo's crew is disciplined enough, the Niners have experience, and Iron Triad will back us. It's actually perfect."

Keagan holds up his hands defensively, amusement flickering in his eyes. "So, no bakery coffee shop then?"

Ryder grins wickedly. "We can discuss Crime and Grind later."

Thorne sighs, rubbing the back of his neck. "Let's focus, please."

I step forward, finally breaking my silence, feeling a rush of confidence fill my chest. "Look, I know this is new and different. Legitimate isn't exactly a word any of us have experience with. But it feels right. Especially now." I glance briefly at Thorne, Ryder, and Blaze, gathering strength from the quiet certainty in their eyes. "We're gonna have a family soon. I'm pregnant."

The room goes still—like really fucking still. Gabe's expression falters for a heartbeat, his usually steady eyes flashing with something fleeting and sad before he quickly schools it into a quiet, supportive smile.

Keagan, naturally, is the first to break the silence, brows shooting up as he looks between me and the guys. "Holy shit. You four didn't waste any time, did you? Who knew gang wars and gunfights were such an aphrodisiac?"

Marcus clears his throat, voice cautious but undeniably curious. "Congrats, Tori. But, uh—who exactly is the dad?"

Without missing a beat, Ryder smugly chimes in, leaning back with an air of confidence. "Obviously me. My swimmers are elite-level athletes."

Blaze just rolls his eyes, but I notice the slight tug at the corners of his lips. Thorne's grip on my hand tightens subtly, and I know he's suppressing a smirk of his own.

Juan, silent until now, steps forward with quiet concern in his eyes. "A child changes things. Are you sure about this? It's not just about you four anymore."

"I know," I say softly, giving him a reassuring nod. "That's exactly why we're doing this. I don't want our kid growing up always looking over their shoulder. I want them to have normalcy. Real, boring, beautiful fucking normalcy."

Blaze finally moves forward, gently brushing his thumb against my cheek, his expression softening into something deeply tender. "Normalcy, huh? Sounds like the best thing we've never had."

Thorne exhales slowly, his voice even but quieter than usual, thoughtful. "Yeah. And we'll make damn sure our kid gets it."

Ryder leans forward, dropping the cocky facade for once, expression earnest and uncharacteristically vulnerable. "I'm not gonna lie—I'm fucking terrified of being a dad. But if we're really doing this, if we're bringing a kid into the world, I want to do it right. Safe."

Gabe nods slowly, his voice quiet but reassuring. "You won't be alone. This is a good path. Trust me, I've seen enough violence and chaos to last a lifetime. A legitimate business isn't weakness—it's strength. Stability."

Marcus finally smiles softly, the first genuine expression of happiness I've seen on his face ever. "So, private security then?"

Keagan sighs dramatically. "Alright, fine. Private security. But if we get bored, Crime and Grind is still an option, right?"

I roll my eyes again, laughing softly. "We'll keep it as a backup."

A comfortable silence settles over the room, tension fading, replaced by something warmer, safer. A shared sense of hope, I realize, as I look around at the men I love, the family we've built from scratch.

"So, when do we start?" Thorne finally asks, breaking the silence, voice firm with determination.

Blaze shrugs, the hint of a smirk playing at his lips. "Tomorrow. Marcus and I will handle the logistics. Licensing, training programs, permits."

"Keagan and I will handle outreach, recruitment, and client management," Ryder adds, clearly excited. "Imagine me, respectable and business-y. It's gonna be amazing."

"God help us," Thorne mutters softly, though his tone holds affection rather than true worry.

Gabe chuckles lowly. "I'll supervise. Keep you all in check."

I get cozy, leaning into Thorne's side. "And I'll make sure none of you idiots get killed."

Blaze's eyes soften as they settle on me. "Sounds perfect, Doll."

A sense of peace washes over me. This is what home feels like—safe, crazy, and imperfectly ours.

Ryder sighs dramatically, sprawling further into the couch. "Now that we've solved our life problems, who wants pizza?"

"Always," Keagan answers immediately.

Gabe looks unimpressed. "Do you ever eat real food?"

Ryder waves a hand dismissively. "Pizza is real food, Gabe. Stop disrespecting my religion."

Thorne's arms slide around my waist from behind, pulling me close against him. His voice is soft, lips brushing my ear. "You okay?"

I tilt my head back to look up at him, smiling gently. "I'm perfect."

His expression eases fully, relief flooding his dark eyes. "Good. Because this...this feels right."

"It does," I agree softly. "For the first time, I'm not scared of the future."

He presses a soft kiss against my temple. "Me either."

My hand settles over my stomach unconsciously, warmth spreading through me. We're creating something better, something new. Not just for us, but for the life growing inside me—the child who'll never know the fear, loneliness, or darkness we grew up in. The child who'll have a real family. Real happiness.

The realization settles firmly in my chest, and I've never been more ready.

"Hey," Ryder calls, drawing our attention, beaming from ear to ear. "Family movie night?"

Keagan sighs dramatically. "Just promise me it's not another anime."

Ryder scoffs, offended. "Anime is an art form, Keagan. You heathen."

Blaze shakes his head slowly. "Movie night sounds good."

I nod, leaning back into Thorne's solid presence, letting the happiness fully settle into my bones.

Our future begins now, and honestly?
I can't fucking wait.

Epilogue: Tori

Sunlight pours through the wide bay windows, scattering gold across the living room floor. It's a lazy Sunday morning—the kind that used to feel like an impossibility. The scent of fresh coffee drifts from the kitchen, a warm invitation pulling me out of sleep, even as tiny feet kick gently against my ribs.

Three years and one very stubborn toddler later, and somehow, this is our life. Quiet mornings. Warm coffee. The low murmur of conversation drifting through the halls, punctuated by laughter that's become as familiar as breathing.

I run a hand softly over the gentle swell of my belly, already feeling the stirrings of another impatient child. This one is Blaze's—a secret thrill he tries and spectacularly fails to hide every time he glances my way. I'm pretty sure he's already mentally bought out half of the local bookstore, determined to raise a tiny genius.

"Mommy!" a little voice calls, right before chubby fingers press sticky Cheerios into my palm. "Breakfast!"

I glance down into bright blue eyes—eyes so unmistakably Ryder's that he loves to tease Blaze and Thorne about their "inferior genetics."

"Thanks, buddy," I say, lifting the soggy cereal and pretending to eat. Ryder Jr.—RJ as we all call him—giggles, pleased with his culinary offering. His little blond curls bounce wildly as he climbs onto the couch beside me, jabbering excitedly about dinosaurs and something that sounds suspiciously like Blaze taught him quantum mechanics again.

The guys swear up and down that RJ's cuteness comes from me, but with that mischievous behavior and devilish charm, there's no denying he's Ryder's clone. *God help us all.*

"You shouldn't be eating cereal in here, RJ," Thorne says, appearing from nowhere like the health-conscious ninja he's become. "Mommy needs real breakfast, not your leftovers."

RJ giggles again, unfazed by Thorne's serious dad face, scrambling from the couch to latch onto his leg. Thorne scoops him effortlessly, lips twitching with a suppressed smile as he shakes his head. "You're trouble, little man."

"Daddy's trouble!" RJ counters, pointing straight at Ryder, who emerges from the kitchen with two steaming mugs of coffee. Blaze trails behind him, carrying a plate of pancakes with enough fruit to satisfy even Thorne's exacting standards.

"Kid's got a point," Blaze murmurs, setting the plate down carefully on the coffee table. Ryder scowls playfully, handing me my coffee and ruffling RJ's hair before sitting beside me. He kisses my temple, lingering just long enough for me to feel his lips stretch in happiness.

RJ reaches for Blaze, bouncing impatiently until Blaze relents and scoops him from Thorne's arms. Blaze pretends to grumble about sticky fingers and crumbs, but the look on his face gives him away completely—soft, gentle, and more open than I'd ever dared to imagine.

"You good?" Thorne asks softly, settling beside me, one hand gently coming to rest against my belly.

I cover his hand with mine, leaning into his warmth. "Never been better."

Thorne nods quietly, the small crease between his brows telling me he's still worried—always worried—but getting better at trusting that things will be okay. Pregnancy hasn't been easy for him, even though the last one was a piece of cake. I know he still carries his fears, even if he won't voice them.

"Hey, Thorne," Ryder calls casually from my other side, nudging my shoulder gently. "Relax, man. You'll wrinkle that pretty face of yours worrying about something that's not gonna happen."

Thorne snorts, relaxing fractionally, his thumb gently brushing over my stomach. "You'd know all about pretty faces, Ryder."

Ryder flashes him a cocky grin, slinging an arm over my shoulder. "Damn right. RJ gets it from me."

Blaze groans from across the room, making RJ giggle again. "Stop reminding me. I'm still holding out hope this next one has Tori's brain."

I laugh softly, relaxing back against the couch, the warmth of Ryder's arm around me and Thorne's quiet strength anchoring me in place.

We've built something here—something none of us ever dreamed possible. Marcus, Juan, and Keagan are thriving in the security company. Legitimate, profitable, and somehow exactly what we needed. Even Gabe found his own place, managing operations with a quiet confidence that has the others finally calling him by his name instead of "new guy."

There are no more shadows, no more hidden daggers, no more waiting for it all to crumble.

It's solid. It's safe.

It's ours.

A year ago, we got news about Diablo—gunned down by some newer, hungrier gang trying to carve out their place. It was strange, hearing the boogeyman of our past was suddenly just...gone. But by the time the news reached us, it felt distant, like an echo of another life. We toasted to his memory, not out of sadness or triumph, but in quiet acknowledgment. We'd moved on. The world he'd ruled with fear and bloodshed was no longer ours. And that felt right.

I watch RJ shriek with laughter as Blaze flips him upside down, Thorne unsuccessfully fighting a smile, and Ryder leaning into me, lips brushing softly against my ear. "You think we're ready for another one, KitKat?"

I squeeze Thorne's hand, draw Blaze's gaze to mine, and feel Ryder's smile against my skin. "Absolutely not," I tease, even as the truth shines plainly on my face. "But we'll figure it out."

Because we're good at that—figuring it out. Loving fiercely. Protecting what's ours.

We're messy. Complicated. Completely unconventional.

But damn if it isn't perfect.

This is your happily ever after, Tori. Enjoy every minute.

Afterword

This is it. This series is over, but if you want to know more, email rae.knight.author@gmail.com and ask for the bonus epilogue chapter.

Make sure to follow Rae for the upcoming spin off series featuring your very own Keagan, Marcus, and Gabe. Who will the lucky lady be?

About the Author

Rae is a woman trying to get her shit together. She's disorganized, chaotic, and due dates are her enemy, but she's kind and empathetic. She loves to loves to hear from her readers, and get to know them, so follow her on Instagram, join her reading group, or friend her on Facebook. She'd love to get a message from you.

Facebook Reading Group: **The Knightly Page Turners**
Facebook Profile: **Rae Knight**
Instagram: **Rae.Knight.Author**

Made in the USA
Columbia, SC
02 June 2025